OF LOVE & FORGE

OF

Love

AND

FORGE

Beyond A CONTEMPORARY MYTHOS

CARLY SPADE

OF
Love
AND
FORGE

BEYOND A CONTEMPORARY MYTHOS
A NEOSPHERE NOVEL

WORLD TREE
PUBLISHING, LLC

Destiny grants us our wishes, but in its own way,
in order to give us something beyond our wishes.

JOHANN WOLFGANG VAN GOETHE

THE FRINGES

HEPH'S APARTMENT

DESOLATION ROW

ULUU'S EATERY

NEOSPHERE
DISTRICT

ONE

HEPH

HARPIES.

Screeching. Meddling. Stinking bloody fucking harpies.

But the sound of an axe blade as it stops said screeching? Bliss.

Leaning against a nearby alleyway wall, I dangled a pair of enchanted shackles between two fingers. The funny thing about harpies was…they could fly. But with the right incentive, also known as yanking their asses back to solid ground, you could easily kill 'em. Not many guys could handle the job, so they came to *me*. Hephaistos. God of the Forge and blacksmithing extraordinaire. With every bounty I took, with every being I dragged in or pulverized, there was also the right weapon for the job.

The harpy screeched as it spotted me, flapping its bat-like brown wings.

I winced and chewed on the toothpick hanging off my lip. "Screech again. I double dog fucking dare you."

1

"You killed my sisters." The harpy bared her pointy teeth with a hiss, those bulging blood-red eyes widening, her spotted puke green skin muted to a drab olive from the darkness spilling through the alley.

Spitting the toothpick out, I pushed off the wall. "It's nothing personal. But a piece of advice from me to you, stop being a fucking menace, and maybe, just maybe, people wouldn't hate your ugly as sin green guts."

Rule number one when dealing with harpies: Get them angry.

She let out a cry that'd put banshees to shame and nose-dived. My black duster jacket shifted as I swiveled, and hurled the shackles at her feet. At the last possible moment, she dodged.

"Bugger," I mumbled, swinging the cuffs by their chain round-and-round.

Rule number two: Be faster.

The harpy's curved claws sprung out from her grotesquely long and gnarled, slender fingers as she dove and swung her hand at my face. The few strands of black hair she possessed fell over her eyes in inky tendrils.

I leaned back with a smirk. "Trying to make the other half of my face match, love?"

Would it ever kill anyone to aim for the side of my face that *already* looked like a half-sucked mango?

Rule number three: Don't let them get too close.

As a Greek god, not a lot could hurt me. Harpies, however, had a toxin in their claws that hurt like a son of a bitch and left a memento in the form of a nasty scar. Several gnarled tears over my left shoulder reminded me every day not to let it happen again.

2

The harpy flew high into the air as if retreating. Giving the chain more slack, I continued to twirl it, waiting for that opportune moment.

Rule number four: Harpies never surrender.

She folded her wings back and flew at me like a dive bomber, giving a shrill cry that made my head pound. Grinding my teeth, I threw one shackle at her, latching onto her wrist. Pulling the chain toward me, I tossed the other shackle, grabbing her ankle.

"No," the harpy bellowed, furiously flapping her wings.

A sinister grin pulled at my lips as I wrapped the chain around my forearm bit by bit, reeling her in like a giant bass. Once secured in my grasp, knowing she couldn't escape, I made my infamous golden axe hammer appear in my hand.

"Who are you?" She hissed, her long forked tongue poking out from her teeth, making her words serpentine.

"Most call me Heph, but I was born as—" I leaned forward, narrowing my eyes at her. "Hephaistos."

The harpy let out a blood-curdling scream, rattling the neon signs hanging above. It was all the incentive I needed to lop her head straight the fuck off. Her green blood splashed over my face and arms, coating my lips. I'd closed my eyes before dealing the blow, but it still did nothing for the putrid stench their blood exuded.

Rule number five: Unless you want to smell like a shit-infested sewer laced in rotten eggs, don't let a harpy's blood get on you.

I never was much good at rule five.

Sputtering, I yanked my wrist back, snapping the shackles

off the dead harpy. I wriggled my fingers, making the axe and cuffs materialize into the air and back into my ethereal storage box. Blood covered my face and beard, and I flicked some at the ground after dragging my fingers through it.

It was no surprise how much I hated harpies, but they never failed to get me a paycheck, and they'd spread *every*where. Once your town became infested with harpies, it was hard to get rid of them, if not impossible, and I knew I'd be back weeks later to deal with the problem yet again. Scooping the head by its ear, I slapped my palm against the device on my hip, sprouting the blue portal to life.

Jumping in, I reappeared in the year 2104 in the Neosphere District. I fucking loved it here. Most of my godly brothers and sisters preferred to stay in modern times on Earth. Not me. Do you know how much of a pain in the ass it was existing in the modern age? They all had to disguise themselves. Take on aliases. Work mundane jobs. Me? I preferred the future. So much had changed that people never batted an eyelash at me making a hammer appear from thin air. By Olympus, I could rub one out in the corner of a pub, and no one would give a rat's ass.

Not that I have.

Or thought about it.

On Earth, in modern times, I'd simply be your friendly neighborhood blacksmith—swords for live-action role players, the occasional knife, horseshoes, fuck, I don't know, wrenches? No. Thanks. Dimension hopping allowed me to be my own person. My own god. And I'd made a life out of bounty hunting, made a name for myself without the inconvenience of pretending I'm anything but what I am. It suited me fine.

The harpy head dangled at my side, leaving a trail of green blood. The occasional passerby would quirk a brow, but one half-assed salute from me and a charming grin made them continue without a second glance. Skyscrapers lined the streets, blazing with neon signs glowing in blue, purple, and pink—advertisements for clothes, food, vehicles, and sex toys—all the essentials. Holocycles and hover taxis glided past the pavement to the faint, steady beat of techno music from the varying businesses blasting it. The occasional fabricated palm tree sprouted from between buildings, giving inhabitants a false sense of place. There are palm trees! I mean, we *must* be in paradise, right?

Still. Home sweet bloody fucking home.

I always believed a person was only as interesting as how they presented themselves. Their manners. Their voice. At first, one might say I spoke like a Brit. And they wouldn't be wrong if this were the eighties on Earth. Over time, I began to borrow words, phrases, and variations of accents from places I traveled, lived and liked. All part of the shades of cultures, dialects, and experiences one is exposed to being a well-traveled Greek god. And sometimes, I'd completely make it the fuck up—or what those closest to me so eloquently called "Heph-isms."

My stomach rumbled, and I glanced at my watch—a simple black, eighties variety digital Casio watch. I had precisely forty-three minutes before Olaf would close up shop for the night. Plenty of time to grab some grub before turning in the bounty and taking another.

Uluu's Eatery was a slap and tickle down the street. For once, there wasn't a line wrapped around the block. Approaching the vendor, I rested the harpy head on the counter with a smile.

Uluu glanced at the head and looked back at me with a raised brow. "What have I told you about bringing dead things around my food?"

"Aw, come on, dear. Where else am I supposed to put it, hm?" I flashed a pearly grin, squinting my eyes just the right amount to make them endearing, or what I'd heard them referred to as my "Sexy Squint."

"I could think of a couple of places," she said, tossing black hair from her eyes.

My smile faded into a frown. I knew I had an ugly mug because of the scar covering half of my face, but I found the ladies were quite a fan of the full beard I kept up, so at least I had that much going for me.

"What'll it be, Heph?" Uluu kept looking at the harpy head with a grimace.

Not bothering to glance at the menu as I always got the same thing, I pulled back my jacket sleeve to scan my wrist over the device resting on the counter's corner. "Noodles. And don't skimp on the sauce this time, eh?"

She rolled her eyes and smacked her lips together as she grabbed a square paper carton, the pink symbol on the side glowing and pulsing to the beat of the music nearby. Using a ladle, she shoved some into the carton, making that suggestive sloshing sound before smothering it with red sauce.

I licked my lips and pointed. "Would you be an absolute doll and give me a jizz of the white stuff too?"

She slow-blinked, making the dark bags under her eyes that much more haggard, and proceeded to squirt the white sauce on top. With a smile, I made "grabby hand" gestures as she slid the carton into my hand.

"And this is why we're biffies, Uluu. Don't you forget it." I winked at her and scooped the head into my other hand.

"Uh-huh, we're about as close pals as you and that harpy head," she replied, growling when she saw the pile of green goo on her counter.

I let out a fake gasp, pressing a hand to my chest. "I, for one, am offended." After flashing her a cheeky smile, I wiggled the head, and turned away.

Continuing to my destination, I walked down the street, slurping the wet noodles into my mouth from the corner of the carton. Sauce dribbled down my chin, coating my beard— another advantage to having a spinach chin—a natural bib. I dragged my jacket sleeve over my mouth and paused at the crosswalk. The man beside me with a bun and shaved sides of his head bounced on his heels to the music blasting through his metallic headphones, every bit of exposed skin covered in colorful tattoos.

I flicked the ear of the harpy head, fidgeting as I impatiently waited for the walking lights to illuminate. On Earth, I'd jaywalk to my heart's content, but dodging gas-powered vehicles was easy. Electric cars? Even easier. But here? Ignoring the walk signs was a surefire way to get your limbs blown off from hover car exhaust. Or worse—decapitation if one of them were shifting to the vertical lanes above us. Yeesh. That'd ruin your fucking day. An ad played on a loop over the adjacent building—an animated chrome arm flexing, the words "How Minty are you?", flashing. A world where they coerced you into replacing as many organs and body parts with cybernetics as possible. Some folks would go pure broke over it, but they got to be the most "Minty" of them all, and to them, that's what mattered.

After slurping the rest of my noodles, I tossed the carton in the trash, the lasers singing it into oblivion before it hit bottom. My eyes shifted to the side as I passed The Firefly—one of the more renowned strip clubs in the District. I forced my gaze away. If I wanted to turn this bounty in and grab another, I needed to keep moving, as much as I enjoyed watching a glistening, jiggling naked lady ass. Fake holo screens replaced the club's windows, a shadowed woman in the buff gyrating on a video loop. I paused, eyed the club, and turned on my heel. I'd made it three steps toward the entrance, and when some of the harpy's goo leaked onto my finger, I turned right back around. Bounty first. Booty later.

"Oh, my—Heph?" A woman's voice called out.

I turned circles, the harpy head bouncing in my grasp.

"Heph, it's me, Daphne," a blonde woman in a skin-tight glossy white dress wobbled toward me in eight-inch heels.

Daphne. Daphne. Should I remember a Daphne?

I quirked a brow. "Daphne…of course." Wincing, I rubbed the back of my head, my response hardly even convincing *myself*.

"You don't remember me." She gave a muddled smile. "Not surprising. It's been a while."

Well, at least she gave me an out.

"Last you probably heard of me—I'd been turned into a tree."

Bloody Tartarus.

"That Daphne? How are you not a tree?" I spun on my heel. "How are you—here?"

"Funny story. I'm still a tree back on Earth, but one day, I sort of…appeared here. I have no idea how. I'm so glad to run into someone I know."

A grimace pulled over my face that probably resembled a similar look to when I had to take a shit, and someone had me engulfed in unwanted conversation. "Funny indeed. I'm laughing on the inside. But uh—welcome to the future." I threw my hands out to my sides and turned away.

I'd be lying if I said I *wanted* to know other mystical beings here. There was a sense of comfort knowing how far away I was from all of them. I could count on one hand the gods I gave a flying fuck about.

"Heph," Daphne beckoned with an outstretched hand.

With a sigh bordering on a snarl, I glanced at her over my shoulder. "Mm?"

"You're not going to show me around?" Her feet turned toward themselves, pigeon-toed style.

"Look, sweetheart. You've got a history with a sun god, and quite frankly, I learned a long time ago not to get mixed up in any form of a family affair. You won't have difficulty finding some dude to show you the ropes." I scanned her body before snapping my gaze back to her face. "Trust me."

She frowned and bit her lip as if she were about to cry. But she couldn't fool me. I'd been around long enough to know when a woman tried to piss on me and tell me it was raining— and even fewer affected me.

"You'll be fine, champ." I tipped an imaginary hat and left her stunned on the pavement.

When I turned around, a woman with a spiked bright green mohawk hitched her elbows and glared knives into my skull.

"What. The. Fuck?" She asked, her voice damn near lower than mine.

Shifting my eyes from left to right, I held my palms up, suddenly feeling the need to go on the defense. "I'm sorry?"

"You got fucking goo on my new sneakers." She pointed at the glowing purple and teal shoes adorning her feet with a healthy splattering of harpy guts.

Making a hissing sound, I rubbed some of it away with my boot. "Yikes. Sorry about that, biff. Shit gets everywhere."

Miss Mohawk rolled her eyes, making her lashes vibrate. "Suck my dick."

Uh, rude.

As she passed, I furrowed my brow. Taking a moment to process her words I finally retorted, "Yeah? Well, eat my twat."

I couldn't be sure if she'd heard me. Not until she flicked me off, of course.

The Bounty Emporium. With how colorful everything else was on this block, the emporium looked drab by comparison—rusted doors, a monochromatic sign falling off its hinges, and one singular wide window where Olaf sat handling transactions. They'd be closing up shop within minutes, so it didn't surprise me there were several people in line.

I tossed the harpy head from one hand to the other, whistling a random ditty as I waited. A man no taller than my hips in front of me twisted his torso to gaze at the harpy head staring back at him.

"Another harpy, Heph?" His bushy white brows bounced as he leaned away.

And now, who was *this* asshole, and why did everyone know me today?

"Pays the bills, dunnit?" I shoved the head at him, wiggling it. "Think you'd know how to take care of 'em?"

The man coughed and gagged, waving the head away. "Not sayin' I could but figured you'd get bored with the same score all the time."

"It keeps me—" My right eye twitched. "—occupied."

The small man chuckled, rubbing his fingerless gloves together as he faced forward.

"What about you? What you turning in?" I honestly couldn't have given a bleedin' fuck, but small talk was better than staring at the cracks in the footpath.

The man adjusted an invisible tie. "Frank Banaducci."

The bounty hunter looked rather proud of himself, and I leaned from side-to-side, looking for his "proof."

"I don't see a head or a limb. And I certainly don't see Frank in cuffs standing beside you." Frowning, I swatted the air in front of me as if Frank were camouflaged.

"Wasn't that kind of bounty," the hunter muttered, opening his satchel for me to look in.

As I peered, bile worked up my throat, and I slapped a hand over my mouth. "Fuck. Is that what I think it is?"

"His dick? Yup. Hell hath no fury like a woman scorned, huh?" The man snickered and let the bag drop back at his side.

Ignoring the blood staining the corner of the pouch from

the cut-off cock, I focused my gaze in front of me as I adjusted my *intact* meat and tackle. "No kidding."

The small man slapped the bag onto the counter with a wide grin, and I ignored the gurgling sound it made as it hit the metal. Normally, that sound brought me a strange sense of comfort but knowing what was inside the bag made me nauseous again. After receiving his payment from Olaf, the mini man saluted me and went his merry way.

Olaf grimaced as he picked up the bag with two fingers, turned on his hover chair, and absently dropped it in a nearby drawer. "Ah, Heph. Good to see ya."

Olaf, the poor bastard, only had one leg and one arm. Despite this day and age having advanced prosthetics, he refused to have anything to do with them—some conspiracy theory mumbo jumbo about the government tracking him. Instead, he floated everywhere on his chair and kept the loose garments pinned from his absent limbs.

After slamming the harpy head onto the counter, I peeled back my sleeve, exposing my wrist to await bounty payment.

Olaf peered at me over his wire-rimmed glasses. One lens cracked down the center. "I'm glad you keep taking these harpy bounties. No one else has the balls to deal with them." He slid the head into another drawer and scanned my wrist.

"It takes a special finesse to deal with harpies, Laf. And I've got enough balls to cover for everyone." I winked and pressed my forearms on the counter. "Please tell me you got another bounty for me."

"Already? Making a habit of doing these back-to-backs, are ya?" His stringy blonde hair bounced as he chuckled, flipping through screens on his tablet.

A teenager zoomed past on a hoverboard, and I side-stepped out of the way when they almost ate shit. "You know I like to keep busy."

"Well, I have one, but the image is pretty blurry. You can't really make out her face." Olaf transferred the image to the holodisplay facing me.

My face fell as soon as I caught sight of the blonde woman in a pink dress, her breasts bulging from the top of it.

"A man named Riley Cortez put a bounty on her to bring her in alive. He's been trying to apprehend her himself, but she keeps escaping. Something about misleading services or something. Gonna be a challenge."

Hardly.

"Virto. I'll take it," I said with a wicked grin.

Olaf blinked. "You will? You can't see her face."

"I don't have to, Laf." I stared at the holoimage of a woman I knew all too well. And she wasn't a *woman* at all. "I'd recognize those tits any day of the week."

two

APHRODITE

LEADING MORTALS TO LOVE day-in-day-out could get dreadfully boring. Mundane. Dull. And yes, this is coming from the goddess of love herself. There were so many other emotions that were far more fun to play with, such as lust, attraction, or passion. Or, if you wanted to boil it down—pure carnal ecstasy. Since when did mortals feel they had to trade one for the other? Or what was so wrong with flings? Or one night stands? Practice the art of "safety," and the world could be your absolute *clam*.

All of the gods still existed in the modern age, but with very few humans believing in us, it drove us to create aliases for ourselves. That is if we wished to be out in public amidst the crowds. Give me living with the humans any day over living like a hermit in a cave like Hypnos did. Big negative Ghost Rider.

I'd adopted the name Vena Milo and ran one of the most

prestigious companion companies in Los Angeles: *Sans Solo*. Needed a date for a wedding? You got it. Someone to hold your hand at a funeral? Most certainly. We could even provide a companion for a Friday night Netflix and chill. The "chill" part is one hundred percent under the companion's discretion. We didn't deal in hired sex, we sold provided company.

"Yes. Yes, absolutely. Could you repeat that address?" Cradling the phone on my shoulder, I yanked the stack of pink Post-Its from my desk and rummaged for a pen. The man on the other line rattled off the address faster than a Hermes sprint, but I managed to jot it all down. "Perfect. As instructed, I'll send a man over in a town car at seven this evening."

Sulking in my chair, I tossed the pen onto my keyboard and played with the gold heart pendant hanging from a chain around my neck. There were times I missed openly exhibiting my powers—hanging out with the other gods drinking Ambrosia wine, and partying in the middle of an agora until we couldn't see straight. But then, I catch sight of the photo of my son Eros on my desk, his proud smile bringing a smile to *my* face, and I remember the reason I changed my tune. I remembered the day I took that photo of him leaning on the bar like yesterday, the prideful gleam in his eye on the opening day of *The Arrow Sports Bar and Grill* in Toronto. His *own* business. Despite my meddling, as he grew up, he somehow managed to become a wonderful man, a god of love and passion, a husband, and even—a father.

One of my assistants, and one of the three Graces, Tina, anciently known as Thalia, burst through the door, her emerald eyes widening behind her glasses. "Oh my—I'm so sorry." She disappeared, pulling the door shut with a yelp.

The Graces, in ancient Greece were actually known as the Charites, but when the Romans dubbed them as Graces, I rolled with it. Not only did it sound prettier, but flowed off the tongue far better.

Tapping a pink fingernail, I cocked my brow.

Tina knocked three times.

Smiling, I leaned forward, clasping my hands on the desk. "You can come in, Tina."

"I'm not sure where my manners were, Miss Milo, my apologies." Tina walked in with her head held low, her auburn bangs falling over her eyes as she pushed the sleeves of her grey cardigan to her elbows.

"Tina, you've known me for how long now?"

She fidgeted at the hem of her pleated black skirt. "Which—" She paused, cutting her gaze to the open office door. "—life?"

Rising from my roller chair, I circled the desk, moving to stand in front of her. I lifted a finger to her chin so her gaze met mine. "The answer is a very, very long time. You might work for me, but you're also one of my best friends. Anything I'd be doing in this office wouldn't embarrass me if you walked in. Besides, what haven't you seen at this point, right?"

Her eyes shifted from left to right. "Even when you have… company?"

"Even then." I shrugged and tossed my hair over one shoulder. "I'm an open book sweetie. And quite frankly, sex is sex."

I'd had my fair share of mortals in my office but brought them less and less. Choices amongst the gods were slim,

16

especially if you weren't a fan of screwing a brother, sister, cousin, uncle...and *that* was not my bag—in spite of what certain ancient scribes say.

Tina clutched the string of her lanyard as she stared at me wide-eyed and silent.

Despite her centuries of existing in the universe, I'd forgotten how genuinely virginal she was. She was the most innocent of the three Graces, and I couldn't be sure if she'd ever had someone go down on her, let alone go the whole way. But her pillow business was her business.

"Did you come in here to tell me something, Tina?" I folded my arms, running my fingers over the smooth silk of my pale pink button-down dress shirt.

She jumped, and her palms flew up. "Right. Yes. Mr. Peters filed a complaint. He didn't read in the contract that, um—" Tina cleared her throat and pressed her fingertips together. "Sexual...acts...were not...guaranteed."

If I had a drachma for every time we heard *that* particular complaint.

Sighing, I pinched the bridge of my nose. "You know the drill. Provide a copy of his signature on the contract along with the exact clause that states it and CC our corporate lawyer in the e-mail. Make him sweat a little."

"Or a lot," Tina said with a snort, followed by a chuckle.

I grinned and bumped my hip with hers. "Or a lot."

"Oh." Tina yelped and snapped her fingers. "There's also someone waiting in the lobby for you."

For whatever reason, my belly fluttered.

"Who?"

17

Tina shrugged and pried the door open. "She didn't say but specifically requested to speak with you."

She. I couldn't be sure who I'd been expecting, but the peculiar anticipation deflated as soon as it'd risen.

"I'll follow you out then." Gesturing at the door, I made my way to the posh lobby of Sans Solo, outfitted with black leather seating, plush eggplant carpets, and throw pillows to match. Various ancient Greek-inspired paintings lined the walls, and my mysterious guest ogled *The Birth of Venus* by Alexandre Cabanel.

Any other goddess may have felt exposed, knowingly having mortal depictions of themselves in the workplace. But I'd always adored how close Cabanel painted my likeness without having ever met me.

"Excuse me?" I interlaced my fingers behind my back. "You asked for me?"

The woman's eyes widened as soon as her gaze landed on me, and she shot to her feet. "Yes. Miss Milo. I hoped to have a chance to speak with you?"

"Of course. I'm all ears."

She clenched her jeans with tense fingers. "In...private?"

When a client asked for privacy with me, it usually meant one of two things: They wanted some action, or wanted to ask for a service not advertised.

I hadn't particularly felt like a sexual encounter, so I sorely hoped it was the latter.

Stepping aside, I held my arm out toward my office door. "By all means. Come on in."

She kept her hands against her legs as she walked, stiff as

an arrow. Silently following behind her, I shut the door once inside and locked it to avoid interruption. No client had yet to threaten my life in my office—not that they'd have much luck killing me anyway.

"I know what you are," the woman blurted, slapping her hands over her mouth with widened eyes.

Pausing with my back to her, I tensed.

How could she have possibly known I was a goddess? The only few who knew were of the same godly variety, moreover, they were deities I trusted. No one would've told her and I'd been extra careful to keep myself under wraps with my powers being unpredictable lately.

I turned on my heel, crossed my arms, and struck my best power pose. The office was the Batcave, and I—was Batgirl. "And what would that be?"

After dropping her hands at her sides, she paced the length of my desk. "There are many names for it—heartbreaker, Black Widow, a player."

My shoulders relaxed, but I hid the motion by flicking my hair. Good. This wasn't about my being a goddess. This was about my—sensual rap sheet. That I could handle.

"Such accusations, and I don't even know your name." Locking her gaze with mine, I tapped my heel against the hardwood floor.

An older version of me—the ancient one—may have taken this opportunity for some fun with an ignorant mortal. But the present me? I think I wanted to help the poor sap and it made me nauseated.

The woman's cheeks flushed, and she forced her eyes to

look away, her hands wringing together. "Sorry I—my name is Brittany. Brittany Fowler."

I moved past her, letting my shirt sleeve brush her exposed forearm. She gasped, but it wasn't of the erotic variety—an easy way to clear *that* particular air. This wasn't about sex. Sitting on the edge of my faux ivory desk, I leaned back and propped one knee. "With all due respect Brittany, I'm a very busy woman, so I'd appreciate it if you'd be so kind as to inform me of your intentions."

"I'm ashamed to ask this, honestly. I know you don't run a business giving people love advice, but I don't know what else to do and I've heard you've helped others."

A lump collected in my throat, and I tapped my nails against the desk—a twitch of mine. It was a handful, but sure, I did help a mortal or two like times of old in the love department—an ingrained part of me I'd never lose.

"You have ten minutes of my time. Explain." I gave her a firm nod, lifting my chin to give my full attention.

Brittany clenched her fists at her sides. "I'm tired of having my heart broken. Laying it all on the line, wearing my heart on my sleeve, love with everything in me only to have it all taken away in a blink of an eye." Her eyes glazed over. "I can't take it anymore."

She *thought* she wanted to be frivolous—that it was a carefree lifestyle without risk of hurt. She'd be mistaken. But we all needed to make mistakes to grow—mortal and gods alike.

"If you're convinced this is the right path for you, I need you to come right out and say it. Ask me what you want to ask, Brittany." Pushing from the desk, I strode to stand in front of her, the fabric of my light gray pencil skirt pulling tight across my legs as I widened my stance.

She sniffled. "I want to know how to be with men without loving them—to just…have fun."

I chewed the inside of my mouth.

There were expected stipulations to be a love goddess. There were the obvious elements of beauty, but not only beauty—pristine, dressed to the nines at all moments. You were never regarded as particularly intelligent, expected to be a phenomenal kisser and the *best* in the sack because nothing less would do. Gods of love were meant to be hopeless romantics and knew how to navigate all forms of love. And fighting? We "supposedly" couldn't spar our way out of a paper bag. It was a role I'd grown far too used to playing.

In reality, what I wouldn't give to throw on a pair of sweats, not care about make-up, and curl up on the couch with a Titan-sized bowl of popcorn to watch *Pretty Woman* until my eyes bled. And afterward? Ambrosia wine while we talked about global warming. And this wouldn't be with my man of the hour. It'd be with my *forever*.

That scenario had played in my head since I was a teenager, with the movie and snack changing to fit the times. And it lived in my head rent-free because that's the only place it could exist. A life like that—wasn't in the cards for me. Everyone wanted a piece of the goddess of love but never tried to keep it.

Flashing my most radiant Aphrodite smile, I ushered her closer to me. "When you zero in on the man you want, you make eye contact. Flirt, dance, possibly even a little over-the-clothes action, but at the end of the night, you give him a peck on the cheek and cut it there."

Brittany's brows arched as she stared off into the distance. "But what if I'm—"

"Horny?" I picked one of her limp hands up and wiggled it in her face. "That's what this is for. The idea is to leave them wanting more. Ideally, you also exchanged phone numbers. Make sure *he* is the one to text first."

She nodded vigorously.

"After your first date, it's crucial what you wear. You want to come across as hot without being slutty. Pure but not virginal." I paused and snapped my gaze to hers. "You're not, are you?"

"Am I what?" She gulped. "A virgin? Uh, no."

"Good." I raked a hand through my hair. "Because then this would be an entirely different conversation. Now—" Breezing to my desk, I scooped a notepad and pen into my palm and held them out to Brittany. "You probably should be jotting this down."

"Right," she yelped before jumping and grabbing the pen and paper.

"At some point, before you seal the deal, when he's kissing your neck, buttering you up and all that, you'll want to act aloof."

The pen in Brittany's hand stopped writing, and the skin between her eyes wrinkled. "Aloof?"

"Yuh-huh. As if what he's doing to you has happened a hundred times before, and he ain't nothing special. Easy way?" I reached across my desk to grab my cell phone and displayed it. "Pretend you're texting, randomly start scrolling through social media, or even something as simple as checking your grocery list. The point is to make him try harder. *You're* the prize."

She snickered to herself as she wrote.

"After you have sex with him, is when you decide on whether or not you want it to happen again. If not, I suggest blocking his number and letting it fizzle away, but if you do—" I stepped in front of her and pressed a knuckle under her chin, urging her to look at me. "And this is the most important part, so listen up, chica."

She nodded and, with a wispy sigh, let her eyes roam my hair.

"If you see him more than once, it has to only be about the physical connection. No emotional attachment. And do not under *any* circumstance *ever* say those three little words."

Brittany cocked her head to one side. "I miss you?"

A knot the size of Olympus formed in my gut. "Don't ever tell him that you love him, Brittany. Do you understand me?"

"Oh." She gulped and leaned back. "*Oh.*"

Clearing my throat, I tugged on the hem of my shirt and moved toward the door. "You asked how to go about it, and that's my best advice, but what you do with it is entirely up to you."

It felt slimy passing on the tools of the trade I hadn't used in eons—tricks I'd used in ancient times where orgies weren't entirely out of the question and I'd get with mostly any mortal who worshiped the ground I walked on. But secretly, deep down, I hoped she'd take the advice and find the love of her life with it. I've always been a sucker for the enemies-to-lovers trope.

"Miss Milo, I truly appreciate your time. Thank you so much." A warm smile pulled at Brittany's lips as she paused at my office threshold.

The smile put me at ease—a grin that told me she'd try this method a time or two and soon realize she missed the connection. It's the type of person she was. And soon she'd discover that not every relationship ends in heartbreak.

"Go get 'em, tiger," I jested, waving her off.

Once she left, I shut the door behind her and sighed. It would've been so much easier to use my powers on her. To make her see what she needed to be happy. To guide her in the direction of true love, but—my magic fizzled.

I sulked onto the stool facing the vanity mirror in the corner. Lifting my hands, I stared at my palms, conjuring my powers. They popped and crackled, soon fading away.

"I don't understand it," I growled through gritted teeth, grabbing a hairbrush from the vanity, throwing it at the mirror, and cracking it.

The door creaked open, and I forced my chest to stop pulsing.

"Ma'am? Sorry to disturb you, but you have another visitor?" Tina's mouse-like voice said from the doorway.

"Who?" The question came out more haughtily than I intended.

"All he said was to tell you that it's Heph."

My insides bubbled, a caressing chill cascading down my arms.

A smile begged at my lips, but I wiped it away. "Tell him I'll be right out."

"Yes, ma'am."

The door clicked shut, and I swirled an arm around myself, successfully making a skin-tight pink dress appear on my body. After flicking my wrist at the mirror to fix the crack, I bent forward to adjust the girls, pushed them up and together, checked my teeth for food, and scurried to the door.

Heph. Hephaistos. God of the Forge and someone I've known since childhood. I'd always had a soft spot for him and could never pinpoint why. He and I would never work out, though. I knew it, and he knew it. His track record alone proved that theory. I was neither warrior nor a scholar and never had been keen on dirt.

As I rounded the corner, he stood in the lobby, leaning against a pillar with one boot propped against it. A hand rested in his pants pocket while the other pulled a toothpick from his mouth once those milk chocolate eyes landed on me. A flash of white poked from his dark beard as he smiled at me, causing heat to pool in my belly.

"Hey ya, Ro."

THREE

HEPH

APHRO-FUCKING-DITE. THE MOST GORGEOUS woman I'd ever seen even since we were twee little gods. It was also why I knew I didn't have a snowball's chance in Tartarus to be with her and nipped that in the bud a very long time ago. Not only wouldn't she see past this ugly kisser, but she deserved better—chiseled to perfection, sharpened bone structure, maybe golden strands of glowy flowing hair? Not to mention she wasn't particularly fond of dirt—and I was as filthy as they come, mate.

"Heph. What, uh, what are you doing here?" Her sky-blue eyes widened, and her arms crossed her chest, pushing those two bountiful tits together.

Sauntering toward her with exaggerated swagger, I flashed a cocky grin. Though I'd been well aware she had seen the scar on my face thousands of times through the centuries—*knew* it was there—I still found myself giving her my "good side."

"Aw, I need a reason to see one of my favorite people in the known universe?"

"Now I *know* you want something." She glared at me, her neck flushing.

Thalia leaned on her desk, resting her chin in her hands, grinning at me.

"Thalia." I nodded at her, not letting the smug smile fade.

She gasped and giggled, making a zipper gesture across her lips.

"Mortal names, Heph. This isn't your neon-crazy town. And for the love of—" She stomped a pink heel against the hardwood floor. "You're tracking green stuff from your stupid boots."

Shooting my gaze to my feet, I lifted one boot and winced. "Shit. Sorry."

"Tina, would you please call someone from the cleaning crew to get rid of it? And tell them to start in the hallway." Aphrodite grimaced at the boot-shaped green splotch I'd left on the purple carpet.

"Yes, ma'am."

"Heph, my office." Her honey hair flowed around her as she turned on one heel, heading for the door.

"See?" I said to Thalia, strolling past her desk once she cradled the phone against her cheek and shoulder. "Not here but five minutes and she already wants me to herself."

"Tina" smiled at me and shook her head, shifting into business mode as soon as someone picked up on the other end.

No sooner had I passed the threshold, Aphrodite slammed the door shut and locked it. Her scent as she brushed past me made my head fuzzy for a beat—sweet and sultry. It'd been some time since I'd been this close to her particular aroma. It flooded my mind with distant memories previously buried deep—endless bantering, that one time we engaged in a food fight with grapes, pies, and Olympus knows what else, that oil slick incident that made her dress cling to her like a second skin.

My cheek twitched and I shook my head, keeping my expression neutral and forcing myself to the fucking task at hand.

"Listen—" I started, taking a step forward.

She poked my chest with a stern finger. "You stay on the mat. Do not deviate, clear?"

"Like freshly scrubbed glass, love." Smirking, I broadened my posture. "I see you're still dealin' in the hooker business, eh?" Taking a moment to scope her office décor, I smiled to myself. Everything from the rose paintings to speckling of white furniture and pink accessories *screamed* Aphrodite.

She sighed and leaned a hip against her desk. "For the hundredth time—I'm not a madame of a whorehouse. This is a legitimate business offering companionship."

Making sure to keep my boots on the mat, I leaned to the side, reaching and stretching my fingers for a pink *Power Ranger* figurine resting on a filing cabinet. "And you're telling me these encounters never *ever* end with the two screwing each other's brains out?" I wiggled the toy at her. "I didn't know you collected toys."

She lurched forward and snatched it, resting it on the desk without further explanation.

Hmph.

"Sex is entirely up to the companion, but it is not a

stipulation per our contract with them." Her cheeks turned a darker pink than the blush she wore.

I'd be lying through my teeth if I said I didn't enjoy the shit out of getting under her skin. Always have, really. I remembered the one time over a hundred years ago I ragged on her for *days* claiming she had a crush on a tubby satyr named Barnabus after she touched one of his horns and made his hoof bounce like a damn dog. After a week, she stomped her foot and full-on shrieked at me to "Quit it." It was fucking adorable.

"And you—" I let my eyes roam her body, masking the need to swallow at how the dress hugged her every curve, leaving very little to the imagination. My brain, however, did just fine in that regard. Enough to make me discreetly adjust my trousers. "—you always dress like this?"

"I—" She paused, haughtily tapping her foot before slicing her hand through the air. "What are you doing here, Heph? I can count the number of times you've decided to make a physical appearance. You usually prefer texting?"

Yeah, I did purposely stay out of her company. A constant reminder of something I couldn't have? *Someone* I couldn't have? No. Thanks.

Taking the job had been easy at the time, but now, standing in front of her? Bloody fucking Tartarus. I rolled my shoulders and snapped my gaze to hers. "You're right, Ro. This isn't a friendly visit."

She stood straight, and her face fell blank, the realization traveling over her features like lava from the top of a volcano. "Heph…you didn't."

Not caring about her mat rule any longer, I took a step forward and held my palms up. "Listen, it's not a big deal. The guy wants you alive, probably to give his tuppence worth on your no hanky panky rule, and that's it." I made a crisscross gesture over my heart. "Promise."

Her jaw dropped, and she closed the distance between us, flaring a finger in my face. "I cannot believe you."

It really surprised her that much? Huh.

"Look, this guy has been after you for weeks. He's probably confused about why he keeps losing sight of you. I'd hate for him to find out—why. And me? Well, we both know I'm equipped to handle ya." Against my better judgment, never being one to read the room well, I winked at her.

She didn't say anything, her chest pulsing up and down, nostrils flaring.

Continuing to hold my palms up, I suppressed a gulp. "Come with me, talk to the guy, and we can both be on our merry way, yeah?" I shimmied my hips with a grin.

Still holding a pink fingernail in my face, she slowly narrowed her eyes. "There's something else, isn't there?"

Damn.

Wiggling my fingers, I averted my gaze to the fluorescent lights hanging from the ceiling. "Part of the reward is an ample supply of Ostilanide."

Her eyes fluttered as she rolled them, letting her arms fall slack at her sides. She turned away from me and slapped a hand on her forehead. "Seriously? Oz? You're trading me in for some stupid forging metal?"

I held my index fingers up, stepping close to her again. "It's not just any metal, Ro. It's one of the strongest in the known universe. And extremely rare. Do you have any idea what I could do with metal like that? What I could forge?"

"Get out of my office, Heph." She pointed at the door, her brow drawing together.

I don't think she entirely understood how the whole bounty-hunting deal worked.

"Sweetheart, we can either do this the easy way or the hard way. I already took the bounty, and have a reputation to uphold." Locking her gaze with mine, I made a pair of silver shackles dangle from my fingers.

"You wouldn't." She eyed the cuffs before flashing her gaze back to me.

"Don't test me, Ro. Come on."

Her eyes darted back and forth between the shackles and my face, panic plain as day making her limbs shake. When her eyes glowed a fiercely radiant pink, I knew what she was about to do—make this difficult.

Clenching the cuffs in my hand, I pointed at her. "Ro. Don't."

After a whimper from her, gold and silver glitter plumed the air, covering my face, and making me sputter sparkles. After wiping the back of my hand over my eyes, I opened them to find her gone.

Of course.

"I always knew she liked things *hard*."

There were numerous perks to being a god of the forge. And having the power to create, to build, and to mold damn near anything your heart desires was above them all. I'd taken the liberty of slapping a small tracking device when she pressed her hand to my chest.

Her touch.

I chewed on the hair skirting my upper lip, my mind delving into treacherous territory, imagining those porcelain hands on parts of my body that'd never had the luxury of feeling her, tasting her, *having* her. The beeping from my ethereal tracking device jolted me from my imaginary wet dream.

"There you be, my buxom love-y goddess." I snapped my fingers at the red blinking light from a shopping mall three blocks away.

Three bleedin' blocks? She could port anywhere on the planet, and she picks a mall in the same town?

Shrugging, I shoved the device into my back pocket and produced the porting device. The blue swirls warbled before me, disappearing as I stepped through. I'd almost made the mistake of appearing in the middle of the food court but remembered at the last minute when and where I was. The back alley, lined with shop dumpsters, welcomed me.

"What the?" A skinny teenage boy with a mop of dirty blonde hair covering one eye said, a cigarette dangling from his mouth.

I curled a lip at his apron displaying the coffee shop name *Cupid's Corner*, his heart-shaped name tag hanging crookedly from the strap. Todd.

Just my luck. One singular employee on their godsdamned cigarette break.

"Those'll kill ya, mate." I pointed at the cigarette, gave a half-hearted salute, and strolled past him as if I had *not* walked out of a portal.

He stared at me, unblinking and silent.

Walking through the rusted metal door propped open with a folded paper coffee cup, I paused in the hallway to check the tracker. The mall bustled with dozens of shoppers, most of them in their formative years taking selfies with each other and twiddling their thumbs on their phone screens, giggling. Keeping the tracker in my pocket, I glanced down, the dot blinking faster in the precise place I stood.

I turned my gaze skyward, grimacing at the name of a lingerie store: *Secrets of Venus*.

Fucking perfect.

With my chin held high, I waltzed in, grinning and tipping an imaginary hat at the stares and lingers most of the women shopping gave me.

"Shoppin' for the missus," I said to an employee who eyed me like a creep-o had entered the establishment.

Another woman gasped nearby. "Omigod, I *love* your accent."

"Oh, I, uh—" I peered at her over my shoulder, the face scar on full display. "Thank you?"

The woman's smile faded into subdued horror before she turned around, absently fumbling with the lacey under-roos on the table in front of her.

The looks of disgust, fear, and remorse of mortals and gods alike didn't faze me anymore.

Who knew a bloody scar could say *so* much about a person? And I ain't talking about me.

Her scent fluttered through the air, infiltrating my thoughts and luring me to her like a fucking Siren's call. Aphrodite stood in a back corner, pushing hangers aside of varying lacey numbers with clasps and doodads.

I stood, watching her for likely longer than I should have before sidling up beside her and leaning on the wall. "You should go with the white one. I've always fancied you in white."

Aphrodite jumped, her hand raising to her mouth. "Eris's hair roots. You startled me. How did you find me so fast?"

Squinting at her, I leaned forward. "You're being hunted, Ro. By a seasoned hunter, need I remind you. And you flee three blocks down the damn road?"

She plucked her finger against the plastic of one hanger before she rolled her shoulders back and continued to peruse the lingerie. "We're in public. Plenty of witnesses. You can't do a damn thing here."

"I think you underestimate my level of commitment, my dear." I coated my words with gravel, a spark igniting in my gaze from the volcanoes I commanded.

Her throat bobbed, her bottom lip quivering as she stared up at me like a deer in the crosshairs. She grabbed a handful of hanging lingerie, tore them from their rack, and threw them at my face before bolting out of the store.

Grumbling, I peeled the lacey garments away and rested them on a nearby counter before power-walking after her. The glares I received of absolute death from the women in the store witnessing her sprinting away from me were enough to make me whimper under my breath.

"That's the missus," I said to them with a smirk, picking up my pace. "Said she left her curling iron on at home."

Before a lynch mob formed, I exited and snapped my gaze from left to right, looking for signs of wheat-colored hair whisking through the air. I caught a faint wisp of it as she took a corner turn. Chasing after her, I snarled under my breath.

This is precisely why I hated it here. Forced to *run* after my mark? This was for the godsdamned birds.

Despite her taking the tiniest steps from the dress constricting her stride, I couldn't help but be impressed by the speed she achieved in a pair of pumps. She ran against the traffic of shoppers, expertly cutting through them and no doubt brushing her tits against some of them to get them staring. A failed attempt in hoping I'd run into them. We'd both come a long way from playing Tag in Gaea's gardens as kids—minus the same dynamic of me chasing her. Only back then, I pretended she could outrun me, gave her that false sense of security before tackling her into flowered meadows in a fit of barrel rolls and giggles.

Aphrodite ducked into a department store, making a beeline for the make-up counters. She passed a line of perfumes and took one in each hand, turning toward me and spraying smelly vapors in the air. A pungent misty cloud of overlapping smells slapped me in the face, making me cough, sputter, and gag. I waved a hand, squinting through the haze to keep an eye on where she went.

Was she so reliant on witnesses she wasn't bothering to port? *Not that I should complain.*

"Vena," I shouted as we dodged mannequins, and entered the women's clothing department. "Let's *talk* about this."

Aphrodite ducked behind a circular rack of jeans, putting it between us. "There's nothing to talk about. You made it abundantly clear where you stand."

"Abundantly? Wow. That's a big word." I bobbed a brow at her, pausing on the opposing side of the rack before pretending to lurch right.

She bobbed left and stopped when I did. "Do you ever take anything seriously?"

"Of course I do." I frowned.

Far more than she realized, but acting aloof to the happenings around you kept people guessing. In my line of work, in a celestial existence, it made the day-by-day that much easier.

She faked, running to the left. I fell for it and jerked right, but she stopped, glaring at me. "Name one thing that doesn't involve forging, strippers, or bounties."

She knew me far too well for comfort—especially someone I hadn't seen in the flesh for years.

"Pasta."

Her scowl deepened. "What?"

Flashing a sly grin, I patted the metal bar of the clothing rack. "Pasta. I take it very seriously. Especially when they don't give me enough sauce."

"You're unbelievable." After letting out a frustrated feminine growl, she bolted, shimmying between racks of shirts.

"Shit," I grumbled, following her. The rows were so tightly packed I had to turn to the side to fit through, and my damn jacket kept getting caught on hangers poking out from the rest.

One hanger looped into my pocket, hurling me backward. With gritted teeth, I yanked once, twice, and tore the pocket clean off on the third attempt. Aphrodite cackled into the wind, continuing her maze-like sprint through the racks.

"You're not going to be laughing in a moment, sweetheart," I shouted to her, fingers grazing the porting device in my pocket.

Witnesses be damned. They would never see me again. And what soul would believe any of them were they to tattle?

Grinning like a jackal, I yanked the device from my pocket, pointed it at her, and a warbly blue portal appeared directly in front of her. I'd made it pop up so fast she had no chance of avoiding it.

"Son of a—" She screeched before disappearing to the other side.

four

APHRODITE

I APPEARED IN THE Neosphere District within a single breath, stumbling out of the portal, and landing on an uneven sidewalk. If I were mortal, I'd have twisted a damn ankle. I'd only been here once before, when Heph invited me to some moonlight festival they held yearly. At the time, I couldn't be sure if he wanted me to witness the spectacle or if he knew the nature of the town would give me the heebie-jeebies. Considering his complete disregard for my well-being and his desire for rare metals overshadowing our semblance of friendship, the answer became obvious. Hephaistos had some nerve taking my bounty. It had me fuming inside, but I couldn't let it distract me. Not now. I had to keep moving.

"Now, what did I tell—" Heph started to say as he leaped from the portal.

I bolted, not letting him finish his sentence, avoiding people moseying like a herd of sloths. Mohawks, shaved heads, tattoos, tattered clothes, bright metallic garments, and anything studded were all the rage in this century—not appealing in the slightest to me.

"Aphrodite," Heph beckoned, chasing me and elongating the "e" part of my name. "We're on my turf now, sweetheart. Don't make this more difficult for yourself."

Oh, I'd make it *plenty* difficult. I didn't doubt he'd end up catching me, especially with my powers dwindling, but I'd make him *work* for it. And in some warped sense, I kinda liked him chasing me.

The pulsing bass from a nearby building had my mind reeling—a nightclub called *Mirage*. Deafening music, blurred vision, strobe lights, and a sea of people—precisely what the love doctor prescribed. Grinning at Heph over my shoulder, I ducked into the club, the booming music and rotating lights of varying shades of green, purple, and blue smacking me in the face all at once. A dubstep version of Blondie's *Call Me* overtook the speakers. Was music from the eighties considered classical in this time? Huh.

Bodies jumped to the beat of the music, their hands raised, glowing necklaces, bracelets, earrings, and hats bouncing along with them. Grimacing to squeeze past and avoid an elbow to the face in the process, I kept shooting glances behind me at Heph.

An arm wrapped around my lower back, and someone pulled me against them. My heart raced as I blinked against the dizzying strobe light.

A man with a flavor-saver goatee, shaved head, dirty ribbed tank top, and one eye covered by a microchip grinned smugly at me. "You are fucking gorgeous, honey. How's about a dance?"

I did *not* have time for this.

"No," I chastised him like a puppy, flicking my hand at his face, and sending a glitter bomb spraying.

Flavor-Saver let go, sputtering the glitter that'd managed to make it past his openly smiling lips. He rubbed his one good eye, cursing at me as I shoved past, my heels scurrying across the slippery dance floor coated with sweat, and Olympus knew what else. As a love goddess, the emotions swirling through this place had my skin itching. There wasn't exactly a lot of "true love" floating about, but the lust and passion borderline suffocated me. And I could *not* be prouder.

Finding a quieter, carpeted hallway, I pressed my palms to the walls, steadying myself. Somewhere between the bouncing bodies and me glitter-bombing the sleazy guy, I'd manage to lose Heph. Blowing out a breath, I pressed my back to the wall and let the rhythmic surge of the bass calm my erratic ethereal heartbeat.

A presence loomed over me, a warm current passing my cheek. The faint scents of ash, metal and spicy masculine musk filled my head, making my nails dig into the cushioned wall behind me.

"I think you're losing your touch, love-y goddess," Heph whispered.

I fluttered my eyes open, staring up at him only a breath away from me, one hand pressing into the wall near my head. "Or maybe I was going easy on you."

He could've caged me in with his other arm but chose to give me a way out—a retreat. And why, oh why, wasn't I taking it?

"Nothing with you is ever easy, Ro. And I do mean *nothing*." He edged closer, those mahogany eyes roaming my face and hair—his gaze harboring a sense of comfort, familiarity, and a home-steady toughness that had my knees pinching together.

I couldn't recall the last time we were physically this close to each other. And the flirting? It had always been there—innocent, playful flirtation that became a game between us. And neither party ever succumbed to it—a simple game of eternal back-and-forth.

"I could easily start running again." I puffed my chest, causing the top of my dress containing my boobs to creak. Heph had always been nearly a foot taller than me and never stopped taking it to his advantage, mainly because he *knew* I had a thing for tall guys.

Not disappointing, his gaze fell straight to my cleavage, and he chewed on his bottom lip before raising his eyes. "But you aren't. Funny thing that, hm?"

There'd been a reason for my running versus porting. The last port I performed ended in the shopping mall, and I couldn't do it again. What started as sporadic unreliable porting became a complete inability. But he couldn't know that. And wouldn't.

"This whole cat and mouse routine is far more fun anyway. Don't you agree?" I brushed my bare knee against his leg, flashing one of my trademark sultry smiles.

He dropped his face to mine, turning his head to show the non-scarred side. He'd always been self-conscious about that scar, not that even his own mother had ever made having it easy on him. To me, though, it gave him character and only added to his rugged handsomeness. I liked that he wasn't perfect. He never saw it, but I did. The man was hotter than the very volcanoes he commanded, making the innocent flirting that much easier.

Most of the time, I forgot all about his scar. It was as much of an accessory on him as the heart pendant I wore. And it suited him. He wasn't the stuffy, clean-shaven type I often kept company with. And secretly—I pined over it.

"Know what could make it more interesting, Ro?" His breath traveled my forehead, my stomach tightening.

Rolling my shoulders back, I tilted my chin, bringing our lips inches apart. "You calling this whole thing off so we can continue elsewhere?"

It was part of my genetic makeup to use my feminine wiles to escape a harrowing situation. I had the power. Had the charisma. And as others never let me forget, I had the looks. What did people expect?

Heph's free hand traced one of my wrists, followed by the other, until a tight pressure cursed my skin. "Nice try, babe."

Handcuffs.

I lifted the sparkly glowing cuffs and hissed at them. "You've got to be kidding me." Rattling the shackles in his face, I seethed. "Take these off."

"Not a chance, Flashdance. This wildcat has needs, and you're the ticket." He bumped his knuckle under my chin with a devious smile.

I shrugged away from his touch, snarling. "Is there a reason they're so godsdamned flashy?"

"Not that you've ported that much—still strange, by the way—but these impressive little babies—" He lifted the cuffs by the chain. "—subdue your abilities. I've used them quite a few times through the years. Work wonders."

Rolling my eyes, I didn't budge, pressing my shoulder blades into the wall, and hoping by some twist of the Fates it'd swallow me whole. "Not sure I can ever forgive you for this one, Heph."

"Right. It took a century, but you eventually forgave me for that oil spray incident. I think you can get over this one too." He winked before gently wrapping a hand over my shoulder, gesturing me to walk.

It wasn't as if I could ever call myself innocent, especially in my youth. We'd pulled some fast ones through the thousands of years we'd known each other—pranks, practical jokes, pure spite, and sometimes, we'd exploit each other because we *could*. We knew each other that well. And yet we both continuously let it happen.

Back-and-forth.

He guided me to the dancefloor, smiling and nodding to any patrons who smiled at us and gave Heph a thumbs-up gesture.

"This is so embarrassing," I grumbled.

"Ah, you're of the kinky variety. Now I get it," Flavor-Saver said, raising his hand for Heph to high-five it.

My vision flashed pink, and I opened my mouth to retort, *really* retort, but the cuffs sparked at my wrists, and I yelped.

Heph's grip skirted up my neck, idly massaging it. "Now, now, Ro. You *do* like it kinky at times. Why does that piss

43

you off?"

"As if you would know what I like, lava breath?"

"Lava breath. Wow, bringing out the old stuff, eh?" He led us to the exit. "And simply because we haven't screwed, doesn't mean I don't pay attention. You've never been that tight-lipped about your—escapades."

Pinching my lips together, I blew the hair out of my eyes once we were on the sidewalk. Hover vehicles whizzed past, and the dozens of holoimage ads in every rainbow color rotating on a loop had my head spinning.

"How can you possibly stand it here, Heph? It's dirty. Noisy. Way too animated." I interlaced my fingers in front of me, and Heph curled his arm with mine.

"The Emporium is right down here." He turned us to the left, and side-by-side, we strode through the Neosphere District. "For starters, do you see how we walked past dozens of people with you in a pair of magical glowing shackles, and not a soul gave a flying fuck?"

"I suppose I may have noticed that."

He hugged me to his side and displayed his other hand toward palm trees framing an advertisement for enhancement drugs. "It's freedom, Ro. And so many unique mortals at any waking moment."

A person with a portly belly sticking out from the bottom of a Holo Halos tee danced past us, moving to the beat of his own drum. He snapped his fingers offbeat with every raise of one knee, hitch-kicking the other.

"Ah, see there." Heph pointed at the flamboyant individual who stopped to jump in a puddle in the gutter.

Curling my arms around my stomach, bringing one of Heph's hands with them, I tossed hair from my face. "You, of all people, should know this is entirely not my scene."

"Me, of all people, hm?" His eyes formed that squint. That damn squint which never failed to make my knees feel like caramel.

"You know what I meant. Stop fishing for compliments."

"I wouldn't dare." His gaze lifted to a row of brightly-displayed machines making obnoxious buzzer and foghorn sounds. "Here's the machines. Want anything before we do this? Chimichanga? A fizzy pop?"

I stomped my foot with a snarl. "No, Heph. I don't *want* anything. All I want is to go. Home."

"And you will." He pulled me to one machine, wiggling his fingers at the selections before swiping his wrist over the purchase scanner. "As soon as I get payment and the Oz."

Was he not *leaving* me with this person?

"But you—you're not—how do you—"

He bent forward to scoop the can that'd appeared from the machine into his hand. Pink animated images surrounded the drink, and he popped the tab. "Did you think I was going to strand you here? Especially with a complete godsdamned stranger?"

"The thought did cross my mind, yes."

"Ouch." He pressed a hand over his heart. "I *can* be a right cunt, Ro. But I try to make a habit of not *being* a cunt."

I couldn't be sure why this particular time had caught me off guard or why I thought he'd purposely put me in danger. In the past, we'd *both* taken advantage of the status of our relationship, our friendship, to gain favor. As much as we ribbed each other, we'd always been too close of friends ever to wish any ill will. Or if we'd said it, we certainly weren't being serious.

We continued to walk, and I swatted him on the shoulder, the shackles jingling. "Stop saying that word."

"What? Cunt?"

I thwacked him again with a furrowed brow.

He chuckled and lightly shoved my shoulder. His warm fingers brushing my bare skin launched my stomach into endless tidal waves, but I gulped them away.

"Why do you still use that accent anyway? You only started using it because of your Ian Dury and the Blockheads fixation." I blinked rapidly at a woman with a purple pixie cut, half of her head shaved, walking past us. She wore a see-through plastic dress, the pasties over her nipples and silver g-string the only things keeping her from being *completely* naked.

"If you haven't noticed, sweetheart, it's *progressed* through the ages. I let the accent roam where it pleases and use whatever fucking word springs to mind at the time." He tugged at my arm, garnering my attention away from the bold woman swaggering down the street. "While we're being so judgmental, why don't you use a Greek accent anymore?"

It irritated me how often he made a point—good ones, for that matter.

"I haven't since the twentieth century. California kind of settled into my bones."

He lifted some of my blonde hair with a snarky smile. "No kiddin'."

Elbowing him in the side, I stifled a laugh. I could never recall a moment where Heph failed to make me smile. I could be in the shittiest mood in all of the known cosmos, and he'd find a way to right every wrong. He even went as far as rigging a device to dump glue over Eris's head when she walked into a room followed by a puff of feathers. Pretty sure I laughed for three days straight after that particular stunt.

"You want some?" He offered the can of soda, wiggling it, making its contents slosh. "I know you gotta be thirsty. And it's your favorite. Strawberry." He dragged out the "a" in favorite, his eyes sparking with embers.

Strawberry *is* my favorite.

"Fine. I'll humor you." His callused fingers brushed my skin as I took the can from him. Calluses forged through the ages by the forge itself, hammering away with whatever legendary weapon the gods and heroes desired.

A roaring chuckle escaped Heph's chest. "Humor me? Gee, thanks."

Grinning at him over the can's rim, I took a long gulp. Sweet carbonated strawberry flavoring burst across my tongue, and a peculiar hum vibrated in my chest. I narrowed my eyes and turned the can to view its ingredients. "What the Tartarus is in this?"

Heph slipped the can from my grasp. "This particular flavor is said to be laced with a sort of aphrodisiac." He bobbed his brow before tilting his head back and downing the rest of it.

There'd definitely been more than sugar, artificial flavors, and carbonated water. And given whatever the source, it was powerful enough to affect the goddess of love—it had to be potent.

I wonder…

As Heph turned his attention away, throwing the can in the nearest trash receptacle, I pressed my hip against him, finger-walking up his arm until I reached his chest. "We could always grab a few more cans. Maybe find a motel somewhere?"

A low growl vibrated at the back of his throat, his gaze dropping to my fingernails scraping the cloth over his pecs. "Mm, is Aphrodite herself being affected by a synthetic aphrodisiac?"

"I do feel a kind of—" Tracing my hand down until I reached his belt, I flicked it. "—flutter. Imagine what three more cans would do?"

He pulled me against him, his nose nuzzling my cheek.

Here we go.

"Baby. If I was going to *fuck* you, you better well believe it wouldn't be because of some pharmaceutical love potion." He gave a quick peck to the corner of my brow and tugged the shackles. "Stop stallin', Ro. Let's get it over with."

Damn it all to Cerberus.

"I hope you realize how incredibly infuriating you can be." Clearing my throat, I rolled my shoulders back and followed him to my fate.

"And yet I still manage to make your chest flush." He pointed at my boobs.

Taking the bait, I gasped and dropped my gaze. No redness. Not even pink.

"Caught ya." The skin at his temples crinkled as he flashed a wide grin, wrinkles showing I couldn't recall being there before.

Ironically, we had control over our appearance, save for

the fated parts of us we couldn't touch. My hair could never be any other length or color thanks to my dear father, and Heph could never get rid of that scar. But why did he insist on wrinkles?

"Hey, hey, Heph. That's a far prettier score than I'm used to seeing you bring in," a random person with a floppy purple hat with rabbit ears said as they passed, pointing at me.

"Smells better, too," Heph answered, bowing.

I scowled. "What do you usually bring in?"

"Harpies."

"I'm *so* glad I'm somewhat prettier than a screeching, scaly she-bat."

Heph chuckled and grazed a knuckle over my cheek—quick and non-committal, but still didn't fail to make my insides twist. "You know you're gorgeous, Ro."

"A fact no one seems to let me forget or live down." I stared at the concrete, suddenly interested in counting cracks and grooves.

I caught a subtle frown pulling at Heph's lips from the corner of my eye.

"Here we are—The Bounty Emporium. And look, there's not even a line. This'll be over in a jiff. Easy peasy money needsy." He guided me to the Emporium counter, where a man on a floating chair approached us.

"Holy barnacles, Heph. You nabbed her," the man said, adjusting his cracked glasses with his only hand.

"He didn't *nab* me. He got lucky," I seethed, tapping my foot.

Heph leaned on the counter and raked a hand through his dark hair. "You bet your ass I did."

The man barked with laughter, and I elbowed Heph in the ribs with a glare that could crack the marble flooring on Olympus. Heph made an *oof* sound, and his chuckles dampened.

"I take it you two have a history?" The man gave a toothy grin as he tapped his fingers on the metal countertop.

"To put it mildly, Olaf. So, how do I turn this in?" Heph lifted my shackled hands, slapping them on the counter.

"This?" I leaned my face toward him, sneering.

He made a shoosh gesture with his finger, and I about choked him with the shackle chains.

Olaf swiped through several holo screens, rubbing his chin and scratching what little hair sprouted from his head. "Huh. This is rare. Not unheard of, but rare."

"Talk to me, Laf." Heph tapped a single finger to the familiar beat of *Addicted to Love* by Robert Palmer.

"They want her brought to them." Olaf flew his hand forward, and a device on Heph's wrist brightened. "There's the address."

"You serious, Laf? Curbside service?" Heph grumbled after glancing at his watch and slapping his palm over it to turn it off.

"I'd love to be referred to as something other than a material object." I pound my fists on the countertop for emphasis.

Heph patted my forearm. "Nature of the beast, sweetheart."

"It's a couple of blocks down the way. Shouldn't be too much of a hassle, Heph."

"Virto," Heph responded.

Olaf nodded at me with a solemn expression. "Ma'am."

My jaw dropped, and Heph yanked me away before I could

say anything. "*Ma'am?*"

"At one moment, you're complaining about being eye candy, and another, you're miffed about someone calling you anything other than *miss*. Pick a lane, woman." Heph peered at the neon street signs blazing at the corner and turned us to the right after a beat.

"Oh, don't even start with me. At one moment, *you* come across as this charming playboy, and the next, you're shying your scar away and begging people not to look at you."

Heph stopped and cocked his head to one side. "You think I'm charming?" A lopsided grin played over his lips.

"And then you cover it up with jokes." I tightened my jaw.

"Well, you have it all figured out now, don't ya, goddess of love?"

We stared at each other long enough to make it uncomfortable, heated and we flared our nostrils. Grunting, Heph continued walking with his hand wrapped over my bicep. We remained silent for the few minutes it took to get to the shiny skyscraper erected so high it almost reached the stars. Heph tugged me into the building and onto a transparent elevator with blue beams of light at its corners. Numbers one through five hundred were displayed on a holomenu, with only numbers one through twenty-five showing blue, the rest red.

Heph pressed the intercom button, and a generic feminine voice asked, "Name and nature of business?"

"Heph. Collected bounty," he responded, gruff and to the point.

Number ninety-nine turned blue and Heph bumped his fist against it.

"I've got a bad feeling about this, Phai." A lump formed in my throat, a nickname I hadn't called him in centuries, falling from my lips.

I caught Heph's face in the clear panes of the elevator. His expression resembled someone who'd been hit in the gut and *wasn't* a Greek god.

"Ro, I told you—" He turned me to face him, gripping my shoulders. "In and out. I know we talk shit and have had our fair share of arguments, but when have I ever given you a reason *not* to trust me?"

For a brief, vulnerable moment, I let myself bask in his gaze and swim in those silky chocolate pools like a kid in Willy Wonka's factory. Scowling, I turned away from him, staring instead at the numbers getting higher. "Like you said, let's get this over with."

The doors hissed open, and a titanic loft greeted us—contemporary ala early two thousands via Earth-styled furniture in every corner. A massive red and black leather l-shaped sofa curved through the middle of the room, various throw pillows in white, red, and black haphazardly strewn. Pine tea tables rested at varying points with fluffy white stools—no high backs, no armrests. A roaring center fireplace cascading from the ceiling encapsulated within transparent glass served as the only illumination with the few hanging sconces, making the ambience inviting, intimate, and bone chilling.

"Who did you say put the bounty on me?" I whispered to Heph, wringing my hands together.

"I didn't say. But Riley Cortez."

A sense of relief washed over me. I didn't recognize the

name. Not that I put to memory all of our clients, but not having one that stood out as particularly vile or threatening served as a plus.

"What an absolute sight for sore eyes," a voice sounded from the shadows. When they stepped into the firelight, it was a man with long blonde hair, donning a white billowy shirt and black leather pants. Bile collected in my throat when those glacier blue eyes darted directly at me.

Hippolytus.

How. In the. Ever-loving. *Fuck*?

"Mr. Cortez, I assume?" Heph asked, widening his stance.

"The one and only. Your reputation proceeds you, Heph." Hippolytus grinned at me, sipping on his wine. "Well done, indeed."

"Right then." He gestured me forward, pressing a hand at my lower back. "Give her a piece of your mind, give me what I'm owed, and we'll be outta your hair."

"Oh." Hippolytus placed the back of his hand over his mouth, cackling. "Oh, my. I think you've misunderstood me. *Vena* isn't going anywhere." His laughter fizzled, replaced by a steely glare.

"Come again?" Heph licked his lips and squared his shoulders.

Hippolytus moved forward, his steps resembling the stealth of a tiger stalking its prey. "You've done your job, Heph. You'll receive payment, don't you worry. Vena here, however, stays with me." He stepped in front of me and lifted the chain of my cuffs before dropping it, letting my hands fall limp. "As a sexual servant."

All sounds around me turned into a deafening buzz.

Sexual servant? It made no sense. The idea of sex with anyone or *anything* had always revolted Hippolytus.

"A bloody sex prisoner? For *you*?" Heph snorted and settled beside me, his jacket brushing my forearm.

"Me? Goodness no. I find sex—dissatisfying." Hippolytus's nose scrunched like he'd caught a whiff of harpy guts. "No, no. For them."

Several people began walking out from a back room—men, women, and otherwise. The lust wafting from them made me whimper and stumble backward, only to be met with Heph's steady grip, his arm curling around me. An action performed out of protection as if—claiming me. He was the one who got us into this situation.

A little late for that, *jack*.

FIVE

HEPH

BEFORE TAKING THIS BOUNTY, I'd thought to myself: Heph, you're going to be stirring up old times—making connections with Olympus because Aphrodite has such close ties. Did I listen? Obviously not. And now here I am—getting wrapped up in Pantheon affairs again while dealing with a psychopathic creep who wants to make the goddess of love his crew's sexual plaything. I'm my own worst enemy, I swear it. But I sure as Tartarus couldn't go through with the bounty now.

I tightened my grip on Aphrodite's waist, her appreciative whimper making my chest tighten.

Nah. Fuck the bounty.

"Well, now, see. *That* is going to be a problem." After coaxing Aphrodite behind me, I rolled up my jacket sleeves.

"Excuse me?" Riley the perv asked, raising one brow and swirling the wine in his massive goblet.

It started as molten lava above my bicep until hardening

into blackened volcanic rock, my hammer axe materializing in my palm. "The bounty. It's off."

Riley stared blankly at me before bursting into hysterics, his goons behind him soon following. "Heph, come now. Be serious. You've *never* backed out on a bounty."

"First time for everything. As I told the lovely woman behind me not even a tick ago, I can be a cunt, but I sure as shit ain't *a* cunt." Directing the pointy end of the axe in Riley's direction, I glared at him, lava erupting in my gaze.

Aphrodite nudged me in the side, momentarily dampening my threat.

"Need something?" I said to her over my shoulder through gritted teeth.

She poked me again. "I told you not to say that word."

"Not sure now's the time for that particular fight, sweetheart." I flashed a smile at the awaiting baddies staring at us.

Riley tapped the sharp metal poker situated over his index finger against his glass, obvious irritation pulling his face tight. "You do know the protocol for breaking a contract, I assume?"

"I'm aware," I growled, spurring the hammer to life, the symbols and Greek lettering glowing a fierce orange.

His goon squad produced their own weapons—rifles and shotguns hissing with shock rounds. It wasn't enough to kill a god, probably not even incapacitate us, but it'd hurt enough to piss us still right the fuck off.

"I'm going to give you precisely ten seconds to change your mind, Heph. We're talking about Oz here. I know how rare the metal is. Why do you think I made it part of the reward?" Using the point of his finger jewelry, Riley scratched his cheek, not pulling his gaze away from mine.

"Heph, take these off. I can help." Aphrodite shoved the shackles in my face.

"And do what? Throw rose petals at them?" I countered, still keeping my eye on Riley. "I have it under control." Reaching into my jacket pocket, I produced the porting device. "I don't need ten seconds, biffies. Ta." Curling my arm around Aphrodite standing behind me, I pressed the button with a devious grin.

Nothing happened. No portal. No sparks.

Riley raised a brow, and the goons exchanged perplexed glances.

"Is it dysfunctional?" Aphrodite whispered.

I cleared my throat, flashing another smile at Riley as I feverishly pressed the button over and over to no avail. "I swear this has never happened before."

"Three, two, one," Riley counted down on his fingers. "Apprehend them."

Reaching behind me, I clamped my hand over Aphrodite's cuffs, making them disappear. "Port us. Quick."

"I—can't." Aphrodite stared at her hands like giant oysters.

"What do you *mean* you can't?" I said through a snarl, lifting the hammer as the goons gained ground.

"I don't think right now is the time to explain," Aphrodite growled back.

Shit. Fuck. Bloody shit.

"You all have been such generous hosts this evening, but—" I bowed, backing Aphrodite to the nearest exit. "Run," I bellowed.

We hurried through the door to the hallway while I beat my palm against the porting device, repeatedly cursing at it.

"Oh yeah, beating it to death will fix it." Aphrodite paused at the corner—three routes to take.

Mumbling, I shoved the device back in my pocket. "You say to the man who beats a hammer against an anvil to create killing devices."

Aphrodite turned on her heel, winding some of her hair around one finger. "You still use a hammer and anvil?"

I may have been far too distracted by the looming killing machines on our tail to take the question at face value. "Yeah, sure. Sometimes."

"Huh." She bit her lower lip and threw her hair over one shoulder.

Huh? I feel like I should be taking advantage of something but I wasn't sure what.

"We better pick up the pace." I pressed a hand to the small of her back, urging her to run faster.

We reached the opposite exit door and clamored outside to the adjacent alleyway. Perpetual night blanketed the District, the white moonlight blending with the bouncing neon colors of signs, advertisements, and hover vehicles still bustling. There was Las Vegas, and then there was the Neosphere District that never truly slept. Establishments were open almost twenty-four seven with rotating schedules to achieve ultimate profit.

Aphrodite's heels clicked loudly against the uneven pavement, and I winced, wishing nothing more than to cover the bottom of her damn shoes with cotton balls. I made the axe disappear as we rounded the corner, greeted by a sea of patrons kicking off the party scene in the town center known solely as The Centrum. As we neared traffic, I gently took hold of Aphrodite's arm and moved her to the inside portion of the pavement.

We hadn't made it an entire block before Aphrodite yelped beside me, and I halted.

"Godsdammit," she groaned, hobbling toward me and shoving a heelless pump in my face. "I broke a heel. I *love* these heels."

Making a hissing sound, I took the shoe and tossed it. "Tough go. But we need to keep moving."

"I can't run like this." She pointed at the ground, balancing on her one foot in the one good heel she had, the bare one resting atop it.

Furiously scratching my beard, I peered around her, eyeing the shadows of our annoying goon chasers. "I don't suppose you're willing to run barefoot?"

She gulped, eyeing the mysterious color liquids skirting the ground, a needle or two, and a glowing condom. "Um. No."

"Didn't think so." Growling, I scooped her into my arms, cradling her back and knees, and ran.

She let out a girlish shriek before a shaky breath pushed from her nose. It was subtle, but I certainly caught it. This woman could be a bleedin' traffic light. She gave so many mixed signals, and it'd been that way for centuries.

She wrapped her arms around my neck, her slender fingers brushing the baseline of my hair. Even the tiniest of skin-to-skin contact had my nerves frenzied.

Oof.

My gaze panned over the porcelain stems she called legs

poking from her dress and resting in my arms. Her intact pump hung loosely from her heel, dangling as we turned a corner. A tightness formed in my throat, and I gulped it down, adjusting her in my grasp with a light toss.

"Heph," Aphrodite yelled, pointing behind us with her naked foot.

I whirled around, tightening my grip on her. The goons emerged from the shadows, charging their shock rifles, and grinning. Eyeing them, I pegged the three manly-looking blokes for human, but the more feminine one? She proved harder to crack.

"I'm going to need my arm, love. I suggest you make like a spider monkey and hold on tight." My portable forge fired in my arm, lava from Olympus' mountains boiling and churning.

Her arms tightened around my neck to the point of suffocation.

"Maybe not *that* tight," I squeezed from my throat.

Her grip loosened, and she interlaced her fingers behind my neck. "Sorry."

The mystery lady goon morphed into a grey wolf—or should I say *shifted*.

Every supernatural creature called for a different weapon. Silver would be essential here.

"Ah, a werewolf. Been a while since I skewered one of your kind." Forging a silver sword, materializing it in my palm, I pressed my lips to Aphrodite's ear. "Hold on." I moved my grip under her knees closer to her ass, freeing my other hand to do the *dirtier* work.

The she-wolf howled before charging us, me swirling on

one heel, hitting the dog in the hind legs with the hilt of my sword. From the corner of my eye, I noted one of the human goons raising their shotguns. Aphrodite flicked her hand at him, launching glitter into his eyes.

The man squealed, dropped his weapon, and rubbed his eyeballs. "What the fuck, you *bitch*," he shrieked.

When this guy woke up this morning, I doubt he knew he'd make as big of a mistake as he had just then.

Stabbing the sword into a nearby wooden pole, I produced a knife and hurled it at the glitter-bombed goon, launching it into his trachea. The man gurgled and covered his neck with his hands, blood spilling over his fingers in unrelenting spurts. When he fell to his knees, I yanked the sword free in time to block a slash of ferocious claws from the she-wolf. Aphrodite's face pressed into the crook of my neck, and I grunted as I adjusted my grip under her thighs, twisting to meet the wolf's amber gaze.

A surrounding group of people near us partying in the streets caught wind of the epic battle ensuing around them. One person, sporting a bright yellow biker jacket with silver spikes on the shoulders, pushed a set of speakers closer to us, blasting some form of rave music. The wolf slashed again, but I miscalculated the direction. Avoiding the claws landing on Aphrodite, I turned my back to it, letting them tear through my jacket, digging into my back.

"Bugger it all to Tartarus," I roared, ignoring the stinging pain blazing from my back. It'd heal.

Aphrodite lifted her head with a gasp, her hand pressing between my shoulder blades. A tingle fluttered across my skin before disappearing, the pain still radiating. "Shit. This power deal is getting *so* old," she cursed. "Are you okay?"

"I'll be fine." Shifting her in my grip again, I sliced my sword in front of us as the wolf leaped, nicking its shoulder, and making it cry out. "I'm a tough breed."

Boots scraped the concrete behind us, and I swiveled. Aphrodite kicked her covered foot, landing a hit across the goon's face. It gave me enough time to launch my elbow into his gut, render him weaponless, and slice vertically up his abdomen with my sword, spilling entrails.

"Oh, my—" Aphrodite started before burying her face in my shoulder.

One more goon. And one giant canine pain in my ass left.

The she-wolf took a running charge, claws clacking against the concrete before slashing right, left, and across. I'd met its advances with varied sword blocks. Roaring, the werewolf shot both arms forward, launching them into my chest, and causing me to lose my balance. With Aphrodite still in my arms, I fell on my back, ensuring she landed on top of me, not the ground.

Her sunshine hair grazed my cheeks as she peered down at me, the pink neon lights from surrounding signs giving her that raspberry glow I remembered her having during the times of Olympus. She half-smiled before her eyes widened, and she pushed away, her bum landing on the ground next to me. A goon had snuck behind us, and she threw a foot upward, landing the heel of her pump through the man's eye socket.

"Olympus," I breathed out, watching the man writhe back on his heels, screaming bloody murder.

Aphrodite grimaced as she lifted her hands coated with green and black blobs. Digitalized sirens blared from every direction, making the party-goers yell to one another, scattering. The she-wolf froze, her nose sniffing the air before trotting off.

"What's going on?" Aphrodite asked.

Grumbling, I leaped to my feet and made the sword disappear. "You can get away with a lot here, but the enforcers occasionally become a nuisance." I held my hand out for her to take. Once she did, I hoisted her up and pointed to my back. "Hop on, love-y goddess."

Her tits pushed against my shoulders as she jumped on my back, her arms lightly wrapping my neck. Holding each of her legs by the backs of her knees, I ran us to the nearest alley as the enforcers rolled onto the scene in their sleek shiny black hover cars.

Out of sight. Out of mind.

I tapped her calf. "Nice work back there, by the way."

Silently, as if surprised by my words, she lifted her chest from my back before settling on my shoulders. "Thanks."

It was rather nice having a moment to "catch my breath" and stroll down the street versus running like a harpy outta Tartarus. The company pressed against my back didn't hurt either. We stopped at a crosswalk, and I hitched her higher past my hips—if only to feel her jiggle.

"What—is that?" Aphrodite pointed to a shop across the street called *X-Dreams*. The blinking neon sign was a man wearing a device over half his head, a broad grin on his face, squeezing the air in front of him with two hands.

"Simulated sex, love." I smirked, unconsciously dragging a finger around her ankle.

She guffawed. "Simulated? What kind of fun is that?"

"Not everyone can bag any man, woman, or centaur with a practical snap of their fingers, Ro. In an X-Dream, they can experience *anything* they want—literally."

The walk sign illuminated. As we crossed the street, a businessman in a pinstripe suit and slicked back-hair eyed the woman on my back like his next quest. I glared at him, igniting lava in my gaze. He lowered his eyes to his equally slick shoes and picked up the pace.

"To clarify, I've never screwed a centaur. Screwed *over*? Maybe, but never—ew, no."

Chuckling, I turned down the street, heading for the slummier part of town known as Desolation Row, or what the locals preferred to call—The Dez. I called it home. It was an immediate and vast change of scenery—from the neon radiance of the District to dimly lit muddiness. A straggly cat screeched as it ran past us, patches of its fur and one eye missing. It stopped to hiss before continuing. Aphrodite jolted on my back, her knees pressing against my ribs—the heat between her legs like magma, reaching my skin through the fabric.

Heph Junior stiffened and I closed my eyes trying to imagine something, anything to calm him down. Ares naked. I gagged.

That did the trick.

"Did that cat give you a furball or something?" Aphrodite asked.

Oh, a certain pussy certainly did something…

"Nah. Just thought about that poor dude's guts pouring onto the street."

Blood, guts, violence—none of it bothered me anymore.

"Ugh. Why'd you have to remind me?" Aphrodite blew out a breath, the warmth of it trickling down my neck.

This woman was going to drive me mad, and didn't know it.

"Where are you taking us, Heph?"

Thankful for the snap back to reality, I cleared my throat before answering. "My place."

"Your place. Is—there?" Her hair shifted against my shoulders as she looked around. "It's so—charming."

"Aw, come on, Ro. You know I never liked anything too fancy."

Except maybe—her.

"Too true."

I couldn't see her face, but the way her words had a tilted uplift in tone was almost as if she said them with a smile. And then…her chin rested on my shoulder.

Once in front of my building, I bumped my shoulder into the door, making it swing open. After two flights of iron-grated stairs, we reached the floor with industrial elevators. Several residents hung near the entrances leading to the subways, trading and purchasing all forms of illegal drugs through the gates with dealers waiting on the other side.

"Eileen. Marcus," I greeted them with a stiff nod.

Eileen rubbed the bags under her eyes, her stringy brown bob cut hanging over half her face. The dirty crop top slung off one shoulder, and given the short length of the hem, it clearly indicated she wore no bra. "Heph with company for the night. Virto."

"You know it," I answered, pressing the button again to call the elevator as if it'd make it arrive faster.

Aphrodite pinched my nipple through my tank top, making a playful snarl escape my throat. I cut her a glare over my shoulder, and she grinned at me—radiant and fucking beautiful. The elevator lurched to a stop. Holding her briefly with one hand, I pushed the gate to the side, stepped in, and closed it behind us.

"Mind hitting four, dearest?" I jutted my chin at the glowing buttons on the control panel.

Obliging, she pressed a pink fingernail to the number four. "All the technology in this time makes this place seem ancient."

"It is by comparison, but I don't know. It gives me a sense of familiar comfort, I guess?"

She rested her chin on my shoulder, her bare feet bouncing to the beat of the music playing over the speakers—a light techno song with repeating riffs. As we climbed closer and closer to my floor, a sense of anxiety bubbled under my skin. I'd never had a woman in my apartment, let alone *this* woman. But there wasn't any other choice. I needed to gather supplies and plan to avoid Riley and his crew while trying to figure out a way to fix my teleporting device. Piece of fucking junk.

The elevator chimed, and I pushed the gate open with my foot, strolling down the hall with one working overhead light. I paused in front of my door, staring at the metal five hanging cockeyed below the peephole.

"Are you going to invite me in?" Aphrodite whispered against my ear.

Taking a deep breath, I swiped my wrist over the locking mechanism. The door hissed open, and I carried the goddess of love piggyback across the threshold of my humble abode.

six

APHRODITE

THE MUSKY, SWEET SCENT floating from Heph's skin was enough to make my legs feel numb. Or it could've been the amount of pressure I'd put on them, pinning my knees to Heph's sides, knowing I'd have to dismount him once inside the apartment. Frowning, I pressed my nose against the back of his neck.

Heph patted my bare knee, forcing me to hold back a shiver from the calluses on his palms brushing my skin. "You can hop down, Ro. This floor is far cleanlier than the outside. You can't eat off it or nothin', but still cleaner."

"Aw, but I like having a stallion," I whined, sliding down Heph's body until my feet reached the cool resin floor.

He flashed a cheeky grin over his shoulder. "I bet you do."

Playfully swatting his arm, I swiveled on my heel, turning my back on him and scoping his pad—a modest sized studio glowing in radiant shades of pink and blue from the overhead lights and a pink neon sign hanging over the bed: "But Did

You Die?" The sheets were unkempt, balled up at the foot of it, dingy white sheets with a simple blue comforter. A circular seating area resided in the center of the room, rotating holographic screens playing various television stations. On the back wall was a jumbotron-sized television mounted with cubicles bordering it—each cubby had a different gaming console from the past few hundred years, a different color glow behind each.

"Ro, you may uh—" Heph started.

I turned to look at him, and he swirled his hand over himself.

"You may want to change your clothes?" He waved his finger at the back of my dress.

Grimacing, I craned my neck over one shoulder, eyeing the splotches of green and black across my ass. With a defeated sigh, I swooshed my arm over the garment. I'd meant to conjure a different dress. Instead—I stood fully nude. Pinching the bridge of my nose, I closed my eyes. The wind blew from Heph's lungs and our gazes locked. His eyes lazily roamed my curves before traveling back to my face.

Neither of us said a word, and I wanted more than anything to have the power to read people's minds just this *one* time.

After a forced cough, Heph slipped the jacket from his shoulders and held it to me, looking away. "Here. There's a threads shop on the other side of town. Once I've gathered supplies, we can head there."

"Since when are you the shy type?" I asked, taking it from him and slipping it on with a coy grin. With his gaze elsewhere, I took the opportunity to ogle his toned, tanned arms, biting my lip at the sight of the crane in flight in a surge of embers tattoo gracing his right bicep.

"Not shy. Trying to be respectful." After a glance in my direction to ensure I was clothed, he stepped closer. "Do you want to explain what's going on with your powers? You can't port. Can't summon clothes. What's going on?"

"I—" I tugged Heph's jacket tighter around me, its security calming me. "—don't know."

Lie.

Distracting myself with a rusted red toolbox in the corner, I ran my fingers over the various worn stickers. There was Gizmo from the movie *Gremlins* sporting old school 3D movie glasses, a *Goonies* sticker that said "Never Say Die," and Dorothy from the show *Golden Girls* with a David Bowie-styled lightning bolt over her face.

"That's…strange." He quirked an eyebrow and leaned his face near mine before digging into his jacket pocket and producing the broken teleporting device.

A stray piece of hair fell over my eyelashes, and I batted it away, disguising the gulp he'd pulled from me given his proximity. "Tell me about it. My powers have been fading for the past few months."

Another lie. More like half the year.

But how embarrassing is it to admit you're becoming powerless because the goddess of love is unloved? And I don't mean in the platonic sense—true, passionate, the moon and stars—*love.*

"We'll have to figure that out. As soon as I get this hunk of junk working," Heph grumbled, holding the device up to the light with a snarl.

I plucked the jacket's collar. "I don't understand, Heph. You're a god of technology. Why can't you—" I snapped my fingers near the device.

"Doesn't work like that, love. 'Sides, you know what the main component this is made of?" He held the device between us and arched a brow.

"What?"

"Oz."

I'd never been punched in the ribs, but the realization had to feel similar. "Oh. Shit."

"Shit is right. So, we're sitting ducks until I can get my hands on some of it, or your powers somehow miraculously decide to work again." He sneered and threw the device at a nearby table, toppling over one of several buildings made of Legos.

Cocking my head to one side, I moved to the display, letting my fingers graze the skyscrapers, bridges, castles, and tiny Lego people. "Did you build all of this?"

Heph rubbed the back of his neck as he stepped beside me, putting the building he'd demolished with the device back together. "Yeah. I don't get to forge as much as I used to, and I always need to tinker—to do something with my hands. Hence the Legos, the video games…"

I could think of plenty of things to keep his hands busy.

My pinky brushed his hand as I pointed with a gasp. "Ooo. What's this one? I think it's my favorite." A dark stone castle complete with spires, towers, and a dragon-looking head with its mouth open, and a draw bridge leading into it.

"Ah. That would be Bowser's Castle from the *Super Mario* game." He snapped his fingers near it, and the eyes glowed

71

orange, a lava moat forming around the castle. "The lava completes it, but I don't like to leave it going when I'm not around. Don't want to burn down the damn place."

My gods, he was adorable.

He'd been grinning at his creation before turning his gaze, catching me staring at him with a gooey smile pulled over my lips. "What?"

"Nothing." I turned my attention back to the Lego fantasy city. "I guess I didn't know all of this about you." Flicking my wrist at the gaming console wall, the entire apartment, and finishing with twirling a finger at the Legos, I shrugged.

"How could you?" He bumped his shoulder against mine before turning and walking toward a closet next to his bed.

I'd known the ancient Heph, the old version of him who'd build forts out of anything available to him—sand, mud, twigs, and leaves. In a time when the gods still called on him for weapons, shields, armor, and the like. And despite the Olympians shunning him from Olympus, Heph still made every one of them. I'm not sure if he'd ever admit it to me, but I always figured he did it because it was a sense of pride to him—to continuously hone his craft. But as modern technology arose, making it easier to communicate from afar, we succumbed to it more and more until years had passed since I'd seen him in the *flesh*.

"Is there a reason you don't port? I mean, why the need for a device at all?" I leaned against a counter in the kitchen area. Well, what I assumed was the kitchen, given the single metal sink and rusted fridge.

He yanked a duffle bag from the closet and breezed around

the room, shoving various items into it. "Seriously? You don't remember?"

Frig.

Not having the heart to say I didn't, I raised my brows.

"We all have the things that ground us. Ares might explode at any moment. Your cherub son can only disguise his wings for so long, you apparently start to lose your powers for whatever reason, and me? I can't port like the lot of ya." He pulled several shirts from their hangers and stuffed them in the bag. "It's why I designed the teleporting device. Not only can I go wherever I want, but also *when*ever." He walked past the Lego table, pointing, and glaring at the device. "When it fucking works."

He'd had the chance at Oz only mere moments ago. I was the reason he couldn't fix it. Me.

"Heph." I slipped a hand over his shoulder, halting him.

He glanced at my fingers resting against his bare skin before his gaze lifted, those brown eyes like a worn leather journal—scarred, pained, but inside, beauty, secrets, and history blossomed. "Yeah?"

"You know where you can get Oz. I'm a big girl. I can handle myself. You get what you need to get."

He bent forward, bringing our faces a breath apart. "Olympus, Ro. Are you out of your damn mind? I couldn't live with myself, leaving you with that psycho freak. We'll find it somewhere else." Furiously scratching his beard, he turned away with a wince, continuing his rummaging.

If my heart had wings, it'd be soaring right about now.

I bunched the jacket below my chin. "But you said it's rare.

Hard to find. If that's the only thing keeping the device from work—"

"Aphrodite," Heph snapped, standing up straight and giving me a stern look from across the room. "We'll find another way."

The only time Heph ever called me by my full name was out of frustration, irritation, or impatience. Something told me this time it was all frigging three. He didn't look away from me until I nodded confirmation.

"Are we—going somewhere?" I rubbed my bare feet against each other, watching him paddle around the room like an unruly tornado.

"We can't stay here. It's only a matter of time before they find it. Have to keep moving." Heph whisked open the fridge, grabbing random jars and bottles, and checking their expiration dates before throwing them in the bag.

"But what about all your stuff?" Frowning, I moved toward his gaming console wall, squinting at a figurine glittering from the pink light glowing behind a Nintendo console.

"It's only stuff. Not worried about it."

The sparkling object was a small pink crystal swan, its wings flared. I picked it up with extra care, the delicacy of it evident as I held it in my palm. "What's this, Heph?"

It looked *so* familiar.

He bolted across the room in two strides and swiped it from my grasp. "Nothin'. Another toy. That's all." Chewing on his upper lip, he slipped it into his pocket.

Something furry leaped from a shadowed corner of the room, landing at our feet between us. I yelped and jumped backward, letting go of my hold on the jacket. The creature turned its head, looking up at me with a large pair of brown eyes, its white nose twitching, the long grey floppy ears hanging past its shoulders—a rabbit?

"Hey, Coney. Where'd you hop off to?" Heph asked the animal, smiling. His grin slid away once his gaze landed on the revealing slit in his jacket draped over me.

After clearing my throat, I pulled the jacket tight, securing the gap. The rabbit sat back on its hind legs, lifting its front paws tipped with white to his chest, nose still twitching.

"Heph? This isn't some futuristic experimental rabbit that will turn into a deranged killing machine or something suddenly, is it?" I took a step back.

"Coney? Tartarus, no. He wouldn't hurt a bleedin' fly." Heph squatted and held his palm out to the rabbit, who hopped onto his hand, still eyeing me as Heph stood. "Ro, this here is Coney. My pet slash sidekick. Nothing magical about him."

As if this man couldn't give me any more reasons to want to jump his bones.

"Aw, Heph. He's *adorable*." I scratched the white patch of fur under Coney's chin, cooing. "You are just the tootest thing I ever did see. Yes, you are. I've always loved rabbits."

Heph froze, his eyes rapidly blinking. "Huh. You *have*, haven't you?"

"Yeah." I squinted at him with a quirky grin. "People used to give them to each other as love tokens in honor of me back in the day. Remember?"

Heph rubbed his fingers together, his eyes still wide and

staring into the distance.

What in the Tartarus had suddenly gotten into him?

"Heph?"

He cleared his throat, and a dopey smile pulled at Heph's mouth before he held the rabbit out to me. "Wanna hold him while I finish packing?"

"Is Artemis celibate?" I made grabbing gestures with one hand, keeping the jacket secure with the other.

Heph moved in front of me and, with gentle care, picked the rabbit up and nestled him in the crook of my arm, like cradling a baby. "There you are." Grinning, he wiggled the tip of his finger against Coney's nose. "He already likes ya." Heph turned away to finish shoving random items into the duffel, a red, black, and white patch sewn into the side that read: My other car is the Normandy SR-2.

"I never imagined you owning a pet, let alone a rabbit. Thought you'd always had a thing for dogs or donkeys." Making kissy faces at Coney, I scratched his belly with my fingernails, causing his back leg to thump against my arm.

Heph chuckled and shook his head. "You remember *that*, but not my inability to port? And why would I have a pet jackass?"

Why *had* I remembered that?

"Because they're as stubborn and stoic as you are?" I shrugged.

Heph ran the tip of his thumb over his bottom lip. "Yeah. Alright."

"Do you have an idea of where we can go?"

"Nope," he responded. "But that's half the fun of it."

"Fun?"

He strolled past me, nudging his knuckle against my cheek.

"Yeah. Still not the adventurous type, I take it?"

I'd always dreamed of going on adventures. But my dad and stepmother at the time made damn sure I knew how disreputable it would've made me. Times were different now, however, so what was stopping me?

"I never said that." I lifted my chin and lightly rubbed one of Coney's velvety ears between my fingers.

"Oh, yeah?" Heph flashed a brilliantly white smile, his gaze sparking to life. "I'll have to remember that."

My confidence soon morphed into anxiety. What the Tartarus was that supposed to mean?

He winked at me before plucking a toothpick from a Hello Kitty dispenser on the counter and shoving it in his mouth. "We should get going. We'll stop to get you some clothes first, but Ro, when I say you have five minutes. I *do* mean five minutes, yeah?"

"Oh, yes, of course. Five minutes. Tops." I crossed my fingers behind my back.

Heph walked past the Lego table and snapped his fingers, backing up to pluck one of the small yellow Lego people from it.

I tilted my head to one side, eyeing the figure with blonde hair and a giant sword.

"For whatever reason, Coney loves the He-Man one. Figured I'd bring it along." Heph wiggled the figure between two fingers before dropping it in his pocket.

"He doesn't chew on it?"

"Nah. Just likes to hold it in his mouth or paws. Funny, eh?" A flash of white beamed from his beard as he smiled at me. "Right. Come on, Coney." Heph whistled for the rabbit, holding open a side pocket on his duffel bag.

After the obedient rabbit hopped into his makeshift transport, I leaped onto Heph's back again, and all three of us headed off to the clothing store *Bows Before Hose*.

Thirty minutes later…

I stood in a fitting room outfitted with a three-hundred-sixty-degree holo mirror allowing the customer to switch out accessories by selection without grabbing them from the shop floor. It was a gal's dream zone. The style, however, of this particular era didn't seem to settle with me as the leopard print dress I currently wore was the tenth dress I'd tried on, and it still didn't sing to me.

"Ro, please, for the love of Olympus, you need to pick something," Heph groaned outside the room. "These clothes are *not* going to be what you're used to."

Sighing, I turned to look at my ass, snarling. "I know, I know. I want to look at least somewhat good, though."

"For who? The bad guys after us?"

For you. Maybe?

Tapping my finger against my lips, I slapped my palm on the locking mechanism, and the door hissed open. Heph had been slumped on a bench with the collar of his jacket popped but sat up straight, shaking the sleep from his eyes. "What about pants?"

"What about them? I quite like trousers." He pointed at his crotch. "So long as it leaves plenty of room for the hammer, if y'know what I mean."

I leaned against the doorframe and folded my arms in a huff. "Yeah, but you're a guy. I can't remember the last time

I wore pants."

Heph stood and sauntered toward me, pressing his hand above my head, his height creating a whirlpool of nerves and lust in my stomach. "Then live a little, sweetheart. You know your ass will look good in anything."

Maybe he was right. And adventuring seemed far easier when you didn't have to worry about a random gust of wind showing off said ass. Yes. I could make it cute. Clothing had always been a specialty of mine.

"On it," I said with a nod, hissing the door shut.

"Finally," Heph breathed out.

Shimmying out of the leopard dress, I smiled. "I heard that."

"While you're in here playing dress up, the closer these goonies are to finding us. I'm only being cautious."

Hephaistos, right again.

"Okay, I'm hurrying, I promise," I yelled back to him through the door.

Slipping on a pair of black skin-tight shiny pants I'd tried on earlier, I looked at myself in them with newfound appreciation. Yes. A new love goddess. I paired it with a prism belt that changed color from blue, to pink, to purple depending on what angle you viewed it, a zip-up cropped halter top that bared my midriff, and a cropped hot pink jacket. The shoes, however—were another matter.

I chewed my lip as I stared at three pairs lined up on the floor—clear high heels, wedged mid-shin high black boots, and a modest pair of white sneakers. The decision was so harrowing it made me pace. On the one hand, I've always been able to sprint in heels without issue, but there was the risk of it breaking like earlier. On the other hand, sneakers were ideal footwear for running and made for more traction. I rubbed my temples.

"Ro," Heph beckoned, dragging out the "o."

Slapping my hands over my face, I grabbed the boots. "Fine."

Finally tumbling out of the changing room, I pushed the jacket sleeves up to my elbows and tossed my hair.

"Damn," Heph breathed out, his lips parting as he pulled the toothpick from his mouth, staring at me.

"What?" I played with the o-ring attachment on the zipper of my halter top. "Do I look bad?"

Heph slowly shook his head and adjusted the bag on his shoulder. "I don't think that's possible for you. You'll blend right in with that getup."

"Yeah?" I grinned and clapped my hands.

"Definitely." He nudged his head toward the cashier. "I'll treat ya, considering I assume you're not storing any drachma in those pants."

Flashing a sultry upturn of lip, I turned on my heel, walking in front of him. Warmth coiled through my chest when I caught his gaze falling straight to my ass.

Meeting me at the register, Heph peeled one sleeve of his jacket back far enough to reveal his wrist. "All this, please." He gestured to me from head to toe.

The cashier, a bald woman with rose tattoos surrounding her skull and a nose ring with a chain from one nostril to an earring in her upper ear, nodded and lifted the scanner.

"Oo—and this," I said, plopping the white sneakers on the counter at the last minute.

Heph raised a brow.

"Just in case?"

"Fine. Those too," Heph lifted his wrist to the device.

A display with various glowing, colorful lollipops resided near the exit, and I jumped. "Oh, and one of those? Please?"

The cashier eyed Heph like he was my sugar daddy, patiently waving the scanner back and forth and trying not to smile as she waited for Heph's answer.

Licking his lower lip, he gave me a sardonic grin and nodded. "Fine." He turned to face me, leaning an elbow on the counter and inter-lacing his fingers in front of him. "Anything *else*, my dearest?"

Taking one last glance around the shop as I popped a strawberry lollipop in my mouth, I shook my head. "Nope."

"Grand." Heph turned back to the cashier and lifted his wrist for scanning before grabbing the sneakers and shoving them in the bag.

We waved at the cashier as we exited and once back on the sidewalk, Coney's head poked out from the bag, his whiskers twitching.

Heph patted the rabbit's head with two fingers. "Not yet, bud. I'll let you know."

The rabbit's ears drooped lower before his head disappeared into the pocket.

"You're right. This'll be fun." I curled my arm with his and pushed the lollipop to one corner of my mouth.

"I know I joked about that earlier, but Ro, we're on the run from the fucking mob or whatever they are. This will be anything but a carnival ride." Heph scanned our surroundings before pulling me away from the street side of the sidewalk, situating me near the buildings we passed.

A truck ran a stop light at the intersection ahead of us, its headlights blazing, engine roaring, and heading—straight for us.

I may have spoken too soon.

SEVEN

HEPH

IF I HAD A drachma for every time I'd been in a situation with a speeding vehicle, I could build my own Olympus. Cortez made it clear he knew of my reputation which meant he knew I wasn't human. And yet here we stood, watching a truck screech at us as if it wasn't one of the easiest attacks for me to overcome.

Coaxing Aphrodite behind me, I stood my ground. The plasma sword I conjured from my arm started as a hilt, gradually materializing the blazing blue plasma blade, its length the entirety of my torso. As soon as the vehicle's tires hopped the curb, I swung the sword forward, slicing through the metal with ease and tearing it straight from its axle. The wheels rolled into oncoming traffic, causing civilians to honk and swerve. And the cabin plopped onto the pavement, the driver inside staring at me wide-eyed, still clutching the steering wheel.

"Jesus Christ," the man squealed, refusing to let go of the wheel as if it would save him.

Leaning on the car's window seal, I patted the door and twirled the sword in my palm, the plasma hissing as it cut through the air. "Now that's a name I haven't heard in a while. Cortez sent you, I presume?"

"And why the fuck would I tell you that? You damn near made me a double amputee." The man wrung his hands on the wheel.

That'd be a yes.

Sniffing the man, I frowned. Another human. "The only reason you're alive and still have both your legs is so you can run back to Cortez and deliver a message."

His Adam's apple bobbed as he stared me down, surely trying to gauge if I was full of shit. After scanning my face, the stiff posture I maintained, and the absent twirling of my sword, he narrowed his eyes. "What's the damn message?"

I pointed at his wrist. "You may want to record this. I'd hate for you to get anything wrong. Nothing like being misquoted, y'know?"

The man rolled his eyes but obliged, tapping his wrist and making a holographic recording device spring from the chip beneath his skin.

"I don't think you realize who and what you're dealing with, Cortez. You're in way over your fucking head and I can handle anything you send my way. Why don't you be a good biffy and quit while you're ahead? Save yourself some bloodshed and the need to hire recruits. Sincerely, Heph." Smirking, I nudged my chin at the man. "You can stop there. Now use those two legs I spared you and sprint back to your little base and deliver the message. Got me?"

"Whatever, Freak," the man grumbled.

Volcanic lava boiled in my veins, my gaze turning crimson, the orange glow radiating in my eyes as I glared at him. With a snarl, I stabbed the sword through the open window, slicing through one of the man's forearms resting on the steering wheel. The plasma cauterized it on contact, leaving him one-handed. The man cried out, holding his stump, and staring at it.

"I sure hope you're a righty, champ." After patting the fuckwit's shoulder, I made the sword disappear and turned to face Aphrodite.

"Was that entirely necessary?" Aphrodite asked, pointing at the man still wailing and holding his handless arm.

After rolling my shoulders and cracking my neck, I motioned for her to follow as we continued down the footpath. "Yes."

"You don't think that was slightly over the top?"

"No," I growled, still stewing over the man's audacity. "People always seem to forget that words have consequences."

Aphrodite went quiet, falling behind stride and trailing behind me.

I stopped, turned on my heel, and canted my head at her. "Ro?"

"You saying that makes what I need to stay that much harder." She clutched her pink jacket at her neck, unable to make eye contact with me.

Fucking Tartarus. I knew that look. Whatever she was about to say was going to turn our situation into shit the size of Cerberus's. The last time I remember that expression was when she ported from Olympus to my forge, confessing that she inadvertently caused the Trojan Wars over some godsdamned golden apple. Only it'd been two years since it had happened.

"Excuse me," a woman's voice screeched from behind me.

After pointing my finger at Aphrodite to signify the conversation wasn't over, I turned around. A black-haired woman with sunken eyes wearing a dingy olive military-style jacket, cargo pants, and high-top yellow sneakers greeted me. A young boy stood at her side, his head reaching her hips, his tiny fingers plucking at his baggy black pants, the sleeves of his red shirt traveling over his knuckles, and the hem falling to his knees.

"Yes?" I asked, the hesitation clear as mud in my voice.

"You almost hit my son from the little stunt you pulled." The woman curled her hands over the boy's shoulders, patting him.

The tyke rubbed his shaved head, his expression bordering on boredom. He certainly didn't *seem* rattled up. My guess? She was after some nakas, this century's most used form of digital currency, and used her poor son's age as leverage.

"Aw, come now. Not even a scratch on him. You got a tough one here." I playfully nudged the boy's shoulder, enticing a proud smile from him.

"That is not the point, and you know it. I demand monetary compensation to take him to a med station." The woman's elongated nose raised, her nostrils flaring as she puffed her chest.

Bingo. Don't get me wrong. It got tiresome being right about damn near everything.

"Compensation? Sure. I can do that." Sniffling, I cupped my hand behind my back, wiggling my fingers as I summoned steel, molding it into a horse. Once done, I produced the toy and held it to the boy. "There you are, son. How's about that, eh?"

The boy's eyes beamed as he took the shiny horse, the dozens of neon lights from signs hanging overhead glinting from it.

"Look, mommy, look," the boy bellowed, holding the toy up for his mum to see and neighing.

"I can see that, Tommy. How very…gracious of this stranger." The woman glared at me before turning her son around and walking away.

"You're welcome," I shouted, waving.

Aphrodite stepped beside me with folded arms. "You're pretty good with kids. I never would've guessed."

"Eh. Kids are cute and all, but—" I rubbed the back of my neck, heat flushing my skin that had nothing to do with lava. "—can you imagine a guy like me with a kiddo?"

A sparkle glinted in Aphrodite's gaze as she seriously pondered my question. When those plump, glossy pink lips parted to answer, I held a finger up. "Don't think I've forgotten you were going to come clean about something. Out with it." I made a "let's have it" gesture.

"I know this is the worst time to bring this up, but after the message you left and the—I mean—what if I told you Riley Cortez wasn't Riley Cortez?" She kicked a pebble, her gaze concentrated on the ground.

Fuck me dead.

"What are you goin' on about, Ro?" I combed my beard with three fingers, the lava simmering under my skin.

"He's…Hippo." Those sapphire eyes finally lifted to mine.

"He's a hippo? Like a shifter? I never fucking heard of a werehippo that's—"

Aphrodite stepped forward in a huff. "No, Heph. He's Hippolytus. Hippo."

The lava hardened, making my entire body stiffen before melting away.

"What?" I growled, closing the distance between us with a single stride.

Aphrodite hugged the jacket tighter around herself. "Hip— Hippolytus?"

"I heard you the *first* time, but let me make sure I understand you. Hippolytus, the ancient Grecian fuckstick?" I'd said it through gritted teeth, forcing the lava to stay at a simmer and not catapult to a feverish boil in a nanosecond.

Aphrodite bit her lip and leaned away from me. "Yes?"

"Fucking shit, Ro," I roared, raking a hand through my hair and turning away from her before spinning back. "Why didn't you say something sooner?"

The skin between her eyes creased, and she stomped her foot. "Don't yell at me."

Pressing my palms together as if I were a mortal praying to the very gods I belonged to, I stepped closer to her. "Aphrodite. Sweetheart. It would've been imperative information to know, preferably before I made an ass of myself unknowingly in that message. Not to mention, I thought we were dealing with an average mafia boss who had nothing but humans and shifters in his ranks. Here I come to find out—he's an immortal shit stain."

"I'm sorry, but you've dealt with plenty like him. Is this not the same thing?"

Shaking my head, I quickly snatched the porting device from my pocket. "If this worked? Not a big deal. If you worked—" I poked her in the shoulder. "Even less of a big deal. But *neither* work."

Aphrodite groaned and pinched the bridge of her nose. "I didn't say anything because I was embarrassed, alright?"

"What could you have possibly done?" I threw my hands to my hips.

"I made him fall in love with his stepmother."

Blinking, I did quick calculations in my head, moving my forefinger to and fro. "Ew."

"Exactly." Aphrodite slapped a hand over her face with a deep sigh. "It was a long, long time ago. Clearly, the bastard still holds a grudge. I thought Uncle P trampled him with horses, but here we are."

If any other person had dropped the nuclear bomb Aphrodite had, I might have blown a gasket. And she was not the same goddess of love from years ago. Something about her changed—evolved even, and it made me that much more drawn to her.

"Alright. This is fine. We can handle it. However, I need you to follow my lead, Ro." I scooped Coney from my pocket, cradling him in the crook of my arm as I scratched his head. Still can't fucking believe I felt compelled to buy a rabbit because of the woman standing in front of me, and I didn't realize it at the time. "No questioning. No deviating. No being a hero. I know you're capable of more than you pretend, but now's not the time to prove it to me. Understand?"

She frowned and nodded. "Yeah, Heph."

"Alright. We need to find a place to stay where they won't be able to track us. I know of a few that don't require digital payment, but I'll warn you—they're not the cleanliest." Raising a single brow at her, I slid Coney back in my pocket, jerking when I realized I'd slipped him into the torn one and quickly corrected.

Aphrodite gulped before lifting her head in defiance and flicking blonde wisps from her eyes. "I can deal."

"Grand. Let's get on with it then, yeah?"

We walked with our elbows brushing, Aphrodite sticking to my side as promised. An illuminated red crosswalk halted our efforts, and I stopped walking, waiting with the rest of the crowd for it to turn green. Aphrodite, however, after looking both ways, went to cross the street. I threw an arm in front of her, desperately trying to ignore the feel of her tits pressing against my arm as I coaxed her back.

"Are you serious? The rebellious Hephaistos doesn't dare jaywalk?" Aphrodite bit back a smile.

"Not here, I don't." I pointed up without bothering to look. "This is what you were about to walk into."

An aerial patrol car whizzed past us with such speed it made our hair plume.

Aphrodite followed it with a quick whip of her head, and her jaw dropped.

"Think a god can survive a decapitation? 'cause me? I don't care to find out."

The green walk illumination chimed around us, and I held a hand out for Aphrodite to move first. She didn't budge for a moment, the shock still washing over her features. After wrapping my arm around her waist with a light chuckle, I guided us to the other side of the street. I'd led us several blocks, going off memory and sheer determination alone in finding one of only a handful of joints that accepted physical currency. Any time you swiped your wrist for damn near anything, you announced your position to the world. We needed to keep a low profile. And in a highly tech-based culture? It was far easier said than done.

"Let's cut through here. The motel should be on the other side, and it'll save us a few precious minutes." I led us through a nearby alleyway littered with a dozen dumpsters overflowing with trash and overlapping stenches, which rivaled a decaying corpse lying on top of a bed of moldy cheese.

"Minotaur's balls, Heph. It reeks in here," Aphrodite said, pulling her jacket over her nose and mouth and fanning the air in front of her as if it'd make it somehow go away.

"Get used to it, sweetheart. Until we're out of this mess, no more high-life living."

The spine-tingling sound of metal scraping against metal echoed off the alley walls. We froze, and orange sparks sprouting from a nearby dumpster flashed in the corner of my eye. I slowly turned around, balling my hand into a fist behind my back, waiting to spy what brand of weapon I'd need to forge.

A being with a spiked blue mohawk, a Hannibal Lecter mask over his mouth, a dingy white ribbed tank, and bright orange punk pants edged toward us. The sparks came from the two long pointy claws protruding from the knuckles of their cybernetic arm—replaced from his shoulder to his fingertips. Silver hoses with a glowing blue substance weaved through the arm, the pistons purring and hissing as the arm moved at the command from its host. They continued to drag their claws across the dumpsters, putting the sound of nails on a chalkboard to shame.

"That you, Skunky? What's it been? Ten years? Aren't you 'Minty-fresh' nowadays." I smiled. Tobias Flynt, nicknamed Skunky, don't ask me why, had been a bounty hunter I ran into on numerous occasions. The cybernetic implants were a new addition.

Swirling and molding an EMP baton into my palm, I kept it hidden behind me, waiting to jolt this fuck's entire circuit board system. He'd become more machine than man, which made him stronger, sure, but also more vulnerable to the people who knew how to handle him.

He laughed a deep, echoed chuckle that made my skin crawl. "Such jokes from the number one wanted man in the district." He reached the end of the last dumpster and sunk his claws into it, carving huge slits.

"Pardon me?" I gripped the baton tighter.

He appeared in front of us within a blink—or a "glitch," as most cybernetic outfitters labeled it. Aphrodite gasped beside me and gripped my forearm.

"Heph, the infamous galactic bounty hunter, doesn't even know of the insurmountable bounty on his own head." Skunky flashed a holoimage from his wrist—a glance at the *new* pain in my ass. Now *both* cheeks were covered.

"Ah. How nice of someone to set up an opportunity for me

to take out my competition." Still smiling, I tossed the baton in my palm, waiting for the right moment.

His cybernetic eye twitched as it scanned Aphrodite. "Two Greek gods. Finally, some fun for once."

"How did he—" Aphrodite started but stopped when I bumped my hip against hers.

"Fun, eh?" Snarling, I stirred the baton to life, swiping it overhead and toward Skunky.

He let out a menacing laugh before glitching away. "Today wasn't about bringing you in yet, Heph. I simply wanted to see what I was dealing with. The next time we see each other, however, will be the last."

Skunky slammed his claws into another dumpster and disappeared around the corner amidst the sparks.

Pulling on my jacket sleeves, I made the baton disappear with a huff. "So dramatic."

"Heph, you'll have every bounty hunter in the District looking for you. How the Tartarus are we going to handle that at half strength?" Aphrodite grabbed my shoulder, turning me to face her, panic lacing her words.

"We are going to have every bounty hunter after *us*. You're still part of the deal, too. which tells me 'ol Hippo is the one who assigned it." I popped the collar of my jacket. "Oh, and love, it won't be only the District. With that reward amount? We're talking universal."

Aphrodite's bottom lip quivered. "Heph, what are we going to do? How are we going to beat this?"

I couldn't recall the last time I'd seen this goddess frightened. *Truly* scared. Probably when she'd come to me sobbing to tell me how Medea murdered her brother and the two sons she had with Jason. She swore it was her love spell that'd gone wrong and compared the sight of the two young boys to her own son, Eros. It took me hours to calm her down.

Sighing, I pressed my hands to each side of her face and held her gaze. "I know your power is being an outright cunt right now—" She nudged me in the stomach, and I winced. "—but you're still a Greek god, Ro. We got this. We just need to be careful. The first step? We keep moving. It makes it harder for them to track us. But tonight? We bunker down and make for it again in the morning."

She nodded, and I could've sworn she nuzzled her cheek against my palm for a beat. "Alright, Heph. I *do* trust you."

My heart lurched in my chest like a hammer striking iron, and I lifted my hands from her face. "You do?"

She swatted me in the chest. "Of course I do."

She waltzed past me in the direction I'd been heading before Skunky interrupted us, leaving me dumbfounded in a stinky alleyway. After I hadn't budged, my mind reeling at her words, she cleared her throat. "Heph? Are we going to get a room or what?"

Aphrodite asking to get a room with me still wasn't helping my mind to focus, that's for damn sure. I sniffed, snarling and wiping a hand down my face before slapping myself. "Right. One five-star luxury suite coming right up, Ro."

And a god of the forge fighting every compulsion Aphrodite's scent sparked—in close proximity.

Bloody. Fuckin'. Tartarus.

eight

APHRODITE

I COULDN'T RECALL THE last time Heph and I had ever "roomed" together.

Scratch that.

We've *never* roomed together.

The realization bubbled as we walked into the room, and it nestled under my skin when I heard the door click and lock behind me. Nerves I never knew existed prickled my skin, but I kept my "goddess of love cool" expression.

The room's size barely rivaled a refrigerator box with yellow carpeting, a single floor lamp, a *single* bed with a gaudy green swirly-patterned comforter, and a round table with one wooden chair in the corner. I hugged my jacket around me as if the air in the room would suffocate me.

"Wow. This place is uh—" I started, tapping my feet against the carpet, my heels sinking into it.

"Stinky? Disgusting?" Heph rolled his neck as he moved to

the singular window in the room with metal grating over it.

"I was going to say—homey."

Snickering, Heph peeled the thin curtain aside, glaring at the distant neon-lit horizon. "Homey? You? Isn't it missing marble flooring, and expensive silk linens? Not to mention, it doesn't have nearly enough pink for your taste? As in—zero pink?"

Ouch.

Though, I guess I asked for that. It wasn't as if I *ever* made anything simple. And simplicity right now sounded frigging blissful.

I shrugged and canted my head at the art hanging above the bed—a warbly painting of what I perceived as a woman bent over, a man railing her from behind. "Sometimes, frilly is too complicated."

"Did I just hear you shun frilly?" Heph said from directly behind me, making me jump.

Clapping a hand over my chest, I whirled around and blew a breath. "I thought you said you couldn't port?"

Heph had Coney curled up in his palm, the rabbit's eyes forming slits as he fell asleep. "I can't. But you were so hung up on staring at that gods-awful painting of a blacksmith and his anvil you didn't hear me walk over here."

"A blacksmith and anvil?" I snapped my attention back to the painting, squinting at it. "Is *that* what you see?"

Heph moved beside me, brushing my shoulder with that torturously taut bicep. "Yeah. Why? What do you see?"

Puckering my lips, I took an extra moment to gaze at it before answering. "Sex."

"I can see that." Heph let out a deep chuckle, and a glint

formed in his eyes as I turned to look at him. "Love and forge, eh?" He pointed between us.

We stared silently at one another until the stale air in the room choked us into looking away.

"We should uh—get some rest. Olympus knows what'll be thrown at us tomorrow with that bounty posting fresh tonight." Heph cast his gaze to Coney as he scratched the rabbit's head. "You know, I always found it ironic that we, eternal deities, still need our shut-eye."

"Maybe twice the lifespan means twice the energy consumed?"

Heph paused, slow-blinking. "That's not a half-bad theory there, Ro."

How disgustingly sad was it that an ounce of praise for something clever I had the nerve to say made me feel weightless enough to float to Olympus?

"I have them on occasion." Playing it off, I stretched a coy grin and brushed off each shoulder.

"More than occasionally."

The smile dropped like an anvil, and I shot my gaze to meet his.

"And yeah. I'm calling you out on it." He used a single knuckle to nudge my chin. "Now then, Coney usually has a bed. I'll need to improvise."

As Heph turned away, rummaging through what little was in the room, I traced a fingertip over my chin, staring at the yellow carpet like quicksand.

"There you are, little buddy. Sorry it's so hard. I can't summon anything—*fluffy*."

Heph had made a square metal box, and he rubbed the

rabbit's chest as it looked at him with saddened eyes.

"Fluffy happens to be my specialty," I announced with my head held high, striding across the room to save the day.

…or so I thought.

Heph wrinkled his nose but stepped aside. I fanned my fingers at the bed, my forehead creasing as I concentrated. A pathetic sputter of glitter drizzled from my palm before making a faint wheezy sound. Gold glitter coated Coney's nose, and he twitched it before releasing the tiniest sneeze I'd heard in my ethereal life.

My shoulders slumped, and I sighed. "Do you know how powerless this makes me feel, Heph?"

The broken porting device appeared in my line of vision, and he wiggled it. "I have a vague idea."

Coney curled up in the corner of the makeshift bed, shivering. Tugging the pink jacket from my arms, I folded it before lifting Coney and tucking him into the cotton comfort. His small furry head nuzzled against the sleeve and he yawned.

"Well, that was nice of you. But aren't you going to be cold?" Heph lazily pointed at me as I rubbed my bare arms and midriff.

I could think of a few ways to keep warm, you big lug.

"I'll be fine. The poor thing was shivering, Heph. He's helpless. I'm not."

We offered small smiles to each other, going quiet again for the second time that night.

Forcing a cough, Heph slid the black duster coat off his back, crumpling it into a ball. I dug my nails into my skin, spying the muscular, tanned, and toned arms on full display. The lighting in the room played off each curve at all the right angles. The crane tattoo seemed to take flight amidst the shadows.

"I noticed there's only one bed." I motioned my head toward it.

"This place typically rents by the hour, if you get my drift. Can't get the job done as easy pushing two twinsies together, eh?" Heph chuckled as his eyes roamed the bed, lingering on the rows of bars in the headboard.

"You'd be surprised." I chewed the inside of my mouth.

Heph's muscles tightened, and he looked away, giving me the non-scarred side of his face as he tossed the coat in his palms. "Right. You can take the bed. Ain't like I've never slept on a motel room floor."

"The floor? Heph, you can't. Look at this thing." I pointed at a large red stain on the carpet near him. "Like that one. Something tells me that isn't wine."

Heph sniffled and lifted his boot from the stain. "Nah. Murder more like it."

"*Heph.*"

"Ro, we're gods. It's not like we can catch diseases." He tossed his coat to the ground and sank to his knees. "I'll be square. Promise."

Grinding my teeth together, I crossed the room and snatched the coat. "Get in the damn bed, Heph. Don't be so ridiculous. We're not only gods but *adult* gods."

He didn't stand at first, remaining on his knees and staring at me. "Al-righty." Heph slowly rose to his feet. "Are we, though? Adults, I mean? Or does living for eternity mean it takes that much longer to mature? Do we ever?"

"Let's save that one for tomorrow." I tossed his coat on the bed and crawled onto the opposite side. "I've expelled my one good theory for the day."

The wall light blazed in the corner, and I extended my fingers. When nothing happened, I let my hand fall to the mattress before shooting it back out, making my whole limb shake with the effort. Growling in defeat, I curled my hand back to the bed.

"What were you trying to do?" Heph asked, making the bed dip as he sat on the edge.

My insides fizzled and popped.

"Turn off the stupid light." With my face shoved into the pillow, the words came out muffled.

I peeked with one eye, catching Heph smiling. He clapped his hands together twice, and the light disappeared.

"Show off," I mumbled, following it with a grin.

Shyness never played a part with me in situations like this, but I turned my back on him to make us as far apart as possible. After crawling under the covers, I wrapped my arms around my torso, gritting my teeth to keep them from chattering. A weight soon settled on me, scents of leather and ash wafting. Blinking my eyes open, I spied Heph's duster draped over me.

"You loaned Coney your jacket. I loaned'ya mine. Seemed only fair. Besides, you were making the whole bleedin' bed vibrate from your shivering." Heph smirked before laying on his side, he, too, keeping his back to me and teetering on the edge.

"Thanks, but what about you?"

He peeked at me over his shoulder. "What about me? I have literal fire in my veins, Ro. I'll be right as rain. Get some sleep."

Nuzzling my head against the pillow, I smiled into the darkness and pulled the jacket higher until it brushed my chin, tormenting myself with the smells of the forge.

When I fluttered my eyes open the next morning, a steady thump beat against my ear, and a radiating warmth coursed through the left side of my body. Heph. I tensed, flattening the hand resting on his chest, a knot forming in my throat. My head rested on his pecs, pulsing up and down with every breath he took. The strong thrum of his celestial heartbeat was enough almost to lull me straight back to slumber town. Risking a peek, I moved only my gaze upward. His eyes were closed—peaceful and serene. One hand rested behind his head, and the other arm…was snaked around my shoulders.

His hips shifted, and when he grumbled, I pinched my eyes shut. His fingers drummed against my arm and I pretended to sleepily open my eyes as if I hadn't been staring at him for the past minute. "Well, uh—g'mornin'."

Turning my head so my chin rested on his chest, I peered up at him. "Morning."

"Not entirely sure how we ended up like this. I'm—"

Normally, I loved to see men squirm, but the sheer awkwardness Heph exuded made me feel terrible. I pressed a finger to his lips. "I didn't mind it a bit, Heph. You're right. You're like a damn furnace."

He gave my fingertip a quick peck.

Gravel coated my throat, and I sucked in a breath, putting

the feel of his lips against my skin to memory. Our gazes locked as I made no move to tear my hand away. The spark in Heph's eyes soon fizzled into a glare, his nose twitching as he sniffed and sat up, pushing me aside.

"Heph? What is it?" I scooted to the bed's edge.

The same silver sword Heph had used when fighting the werewolf materialized in his hand. "We need to get out of here. *Now.*"

Jumping to my feet, I scooped a groggy Coney into my palms before handing him off to Heph and slipping into my jacket. "Is it that same shifter?"

"It's a shifter. Can't tell if it's the same one. Their scents always overlap." He motioned with his hand for me to walk out the open door. "We'll take the stairs. Avoid the elevator revealing our location."

Nodding, I followed him to the emergency exit and grimaced as the heels of my boots made loud thumping noises against the metal steps.

Heph's lips thinned at me over his shoulder. "Try to be light on your feet. It echoes in here."

I mouthed the word "sorry" and proceeded the rest of the way on the balls of my feet, gripping the handrail for purchase.

When we reached the door leading to the street, Heph shouted, "Duck!"

"What?" I screamed back, moving my hands to each side of my head and squatting.

Heph's sword sliced through the air above me, sending a spray of blood floating around us in a blurry mist, a grey wolf head rolling on the ground in front of me. My hands shook near my face, and an invisible vice clenched my spine as I looked up at Heph. Blood splotches stained his tank top, his cheeks, and beard. He said something to me, but all I could hear was a dull buzz.

"Ro? Aphrodite," he said once the fog lifted. Heph knelt in front of me, lightly shaking my shoulder. "Are you alright?"

No. I wasn't. *None* of this was okay.

My chest heaved as breathing grew increasingly difficult and I shot to my feet. "No. No, I'm not, Heph. This is all so, *so* stupid. Stupid powers. Stupid porting device. Stupid bounty hunters. Stupid. Stupid." I growled the last "stupid" and kicked a nearby trashcan. Instead of it toppling over, it spun in a circle and settled back with a defiant clank. "See? I can't even kick over a trashcan."

"Ro," Heph said calmly, dipping his face into mine each time I tried to look away and not stopping until I met his gaze.

"What?" I spat, immediately regretting the tone I used.

He took both my hands and lifted them between us. "You're panicking. Deep breaths. In and out, love."

I could count on one hand the number of times I'd gone to my big brother Ares in times of panic. Miscalculated spells, accidental mortal deaths, regretted decisions—there weren't enough fingers or toes on me to account for how many times I ran to Heph, knowing no matter what it was—he'd make it okay.

After whimpering, I took a deep breath through my nose and let it release from my mouth.

"Know what? Let's go somewhere." He kept hold of one hand and led me down the sidewalk, tugging me along when

I fell behind stride.

"Where are we going?"

"A place I go when I need to clear my head." Heph glanced skyward at one of the tallest skyscrapers I'd seen in the District before leading us through a metal door to more frigging stairs.

I groaned and halted, Heph's hand still interlaced with mine. "More stairs? Reminding me again of my lack of powers?"

Heph sighed and stepped off the one step he'd taken when I made it clear I refused to move. "Apples and pears, sweetheart. You'll get your powers back. But for now, pretend you're mortal with me?"

Mortal. I'd never contemplated the concept. Going to bed every night with the unsettling notion it could be your last. Or worse yet—the last moment the person sleeping beside you could be alive. I tightened my grip on Heph's hand before following him up many, many flights of stairs.

We reached the tippy top with no more stairs to climb, and Heph took us through a door labeled "Roof Access." The rainbow colors of the surrounding city blazed from every direction, the height of the building giving a full three-sixty view of adjacent skyscrapers, advertisements scrolling on a loop from the sides. The stars twinkled above us, making me realize the District never saw daylight—perpetual nighttime ensconced with darkness and twilight.

"It is so beautiful up here." I closed my eyes, hearing only the faint puttering of passing hovercars. "And so quiet."

"Yeah. It's why I like this spot. As much as I love living here, constant sensory overload can sometimes get a bit chaotic." He moved to the ledge and plopped onto his butt, letting his legs dangle. After scooping Coney from his pocket, he patted the spot next to him and urged me to take a seat.

After settling beside him, I let my feet hang over the edge and swung them while shoving my hands between my thighs, warming them. "How did you know exactly what I needed, hm?"

A rhetorical question, really.

"We've known each other a long time, Ro." His radiant grin flashed before he plucked a toothpick from his inside jacket pocket and stuck it between his teeth.

"We have, haven't we?" I smiled back at him. "Ugh. The Fates must be having a laughing riot right about now."

Heph leaned back on his elbows. "Huh? Why you figure that?"

"They know everything that's going to happen to us, right? Two Greek gods stranded and all the while being hunted? They're probably even oink-laughing at this point at us." I shook my head and closed my eyes as the wind picked up, breezing through my hair.

"You honestly think we have no control over our destinies?"

I peeked at him with one eye. "Isn't that the whole point of their jobs?"

"Nah. I don't buy it for a fucking second." Heph scrunched his nose, the toothpick flopping as he spoke.

"Oh, no? Then what do you think happens, god of the forge?"

Coney rolled onto his back, and Heph rubbed his furry tummy. "I think those 'ol crones *do* have something to do with it. But their guesses hold about as much worth as the mortals who wrote, and continue to write all those interpretations of us. It's precisely that—one big fucking guess."

Shrugging, I perched on one elbow, bringing our faces closer. "Sure, but you have to give them *some* credit. They haven't gotten everything wrong."

"Yeah?" He arched a brow and slid the toothpick from his mouth. "Did you screw your war-god brother while simultaneously being married to me?"

I scrunched my nose and made gagging sounds. "Tartarus, no."

Heph turned his gaze away, his jawline tightening.

"I meant the idea of boinking Ares, not the other thing you said." I licked my lips and turned my gaze in the direction Heph looked.

A light unmotivated chuckle floated from Heph's belly. "The other thing is just as absurd. I mean, us hitched? Crazy, right?"

A tornado spun in my stomach, and I pressed a hand over it, not answering straight away. It hadn't sounded all that crazy to me.

"Ro?" Heph's fingers slid under my jaw, turning my face to his. "Right?"

A laugh I didn't want to give forced itself from my throat, and I patted Heph's hand. "Of course. Pssh. Absolutely. That'd be weird. You're like a brother to me."

If it were possible actually to insert a foot into one's mouth, I'd choke myself with it.

"Right." Heph's nose twitched, and a weak grin tugged at the corner of his lips.

We sat side-by-side on the highest point of the Neosphere District, enjoying the deafening silence with hovercars racing under our feet. We'd spent an entire hour without saying another word, and I contemplated every other answer I wanted to give him but didn't have the guts to say.

NINE

HEPH

HER. BROTHER. SHIT. WHAT had I expected her to say? That's the reason I'd kept my distance despite enjoying the Tartarus out of her company. Better for her. Better for me. And mostly—better for my damn ego. After not being able to sit in silence any longer, I'd coaxed her back downstairs, and we took to the streets again. An idea sparked during that awkward quiet time we delved into, and it would be a long shot, but one I had to try—Olaf.

"Where are we going, Heph?" Aphrodite asked, bouncing on the balls of her feet to catch up with me.

I may have purposely walked in a stride I knew she couldn't keep up with because, inside, I still stewed. Sorry, not bloody sorry.

"The Bounty Emporium." I paused at the crosswalk, a familiar stench floating through the air. "I've known the man who runs it for years. Perhaps he'll see it in his crooked heart to drop the bounty on us." Twitching my nose to the wind, I spun circles.

Aphrodite slung her hands over her hips. "That's your plan? You two that good of friends he'd be willing to lose that much money in commissions?"

Hmph. Since when did she get so fucking intuitive?

Alright, that wasn't nice. I know she's smarter than she lets on, but at present, it did nothing to fizzle the frustration brewing.

Squinting at her, I flicked my wrist in the space between us. "We don't have many options here, *princess.*"

Heat flushed up her neck, and she folded her arms with a huff. "Princess? I hate being called that."

Dipping my face near hers, I slid my mouth into a devious grin. "I know." Before she could fire back, I turned away, smelling people passing us. Lost the scent. Onward we go.

Aphrodite's boots thudded against the concrete as she sprinted to my side. "What in the Tartarus is wrong with you all of a sudden, Heph?"

"Who, me? Oh, I'm right chuffed, sweetheart." I flashed her a mouthful of teeth. "See?"

She squinted at me as she clucked her tongue against the inside of her cheek. "Uh-huh."

As if sensing my need for a lifeline, the comm device on my wrist buzzed. "And look, Orion's messaging me."

"Orion? I'd say I was surprised you two were still friends, but you always were thick as thieves." She leaned sideways, trying to peek at the message.

Turning my back on her, I squinted at the holodisplay on

my device. "When you help a man get his sight back, you tend to develop a sort of ever-lasting bond, I'd say."

Orion: Yo Tuss. What you up to?

Heph: Runnin' from bounty hunters with the love-y goddess.

Orion: As in…Aphrodite? Seriously?

Smirking to myself, I kept turning my shoulder away from Aphrodite every time she tried to snoop.

Heph: That's what you got out of that reply, mate?

Orion: You sly dog. Was going to ask you to meet me at Firefly, but I can see you're already…busy.

"You could at least tell me what you're talking about if you're going to frigging ignore me," Aphrodite snarled at my side.

I slapped my hand over the device before she could see the repeated eggplant and peach symbols Orion sent last. "Nothin' important, Ro. I port Orion here every other month, and he parties his handsome blondie self into oblivion for a few days, and I cart him back."

"Ah. So, I guess you told him you have no way of sending him back right now, then?" Aphrodite's brow arched.

Bleedin' shit.

"Of course. What do you think we were talking about?" Chuckling, I pulled my jacket sleeve over the device, banishing it to darkness for the foreseeable future.

Aphrodite sighed as we stopped at a crosswalk, her gaze focused on her boots. "Speaking of friends. Thalia is probably worried sick by now. I did *disappear* thanks to a certain someone."

I slipped several fingers into my pocket, stroking Coney's

soft head before clearing my throat. "Yeah. I uh—sorry and all that." The rabbit's tiny wet nose brushed my knuckle as he re-positioned himself. "You still friends with all the Graces?"

"Forever and always." Aphrodite offered a weak smile. "They're the only ones that 'get me.'"

"I don't know about all that. I think I get you pretty well."

The dampened smile brightened somewhat. "Maybe. But—they're not dirty."

"That's what makes taking those hot showers so fun, though. More time with the suds." I bobbed my brows at her, eyeing how she discreetly bit the inside of her lower lip.

Back to our dynamic.

To. And. Fro.

It was, by far—safer.

The blazing orange sign for The Bounty Emporium shone in the distance, and I picked up my pace. Golden hour neared, and soon there'd be dozens of hunters lined up to turn in bounties, and, no doubt, they'd recognize us.

"Chop, chop, Ro. We're on a time crunch." I gestured over my shoulder at her before flicking my collar up once I reached the grated podium.

Olaf slouched in his floating chair, his arm dangling off the backrest, mouth open and snoring—loudly. I thudded my palm against the counter. *Still* snoring. After a few seconds, I beat my fist against the metal. Aside from a minor lip twitch, he snorted and returned to snooze fest.

Aphrodite made a shrill whistle behind me, making my head buzz. Blinking, I wiggled a pinky in my ear before cocking an eyebrow at her. She grinned and pointed at Olaf.

Olaf stirred, smacking his mouth open and closed before rubbing the inch of his stomach poking from his stained shirt. "Bounty claim isn't for another twenty minutes."

"Not here to claim, Laf." I leaned an elbow on the counter, displaying boredom but still acutely aware of our surroundings.

Olaf jolted in his chair, his eyes widening behind his glasses. The stool floated closer, and once Olaf spotted the bodacious blonde standing next to me, he licked his hands and used spit to smooth out his stringy hair. "I uh—thought she was the bounty, Heph?"

"Don't even try taking the piss with me, old biffy. You know I backed out on the contract, and you know there's a bounty on *both* of us now." I tapped my finger on the counter, keeping our gazes locked.

Olaf tugged on his already loose shirt collar. "You're right. I do. No hard feelings, Heph. Only business."

"Is that so?" Glaring at him, I pulled at the lava raging through my veins, flashing it in my eyes. "And there ain't no chance of you calling it off? For old time's sake?"

Olaf floated backward, feverishly working the controls of his chair. As if the thin metal separating us was a challenge for me. "You know I can't do that. I do it for one hunter, even you, and more and more will expect it. That's not how someone makes money, Heph. It's how they go broke."

"Now ain't that a downright shame. I thought we had a good thing going." An urgent fury roared in my chest, my hand balling into a fist on the counter.

Who knew how long it would take us to find Oz—if we ever found it—and all the while fending off hunters from across the known galaxy? Fucking Olympus.

"Olaf, please." Aphrodite leaned on the counter, her pink jacket falling from her shoulders, that pearlescent skin showing itself. "I'm only trying to get home. That's it."

Olaf's eyes drifted to Aphrodite's tits resting on the counter. I fought every ounce of my inner soul not to melt the fence separating us and kick his floating stool straight from under his ass. "I—I'm sorry, my dear."

Aphrodite's smile faded. She threw the jacket back over her shoulders and sighed. "After this blows over, then, Heph won't be taking any more of your bounties."

I straightened. "I—won't?"

"Nope." Aphrodite crossed her arms.

Olaf laughed. It started contrite before exploding into a barrage of cackling.

Aphrodite leaned over and whispered, "There are other places to pick up bounties, right?"

I leaned closer. "No."

"Oh. Um. We'll figure it out." Aphrodite stood taller and flattened her palms to the counter. "Not sure what you find so funny, Olaf. Heph is one of your highest-performing hunters. Think about the chunk of commission you're going to be losing."

I had no clue where this side of the love-y goddess came from, but all signs pointed to: Yes. Please.

Olaf tapped his fingers against his teeth before rapidly shaking his head, his glasses edging down his nose. "No. Nope. I'll have to take the loss. Reputation is worth its weight in gold in this business."

Aphrodite's mouth fell open. "You can't be serious."

Hooking my arm with hers, I coaxed her away. "Not worth it, love." After she numbly turned away from Olaf, I shot him a wicked grin over my shoulder. "Good luck finding hunters to take those harpy bounties, Laf."

"Damn it all to hell. Heph, come back. Come back. I can't drop the bounty, but I'm sure we can negotiate something. We can—"

After flashing him my middle finger, I gave a curt head shake. "Ship has sailed, champ."

Olaf's fist shook before slamming down on his chair's remote. The stool spun out of control, and I turned my head away, focusing my attention forward.

A pair of lips brushed my cheek—Aphrodite's lips.

Rubbing the spot our skin met on my face, I eyed her sidelong. "What was that for?"

"Proud of you." She beamed at me.

My palms grew clammy. "For?"

"Old Heph would've marched back over there to listen to what he had to offer."

A kink formed in the back of my neck, and I rubbed it. "Yeah. Guess I would have."

The all-too-familiar sound of a laser rifle hissing to life echoed in my ears. Snapping my chin in the appropriate direction, I shoved my jacket sleeve and materialized a shield large enough to cover me and Aphrodite. Several rounds of laser fire whizzed through the air, clanging against the shield. I'd peeked from the side, angling the shield enough to ricochet the shots back at the shooter. All three launched into their chest, killing them.

"Where did he come from?" Aphrodite lowered the arm she'd raised to cover her head.

Flexing my bicep, I made the shield disappear and furrowed my brows as I latched Aphrodite's elbow to urge her. "It's started. Be prepared."

When I said it started, I thought we'd run into a hunter, possibly every few minutes. What I didn't expect was running into one nearly every other block.

I'll admit, at first, it was fun, and mostly, all were human, which made it easy. One would lurk from the shadows armed with a rifle, knife, or bat, and I'd spin on my heel, launching several throwing stars or knives into their chests and guts. It became a sort of deranged waltz. The song *Separate Ways* by Journey sprung to mind. They came in such frequent spurts I began timing my throws to the beat of the music playing in my head. Aphrodite clutched my jacket from behind me, keeping stride. At one point, I scooped Coney from my pocket, handing him off to her, so he wasn't getting swung around like a freed ball sack.

A young girl no older than ten rounded the corner, standing in our path and making me pause. Aphrodite ran into my back. The girl wore her hair in pigtails, sporting a yellow-flowered jumper. She stood pigeon-toed as she stared at us wide-eyed, fidgeting with her fingers. I sniffed the air, squinting at her. Something smelled off.

"Heph, what are you doing? She's probably lost her mom." Aphrodite inched past me, kneeling in front of the girl with a canted head, Coney lying in the curve of her arm. "Hey there, little one. Are you lost?"

The girl nodded but said nothing, her gaze focusing on my rabbit in Aphrodite's arms. Aphrodite scooted closer, a breath away from the girl. The hair on the back of my neck stood on end, and I lurched forward to yank Aphrodite out of harm's way. The girl's eyes turned pitch black and lifeless. She shrieked, baring two rows of razor-sharp, pointy teeth and shoving both hands against Aphrodite's shoulders, launching her several feet in the air.

"An acheri," I snarled, producing an iron sword with one flex of my forging arm. "Ro, you alright?"

Aphrodite groaned behind me, her jacket rustling as she stood. "I'm fine. Deal with the little nightmare."

"Righty-o." Giving the sword a twirl, I advanced toward the acheri, knowing it was about as much of a human child as an angel, but its girl-like form made me uneasy.

The acheri hissed and screamed, growing knives for nails and circling me. It lunged, slashing its claws, and I deflected with the sword. It kept me on the defense for another full rotation, and every time I'd go for the victory blow, *knowing* I had the window, I'd pussy out.

"I'd really prefer if you'd shift into something else. Literally *anything* else." I lifted the sword to cut off the demon's head but grimaced and lowered the weapon. "Shapeshift," I yelled.

Instead of simply doing as I asked, the little hellion cackled.

"Heph, what are you doing? Kill it," Aphrodite bellowed behind me. "More hunters are going to show up at *any* moment."

For a brief instance, the acheri shifted into a man walking on the other side of the street wearing only a speedo and flip-flops. No doubt, a glitch in its cerebral cortex, but the one solid second I needed.

"Good enough," I said with a sly grin, slashing the blade horizontally through the air and separating the acheri's head from its body. Its black blood sprayed a radial pattern on the pavement, and I closed one eye as some misted my eyelashes.

"What in Olympus was that?" Aphrodite breathed out, nudging the acheri head that was still in mid-shift from the man back to the little girl with her boot.

The iron sword fizzled from my grasp, and I yanked my sleeve down. "An acheri. A demon." On the move again, I tugged Aphrodite by the wrist, pulling her into the closest alley. "Even being gods, we can't keep this up. We've gotta get out of the main streets. Find alternative routes."

Aphrodite pointed behind me. "There's a cracked open door. Maybe we can lay low in there for a while? Throw the hunters off our scents before moving on?"

"Now you sound like me." I snuck a whiff of her hair as her gaze remained in the other direction and leaned back when she turned to face me.

"You make that sound like a bad thing."

"Not at all."

But it was also an odd feeling to be turned on by…yourself? Anyway.

I offered her my hand, and once she took it, I led us to the door. Wherever we snuck into was dark enough that I could hardly see my hand in front of my face. I made a conscious effort to close the door the same amount it'd been before we crept in and winced when it made a loud *creeeak*.

Bugger.

A blinding spotlight shone on us and I squinted against it.

"Oh, my. It seems we have some visitors through our... backdoor," a mysterious voice said beyond the bright light.

That tone sounded far too double-entendre for my liking.

Aphrodite lifted a hand to shield her eyes. "We're sorry. We were feeling a little frisky, saw the open door, and didn't think anyone was in here."

What in the actual fuck?

"What the Tartarus are you doing? Frisky? That's what you go with?" I leaned toward her, speaking in loud whispers.

Aphrodite shrugged. "I panicked. It was the first thing that came to mind."

Godsdamned love-y goddess.

"Frisky, you say?" The voice said with an unsettling hopeful pitch before the bright light disappeared.

After the few seconds it took for my eyes to refocus, dozens of people scattered the room. They were separated into pairs, stroking each other's arms, legs or leaning over the other's laps. They stared at us like two succulent steaks, licking their lips and biting fingernails. Pillows of rainbow colors littered the floor, chaise lounges, couches, and beds. A sign hung across the back wall: *The Barter*—neon green arrows animated in a never-ending circle.

Wait a minute. I recognized the name of this place...

Aphrodite went to walk forward, and I caught her forearm. "We need to leave."

"What? Why?" Her brow creased.

I jutted my thumb at the ravenous crowd. "Ro, this is a

swingers club."

"Your point?" She flicked her hand at me before returning back to the awaiting horn dogs.

I caught her wrist. "I don't think you heard me. It's a *swingers* club."

"I heard you the first time, Heph. I'm saying, what is the big deal?"

I looked left, right, then stared at her like she suddenly became a hydra. "It's a godsdamned swingers club."

"Hephaistos." She turned to face me and placed her hands on my shoulders. "This is the perfect opportunity to hide out for a bit. They already think we're a couple. You're acting like we've never played pretend before."

"Pretending we were galactic space pirates when we were kids is not the same as a fucking swingers club." My tone became haughtier with each passing minute.

"Why do you keep repeating that?"

"Because I don't think you understand the gravity of the situation, love." I pressed my palms together in prayer between us. "Say we do this. They *will* expect us to follow through to—completion."

"Phai, this isn't any different than when you faked being my big alpha boyfriend to scare that creepy Adonis guy away."

Making my eyes form slits, I folded my arms over my chest, causing my form to broaden. "He wasn't creepy. You were just done with him and wanted him gone. And all I did was stand as I am now with a mean face." I leaned forward, bringing our faces inches apart. "This is too risky."

Aphrodite slid her hands to my forearms, the contact making

my skin crackle with heat. "So, we stall. Let's say we're newbies at it. This is our first rodeo. And you—are the jealous type."

I furrowed my brow and shoved my hands at my sides. "Why do I have to be the jealous type? Maybe *you* are."

"Why would I be the jealous type?" She folded her arms in a huff.

Not answering, I mirrored her pose, crossing my arms over my chest and glaring at her.

"Fine," she spat. "We're *both* jealous."

I nodded. "Alright then."

"Are we doing this?" She extended her hand, wiggling her fingers. "Pretend to be my kinky lover for a few hours to ward off bounty hunters?"

I placed my hand in hers and gripped it tight, tracing my forefinger in a circle over the skin at the inside of her wrist.

I'd been in far more difficult situations. This would be fucking crumpets.

ten

APHRODITE

THE LUST COURSING THROUGH the room made me feel like my old self again—fooling me into thinking my powers were back in full swing. But I didn't need my abilities for what we were about to do. Because of my charisma. My sensuality. Those were still *very* intact. It shouldn't be hard to fake it with Heph. We'd known each other so long it should be like settling into a well-worn couch.

I kissed Coney's cheek before slipping him back into the safety of the duffel bag. Heph rested the bag at our feet before we looked on at the impatiently awaiting crowd. Slipping the jacket from my shoulders, and letting it hang, I curled my arm with Heph's and curved a sultry smile.

"I'd have to say this was somewhat fortuitous. My man and I have been discussing venturing into wider territory with our sex lives. Isn't that right, honey bunny?" I elbowed Heph in the side before pressing my chest against his arm and resting my chin on his shoulder, gazing up at him with doting eyes.

He squinted at me before cupping my chin and grinning. "That's right. Whips and chains. Double-ended dildos. *Nothing* satiates this woman. Isn't *that* right, pumpkin?"

Bastard. But gods did I love it.

"I do have quite the—appetite." Sliding my hand over his hip, I didn't stop until I felt the impressive bulge under his pants. Its girth was enough to give *me* pause before squeezing it.

He grunted and snatched my hand, kissing the inside of my palm.

"You two are positively delightful." A man with bleach-blonde spiky hair, golden skin from an evident bottle, and wearing only a metallic gold banana hammock sauntered forward. He kept one hand on his waist and pointed between us as he spoke. "You're both gorgeous. Have incredible chemistry. Those tits. The accents. That *scar*. Mm."

The other couples growled and moaned in sheer agreement.

Heph smiled at the mention of his scar, patting his chest with pride. "I'm Jack, and this here is…Princess."

Heat flushed my neck, but I forced a grin and pinched Heph's ribs, making him let out a small yelp.

Another man walked to Fake Tan's side, wrapping his arms around him in a side hug. He wore matching metallic gold skin-tight shorts, no shirt, and a flowing silk scarf with white stars draped around his neck. "And you're newbies. We'll take extra good care of you. We promise."

"Good to hear. I wouldn't let my goddess in the hands of anything less." Heph snaked a hand around my bare waist, slipping a finger into the top of my pants, and resting it there.

A volcano rumbled to life in my stomach from his skin touching mine, forcing me to mask my reaction. A woman in a relationship that participated in a regular screw fest wouldn't react to her man's touch as if it surprised her. Instead, I traced my middle finger between his knuckles, grinning at him from the corner of my eye.

He licked his bottom lip, his gaze falling to his hand on my stomach, before lifting his eyes back to the club. "How does this all work?"

Mr. Scarf sashayed to Heph, trailing his hand over his chest. "Since you're both new, we understand your desire to peruse before making a choice. So, please." Mr. Scarf drifted behind Heph and swatted his ass.

Heph grunted and tossed me a quick seething glare. I bit back a smile.

"Take all the time you need," Mr. Scarf finished, moving to stand in front of me, tracing a finger over my collarbone, his gaze focused on the crease between my breasts. "And don't be afraid to get handsy."

Fake Tan walked to Heph, flexing his muscles, urging Heph to feel it.

Heph looked skyward, but Fake Tan inched closer. With a grimace, Heph patted Fake Tan's bicep with an open hand. "Ah, yes. Very toned. Very—oily." Heph scrunched his nose as he wiped his palm on his jacket.

Fake Tan let out a wistful sigh. "Oh, those calluses. I knew you looked like a man who was good with his hands."

As Mr. Scarf's finger explored lower, Heph coughed and yanked me away with a subdued snarl. "Did you hear that, sweetheart? A taste test of the merchandise before settling. How thoughtful of them, eh?"

I know we agreed to role-play jealousy, but that seemed relatively fast.

Mr. Scarf walked back to Fake Tan, fanning himself. "It's *so* firm. I mean like a fucking rock, Romeo."

Raising a thin brow, I leaned back to catch a glimpse of Heph's ass, his jacket covering it. I parted it away, but Heph caught my wrist before I could make my own assessment.

"Hey, now. You know all of my nooks and crannies." He grinned at me—seductive and delicious. "Time for others to sample."

I wanted to sample. Me.

No more than five minutes had passed, and I was already questioning my choices.

"Blondie," a woman's voice beckoned from a chaise lounge in the corner. She raised her hand, her gaze laser-focused on me.

Heph's hand touched the small of my back, and he whispered, "I'm not leaving your side. I hope you know that."

"You better not, *jack*," I whispered before blanketing my face with the love goddess persona.

He opened his jacket and curled me to his side within it. We approached a trio of people draped over the chaise, the man seated on the floor, stroking another woman's knee.

The woman who'd called me over stood, clacking her metallic silver fingernails together as she surveyed us. She tossed her blue bangs from her eyes with one flick. "My name is Fiona." She primped the rainbow-colored fur tracing the neckline of her clear plastic jacket. "The woman behind me is

Triss, and the man at her feet is Yohan."

Triss smiled at us, waving. She had her hair in two buns atop her head, the color starting purple before fading into teal. Using one of her bare feet, she pressed her toes against Yohan's cheek, turning his face to us. He'd been distracted by Triss, but his expression turned feral once he took us in. He had a shaved head save for one side covered entirely in circuitry.

"We wanted to get closer to you before the vultures began to swarm." Fiona scanned Heph from top to bottom, circling him.

I clung to him tighter.

Triss rose from her seat with Yohan at her heels. She slipped a slender hand around my arm and tugged it. "No need to be shy, pretty Princess."

Heph's jacket was a safe space I didn't want to crawl out of—not here, not in the outside world, not even if we were on Olympus.

I reluctantly moved from Heph's side, already missing his warmth. Canting my head at Triss, I slipped my jacket down my arms, letting it fall to the floor.

Triss folded her arms across the blue fish scale patterned dress she wore before stepping in front of me and tracing her fingers over my jawline and nose. "You are absolute perfection. Symmetrical in every way. Are you—fabricated? Which company made you?"

Olympus Enterprises?

When your father created you from scratch with no outside interference, especially a god with his size ego, you wouldn't come out of that clamshell anything less than perfect. And I'd grown to despise it.

Taking her hand in mine, holding it, I caught her gaze. "Not fabricated. All me."

Triss sucked in a breath. Her once relaxed demeanor smoldered away, impatience replacing it. "I approve, Fiona."

"And if Triss approves, you know I do," Yohan said, sidling to Triss's side and resting his chin on her shoulder.

Fiona still groped Heph, which already had a pit forming in my stomach. When her hand fanned over his scar, I saw *red*.

Launching toward them, I slapped her grabby paw away. "That particular part of him is more of a look but don't touch accessory."

I spied Heph squinting at me from the corner of my eye, but I didn't dare look him in the face after a stunt like that.

Fiona held her hand over her chest, glancing between us. "Oh, my stars. You two are the possessive type." She bit her knuckle, grinning far too wickedly for my taste.

"Mm, you're right, Fi. I could practically warm my hands from their fire." Triss giggled as she made absent circles with her finger around one of Yohan's nipples.

"We're new to this. Still learning the ropes, right?" Heph slapped my ass, the crispness of it echoing off the damn walls. And I wanted him—to do it again.

"Right. But we assure you when the time *comes*…it won't be an issue." I flashed them all a sultry squint, smiling with my eyes.

Fiona flicked her fingernails. "Good. Then we have an offer for you."

"Offer?" Heph slipped his hand to my back again, and I

wanted to glue it to me.

Triss and Yohan nodded in unison.

"The two of you perform for us, and afterward, we all have each other for dessert." Fiona petted the fake fur around her neck. "We realize performing isn't a normal part of the foreplay procedure at these events, so we would compensate you handsomely. Nakas, of course."

Heph stroked his beard. "We aren't exactly hurting for nakas, love. I'm afraid we'll have to decline respectfully."

Triss and Yohan pouted, urging Fiona on.

"If not nakas, then of what would you ask? Anything."

Heph chuckled and playfully elbowed me. "Unless you have some Oz lying around, we still wouldn't be interested."

Triss and Yohan brightened, their lips stretching into two broad smiles.

"Oz, you say? We have Oz." Fiona dipped a fingernail into the top of her sparkly low-cut dress.

Heph scratched the back of his head. "You—do?"

"Mmhm. So, what do you say? Oz in exchange for a private night with you two?" Fiona swiveled her hips.

"Absolutely," I answered for both of us.

Heph grabbed my elbow and held a finger up. "Would you give us a moment?" He pulled me to a vacant corner and turned me to face him. "What the bloody Tartarus are you doing?"

"Didn't you hear her? She *has* Oz."

"I did hear that. But I also heard not only do they want us to perform but have some crazy fuck orgy afterward. I'm no prude, Ro. I'm really not, but even I have standards, and I haven't exactly bedded something with its *own* meat and tackle." He pointed at his crotch and jutted his thumb at Yohan.

"We wouldn't actually go through with it. Perform, grab the Oz, and get out. Done deal."

Heph squinted at me as he adjusted his stance and folded his arms. "What makes you think for a damn second they'd hand over the Oz before we completed our end of the deal, hm?"

I tapped my finger against my teeth. "Good point. How many thingies of Oz does the device need to get it working?"

"Two ingots should do it."

I held a finger up and walked back to Fiona. "How much Oz do you have exactly?"

"Three, maybe four ingots?" Fiona shrugged.

"Would you be willing to give two up front and the rest after the deal is settled?"

Fiona chewed on her nail, grinning. "Sure. Whatever gets you in our bed."

"Perfect. One sec." Heading back to Heph, I held my head high. "Did you hear that?"

"You're serious about this." Heph interlaced his fingers behind his head and blew out a breath.

"It's an easy way to get what we need, Heph. It'll work. Trust me." I placed a hand on his chest and watched his expression melt.

"This week could not get any shittier. You realize that, yeah?" He smirked, causing those laugh lines in his cheeks to deepen.

"All we have to do is some sexy performance. I got it handled. All *you* need to do is stand there and look pretty. Be my pole." I adjusted the collar of his jacket, smoothing it out after straightening it.

"Your—pole?" He inched forward, his crotch hovering near my stomach.

Swallowing the tingles sizzling under my skin, I blinked at him. "My prop. Stand. Sit. Whatever you prefer, but you know, shirtless." My gaze fell to his pecs, wishing I had Orion's x-ray vision to get a preview—to prepare myself for what I was about to see.

The last time I'd seen Heph half-naked, he'd been younger and not near as bulky and *cut*. We'd gone for a dip in the fairy pools when Heph spotted a group of nymphs fawning over him. He asked me to race him—and let him *win* to impress them. I'd obliged but swam naked and the loss had still felt victorious garnering his attention away from the nymphs.

Heph slid a hand over my hip with a deep sigh. "You're right. We don't have a lot of options. But we run like Tartarus the minute we're done performing. Understood?"

"Yup." I jutted my hand to him.

Heph stared at it with heavy lids, and instead of shaking it, he lifted it to his lips, grazing a feathered kiss over my knuckles. "Use me as you see fit then, love-y goddess."

I couldn't recall any other god, man, hero, or demi-god that could turn my insides into gooey confetti from a simple gesture.

After sucking on my lip, I looked at Fiona. "You have a deal, Fiona."

Triss and Yohan bounced on the chaise lounge, clapping their hands.

"Splendid. Once you've gathered your things, meet us

in room seventy-seven. We'll want privacy." Fiona's brow bobbed before the three of them whisked down the hall.

"Stay right here, yeah?" Heph briefly touched my arm. "Going to grab the duffel, and I'll be right back."

Back in the day, I was up for damn near anything when it came to sex. Even what these three swingers thought was about to happen. So why did I feel borderline uncomfortable?

I'd been staring at the ground, unblinking when Heph returned and rested a hand on my shoulder, making me jolt to attention.

"You alright?" Heph placed a hand on my cheek, stroking my chin with his thumb.

"Yeah. I was thinking about how they can't expect me to perform some sexy dance number in a get-up like this?" I stepped back, reluctantly pulling away from his touch, and spread my arms wide.

"What's wrong with it?"

I dropped my hands at my sides. "Seriously?"

"Fine. Summon something." Heph's shoulders slumped, and I waited for the epiphany to happen that never did.

"Sure." I crossed my arms. "If you want me to do the damn thing naked."

Heph's cheek twitched before he slapped on a grin. "Right. But I'm sure there'd be no complaints."

Would it be so much to ask if *he* complained?

"Heph. Make me something."

Heph looked around himself as if there was another person in the room with the same name. "Me? What do you want *me* to make? I can't control fabric. You know that."

"No, but you've forged armor, haven't you? Chainmail?" My stomach fluttered at the thought of Heph making something for me. *Anything.*

Heph rubbed his chin, eyeing my figure not as an ogle but as measuring. "Alright. Hold still."

He stood before me, keeping our gazes locked as his arm ignited into a makeshift forge. His finger traced across my chest, directly above my nipples, making them harden. He trailed his touch down my stomach, stopping once he reached right below my hips. Not removing his hand, he walked behind me, his feral gaze igniting in sparking embers. He dragged a loop pattern above my ass, and for the final touch, he reached his arms over my shoulders from behind, tracing both hands around my neck.

I let out a shaky breath, mind fuzzy and out of sorts. The garment he'd made was heavy yet not, consisting of hundreds of tiny silver links to create a sultrier chainmail dress than even I could've thought up. I trailed my fingers over the cowl neckline, most of my breasts exposed from the opening in the center. It was a mini halter silhouette, my back fully exposed, slits on each leg, giving my thighs freedom. A tie closure wrapped around my neck, and a chain hung from it, the end of it bumping my ass with every motion.

"This is—gorgeous." I traced my hands over my curves, relishing the chainmail's textured feel. "Thank you."

Heph reached for the chain hanging from my neck, letting it run through his fingers with darkened eyes. "You're welcome. Let's go get this over with." He slung the bag on his shoulder, peering in the side pocket at a sleeping Coney before turning to walk away.

I grabbed the bag's strap. "Hold on there, buster. Shirt and jacket. Off."

"I'd hoped you'd forgotten about that." His tone turned husky.

Without saying anything else, I peeled the jacket from his shoulders and shrugged it down his arms. Heph chewed his bottom lip as he reached a hand over his shoulder to grab a handful of his shirt.

Heph kept his eyes locked with mine as he lifted the shirt free, tossing it in a pile on top of the bag with his jacket. I plucked the choker around my neck, allowing my gaze to roam the rippling toned muscles of his arms, washboard abs, and chiseled pecs. Swinging a hammer all these years had most certainly done the man *good*.

He inched forward, letting his fingers trail up my exposed back before dipping his nose near my ear. "Does the love-y goddess like what she sees?"

"How can you possibly think you're not attractive?" I breathed out, stifling a moan from his beard tickling my cheek.

He didn't answer me and took my hand in his.

Several gnarled scars laced his left shoulder, and I touched them. "When did you get these? How did you get these?"

"A harpy."

I frowned. "Did it hurt?"

"Enough to make me never let it happen again."

I peeled my hand away, panning my gaze to the scar on his face that went the entire length of his neck past his beard, and ended at his collarbone. The desire to touch it ran deep, but it'd be far too intimate.

They'd set a single chair in the middle of the room, the three lounging on a bed big enough to fit a dozen people, holomirrors surrounding it. A transparent resin platform elevated the bed, and I waited for it to frigging rotate or something.

"Dear. Heavens," Yohan breathed out, trailing his hand over his chest as he stared at us.

Heph sauntered over, making sure to flex his muscles with every step. He held out his hand to them. "Those two Oz ingots first."

Fiona snickered and a holodisplay sprouted from her wrist. After swiping a screen, a metal drawer opened from the end table. "As promised."

Heph bent forward, scooping two oblong blocks of green quartz material into his palm. He gave a curt nod to Fiona before turning away and depositing the Oz in our duffel. I moved to the chair, trailing my hands over the back of it before beckoning Heph with a single finger. Grinning deviously at me, he took his time walking over before slowly lowering himself to the seat and spreading his legs wide.

A synthwave song with bluesy saxophone overlays played through the room, and I moved in front of Heph, tracing my touch over his shoulders. His skin against mine felt like eternity—a blissful connection of stardust and longing that I couldn't explore. This would have to be enough. This moment. Right here. And I'd take full advantage of it.

Heph made no move to touch me, moving his eyes with every step I took, keeping his arms dangled at his sides. I swung my leg over his lap, lowering myself with as much speed as he took to sit down. Once my thighs met with his, I thrust my hips forward, already feeling his hardness through his pants. We were so close I could make out the specks of gold in his mahogany eyes, the divot in his cheek from a stray spark he'd left there as a reminder. Always the one to chronicle his mistakes with his body. Gripping his shoulders, holding back the satisfied grin I so desperately wanted to play on my lips, I dipped my head backward, my tits on full display for him.

I lifted, ready to go for another dip, when Heph's hands grabbed my hips, pulling me tighter against him. A devilish glint flashed in his eyes, and he dipped me backward on his lap, trailing his lips over the skin between my breasts. He reached for the chain hanging behind me and wrapped it around his wrist, tugging it, and making me gasp.

"What did you think the chain was for, sweetheart?"

ELEVEN

HEPH

OF ALL THE STUPID godsdamned harebrained ideas you've had, Heph, this must take the cake. Why did I agree to this? Was it because it was hard to say "no" to this woman? Or maybe I, like a right drongo, wanted to pretend we belonged to each other, even if for an hour? All the fucking above. And here we were—the god of the forge with the goddess of love straddling his lap—dry humping.

No more than five minutes into the entire ruse, I decided to take the opportunity in stride, considering how often something like it came up. As in, it *never* came up. And the performance? I mainly wanted to keep the others' dirty fingers off her. Have her all to myself.

Ro thought going into this, I'd be a fleshy prop for her, but I had the sinking suspicion she didn't know the fire god had more than a few moves up his sleeve. And let's not forget the simple fact of what she wore. One look at her in a dress I made *for* her, and I got stiff like fucking granite. And yet again, I loved to torture myself, giving her an entirely exposed back for me to caress. Created a sinful hemline showing me her lace panties as she writhed on my lap. And finally, I molded a sparkling chain from the choker around her neck for me to tease her.

Would any of my sly actions *work* on Aphrodite? Fuck, if I knew. Probably not. But it was damn sure fun to try.

When I tugged on the chain, she let out a moaning gasp, and I trailed my tongue between her tits, up her neck, and grazed my teeth against her cheek. "You didn't think I'd be able to sit here and not touch you, did you?"

"I'd have been disappointed if you didn't." She chewed her bottom lip while scraping her nails over my pecs.

Loosening my grip on the chain, I moved my hand to her hair, bunching it, still holding her captive. "Two can play this game, princess."

"*Can* they?" A pink haze glinted in her eyes.

Bloody fuck.

Moving my hands to her hips, I dipped her backward, guiding her into a circle before shoving her to my chest. Keeping our gazes locked, mine scorching with fire, I stood, her legs wrapped around my waist and my palms cupping her ass. The feel of her skin against mine was tantalizing—soft as fine sand and smooth like marble.

A devious smile curved her lips—a mysterious expression that always had me reeling. It impressed me how easily Aphrodite could turn it "on" in any given situation—the seduction, the charm—and it never mattered who or what it was. To the rest of the world, whomever she set to work on was *her* entire world. She warped it into hyperdrive for these swingers. But had I expected anything less from a goddess of passion?

After kneading her ass with my fingers, I plopped her to the chair—not delicately, but not so forcibly it'd come across as anything less than rough play. The wicked smile faded for a nanosecond, surprise, and intrigue somewhat apparent from the quirk of her brow. I leaned over her, gripping the chair's back on each side of her shoulders. After pressing against her, I tugged the chair, making it spin on one leg until her back faced the swingers. I didn't want them to have the privilege of the view I was about to *take*.

Dragging my hands down the tops of her thighs, I yanked her legs apart once I reached her knees. A breath pushed from her throat, and she kept her legs precisely where I'd put them. Placing my hand on the seat between her thighs, I dragged the tip of my nose over her tits, and her stomach, taking a deep inhale of the sweet scents floating from her that had no true comparison. My life consisted of endless days with smells of metal, blood, sweat, and oil. Her scent was Olympus itself and all its shimmering marble. And like Olympus, I could only dream of what being *inside* would feel like.

Growling, I pushed away, straddling her before using one hand to grip the chair's back, the other lightly wrapped around her petite throat. Her hands moved over my forearms, not in action to coax me to stop, but a plea—for more. My heart boomed against my chest as I peered down at her in my grasp, the echo pounding in my ears like one of Zeus's thunderbolts.

Was this what an ethereal heart attack felt like?

Lifting her, I kicked the chair away and lowered it to the ground, looming above her. I trailed a finger over her cheek as I moved my hand from her throat to the floor on each side of her head. Dipping my face to hers, I traced my lips across her forehead, down the slant of her nose, and paused at her mouth.

I wanted nothing more than to kiss her. Devour her. Fuck her mouth with my tongue and have every damn inch she'd give me. But I was no fool. Simulated sex was one thing. A kiss? All too telling. *Especially* for the goddess underneath me. When I finally moved my mouth away, Aphrodite's bottom lip trembled, and I snapped my gaze to it—carved a memory of it like etched metal.

Aphrodite grabbed my waist and pulled me against her, her back arching from the floor. I rolled my hips, rubbing against her, fighting every compulsion not to plunge into her right then and there. Swingers be damned. All that separated us was a bleedin' pair of pants and lace. It'd be far too easy, and there wasn't a doubt in my mind she'd probably let me if for anything but to "perform."

No. Fucking, no.

This had to be enough. It *was* enough.

Yohan slumped from his perch on the bed, crawling to us while biting his lip. "I'm not sure how much longer I can take this. I'm tempted to get involved *now*."

Aphrodite's eyes had grown heavy, and she scarcely glanced at Yohan before looking back to me, her one heel digging into my back as if a silent cue to *deal* with him. Lifting my hand, I swirled power through my fingers, the gray streaks settling over Yohan's wrists until a pair of iron shackles appeared.

Yohan gasped and sat back on his haunches, lifting the shackles, and making the chain jangle. "I like where this is going."

"Wait." Lava ignited in my gaze before the shackles pulsed orange, sending a quick surge of warmth through Yohan's arms and chest. "And I promise it'll be worth it."

Aphrodite's nails scraped my stomach, demanding attention.

Yohan moaned before biting his bottom lip and trotting back to the bed like a good little dog.

I stood, shadowing the love-y goddess. Grabbing her hands, I pulled her through my legs to stand, retaking control of the chain before she could react. Her cheeks flushed pink, and I turned her, pushing her back to my chest, using the choker to cock her head to the side. I kissed, licked, and bit her neck, her ass making torturous circles against my cock, straining through my pants.

As much as I craved this moment could last forever, we'd wasted enough time here. The longer we put on this show, the sooner they'd want to have their way with us, and all we did was feed fuel to the fire.

Not to mention my own raging godsdamned inferno in my balls.

Pressing my lips to her ear, I kept hold of the chain and pressed the other hand to her stomach, both of us idly swaying together to the pulsing synthwave and sultry saxophone blazing over the speakers. "Bout ready to wrap this up, Ro?"

"If we must. You better dip me one last time, though, you tease." She smiled at me, sneaking a hand to the back of my head, scratching her nails against my scalp in languid rotation.

"We're going to keep up the act until we get to the duffel,

then hightail it through the club until we reach the sidewalk. Good with it?"

She nodded, a light purr vibrating from her throat.

Pushing against one of her hips, I spun her away from me. Swooping to her, I slid a hand behind her neck, dipping her to the floor and holding her there. She skirted a knee up my hip, trailing our skin together against my ribs. As I lifted her back, her golden hair crested, settling into sexy as fuck wild tendrils around her face. I kept a hand at her exposed lower back, and she pressed a shaky one to my chest. We stood inches apart, staring at one another with labored breathing for what seemed like a millennium before Triss squealed and clapped her hands.

As if we had both been floating in another dimension, we snapped back to reality in unison, fluttering our eyes.

"Satisfied with the performance?" Aphrodite said, keeping her gaze with mine as if asking me but directing it at the swingers.

Taking her hand, I led her toward the corner where I stashed the duffel, circling my thumb over the top of her hand. "I think they underestimated us, Peach."

Aphrodite's face softened, and I tensed before tugging her faster toward the bag. *Peach*? I hadn't called her that in forever. It started as a cutesy reference to a delectable sweet fruit that also had a double meaning to reference either a woman's pussy or bountiful ass cheeks. Later on, however, when I grew an adult crush on the saucy blonde *Princess* Peach, it really took hold.

"I call dibs on Jack. I want him railing me from behind, pressed against a wall so much I might die on the spot," Triss said, moaning as she slid from the bed.

Aphrodite's brow twitched, and it turned from me dragging her to the bag to her pulling *me* over the last two strides to reach it. Aphrodite squatted, looping her arms through the bag handles, attempting to lift it from the ground.

"Do you have a strap-on in there? Please tell me you have a strap-on," Yohan squealed, jiggling the shackles and biting his lower lip as he looked skyward.

Playfully batting her hands away, I hoisted the duffel to my shoulder with ease and bowed at the swingers. "Ladies and er—*gent*, it's been a pleasure, but we won't be continuing with tonight's festivities."

Fiona fumed as she stormed from the bed, her exposed tits bouncing with each heated step toward us. "We had a deal," she shouted as we scurried out the door.

I flicked my wrist, creating an iron bar across the doorway that'd buy us some time. Multiple exits in the room led to other hallways. I'd checked despite how amazingly good of a distraction Ro had been.

"Faster, faster, love. They're all staring," I said through a smile of clenched teeth, waving as we hurried past bewildered naked people in the middle of every type of position and situation imaginable.

"I know I can run in heels, but could you have seriously made these even an inch shorter?" Aphrodite seethed, taking tiny, quickened steps to compensate for the seven-inch heels I'd created.

"Nope." The sound of silicone slapping flesh resonated. A woman wearing nipple clamps spanked a naked man on all fours with a rainbow-spiraling dildo that looked quite a bit like… "Is she about to fuck him like she's a godsdamned unicorn?"

Aphrodite grabbed the duffel's strap, forcing me away from gawking. "As if we never saw weirder back in the day. Come on, Heph."

We made it to the sidewalk unscathed but still had mountains to climb and couldn't afford to stay still for long.

Aphrodite adjusted the chainmail dress and pulled at the hem. "This is going to *suck* running in this thing."

For a solid thirty seconds, I contemplated letting her do just that. Thirty seconds.

"Good thing I had your old clothes appear in the duffel then, eh?" I unzipped the bag, the hot pink jacket and black pants sprouting out.

She yipped and wrapped her arms around me, giving my cheek a quick peck. We both froze. Slowly peeling away, she kept her hands at the back of my neck. "You were really convincing in there. I didn't know you could *move* like that."

"It's not like I advertise it, Ro." Snickering, I yanked her clothes out and held them to her.

She didn't take them and continued to stare at me. "Why not?"

"Because." I should've known that one-word open-ended answers would not satisfy her at this point. Sighing, I let the duffel fall to the ground at our feet after taking Coney into my palm and feeding him several baby carrots. "Because as a god of the forge and volcanoes, dancing all sexy and gyrating my hips isn't exactly what's expected of me. It's easier to play the game."

Aphrodite's gaze panned down my body until it settled on the concrete, her expression turning solemn. "Yeah. I know what you mean."

Crunch. Crunch.

Our eyes snapped to Coney munching on three of the carrots, trying to fit them in his mouth all at once. He paused when he caught us staring, bits of orange lacing his whiskers. We laughed, the tension in the air melting from my furry companion. For the moment, at least. Aphrodite held her hand out, and I gave her the clothes. She crouched to the bag and fished for the sneakers versus boots.

"Function before beauty? I thought I'd never see the day," I teased.

She swatted my arm. "Shut up. I want to make sure I can run as fast as possible. As much as I *do* love you carrying me everywhere."

"Uh-huh. You just like my hand on your ass." I circled the air in front of her rump with a single finger.

Smiling, she bunched the clothes between her knees and unfastened the choker around her neck.

"Olympus, Ro. Wait." I held my hands up and fished through the duffel for my coat.

"Why?"

Shooting her a glare, I held the jacket in the air to cover her goods as she changed. "Oh, I don't know. We're in public, and not every whack-job in the District needs to see your bibs and bobs?"

The chainmail clinked as it hit the concrete in a pile, and I forced my gaze away.

Don't think about the sight of her bare ass writing on top of you the way it had in The Barter mere moments ago, Hephster.

Rustling sounds bounced off the alley walls as she shimmied into her pants. Several broken pieces of green stone lay in the bottom of the bag, causing me to frown. I picked up one of the Oz ingots, only to have it crumble in my hand from increased pressure. Considering it was one of the strongest metals in the known universe…

"Shit," I snarled under my breath.

A fully clothed Aphrodite pushed my coat down. "Heph? What is it?"

Fury erupted in my gut, and I hurled the other ingot against the stone wall, exploding it into green mist. "Fucking bloody shit," I roared.

Coney whimpered before dropping what was left of the carrot in his palms and scurrying to the confines of a duffel pocket.

"Please don't tell me it's—" Aphrodite started, scooping some green stone into her palm, the dyed residue coating her skin.

"It's fake. Godsdamned bastards."

Aphrodite slowly dusted her hands clean before letting her arms fall slack at her sides. "You should've never taken that bounty."

The volcano within made my vision crimson and I closed the distance between us. "You know what? I'm tired of you pinning this on me. I've already apologized. Did you ever think about if I hadn't taken it, Ro? Hm?"

"Of course I have. I just said that. We wouldn't be in this

mess if you'd ignored it," Aphrodite fired back, her gaze taking on a pink hue.

"Wrong-o." I pointed a finger in her face. "Someone else would've taken it. Another bounty hunter. And then where would you be right now? Playing fuck toy to Hippo's harem. That's where."

Seething, she batted my finger away with a tiny growl. "Don't you try to tell me you acted out of damn chivalry. You had *no* idea."

"No, I didn't. But you should still be gladder I did, don't you think?" I flicked my hands at her before turning away on my heel, only to lurch right back in front of her. "Then again, it shouldn't surprise me. Tell me, when did you finally realize the world doesn't revolve around you?"

The way she glared at me was enough to turn lava into ice. "Excuse me?"

"It must've been a recent development because you put up a lot of fronts. But that?" Dipping my face in hers, I flashed a cheeky smile. "Always true, *princess*."

Her palms flew into my chest. "Look who's talking, Mr. Pity. You've had that scar your whole life, yet you *still* seek pity."

The words felt akin to an axe to the chest. Especially coming from the one person who never dared pity me but raised me up instead. I suppose I should feel thankful only for the number of times we'd fought through the centuries, considering how long we'd known each other—even a hundred fights seemed minuscule by comparison. Fuck, Zeus and Hera would've clocked that number in a week.

"Oh, boo hoo. I didn't have a mommy." She wiggled her

fists by her eyes, frowning. "But Hades stepped in when you needed guidance. You and Ares both. Who did I have? Zeus? Please. Hera? She was about as good of a stepmom as she was a mom, and she only ever truly cared about Ares." Aphrodite's voice grew louder with each passing word until she was fucking roaring at me.

"Pity? Really? I spent my life trying to make this thing—" I pointed at the scar. "—not define me. You think I like people fearing me? Being disgusted by my presence?" Growling, I paused to pace the length of the alley, reining the festering boil back so I didn't all out explode. "You were right. I cover it all up with aloofness and jokes, Ro. You were fucking right."

Aphrodite's bottom lip trembled, her eyes glazing over.

Fuck. How did we get here? I knew exactly where she'd been going with this and what's more—she was right about it all.

Her jaw tightened before she whispered, "I put myself first because I have no one else."

A torrential downpour doused the fire in an instant and I pulled her to me, hugging her, and rubbing the back of her head. "Ro—"

An unmistakable tremor vibrated the ground.

Aphrodite's head shot up with a sniffle. "What the Tartarus was that?"

"Either an earthquake that's never happened here before or a t-rex. I'm seriously hoping for the former."

The concrete shook again. This time, it made us lose our balance. It'd gotten closer. Lifting my chin, I took in the scents floating through the air, sifting through them until I found one I sorely wished I hadn't recognized.

Shit.

A massive being, towering over most of the skyscrapers, appeared on the horizon—fat, ugly, and with a bald, spotted head. It blinked its one cybernetic eye at us, scanning and roaring once it identified us.

"Is that—a cyclops with a cybernetic eye?" Aphrodite backpedaled and gripped my arm.

That Grecian immortal fuckstick.

twelve

APHRODITE

LEAVE IT TO A giant one-eyed monster to kill the mood I was damn sure developed between Heph and me. And unfortunately, I was *not* referring to the one inside the forge god's pants. Electric sizzle buzzed in that swingers' club. I'd been sure of it. But it could've also been my hopes and dreams on a string wishing the situation were something other than what it was—two friends pretending to be swinging lovers as a means of escape from bloodthirsty bounty hunters. I couldn't rely on my powers to see through the haze, leaving me with little to lean on.

"Someone's controlling it. And I'll give you one damn guess who that someone is," Heph mumbled at my side.

"How can you tell?"

The cyclops looked far closer than it was. Mainly because the way they walked simulated wading through molasses. You'd think with their long legs, they'd get to where they needed to go in the flap of a Pegasus wing, but nope. Slowpokes to the extreme. It gave us time to stand, ponder, and watch.

Heph curled an arm around my shoulders and pointed. "You see how he's movin'? Have you ever seen a cyclops move that gracefully?"

Graceful wasn't exactly the word I'd have used to describe it, but he was right. Any cyclops I'd seen flailed their abnormally long arms with abandon and tripped over their feet with every other step.

"Do you think he's being controlled like Krang controlled that giant human-robot thing he was always in?" I cocked my head to the side, looking for signs of unnecessary incisions on its body.

Heph slowly leaned in front of me, aligning our faces. "Krang? As in the *Teenage Mutant Ninja Turtles*?"

"Mmhmm. Think it's like that?"

It wasn't often I let my nerd flag fly—that deeply rooted part of me that I kept buried because it didn't fit the status quo. But for some reason, I knew Heph would not only understand it, but also maybe enjoy seeing that side of me.

"I—" Heph opened his mouth and snapped it shut before nodding. "Yeah. Maybe." He stood back, tugging on the lapels of his jacket. "I'll be sure to spill his guts so we can see if a tiny pink wrinkly alien thing pops out."

Grimacing, I waved my hand. "That won't be necessary."

"We should lure it away from the city center before it—" Heph started.

The cyclops stepped on a vending kiosk at the wrong angle, lodging one pointy end of the structure in its foot. The monster roared, holding its foot and hopping on one leg. He threw himself off balance and fell against a nearby skyscraper, taking a giant shoulder-sized chunk out of it.

"—wrecks something." Heph finished, scratching the back of his head. "Yeah. Let's coax him to the Fringes." After patting my shoulder, Heph strode to someone sitting on their hoverbike, distracted by the holoscreens displayed from a wrist device.

I dropped to my knees by the duffel, fishing Coney from the side pocket. He trembled in my palms, still shaken up from our argument, and I held the tiny He-Man Lego out to him with a smile. After sniffing my fingers, he gently took the plastic toy into his mouth and cupped it with both paws. I unzipped my jacket and nestled Coney within, using it as a makeshift sling to carry him.

"Pardon me, good sir, but we'll need to commandeer your vehicle." Heph clapped his hands together. "Trust me. It's for a good cause." He gestured with his head at the rapidly approaching cyclops.

The biker glared at Heph before dismounting, beating his knuckles against his palm as he approached him. His threatening demeanor blossomed into bone-chillingly terrified once he spied the cyclops over Heph's shoulder. All color drained from the biker's face.

"Holy fucking hell," the biker screamed, sprinting in the opposite direction.

A snarky grin slid over Heph's lips as he breezed past me to retrieve the duffel. "Nice chap to let us use his wheels."

"Yes, I'm sure the ten-story-high monster had *nothing* to do with it." I followed Heph to the bike, keeping a hand on the furry lump in my jacket.

Heph peeled my coat back, grinning once he saw Coney curled up. "Careful now. You're going to spoil him."

"Oh, well." Shrugging, I threw a leg over the bike and settled onto the back.

After securing the duffel behind me, Heph mounted and started up the bike, the blue holo wheels blazing brightly. Compared to gas-fueled bikes, this one was nearly silent except for the light humming when Heph turned the throttle.

"Hold on. Bikes in this century have a Tartarus of a kick." Heph took one of my arms and wrapped it around him.

I slipped the other around, resting Coney on the seat between us, snuggling in my jacket. "Um, Phai, does it seem like 'ol one-eye has suddenly gotten closer?"

Heph's eyes bulged when he looked over his shoulder. "Shit. Here we go," he shouted before peeling away from the curb and into traffic.

The sudden jolt made me yelp, and I held onto him tighter, squeezing my knees at his sides. He slid a hand to my thigh, patting it before returning it to the handlebar. The briefest of touches, and it was still enough to make my stomach flutter. Screams followed behind us as the cyclops traipsed between buildings, not caring who or what it stepped on. Heph weaved through traffic like we were in a damn light bike race in *Tron*, the bike's inner-working pistons hissing and shifting each time he changed gears.

"Wouldn't it be faster if you take that road?" I asked, shouting my words through the gusts of wind blasting over us, my hair flying around me and into my eyes and mouth.

Heph shook his head. "The overpass? Too risky. Dozens of people are always on that thing, and with our luck, the cops would plow right into it before ducking."

Pressing my forehead against Heph's back, I inhaled—leather, musk, and the faintest hint of dirt. The filthy level of the Neosphere District grossed me out beyond measure, but the idea of Heph caked in oil and soot while he forged something? Those bulky tanned arms flexing with each swing of the hammer, sparks flying around him, skin glistening with a sweaty sheen…

"Better not loosen your grip, sweetheart," Heph said, snapping me from my daydream.

Honestly. Who played out a fantasy in their head while being chased by a cyclops?

"Pothole," Heph shouted over his shoulder at me.

"What?"

The bike bounced, sending my forehead colliding into the back of Heph's head. We both groaned the word "ow" in unison.

"I warned you," Heph said, rubbing the back of his head with a snarl.

"Blurting the word 'pothole' is a warning, Heph? Why not 'brace yourself', or 'hold on tight,' or virtually anything else but 'pothole.'" I used Heph's shoulder to soothe my forehead since removing my hold on him was evidently out of the question.

"Listen here, young lady, I will turn this bike right around," Heph teased, beaming at me over his shoulder.

After flashing a smile against his back, I squeezed him with my knees. "Eyes on the road, volcano breath."

How did he make it impossible to be mad at him for more than thirty seconds?

The vibrations from the cyclops' steps grew more frequent. What started as a beat to the rhythm of drums leading into a song turned into an erratic heartbeat, the monster quickening his pace, sprinting. Cyclops never *ever* ran. Like ever.

"Heph," I said.

Heph banked the bike at the last moment, taking us through an alleyway. "I see it."

If Heph intended to force the cyclops around the building…

The cyclops plowed into the alley behind us, its shoulders peeling away rubble from the adjacent buildings.

"Heph," I said again, louder this time and with more conviction.

"I bloody well see it, Ro," Heph shouted. "Hold on."

Heph leaned forward and yanked the throttle, the bike picking up speed as it zoomed to the end of the alley. When the cyclops exited soon after, Heph cut the engine, bringing us to a screeching halt, the cyclops charging straight past us. Heph flicked a switch, the blue holo wheels glowed again, and he slammed his boot down to turn us a hundred and eighty degrees.

"What the Tartarus kind of Maverick *Top Gun* move was *that*, Heph?"

Heph's shoulders tensed. "You recognized that?"

Did I admit this? Would he think me weird?

"Yes," I said, my voice barely above a whisper.

"Huh. Well, I figured it'd confuse the beastie, and if Hippo *is* pulling the strings somewhere, I like the idea of him throwing a fucking tantrum over things not going his way." Heph chuckled, his shoulders bouncing, making my head bob with him.

After re-orienting himself, the cyclops shook its head and held it with one hand, then turned on one heel and continued the chase after us. With each mile Heph drove, the city's chaotic sounds faded away—no pulsing music, no overlapping conversations, no ads on loop from every other building. The once smooth road turned into dirt, the bike bouncing and kicking up pebbles as it shifted to uneven terrain. Heph veered the bike into an open field, the tall grass scraping against the bike's undercarriage, almost hitting a metal sign that read: Now Entering The Fringes.

"Are cyclops vulnerable to certain metals?" I squinted against the dirt kicking up from the bike's holos.

Heph snapped a look over his shoulder as the cyclops followed us into the field as planned. "Nah. Gotta take out its eye. If I had my porting device, it'd be easy. I have to figure out a way to launch something at it from the ground." Heph scratched his chin before making a bow appear in his grasp. "On second thought, my aim isn't the best with a bow, and it might not make it far enough into the cavity."

The bow disappeared, and he swiveled the bike once the cyclops got closer, giving us extra time to come up with a plan as the monster re-adjusted.

"Or maybe…" Heph materialized a javelin, tossing it in his palm. "Yeah. It'll have to do."

"A javelin? How are you going to drive the bike *and* throw that thing at the same time?"

He took one of my hands in his. "Because, dearest, *you're* going to drive."

"What?" I shouted. "Oh, no. No, no, no. I can't, Heph. I'll steer us straight into a boulder." When I tried to recoil my hand, he snatched it.

"We're in a field—no boulders in sight. You'll be fine, Ro. All I need you to do is drive it straight enough for me to aim and launch." He squeezed the top of my thigh. "That's it. Twenty seconds tops. Yeah?"

Snarling, I beat my forehead against his back and sighed. "Fine."

"Good. Get your pretty ass up here then."

My stomach dropped. "Aren't you going to stop for us to switch?"

"Think that's the best idea? That monster keeps picking up speed every time it passes." He shot me a mischievous grin over his shoulder before refocusing forward, an expression I recognized as a warning he was about to say something snarky. "' sides. You trying to tell me you're not flexible enough?"

Glaring at the back of his head, I cupped Coney within my jacket and used the other hand to grab Heph's shoulder. Heph uncoiled his fingers from the bike, only putting them back once I'd swiveled, swinging my leg around and straddling him, our chests facing each other. My knees pressed at each side of his ribs, his arms caging me in as he continued to drive the bike. I stared at him and dryness coated my throat, our faces so close I could feel the heat of his breath on my cheek—a surging warmth emerging from the fire pulsing in his veins.

He wiggled one of my knees. "I know you're enjoying the

view, buttercup, but it's easier to drive this thing facing the other direction."

Nodding and sucking a breath, I shifted my position, using the foot pegs as leverage to swing my leg, and face forward.

Heph pressed his lips to my ear from behind me, his hardness pressing against my ass as he pushed his hips forward. "Ready?"

Gulping, I stared at the handlebars like Medusa's hissing snakeheads and nodded. He took my right hand and rested it on the handlebar, followed by the other until the bike was in *my* complete control. I shrieked, stiffening my arms to keep us going straight, frightened one false move would launch us directly into the dirt.

Extending one arm for balance, I felt Heph straighten behind me. From the bike's rearview holomirror, I saw him glaring at the cyclops. After bouncing the spear in his grasp and aiming, he threw it. It hit the eye but not dead center, only slightly to the right.

"Bugger," Heph growled. "We need to swing around for another pass."

"What?" I shouted. "You want me to make a *turn*? There was no mention of turns, Heph."

He reached past, his arms wrapping around me, his warm chest pressing to my back. "I got it. Let go."

No sooner had the words left his mouth my hands were in the air as if the handlebars had become molten lava.

I held onto Heph's knees once he slammed a boot down, turning the bike toward the other direction. "Do you really have to hit it square in the center?"

"Unfortunately, yeah. Their brains are the size of a godsdamned beach ball and right behind the eye socket. Only way to take 'em down." He tapped my knuckle. "Ready to take over again?"

Nodding, I took control with more confidence than before.

Heph shifted behind me, and with a quick glance over my shoulder, I saw him standing on the bike's pegs. The javelin relaunched through the air, landing dead center in the cyclops' eye and making a few sputters of sparks.

I let out a single *woo* but frowned when Heph plopped back to his seat, not as excited as he should be. "What's the matter? You got it. Didn't you?"

"It didn't go in far enough." He leaned forward, slipping his hands over mine, signaling he'd drive.

Coney spun within my jacket, curling into a ball on the opposite side.

"I may have an idea, Heph." I rubbed my lips together, nerves raging.

The cyclops roared and charged for us, picking up the same speed it had before. After several evasive maneuvers on Heph's part, bobbing and weaving through the monster's legs, we made another loop.

"I'm all ears, Ro."

"Have you seen *Empire Strikes Back*?" I peered at him over my shoulder.

Heph's legs stiffened behind me. "As in *Star Wars*?"

"Uh-huh."

He snickered. "Uh, yeah. A time or a hundred."

"What if we take down the cyclops like they did the AT-AT?

Would it be easier to jam the javelin the rest of the way if he's at our level?" Shrugging, I drummed my fingers on his knee and looked back at him, trying not to display the desperation all over my face.

It hadn't occurred to me how much I valued his opinion until I offered a plan. Did I even have it in me?

Heph chewed on his lip while raking his fingers through his beard, mulling my words. He slowly nodded. "Yeah. Yes. That could work, Ro. Good thinking."

There was no way in Tartarus I could hold back the grin begging at my lips.

Heph wiggled his fingers, and a grappling gun appeared in his grasp. He launched it into the ground before zooming the bike toward the cyclops, driving with one hand, holding onto the hilt of the gun with the other, letting the wire extend. Heph circled the cyclops once, twice, three times, winding the wire around the monster's calves tighter and tighter. The cyclops growled, dizzy as it tried to keep watch on us. After the fourth pass, the cyclops' legs pinned together.

Heph stopped the bike, and we both froze, holding our breath as we waited for the cyclops to fall—or not. Like the universe's tallest tree, the cyclops slowly, ever-so-slowly, fell to the ground in a slump, its chin bouncing when it landed. The fall caused a brief earthquake through the field, vibrating at our feet.

"Stay here," Heph commanded before jumping from the bike to the defeated cyclops. He raised a boot and rested it on the spear sticking out from its cybernetic eye. "Tell Hippo I said cheers, mate." He kicked forward, lodging the weapon the rest of the way. The cybernetics sparked and smoked until the cyclops' arms fell limp at its sides—dead.

I reached into my jacket to check on Coney, scratching his head with the tip of my finger to soothe him. As Heph walked back, dusting off his hands, I gulped at seeing him all badass and imposing with a gigantic dead cyclops in the background.

"That was a prime idea, Ro. We seem to make a good team." A flash of white shone through Heph's dark beard as he grinned at me.

Offering a tiny smile, I continued to pet Coney within my jacket but beamed at Heph. "Who would've ever guessed that, huh?"

Heph leaned on the bike, keeping my gaze.

His wrist device blinked and he stood to attention, swiping his hand over it to read the message. "Ah, it's Rion. Says to feel free and use his place for the night as he won't need it." After smirking, Heph pulled his sleeve down.

"Is it close? Will it be safe?"

Heph mounted the bike and tapped his fingers on the seat between his legs. "It's safe but *not* close. He lives in Daneland on the other side of the District."

"If only I could port," I grumbled.

Heph patted my knee, making my stomach tighten. "We'll take the tube. There's a station only a few blocks away, and traveling underground will keep us out of sight, yeah?"

Nodding, I wrapped my arms around him and nestled my head against his back as he drove us to the subway. A chill settled in the air underground in the District—dark, dank, and mysterious putrid stenches. But we were much safer down here.

"The trains normally arrive about every ten minutes, so it shouldn't be too long of a wait." Heph gestured to a metal bench, and we sat.

As I sat next to my best friend, my fantasy of being simple and ordinary, watching a movie and eating popcorn, sprung so vividly I could taste the butter on my tongue. A holo television hung behind protective glass played a commercial for a product called Scrubber Dubbers—an animated bubble wearing a fedora floated back and forth onscreen. It was questionable whether they advertised for bathroom cleaner or murder scene clean up. We sat close enough that I rested my head on Heph's shoulder to see how it'd feel. And—he let me.

THIRTEEN

HEPH

DID I WANT TO know what possessed Aphrodite to rest her head on my shoulder? For the first time since we'd crossed paths again, I can say—not really, no. Did I try to over-rationalize the action? Thank the fucking Forges, but no to that too. It may have been the exhaustion pulling at my godly brain or the contented silence underground, but for that brief moment, I let my eyes close, rested my cheek against her, and enjoyed the sweet scents of a beautiful woman.

The light whirs of the approaching train caused me to stir, bumping my elbow gently against a sleeping Aphrodite's arm. She let out a moan that woke me up right quick given it sounded far too sensual for my horny self.

"Come on, sweetheart. Train's here, and they don't stick around long." I helped Aphrodite to her feet as she let out that torturous groan.

She rubbed her eyes with the backs of her hands. "Doesn't

the conductor keep an eye on the platform?"

"Not here." The doors automatically hissed open once we stepped into them. "The trams run on an AI system, so that they can operate twenty-four-seven. And wait until you see how clean these things are. Not even any graffiti. All because of the AI."

There were so few people who took the train it wasn't difficult to find a car all to ourselves. Leading her to a corner seating area with more legroom, I sat by the window and popped my jacket collar. I'd expected Aphrodite to take a seat across the way, but instead, she sat directly beside me. I gave her a labored blink.

"What? You said it yourself. You're a furnace. Hasn't this AI heard of central heating?" Aphrodite rubbed her hands together before unzipping her jacket, allowing Coney to come out.

Coney's head shot up, and he sniffed the air several times. The train lurched forward, the orange lights in the tunnel blurring as we picked up speed. Coney scurried across Aphrodite's lap and mine to reach the window, standing on his hind legs to watch the lights. Grinning, I scratched the rabbit's head before settling into my seat.

"Should only be about twenty minutes. Doesn't feel like it, but these things are *fast*." I rested my head back and shut my eyes.

"Hey, Heph," Aphrodite's fluttery voice said.

"Yeah, Ro?" I kept my eyes closed.

"How did you learn to dance like that?"

And they flew right the fuck open. "I'm—sorry?"

"Don't pretend you have no idea what I'm talking about, *jack*." She pointed at me, a hint of a smile creeping her lips, making that single dark freckle near the corner of her mouth disappear into a crease.

Grinning, I rested my head back and closed my eyes again.

All about "aloofness."

"We get bored. You know this." I flicked my wrist in her direction. "There was a period in my life I traveled all over Earth. Trying to be cultured and shit. You pick up a thing or two."

"That was more than a thing or *two*, Heph."

I peeked at her with one eye. "Liked it, did ya?"

"It was—surprising." She traced a finger over her collarbone— an action I came to learn through the years she only did when she felt…nervous.

Well, that couldn't be right.

Letting my eye fall shut again, I interlaced my fingers and rested them on my stomach. "I learned it and held onto it. You have to realize most women think this scar sums up my entire body. And I couldn't have them assuming I was inadequate where it counted." I bucked my hips.

"And are you inadequate?" Her tone took a devious turn.

I flashed my eyes open and leaned toward her. "Love, it falls to me ankles. It's a burden, really." Pressing a hand to my chest, I faked a frowny face.

Aphrodite bit her cheek before her eyes sparkled, and infectious laughter followed—a laugh that brightened her features, melodic and wholesome.

Fucking Olympus, did I love making her smile. "I can't

believe I've never asked this before but I'm curious—what's it like having Zeus for a dad?"

Her eyebrows lifted, and she scooted down in her seat, moving her arm closer to mine. "You mean a *dad*, dad? Beyond him lending his seed to create me biologically, dad?"

"Fuckin' Forges, Ro. Always such a way with words."

She chuckled and slapped her hands over her face. "Sorry. Honestly, he's not as bad as what most assume."

"Oh, no?" I folded my arms and slid down my chair to align our faces. "He had tea and crumpet parties with you then? Braided your hair? Typical daughter daddy shit?"

"Definitely *not*. He's got an entire kingdom to watch over. Not to mention dozens of other children." She shrugged, and we turned our heads, resting them on the back of our chairs to look at each other.

"And that never bothered you?"

She shook her head, a hint of a smile still tugging her lips. "It used to, but he was there when it counted. The first time I accidentally killed a mortal, the time I was so lonely I kept crying and didn't know how to stop, and of course—" Her gaze faded into serenity. "—when I gave the news about Eros."

"No shit. Gotta say I'm a bit shocked." Keeping my eyes on Aphrodite, I rubbed Coney's back as he stayed fixated on the streaking lights outside the window.

"Don't get me wrong, my dad can be a straight dickhead. Especially back in the day before I popped out of my clam, but the past decade—he's changed." She pulled the jacket around her tighter.

Without taking a moment to overthink it, I stretched the

arm near her across the back of her seat, allowing her to move closer to the "furnace" if she wanted. "How so?"

Her shoulder nestled against mine, and the fire in my veins glowed brighter. "When he first became king, it was about the power for him, and now? He's not only accepted the responsibilities that come with it but *embraced* it."

"But he still goes around acting like an arrogant womanizing prick?"

With her head resting on my chest, she tilted her chin to smile up at me. "Going along with what is expected of you is often easier than trying to convince people otherwise. Sound familiar?"

"Yeah, yeah. Smarty pants." I kissed the top of her head.

And we both froze.

It'd happened so effortlessly—so quickly, I hadn't a chance to stop myself.

The train hissed to a stop and I rubbed her arm through her jacket. "Looks like we're here."

And not a moment too soon.

Aphrodite frowned and stood, walking to the aisle. Coney pressed his nose to the glass, his ears drooping further, forelegs falling slack at his sides.

"I know, bud. We'll take the train again soon." After slipping a very sad rabbit into my pocket, we exited the train and headed for Orion's place.

His loft hadn't changed much from the last time I visited. A hexagon-shaped doorframe opened to a yellow triangular geometric-patterned carpet leading to the small kitchen area in the corner, complete with a mini bar and continued through the apartment. On one wall hung the word "Relax" in vibrant yellow neon. Below it was a large holographic television screen surrounded by six holo speakers. A vast circular black leather couch big enough to seat a dozen people filled the living space. Various animal heads mounted to wooden plaques hung from the opposite wall overlooking a billiard table with yellow felt. Upstairs would be the vast white and gold hexagon bed that I'd undoubtedly need to change the sheets of before letting Aphrodite anywhere near it, and one wall with floor-to-ceiling mirrors.

"Wow. Orion has done well for himself." Aphrodite slipped her hands to her hips. Turning circles on her heel, she marveled at the yellow vomit Orion called "furniture" surrounding us.

"Flashy as always, that's for damn sure," I grumbled, resting the duffel on the couch.

"Heph." Aphrodite whipped around to face me, her arms folded. "I have a request. No. A demand."

I tried not to burst into laughter. "A *demand*? This I gotta hear." Facing her, I leaned on the couch's back, crossing my arms over my chest to mimic her power pose.

"I'm sick and tired of standing around when there's a goon or a monster and not being able to help. Not to mention, I want to know how to defend myself. There's not always going to be someone there to look after me."

Not if I had anything to say about it. If anyone so much as split a hair on this woman's head…

"What are you gettin' at, Ro?" I stood tall, keeping my arms folded, but walking toward her.

"I want you to forge me something. A weapon you think I

can handle." Her hands fell at her sides. "And then I want you to show me how to use it."

"Is that so?" I peered down at her, tapping the toes of my boot against her foot.

"Yes." She gave a curt nod.

This goddess and her constant control.

I'd never been the sharpest axe in the shed, but throughout our friendship, I'd always realized she *knew* she could ask anything of me, and I'd never turn her down. Heph, could you talk to Ares for me? Heph, I need a set of cutleries to give as a gift, could you forge some for me? Heph, that minotaur looked at me the wrong way. Could you do something about it? Yes. Sure thing. Straight away.

But now? I think I'll make her *work* for it.

"I've gotta say I'm surprised it took you this long to ask, but we have one problem here, love-y goddess." A spark overtook my gaze.

"Problem?"

Pressing my lips to her ear, I whispered, "You didn't say 'please.'"

Her throat bobbed, and her finger trailed that collarbone again before she pushed out with a shuddering breath, "Please, Heph."

Grinning, I stepped back, rolling up my jacket sleeve to ignite the forge.

Aphrodite snatched my elbow. "No."

My brows drew together. "I don't follow."

"You said you sometimes still forge the old way. I've never seen it. And—I want to." She scraped her fingernails over my exposed forearm.

The volcano within me *roared*.

"You want to see me shirtless, banging a hammer on an anvil, over and *over*, Ro?" I slipped the jacket from my shoulders, keeping our gazes locked. "Watch me dripping with sweat? Growin' more and more filthy with each passing swing? Hm?"

Nodding, she dragged a finger across her lips.

"And you're sure you can handle it?" A devious smile conquered my lips. "It's quite the spectacle."

Aphrodite grabbed a nearby chair and plopped into it. "Show me, *Phai*."

I had no godsadamned clue where this was going, but I sure as shit daydreamed of all possibilities.

Nerves churned in my stomach.

That was new. It wasn't as if I couldn't forge with my eyes closed, ancient way or not. But I'd never had someone watch me forge like *this*, let alone—her.

After situating Coney in a cushioned drawer Orion had set up for him any time I stayed, I pulled my shirt off, keeping my back to Aphrodite…for now. Snapping my fingers, making sparks fly, I materialized an anvil. In a swirl of glowing lava, the first hammer I'd ever created appeared in my palm. A steel ingot shimmered into my other hand, and finally, I turned to face her, slamming the ingot to the anvil with a loud *pang*.

Catching her gaze, I called to the lava coursing through me, willing it to flow from my fingertips. The lava churned and billowed in a circle, forming a fiery hearth. Sweat already glistened on my skin, and as I tossed the ingot into the hearth to warm, I brushed my hand over the coals, dirtying my fingers. As I waited for the metal to form a scorching orange glow, I dragged my hand over my forehead, streaking my skin with coal.

Orion would have an absolute hissy fit if he knew what I was doing in the middle of his living room. And it only egged me on more.

Aphrodite sat with her back as straight as an arrow, her fingers playing with the chain of her heart pendant, knees pressed together. She idly sucked on her bottom lip and hardly blinked, let alone looked away.

Retrieving the heated ingot from the fire with my bare hand, I tossed Ro a smug grin before slamming the metal onto the anvil. Using my hand as tongs, I brought the hammer down, orange sparks cresting in glowing cascades. Every muscle in my arm ignited and flexed with each swing, and once the brilliant orange dimmed, I shoved the metal back into the hearth. Oil and ash coated my hand as I retrieved the ingot. Before continuing, I met Aphrodite's gaze and slid my palm down the center of my chest, not stopping until I reached my pants.

Aphrodite's legs began to part. Gasping, she snapped them back together and gripped her knees like her hands were the only things keeping them from doing what they willed. Her eyes roamed my body, lingering on the tattoo lacing my bicep—a crane in flight from a bed of swirling fire, lava, and embers.

Did this actually…

Could she possibly…

As I hammered the metal into a blade, I stared at her through the bouts of sparks and smoke. Her blonde hair like ancient Greek wheat fields being caressed by the wind as it fell through my fingers, those blue eyes calming, soothing—moonstones.

No.

I gritted my teeth and beat the hammer against the anvil with extra force.

A treasure chest—gems, gold, and filigree. Aphrodite was it all. And a radiant treasure should never be reduced to the fucking darkness where it had no place to shine.

After giving one growling last and final swing and using my power to quench it, a solid court sword blade rested on the anvil. My chest pumped, but not from the energy expelled from forging. I'd allowed myself to be swept into the idealistic dream of Aphrodite being into me. The idiotic thought she'd possibly ever want to see us as something more than friends. And then, I had to throw myself from the clouds of Olympus back to reality for the second time in my life.

Bleedin' imbecile.

The love goddess rose from her chair with the grace of a swan landing in calm waters. Keeping my eyes on her, I fluttered my fingers over the sword's tang, forming a golden hilt.

"Enjoy the show?" I asked with a smirk, lifting the sword horizontally by its blade with two fingers, testing its balance.

Aphrodite's gaze roamed my naked torso, her skin reddening over her collarbone as she rubbed it. "You weren't kidding about it being a—spectacle."

My cock clearly hadn't gotten the memo as it formed half-wood in my trousers. Yesterday, a look like that from Aphrodite may have dulled my senses, but now it only irritated me into continued frustration and confusion.

Looking away from her, I tossed the sword in my palm,

holding the hilt-side out to her. "Here you are."

Aphrodite dipped her face, trying to look at me, but I kept averting my gaze. Out of the corner of my eye I caught her scrunching her nose before taking the sword and gasping.

"Heph, this is—this is gorgeous."

With my focus drawn to the sword and *only* the sword, I pointed to the blade. "This is a short sword, sometimes called a court sword. It's not as heavy and lengthy as a long sword, but this should be easier for you to handle as a first-timer."

"Oh, I don't know. I'm fairly good at handling heavy and long at pretty much *any* time."

My dick betrayed me yet again, and I rolled my shoulders.

"It's still as versatile as a long sword, so don't feel like you're being swindled or anything." I scratched my chin and couldn't avoid looking at her any longer once I caught her mesmerizing stare at the hilt.

She ran her thumb over the symbols I'd etched into it— filigree, hearts, roses, and swans. "This is *so* me." Those moonstone eyes lifted to meet mine, a peculiar anguish hidden in her gaze.

"I pay attention." There was so much more I wanted to say before and after those three words, but I cut myself off. "Let me show you the basics then, yeah?"

Aphrodite didn't answer at first, her fingers still trailing over the swirls and grooves that made up the hilt's design. When she made no motion to move, I held my hand out and gently took the sword away.

"Now. You have your basic movements." As I described each one to her, forcing myself to keep it all business, I showed the motions to her. "Your perry, thrust, block, and slash. As you're fighting, you'll be doing a combination."

She nodded, her eyes on my abs instead of anything I tried to show her.

"Aphrodite?"

Her gaze shot to my face. "Thrust. Got it."

Gorgon's tit. How much longer did I expect myself to keep this up?

"Do you want to try a few moves?" I handed her the hilt. "I can guide you."

She limply took the sword in her palm, a glint forming in her eyes as she widened her stance. "Come show me."

As I moved behind her, something ignited in the space between us. Something that went beyond innocent friendly flirting and banter. The lava surged in my veins, and once I reached my destination, I pressed the rock-hard cock still straining in my pants against her lower back. Slipping my arms around her, tracing my fingers past her elbows, I corrected her hold and proceeded to instruct. Whether she picked up on anything or not, I didn't give a damn.

I should've gone into form and procedure. *Should* have. But I didn't want to. I wanted to make this woman mine and for Aphrodite to claim me as *hers*. I wanted to love her, fuck her, chill with her for all eternity and make her my world. And I was fucking tired of watching, waiting, hoping.

"Spar with me, Ro," I whispered against her neck, the words coated with grit. Reluctantly pulling away from her, I turned my arm into metal, intending to block her swings.

Aphrodite's cheeks turned rosy, her eyes heavy, and sheer

fucking lust blazed in her stare as those eyes flashed pink. "Go easy on me."

"Never." I winked before raising my arm to block her first swing.

Having never worked with a sword before, that'd been a damn good slash.

She tossed the sword from one hand to the other as she slid the pink jacket off, throwing it in a crumple to the floor. Licking her lips, she lurched forward in a perry, poking against my arm and making sparks fly. Those gorgeous tits pumped up and down as she stared at me, her lips parting, baiting me. When I didn't budge, she cinched her brow and lunged. Her swings turned frantic and angry. I'd let her slash and perry against my arm to her heart's content until enough was enough, and I grabbed her wrists with one hand holding them above us.

It was now or never. Either I started life with the love goddess today or spent the rest of that life getting over her. But it was time to come clean. Fuck the consequences. Because these past days had been nothing short of blissful torture that I couldn't rightly stand any longer.

I had, in fact, gone easy on her and now swept her feet from under her. No sooner had her back collided with the carpet, than I was on top of her, peering down. My heart hammered in my chest, and I lowered to my elbows, caging her head with my arms.

"Ro," I managed to push out.

She lifted her hips, but I put more weight on her, pinning her, keeping control of the situation. "Yes, Heph?"

"There's something I need to tell you, but sure as shit don't know how to say it."

Aphrodite blinked, the gold heart pendant hanging from her neck sparkling with the yellow neon lights in the room. "It's only me. Just say it, Heph."

Only her. As if she were any other woman or goddess in the godsdamned universe.

"Ro—" I started before tightening my jaw. "I—" No sooner had I worked up the balls to say what needed to be said, Aphrodite disappeared from my arms, and my hands tore at handfuls of fucking yellow carpet.

fourteen

APHRODITE

HEPH COULD NOT BE any more wrong. The Fates were definitely cackling themselves into oblivion at us. Heph was about to confess something—something huge. And I could feel it with every grain of power left in me, but what happens? I disappear into a frigging floor. You *cannot* make this stuff up.

The world went black in an instant before my back collided with something hard. Groaning, I fluttered my eyes open to blanket darkness. I rubbed my fingers against the surface beneath me—cool and smooth. Metal?

"Imagine my surprise when I heard your name floating through the streets. And here of all places. Hardly the scene I'd imagine the goddess of love would set foot on," a male voice, thick and rich, spoke from the shadows.

I recognized that voice. Why?

"I've been expanding my horizons," I mumbled.

Fluorescent lights flickered overhead, one blazing after the other until unflattering white light brightened the room. I winced from the sudden change before cutting my eyes to the Mystery Man. Tall and utterly handsome with perfectly proportionate chiseled facial features, an impeccably slanted nose at a precise angle, vibrant hazel eyes, and messy chocolate hair.

Narcissus.

"You have got to be kidding me." I shot to my feet with fists clenched at my sides.

A crooked smile curved Narcissus' pouty lips, and he folded his hands behind him before strutting forward. "You sound surprised to see me."

"Uh, yeah? I could've sworn the lot of you were dead a long, long time ago, and yet you all keep turning up."

Narcissus moved closer, still plastering the smug grin that made me want to slap it from his pretty, stupid face. "Spacetime can be a real pain in the ass. Can't it?"

Space, what now?

A crease formed between my brows, and I rubbed my temple. "What the Tartarus am I doing here, Sussy?"

He cringed at the endearing nickname I'd given him eons ago. "I've been searching the stars for decades to find you because you're the only god who can help me."

Laughter poured from my throat, making tears collect at the corners of my eyes. "Help you? Firstly, why would I do that? You're a prick, Sussy. A huge one. Secondly, what could you possibly need from *me*?"

His lip bounced in a snarl, cheek twitching. He appeared in front of me with speed demi-gods usually don't possess.

Cool metal pressed over my wrists. "You *will* help me one way or the other, Aphrodite. I want you to lift Nemesis' curse. I'm tired of not being able to look in a mirror without fear of falling in love with myself. It's been over three hundred years since I dared to try."

The chilled metal against my skin felt familiar yet strange— handcuffs. I lifted them, the chain clanking, and let my eyes roam the handiwork. Heph hadn't made these. One link in the chain remained weaker than the rest, the metal not matching up to form a perfect circle. Heph wouldn't settle for anything less than perfection. And he'd always been that way with everything he forged—weapons, dinnerware, horseshoes—it all had to be flawless or he'd start over.

"What makes you think I have the power to undo anything that winged chica has done? Not to mention, she's a daughter of primordials. We Olympians do *not* stick our hands in that mess." I scrunched my nose. "And if you wanted me to use my powers, why the dampeners?"

"You *better* find the power, love goddess. Because you're not leaving here until this dreaded curse on me is gone. And those?" He flicked his wrist at the cuffs. "Are to ensure you don't use your powers on *me* until you agree to my terms."

Love goddess. Love-y goddess. *Heph.*

I *had* to get out of here.

"Listen, Sussy. I couldn't help you if I even wanted to. My powers aren't at full throttle. Catch my drift?" I ran the shackle chain between two fingers, giving it light tugs, and checking its strength.

Narcissus tossed brown hair from his eyes like Justin Bieber

177

before staring at his well-manicured fingernails. "Convenient."

"*In*convenient. For you. Because I'm not kidding here, Pretty Boy, I can barely make clothes for myself, let alone drop an age-old curse."

Narcissus moved in front of me, so close I could smell the nectar and honey blossom floating from his skin, making my spine stiffen. His nose brushed mine, our gazes locking. "I don't. Believe. You."

Glaring at him, I pushed his chest away with a single finger. "Believe me or not, you're shit out of luck."

He snatched my hand and brought it to his lips. "One way or the other, Aphrodite, I *will* make you agree to help me." He slid my finger into his mouth, sucking on it.

Grimacing, I tried to yank my hand away, but he held firm. "Oh, yeah? What are you going to do? Torture me?"

"No." He bit the tip of my finger before letting go.

Relief washed over me. I'd never been mythologically tortured and didn't care to try it any time soon.

"She is." He displayed his hands, opening his arms wide as he backpedaled.

She?

A wicked high-pitched cackle cut through the air like a rose thorn. When Heph said this week couldn't get any worse, he jinxed us. He frigging *jinxed* us.

"Oh my, oh my, oh my, oh my," a maniacal voice I recognized stammered from the corner.

Lupe. One of the Algea—bringers of weeping and tears. And Lupe's specialty? Pain.

How fortunate for me.

"Have you somehow gotten uglier through the ages, Lupe? Afraid to come out of the shadows?" I tugged the cuff's chain.

She actually wasn't ugly by any means. In fact, if she weren't so maniacal, bloodthirsty, and downright creepy, I'd even call her Beauty Queen material.

She leaped from the darkness, letting out another screeching bout of laughter. Her long raven locks bounced once she landed in front of me, sniffing my hair and running her red and black claws over my bare shoulders.

"I'm going to have so much fun torturing your pretty. Pretty. Skin." She drummed her nails against her lips and hopped in a circle like an excited child. Once she'd completed two full rotations, she shoved her face in mine, staring at me with one white eye, the other—bright blue—rotating in the opposite direction.

I leaned away, but she snatched my chin and narrowed her eyes.

"What? You don't want to *play* with me? Is the goddess of love afraid of—afraid of pain?" Her ruby-red lips slithered into a grin, exposing her vampiric teeth. "You are. I know you are. Want to know why?" Whenever she spoke, the first words were rushed and chaotic.

"No," I seethed.

A quick cackle fluttered from her mouth as if she could scarcely contain it. "Because you've never tasted it. Never experienced it. Never smelled the stench of blood, misery, and war." Screeching, she slashed my cheek with one claw, shoving her hands to her mouth as she skipped.

I hissed at the burn lacing my skin. It'd never held on

that long before—never hurt that badly. Under normal circumstances, I could feel it healing no sooner had it been inflicted. Now? It took its damn time.

Gasping, she pointed at me. "It's taking forever." She elongated the "e." Her chaotic expression appeared in front of me again, and she licked the blood dripping down my cheek, closing her eyes as she exaggerated sticking her tongue out and rolling it over her fangs. Her eyes flew open. "You're—broken," she shouted with far too much enthusiasm.

I chose to remain silent as exhaustion pulled at my brain. All I needed to do was hold out long enough for Heph to show up. He'd be on his way by now.

That is…as soon as he figured out where the Tartarus I was. Frig. Double frig.

Lupe waddled back and forth through the small room with her arms at her sides like a sumo wrestler, cackling. She jumped in front of me, her claws playing with the buckles hanging from her black pleather dress. She gave a high-pitched grunt and dug her claws into my arm, dragging them down until she reached my elbow.

As much as I tried to hold it back, the pain proved victorious, and I cried out in agony, turning my face away to not look at the crime scene my arm had become. Warm liquid oozed over my skin, and I whimpered, forcing tears back.

"Look at it," Lupe squealed after removing her claws. When I didn't obey, she grabbed my chin and tugged it in the opposite direction. "Look. At. It."

Gulping, I cast my gaze downward, a breath pushing from my lungs as I caught sight of the gash she made in my arm.

Cool it, Ro. It's not permanent. It will *heal. Just slower. Keep it together.*

Lupe let out a breathy snicker and clacked her nails together. Canting her head at an impossible angle, she let go of my face, one claw re-opening the slash that'd healed from earlier. "Are you not enjoying yourself Aph. Ro. Dite? Hm?" Lupe's thin dark brows bounced.

The gash in my arm started to seal, the blood staining my arm. "What the fuck do you think?"

Pain brought out grit in me I didn't know existed.

A broad smile quirked her crimson lips, her pale pink tongue skirting her teeth. She brought our faces closer, the tips of our noses touching. She combed my hair with bloodied fingers and kept her white eye on me while the blue one turned skyward. "You know what to do if you want this all to stop." Lupe finished her sentence in slow whispers.

"I've already told Narcissus I can't help him. This is pointless." I spoke through several growls.

She tapped one fang against her bottom row of teeth in a staccato-like rhythm. "Physical—isn't—the only form of pain." Her voice went up an octave on the word 'pain,' and she dragged out the 'a.'

"Is forcing me to figure out your riddles part of the process?" I mumbled it, feigning boredom like I'd witnessed Heph do countless times.

She giggled before giving a harsh tug on my hair, ripping out a lock. A yelp flew from my throat before I could stop it, and I rubbed my scalp with a scowl.

"What does the goddess. Of. Love. Hold dear, I wonder?"

She traced a heart pattern with a single claw in front of my face and tapped the tip of my nose.

How exactly did she plan to crack this particular code? Mind read? Voodoo?

She skipped circles around me, being sure to jab me in the sides with a claw sporadically. After the seventh lap, she let out an exaggerated gasp before diving into my face again. "Hephaistos."

My neck numbed.

"Lupe, you're losing your touch," Narcissus shouted as he stormed into the room. "This is taking far too long. Out of the way."

Lupe tossed him a glare and puckered her lips like a duck.

Narcissus shoved her aside, lifted a black curved talon in the air between us, and used the claw to gouge my left shoulder in the same instance. It all happened so fast the anguished scream started as shocked silence. A tear streaked my cheek, and I seethed at the searing, burning pain striking down my arm.

"What the Tartarus was that?" I yelled, reaching a shaky hand toward the wound.

Narcissus shoved a forearm against my chest, pushing my back against the wall. He lifted the claw, my blood still dripping from it. "A harpy claw. That wound will heal, but the scar it leaves behind?" A villain's grin crawled over his lips. "Permanent."

The pain pulsed and radiated through the entire left side of my body. Even my fingertips throbbed.

"Fucking asshole," I forced out through clenched teeth.

He moved the claw inches from my cheek and pushed his

arm against me harder, nearing my throat. "Do as I asked *now,* or I'll make more scars."

"That's not the way to get to her," Lupe said, standing pigeon-toed and twirling her hair.

Narcissus gave a disgruntled sigh before he glared at her over his shoulder. "What are you babbling about, psycho?"

"You say the sweetest things." She flitted her eyelashes. "I was about to yank it out of her when you came barging in here like Cerberus with the shits."

Narcissus shoved me before finally pulling away and walking toward Lupe, pointing at her with the harpy talon. "Be. Quick. About it."

"Yeah, yeah, yeah." Lupe flicked her hand and rolled her blue eye. "Skedaddle."

I concentrated on the breaths escaping my nose, the faint hum of the fluorescent lights, the honey blossom scent still hanging in the air from Narcissus—anything to tear my focus away from the pain still radiating through me. The harpy venom sizzled under my skin like scorched acid.

Lupe ported in front of me, splaying her hands wide and lifting them to each side of my head. "Ready to have some fun?" She flicked the tip of her tongue against a fang before grabbing my head.

My vision glitched until a black-and-white image of an alley blazed through my mind. It was like seeing through foreign eyes not attached to my body. Heph ran around the corner, speaking to someone through the holo device on his wrist.

Is this real-time?

"I don't care what you have to fucking do. We find her

183

now," Heph said, slamming his palm against the device to end the call.

Is he talking about me?

"Where could she be? Where could she fucking *be*?" Heph yelled into the void, pacing and slamming his fist into the bricks of the alley wall.

Why would she be showing me this? Sure, it sucked seeing him in distress over me, but it was also…relief?

The faint sound of flapping wings echoed, causing Heph to sniff the air and spin on his heel with a furrowed brow. A shriek to rival a banshee sounded, and a harpy loomed over him. Heph glared at it before producing a pair of shackles. The harpy launched at him. Its claws sliced through the air near his head, but Heph dodged and deflected with the chain, grinning at it.

Only he would be smiling over a harpy almost decapitating him—my silly Phai.

The harpy lunged at Heph's side, but Heph swung the shackle chain over his head and sent it flying at one of the harpy's feet, catching it. The harpy shrieked, spun in the opposite direction, and tore its claws across Heph's stomach.

No.

Heph froze—eerily still and motionless. He moved his palm toward his torso, and when he pulled his hand away, red liquid covered it.

No. No this isn't possible.

Terror clung to me, tore at me, consumed me.

The harpy flew away, screaming into the wind with the one shackle dangling. Heph turned around, his steps slow and clunky. If I could've gasped, cried, shouted in denial, I would've at the sight of his intestines spilling from his body.

This can't be real. Heph knew his way around harpies too fucking well. Knew *what could happen from the claws.*

Heph sunk to his knees, holding one hand over his entrails as if he could shove them back in. Blood filled his mouth, and it sputtered in red bursts as he mumbled, "Ro," before falling in a lifeless heap to the ground.

Fury swarmed through me.

No. I refused to believe this. Heph wouldn't go out like this. He couldn't. This was some twisted mindfuck from Lupe. Inflicting an entirely different form of pain. The loss of—the sight of— someone I—loved. Dying.

I couldn't live without him. Couldn't imagine breathing without him. And I needed to get the Tartarus out of here to tell him all of this. Screw it if he didn't feel the same. He deserved to know the truth. And I've been an absolute idiot for not saying it a long, *long* time ago.

I love him.

The alley disappeared in a swirl, and I landed on the ground in a similar-looking alleyway, the cuffs chain clanking, swirls of pink magic glowing around my wrists before fading away. I gasped. Had I…ported? Closing my eyes, I concentrated, trying to port again. The extra grunting I did wasn't helping. Somehow, I'd ported myself from Looney Lupe and made it outside. A one-time deal? I'll take it.

But also—how had I ported with dampeners on? The weak link?

Jumping to my feet, I hissed at the pain striking my arm.

One advantage to Lupe's dreamscape? I couldn't feel my wound. Risking a glance, I surveyed the damage from the harpy claw. The tear was close to sealing but still sore and red. Searching for the weak link in the cuffs, I whipped the chain over a nearby broken pipe and pulled away. The pain throbbed in my arm from the strain, but I ignored it, pulling harder and gritting my teeth until finally, the chain broke, giving me freedom and two new bracelets for the time being.

I rubbed my wrists as I took in my surroundings. All I had to do was navigate through a place I was not only not used to but had no clue where anything was—easy enough. Leaning around the corner, District dwellers filled the sidewalks on each side of a busy road. Skyscrapers lined the streets like ancient Greek pillars, and a blazing neon sign hung from an overpass with the name of the subdivision: Ithaca.

How's *that* for irony?

FIFTEEN

HEPH

"BLOODY FUCKING SHIT," I stammered, staring at the floor as if she'd somehow re-materialize before my eyes. "Fucking. Shit," I roared, slamming my fists against the carpet, making a hole in the wood beneath it.

She'd been right there—underneath me, staring up at me with those baby blues and waiting for me to say it. It was my own damn fault, really. There were countless times through our lives I could've said it, but no, Hephaistos is a fucking coward. I'd come close once—the last and only time before now I'd brought her here several years ago for the Lunation Festival. The memory was so clear in my mind I could remember the smells in the air that night—salt from the sweaty crowds, overlapping food scents from dozens of vendors, and the sweet aroma that never left Aphrodite's skin. The way the moonlight made her hair glow that night, the radiance in her eyes as she took everything in—I *almost* confessed it, but didn't.

And now I'll be damned if I don't get the chance to say what needed to be said.

Pushing to my feet, I swiped the holo on my wrist, typing a short and quick message to Orion.

Me: Your place. Now.

It took no more than ten seconds to receive a reply.

Orion: On my way.

No questions asked. With a friendship like ours, it wasn't a matter of asking when and where to bury a body. Either of us would've already had the hole dug.

"I'm going to guess there's a reason you didn't teleport yourself or teleport me to you?" Orion's voice sounded behind me.

Dragging a hand over my face, I spun on my heel to face him. Orion leaned against the doorframe in his black tech vest, arms crossed, the full-sleeve hunter's tattoo with astrology undertones blazing from his bare arm.

"Device is broken," I mumbled.

Who could've possibly taken her? No hunter I knew had that kind of power.

"So fix it." Orion ruffled his long blonde hair before crouching on the carpet near the new hole I'd made, the various rips in his dark blue jeans stretching.

"It takes Oz, Orry. And it's not like I can dig it out of the godsdamned ground like any other damn metal." I moved to the window, glaring at the glass like it had been the one to take Ro.

"Going to guess your remodeling of my floor has to do with why you asked me here?" He pointed between his legs, sucking on those ridiculously pouty man lips.

I'd been into women my entire godly life, but even I could admit how "pretty" Orion was with his sharp jawline that could cut diamonds, eyes the color of cornflowers, and just enough stubble to get away with rugged.

"Yeah, yeah. I'll fix it later. Right now, Aphrodite is the priority." Even saying her name out loud stirred the volcanic beast, and with a deep breath, I coaxed it back. Best to save that aggression for whoever fucking took her.

"Aphrodite?" Orion stood, squinting at me. "I know you mentioned you were steering clear of bounty hunters, but now I need to ask. Mind filling me in on what the Tartarus is going on, Heph?"

Pushing a breath out, I interlaced my fingers behind my neck and paced. "To summarize, someone put a bounty on Ro. I took it because, one, Oz was part of the reward and two—" I paused and cut my gaze to Orion, ensuring he heard the next part. "—it wasn't for her life. I thought it'd be an in, out done deal. Turns out, it was Hippolytus seeking revenge and hoping to turn her into some gangbang concubine."

Thoughts of that many paws groping her—none of which belonged to me—infuriated me. I dropped my hands at my sides and clenched them.

Orion moved before me, leaning on the wall with crossed arms, the neon yellow of the "Relax" sign hanging above him, turning that blonde hair of his fucking golden. "And you refused to uphold the terms of the bounty because you're head over heels in love with her and the bounty was then set on you too."

And this is why having a best mate could be the absolute

pits. Thinking they knew you and shit.

I chewed on my bottom lip. "…more or less."

It'd been the perfect opportunity to have a go at me, for Orion to call my bullshit with denied feelings for Ro, but all he did was nod.

"Hunting the hunters then, are we?" Orion pushed from the wall and cracked his knuckles.

I ignited my forge arm, gaze blazing with embers. "Damn right we are." A golden bow materialized from my palm, and I held it out to him. "Remember how to use one of these things?"

With a smirk, Orion yanked the bow from my grasp. "Still go hunting with Missy every weekend, you prick."

Artemis and Orion—a pairing I still didn't understand, but those two remained two very close peas in an even tighter pod.

"Still gotta hand it to you, mate. Being with a woman knowing full well there's to be no hanky panky?" I summoned a leather quiver and arrows before handing it off to him.

Orion took the quiver, running his fingers over the fletching on each arrow. "You should know it isn't always about sex. And a man and a woman *can* just be friends."

"Mayhaps." I leaned near him and elbowed his side. "But you can't deny sex is fun." Snapping my fingers, I produced several holo arrows, holding them out to him with a stiff arm. "You'll need some of these. Work better on cybernetics and the like."

Orion took the glowing blue arrows with squinty eyes, flicking the shaft of one with his fingernail.

"I'll need to drop Coney off with someone before our boots hit the pavement. Not sure how long this'll take, and he's not exactly self-sufficient." I pulled the drawer open to find Coney sleeping away. "Come on, bud. Wakey, wakey."

The rabbit's eyes lazily opened, and he yawned, exposing those extra-long front incisors, his pink tongue curling, and stretching.

"You have someone you trust with him here other than me?" Orion slung the quiver's strap over one shoulder and secured the bow on his back.

"Aw, yeah." I grinned. "We're practically family."

"You want me to do what?" Uluu blinked with about as much enthusiasm as Hippolytus at a strip club.

Alright, so Uluu of Uluu's Eatery wasn't exactly like a cousin to me or anything, but she was someone I saw every day. And I kept my "good mates" list to a bare minimum.

"Let this little fur ball sleep in one of your vacant drawers back there, feed him a carrot or two, and let him take a shit when necessary. That's it."

Coney stood on his hind legs with his front paws drawn to his chest.

Uluu narrowed her eyes at him and smacked her lips together. "Oh, yeah. Because I want excrement around a kiosk that serves food."

"They're more like pellets?" I cocked my head to one side. "I swear they're no bigger than the tip of your wee finger." Flexing my pinky in front of her, I smiled. "' sides, look how bleedin' cute he is."

Uluu gave him a once over without so much as cracking a smile. "Do I look like someone who cares about something being—cute?"

"You do look like someone who *loves* making money." I scratched Coney's tummy. "My mate and I will buy extra noodles from you with bountiful sauce for the next few months."

Orion, who'd been quietly standing behind me, edged forward. "Why are you roping me into this?"

Without answering him, I flicked a hand over my shoulder, urging him away.

"I don't know, Heph. I've never even owned a goldfish." Uluu wrinkled her nose at my furry pal.

"Please, Uluu. You'd be doing me a huge favor. I'm about to get into some serious shit, and the last thing I need is Coney getting hurt. Be a biffy and help a guy out?"

Coney hopped from my arm and scurried across the counter to Uluu, placing one paw on the top of her hand, and wiggling his nose at her.

Damn. I hadn't even taught him that.

Uluu thinned her lips before letting one finger pet Coney's chest.

And now she'd be a goner.

Uluu let out a deep sigh. "Fine. But you put in no less than five orders of noodles a week for three months, or the deal's off."

"Virto. Done." I swiped the He-Man Lego from my pocket and handed it to Coney before ruffling his head. "I'll be back as soon as I can, bud. Be good for Auntie Uluu."

"Do *not* call me that," Uluu said, pointing at me with a stern brow.

After flashing Uluu a wink, I turned to face a glaring Orion.

"I hate noodles. You know that." Orion combed a hand through his hair.

"How in the shit are we best mates? Who hates noodles? Honestly." Shaking my head, I turned for the streets, snapping my jacket's lapel around my face. "Eyes peeled. Shouldn't take long for a hunter to sniff us out."

Orion narrowed his gaze, his eyes glowing a fierce yellow as he used his "x-ray hunting power" to scan the area. "Don't see anything out of the ordinary except—"

"Heph," a man's voice shouted from behind us.

I let my shoulders slump.

Now what?

Turning on my heel, a hulking, bearded figure sporting a "manly bun" in his long dark hair stalked toward me. "Ah, Ares. What the Tartarus are you doing here?"

Ares stopped in front of me with his head canted to one side. "Are you serious? Two weeks ago, I had you bring me here to settle a score. Doesn't ring any bells?" He rolled his shoulders, making the fur-trimmed collar on his jacket rustle. The thick Greek accent he still insisted on using always made me think of home—for better or worse.

"Right. Sorry, champ. Have had a lot on my mind as of late." I jutted a thumb behind me. "You remember your cousin, Orion?"

"Vlakás, it's been what? A hundred years?" Ares brushed past to lock forearms with Orion.

"At least. Your big bro here still making toys for ya?" Orion snickered, motioning at me with his head.

"Not near as much as I'd like." Ares cut me a side glance with a smirk.

"Certainly not because I *ever* refuse." I punched Ares in the shoulder. "The Forge is always hot, brother."

"You still using the MMA thing as a cover back home?" Orion stepped aside for a thin as a pole man wearing only tighty-whities and loafers, babbling incoherently to himself, shuffling past us on the sidewalk.

Ares raised a brow at the man scratching his stringy grey hair. "Yeah. Not for long, though. Once I get back and win the heavyweight championship, I'm announcing my alter-ego is retiring. Pop's orders." Ares' jaw tightened at the mention of his dad—Zeus.

Pretending to clean the gunk from my ear, I leaned closer to Ares. "Pardon me, did I hear you say you're doing something because your *daddy* told you?"

Ares growled and tightened the rubber band holding part of his hair back. "I don't like him, don't talk to him, but I sure as shit know not to disobey a direct order."

"What the Tartarus are you going to do then?" Orion asked.

"Bodyguarding. Figured I had more of a chance to kill someone versus the octagon. They tend to frown at skewering someone with a sword in professional sports. Go figure." Ares pressed his back against a wall, crossing his ankles and making his combat boots scuff together.

"Speaking of skewering. We were about to do a bit of it ourselves. Have a big hunt on our hands. You in?" The weight of my hammer axe in my palm already flittered over my skin.

Ares shook his head. "Enticing offer, but afraid I can't. As I said, I need to get back for the fight, Heph."

Orion cocked a brow at me.

"Yeah. About that." I scratched my chin. "I can't just yet, little bro."

Ares pushed off the wall, a scowl wrinkling his features. "What do you mean you *can't*?"

"The device." I met the war god's eyes. "It's broken."

"What?" Ares roared, fanning a hand down his beard. "Heph, I don't think you understand I have to go—"

"They've taken Aphrodite." The words spat from my mouth with the same rage and conviction I had toward whoever took her from me.

Ares's face softened for a tick before swirling into a frenzy, his eyes blazing crimson. "Maláka. Who? When?"

Always the protective brooding big brother—same as I'd been for him—not that he often needed it.

"I don't know, which is why we need to *hunt* for answers." No longer able to keep it sheathed within my mystical arsenal, I made the hammer axe appear in my grasp with an upgrade—a blue holo blade. "I ask again, brother. Will you help?" My arm itched, ready to forge a sword for the god of war.

Ares shifted his eyes to Orion, who gave a stern nod. Ares marched forward, offering his forearm to me. "You know full well any matters that concern my sister, and I'm there."

I gripped arms with him, producing the great sword with a red holo blade in the other.

Still limb locked with me, he pulled me forward, moving his mouth to my ear. "And don't think I don't know that one of those matters is *you*, brother. But we'll talk about *that* after we find her."

Had everyone been in on this *except* for me?

Not answering, I nodded. "Right then. Boys, shall we go to work?"

"Well, well. Looks like someone *has* friends. I'm shocked, Heph," Skunky's slithering voice bounced off the walls.

I spun the hammer axe in one palm, producing the same EMP baton that worked wonders last time in the other. "You'll be more surprised when you realize the kind of company I keep and the reason you're royally fucked."

"You think I came alone?" Skunky held his arms out at his sides, the pistons on his silver cybernetic arm hissing. A dozen hunters appeared from the neon shadows behind him. Some I recognized, others I didn't.

"What's that? I can't hear you from behind that fucking mask. Between it and those tubes, your new nickname should be Bane, I figure." The black Lecter-style mask covered his entire mouth and both sides of his jaw, and his words muffled whenever he spoke.

"Bane?"

I let the hammer axe dangle at my side. "From Batman? A comic, cartoon, movie—" When I received nothing but perplexing blank faces, I shook my head. "Nevermind."

Orion snatched the bow from his back, notching an arrow. "Wow. Easiest hunt I've ever experienced. The prey comes to *you* here."

"Good. That means we can get to my favorite part." Ares slid forward after shrugging the jacket off and tossing it aside. He twirled the hilt of his holo sword once before clasping it with both hands. "The slaughter."

"I do notice a certain clam missing amongst your sausage party here, Heph." Skunky pointed between the group.

Fire engulfed the volcano stirring in my chest. "Yeah. You wouldn't happen to know anything about that, would ya?"

"Moi?" He pressed a hand to his chest while several hunters snickered behind him. "Of course not."

He knew. He fucking *knew*.

"Gents," I addressed my mates, igniting flames in my eyes. "Have at it with the rest of 'em, but Hannibal Lecter there? Keep him alive."

"Yamás," Ares said, using his sword's blade to cheers us like a mug of ale.

Skunky whistled, motioning with the two sharp claws launching from his chrome arm for the hunters behind him to attack. Like the outright fuckwit he was, Skunky let the sea of hunters coast past him, retreating himself to the back of the pack.

Orion lifted his bow and, within two blinks, launched one arrow, then another, dead center into two different hunter's heads. A song I recognized blared from a nearby food vendor—a "Phonk" song called *Neon Blade*—I'd often pipe it through my earbuds during harpy hunts, and it never failed to turn the smoldering fire into an inferno.

That look on Ro's face as she disappeared...

Growling, I lurched forward, swirling the blunt side of my axe vertically like a croquet mallet, flying it into the chin of an approaching hunter. The daggers they'd been wielding fell to the pavement in clinks and clanks. I sliced the axe's holo blade through the air, separating the hunter's head from their body, gaze fixed on Skunky through the chaos.

An arrow from a crossbow launched through the mass, and Ares's sword flared in front of me, batting the arrow away like a gnat. I snapped a quick nod of appreciation before turning my focus ahead of me.

Ares grunted. "Keep your head in the game, old man. I know that look."

"No, brother. I don't think you do." Bouncing my lip in a snarl, I pushed forward to the awaiting hunters, ready to tear them apart with my bare hands if that's what it took to get to Skunky.

A hunter with a crowbar lunged at me, and with a quick slash, I knocked the weapon from his hands, lodged the axe blade in his skull, and yanked skyward. His head gurgled as the face split in two. Ares flew through the air beside me with the sword raised above his head, using both hands to slam the blade into another's chest. Orion stayed at a distance, releasing arrow after arrow with precision, headshot after headshot.

Alright, so he *did* remember how to use that thing.

I continued working through the horde, slashing legs, decapitating some, and maiming others. One hunter went to throw a hatchet at me, but I threw my axe, landing it in his face first. Without a weapon, I hurled a lava ball at the next hunter, making him bat frantically at the part of him melting. Ares had acquired another sword from one of the hunters—a katana. Using it to block slashes from a wrench pipe, he deflected the tube and stabbed the hunter in the chest with the great sword blade. Ares snarled at them, forcing them against a wall. Yanking the sword out, he used both edges, slicing them through the hunter's neck.

The only one left was dear 'ol Skunky.

"You might as well bend over right now, Skunky, and let us jam a sword straight up your ass." I materialized another hammer axe, gripping the handle with such force it made my fist shake.

"I think you underestimate my upgrades." A slimy grin pulled at Skunky's lips.

"Try us," Ares challenged.

Ares and I took turns hurling our weapons at Skunky—slices, slashes, thrusts. With his cybernetic capabilities, the son of a bitch kept glitching out of reach. With each glitch, Ares tried porting after him, but ancient Greek power wasn't a match for advanced tech. Fancy that. Attempts at hurling lava at him also made no difference because he kept blocking them with his chrome arm.

Skunky glitched in front of me and slammed his claws through my shoulder. The volcano roared within me, making my veins glow orange. Blood oozed from the wound, the pain pulsing through my chest. Pain was temporary. I produced two EMP batons and tossed one to Ares, him catching it with ease.

"On three, Ares. Wrecking Ball," I shouted, whirring the baton to life, sending a blaze of electric blue sparks.

"Égeine," he responded with a nod.

Once we both counted to three, Skunky glitched in front of us, and we hurled ourselves at him, slamming the electric parts of the batons against his head and neck, making his cybernetics go haywire. Using our freed forearms, we ran him toward the wall, slamming him against it and pinning him there. Orion leaped above us, the bow glowing a fierce blue from the two holo arrows notched. Aiming, he released the arrows, the points landing at two spots of Skunky's robotic arm, severing it from his body in defeated sparks and smoke.

Ignoring the throbbing pain in my shoulder, the feel of my immortal blood soaking through my shirt, I slid my forearm to Skunky's throat. "Now, you're *going* to talk."

sixteen

APHRODITE

RAINBOW-COLORED HOLOGRAPHIC GREEK PILLARS were erected amidst skyscrapers bordering the streets with palm trees in between. If Ithaca had been a casino on the Vegas Strip versus a place in Greece, I imagined this would be how it looked. Instead of older, rusting vehicles that crowded the streets in Heph's neck of the woods, these were shiny and slick, the rotating spotlights from every direction glinting off the reflective chrome. Citizens passed clad in prestigious dresses or pantsuits, and everyone was well-kept without so much as a hair out of place.

I wrapped my arms around my bare midriff and combed my tousled hair with my fingers. Considering the caked blood on my arm, the current state of my rat's nest hair, and my attire, the stares I received from everyone seemed warranted.

"Of all the places I could've accidentally ported myself," I mumbled.

Would it have killed me to port myself to The Fringes? The filth amount would've complimented nicely.

A woman walked past with black hair pulled tightly into a bun, a thin band of blue holo wrapped around her eyes. Scrolling text whirred up it. "Fine. Fine. But will it be here in time for the Lunation Festival?" She kept her arms pinned at her sides as she moved with graceful steps.

Instead of a hologram, a fountain sprouted natural water from between a set of buildings across the street, several streams bouncing between hexagon-shaped structures. Turning to cross the road, I paused with my sneaker hovering, remembering what Heph said about crosswalks here. A bright yellow Lamborghini-styled car zoomed by the exact moment I stepped back, the wind kicking off it and sending me flying to the ground on my ass.

Grumbling, I sat in a slump, not bothering to hoist myself to my feet. People passed without a glance in my direction, all with those same holo devices stretched over their faces like they were an extension of their bodies.

A man with a shaved head, sporting dark grey slacks and a white button-up shirt, crouched beside me. One of his hands pressed the side of his head, making the radial blue holo on his face disappear. The other hand slipped to my shoulder. "Miss? Are you alright?"

I tensed under his touch and the man snapped his hand away with a grimace, backpedaling on his heels. "Oh, shit. What the hell is that?"

"Sorry. The blood is mine. I swear I didn't murder anyone or something."

Not that I wouldn't have given a chance…

"Not that. The gnarled nasty thing on your shoulder. Are you a leper?" His eyes widened, and he leaned away.

I looked at my shoulder, a peculiar sense of acceptance washing over me at the sight of a crescent-shaped scar on my skin. "The scar? Seriously? That's what you're focused on?"

"Why would you keep that? Get it lasered off like everyone else." The man sneered at me before wiping his palm against his pant leg.

I'd had the scar, not twenty-four hours ago and already felt offended by someone's response. Heph had been dealing with it his *entire* life. "Maybe I keep it as a reminder." Glaring at him, I stood, dusting off my ass.

"Suit yourself, but it's disgusting." He pushed on his temple and shook his head as the blue holo band appeared again.

"Yeah? And you're fucking rude."

The crosswalk turned green, and I brushed past him before he could say anything more. I didn't need "murder on an Ithaca street corner" added to my rap sheet. And I didn't need the drama. What I *did* need was to get my bearings and find a way back to Heph. Who knew you could miss someone so fiercely it made your chest physically ache over their absence? Certainly not me. Not until I'd confessed those feelings to myself. And what goddess of love can't sort out their own emotions?

Once I reached the fountain, I sat on the white resin edge with a deep sigh. The water was cool to the touch as I dipped my hand into the collecting pool, washing away the dried blood from my arm and smoothing out stray hairs atop my head. I traced the fully exposed scar on my shoulder from one end to the other, a surprising smile gracing my lips.

I liked the scar—a warble in the otherwise flawless porcelain. It felt…freeing.

With a newfound hitch in my step, I slapped my thighs and leaped to my feet, determined to find a way out. Did this place not have a city map anywhere? A transportation map even? Considering the friendly nature of Mr. Your Scar Is Disgusting, asking someone for directions seemed out of the question.

A shop on my left glowed brightly in neon pink and mint green lights, the name *Maia's Doves* flashing above with animated twin doves and a woman's curvy lips. Two ceiling-to-ground windows were on each side of the door, but no view of the inside. Scantily clad women wearing only jewel-studded g-strings, bikini tops, and transparent platform heels danced in each window like living merchandise on display. To make it worse, they also had animated neon signs advertising their names.

An auburn-haired woman with freckled skin named Candi gyrated in one window, while the other harbored a woman with pale pink and baby blue cropped hair named—Aphrodite. Narrowing my eyes, I moved closer, prepared to look at the woman's face when she turned toward the window. I'd have lost my jaw were it not attached to my skull.

"Daphne?" I said out loud despite the thick pane of glass between us.

The woman froze, her light eyes searching my face before pushing her hands against the glass, mouthing my name. Needing answers and needing them now, I stormed for the door, stopping dead in my tracks, when a hulking man in

Aviator shades stopped me in the foyer with a hand twice the size of my head shoved at my face.

"You want in? You gotta consent to a weapon check, ma'am." The depth of the man's voice rivaled the echo of a Titan's sneeze.

I lifted my hands and widened my stance, expecting him to wave an electronic wand over me. "Sure. Do what you must."

His eyes glowed red as he started at my face and worked his gaze down my body. After his eyes went back to normal, he nodded and stepped aside. "You're cleared. Have a good time."

"Oh, I intend to." Slipping on the love goddess persona I so desperately did not want to visit right now, I sauntered inside.

There wasn't much to the place except for a front desk and two doorways leading to hallways where I imagined all the "action" took place. A holo sign hung from behind the desk listing all forms of services and pricing—oral sex, both giving and receiving, various positions, and an endless list of kinks, one or two that even *I* had never done. The receptionist hopped from her stool, the long bone-straight silver ponytail swaying. She flicked it over one shoulder and tapped her Indy-red fingernails on the clear countertop with a sparkling grin.

"How may we serve you today?"

I leaned one elbow on the counter and bit my lip as I shifted my gaze to Daphne's window. "I'm quite interested in the pink-haired one."

"Aphrodite, hm? You have quite the eye." The receptionist swiped her hand near the monitor, pulled up a holo screen, and typed something.

A light *whoosh* sounded from the windows, and several

moments later, Daphne entered the space with her hands folded over her bare stomach. The receptionist flashed a sultry smile at me before moving from behind the counter.

She peeled Daphne's arms from her midriff. "Now, now, dear. You mustn't hide the merchandise when a customer has chosen you for their company."

Nausea bubbled in my gut, but I kept up the game as I sauntered to Daphne, walking around her and dragging a single finger down her spine. "Yes. I'll have her."

"Aphrodite, would you lead her to room thirty-four?" The receptionist pressed a hand between Daphne's shoulder blades, urging her forward. "She'll take payment from you once you're satisfied."

Nodding, I fell in line behind Daphne as she walked through the right doorway to a hallway dimly lit by glittering white lights bordering the walkway. Daphne clenched her fists at her sides and didn't look back at me before arriving at door thirty-four. With a trembling hand, she swiped her wrist over the lock, and the grey metal door swung open. I followed her inside to a modest- sized-bedroom—a circular bed with eggplant satin sheets in the center, a filigree-patterned chaise lounge in one corner, and a wet bar with a dozen assorted bottles and tumbler glasses in the other.

Daphne whirled around to face me. "What would you like me to do?"

"Sit down, Daphne. I'm not going to use you for your services." I pointed at the bed's edge.

A crease formed in her brow as she sat, gripping the satin sheets. "Aphrodite, I didn't choose the name. Maia did."

"I don't care you're using my name." I sat next to her and canted my head. "I care that you're working here and don't seem to enjoy the line of work."

Goosebumps littered her skin, and her teeth chattered. "A gal gets desperate when they're about to be evicted."

Olympus.

"Do you have a robe or something you can put on?" I frowned, searching the room for any signs of a closet.

She pointed at the wet bar. "There's one folded in there, but honestly, I'm fine."

"You're not fine. You're shivering so hard you're making the whole bed shake." I pushed to my feet and retrieved the thin silk black robe, holding it out to her.

"Sorry." Her voice weakened as she took the robe and slung it over her shoulders.

"Why are you apologizing?" Sighing, I sat next to her.

"I don't know. Just something they expect me to say in these situations." Her gaze shifted to the floor, tears welling in her eyes.

"How are you here, Daph? I thought that tree curse was a permanent deal." I chewed on my lip, remembering the whole thing started because my son got miffed at Apollo. Back then, I'd applauded his scheming motives. "And I should be the one apologizing. Eros was to blame for all of it."

She shook her head and offered a tiny smile before looking at me, the longer wisps of her geometric-styled haircut swaying over her collarbones. "It was such a long time ago, Aphrodite. I don't have any grudges over it."

"You'd be a first among the Greek deities *not* to hold

a grudge." I flicked a piece of dirt from my pants. "Even hundreds of years later."

"It doesn't matter. I couldn't tell you how I got here, but I'm only thankful someone took pity on me and lifted the curse."

I leaned forward, resting my forearms on my thighs. "You know I have nothing against sex for money, but not when the *merchandise* you're so grossly referring to is not feeling the vibe."

"It's not a big deal. I'll quit as soon as I have enough money to cover rent for a few months and find something else." Daphne hugged the robe around her tighter, her cheeks flushing pink.

"No. You shouldn't have to do this." Raking a hand through my hair, I shot to my feet.

If only I had my frigging powers—I could fix this. Feeling powerless while *being* powerless plain sucked.

"Aphrodite, are you okay? You seem…different." Daphne stood and met me across the room, rubbing the shorter portion of her hair that hung to the base of her skull. "And since when do you have a scar? *How* do you have a scar?"

"It's a long story that I don't have the time to tell. You wouldn't happen to be able to port, would you?" I chewed on my thumbnail, getting antsier by the minute to find Heph. Lupe's twisted nightmare she'd implanted in my mind in an unending spiral.

"Nope. All I can do is enchant plant life." She shrugged her thin shoulders and splayed her hand at the floor, making several yellow daffodils sprout from the carpet. "Why? You can. Right?"

"I lost my powers. And I need to find a way back to Desolate Row and don't know my way around here." I hugged my arms, rubbing them.

"You lost your powers?" Daphne shook her head and pressed a finger between her eyes. "And what's in The Dez?"

I sucked on my bottom lip. "Hephaistos."

"Heph?" Her tone sounded surprised as she let her hand disappear from her face. "I ran into him not long ago. He's looking extra cute nowadays. Funny how immortal men *also* age like a fine wine."

My stomach fluttered. "Yeah. I uh—I noticed."

"Wait. Are you two—"

"No," I exclaimed before turning my back to her. "Maybe? I don't know. But he thinks I'm kidnapped, and I need to find him." I whirled back around and gripped her shoulders. "Will you help me? When I get my powers back, I can make sure you never have to resort to a job like this again, Daph. Believe me."

A half smile pulled at her lips. "I do believe you. And I'll help you, but I don't expect anything in return. You'll need to walk out first. Meet me a block down in the alley between the two megacorp buildings."

I could have cried but forced the tears away. "Thank you, Daph." Squeezing her shoulder, I turned for the door and took a deep breath before donning the façade.

Trailing a finger over my lips as I passed the front desk, I smiled at the receptionist.

"I take it Aphrodite met all your expectations?"

"Beyond them." I continued to grin as I backed toward the

foyer. "She's a treasure."

"Thank you for choosing Maia's Doves. We do hope you'll consider us again for future entertainment." The receptionist bowed her head.

No sooner had my sneaker landed on the sidewalk outside, I let the smile fade away. Whether it had been fake or not, grinning felt so wrong with the absence of Heph. As instructed, I walked a block over and dove into the alley, pressing my back against the cool granite of the adjacent building.

It could've only been minutes I waited, but it felt more like hours—the impatience building to the point of my knees shaking. A black car with tinted windows stopped outside the alley. The passenger window disappeared and Daphne leaned her head out.

"Get in," she shouted.

Raising my brows, I touched my palm to the handle, and the door flung up like a wing. As I slid onto the white leather seat, I held my palms out, afraid to get something dirty.

"Well, now I see why you can't afford rent."

Daphne had changed into skinny red pants and a white vest. She laughed before waving her hand over the holo menu on the car's steering wheel. "This is *not* mine. It's a company car. The Doves make house calls too."

The car whirred to life as she turned the u-shaped wheel to merge with traffic.

"Powers or not, Daph, I'm going to make sure you never have to go back there." A deep sigh pushed from my chest. "You're far too sweet for that place."

Daphne flashed me a sparkling smile, making her green eyes

gleam like glistening emeralds. "I appreciate that. I do. How did you end up here? The Neosphere District doesn't exactly seem like your type of place."

I'd been so pissed at Heph when he teleported me here, and days ago, I may have agreed with her. Everything about the District didn't align with my style or preference. But things changed. I changed. And most importantly, Heph called the District home.

"Hippolytus took a bounty on me to get revenge for what I did to him. Heph took the bounty. And here we are." I spoke to her but kept my gaze at the window, watching the buildings and blurs of neon whiz past as we picked up speed.

"Hippolytus? That was ages ago."

Smirking, I turned my head to smile at her. "I told you. You'd be the only one not to hold an ancient grudge."

"But Heph ended up not finishing the bounty, right? He couldn't—" Daphne trailed off and thinned her lips before guiding the car to an elevated on-ramp.

"He didn't hand me over. No. And now the bounty is on *both* our heads."

Daphne tapped her pink fingernails against her knee, steering with one hand. "Wow. Welcome to the Neosphere District, indeed. Most take years to experience what you have in a matter of days."

A flickering chuckle floated from my stomach. "Lucky me."

She smiled warmly before pointing at a holo menu in the center console. "Mind if I play some music? We have at least half an hour before we get to The Dez."

"Be my guest."

She fanned her palm over the menu, and a light techno song filled the car with a repeating rhythm. I went quiet, both of my knees bouncing, and I continued to stare out the car window, distracting myself with people watching.

A random memory of Heph and me sprung to mind as we drove. Dionysos held his wine festival the same as he had and still does year after year. I'd attended that year with a blonde, baby-faced bard who told the worst jokes and his lyre never seemed to be in tune. Not sure what I saw in the man except for his looks and sparkling smile. I'll never forget how my stomach dipped when Heph appeared—the first time my body sensually reacted to him. The Maenads swarmed him as soon as he'd popped in to give Dion the metal statue he'd requested, mostly ignoring the several women pawing him.

Our eyes had locked that day from across the room, and we both went motionless—his expression, as I recall, perplexed. The Maenads roamed their hands through his dark hair, his clean-shaven chin he used to upkeep, and his chest. The blonde man, whose name I can't remember, had slipped his hands under my toga, and it was at that precise moment Heph scowled and batted the Maenads away. We never spoke about that moment we had; now, look where we were.

After a few minutes, what I caught sight of rounding a street corner and pausing at the crosswalk made my heart leap into my throat.

"Stop the car," I yelled to Daphne, not daring to move my gaze for fear I'd been dreaming it.

Heph stood at the crosswalk, and on either side of him were Orion—and Ares.

"What are the odds?" Daphne said, bringing the car to a halt across the street from them.

Slim. Very slim.

"Are you coming?" I snapped my gaze to hers, impatient for an answer.

Her eyes focused on Orion a beat too long to ignore before she shook her head. "I've got to get the car back before they notice it's been missing without a proper checkout."

"Daphne, I *will* be back. A promise is a promise." I patted her hand, itching to look at Heph out the window but keeping my focus on Daphne to reassure her I meant every word.

A comforting smile etched her lips. "I look forward to hanging out with you again, Aphrodite. And maybe this time, both of us won't be in the middle of shit shows."

Nodding, I patted her hand one last time before flying out of the car. I'd been so distracted seeing Heph that close to me, so hung up on the idea of a chance to confess everything to him that I ignored the crosswalk. Distraction had cast down Heph's eyes but when they lifted, and he spotted me sprinting across the road—he looked relieved and then—mortified. Metal crunched, and glass shattered beside me. Ares ported in time to let the oncoming car collide with him instead of me. He remained crouched, one fist resting on the pavement, the front of the vehicle wrapped around him like a damn scarf.

"Sis." Ares nodded at me before rising, ignoring the yelling and cursing from the driver. "A lot has happened since the last time we saw each other, hm?"

The traffic around us slowed to a crawl, drivers honking their horns and shaking their fists out windows to get us to move. I blinked at my big brother, unable to process his presence, but what's more, Heph's metal and ash scent filled my head—his tall, imposing form towering over me.

SEVENTEEN

HEPH

WE'D FOUND AN ABANDONED building and dragged a woozy Skunky into it. I produced chains to secure him to a rickety wooden chair and sat across from him, letting my hands dangle between my knees, chewing so hard on the toothpick hanging from my teeth I made splinters. Orion and Ares gave me the room, standing outside to watch for any potential unwanted guests. Skunky wouldn't have been too hard to handle now that we'd fried his cybernetics and he'd been de-clawed.

It would've been easy to force Skunky awake. Olympus knows I wanted to beat him into consciousness only to send him into darkness again. But gaining knowledge of Aphrodite's whereabouts would take finesse—painful, intimidating—finesse. I'd taken the opportunity to remove his Lecter mask, revealing an entirely replaced jaw and teeth made of metal.

Skunky groaned and snapped awake, pulling on the chains and frantically searching the room.

"Ah, there we are," I mumbled, using my tongue to flip the toothpick in and out of my mouth.

"Heph, if this is about that bitch goddess, I don't know a goddamned thing." Skunky yanked the chain connected to the one arm he had left.

I launched at him, grabbing his chin, lava boiling in my hand and igniting in my eyes. "I don't think you realize who you're fucking with, *biffy*." The lava burnt against his cheeks, making them smoke.

Skunky cried out in agony. "What the hell are you?"

"You ever piss off a Greek god?" I doused the fire and dragged my chair within inches of him. "Because you have now."

Skunky stared at me, squinting, searching my face for the answer to the burning question: Was this dude insane? "A Greek—what? How is that possible?"

We weren't here for me to explain the nature of my existence.

"Aphrodite means far more to me than I think you realize." I flitted my fingers, creating a pool of lava below the seat of Skunky's chair. "So, I intend on doing whatever I need to do until you recognize it and *tell* me what I want to fucking know."

"Heph, Heph. Hold on a minute here. I'm tellin' ya I have no clue where she is." Heatwaves floated from the lava beneath him, and he picked up his feet before snapping a petrified gaze back to me. "What the hell are you going to do?"

"There's always slitting off your eyelids or shoving hot splinters up your fingernails." Shrugging off my jacket, making my arms visible, I engaged the forge, watching Skunky's eyes go wide as the hardened black rock morphed over it. "But considering I have the means, let's get a little more creative, shall we?"

Crackles of glowing orange lava pulsed down my arm as the chained harpoon spear I envisioned appeared in my palm. I gave it one twirl, not doing much else with it yet.

"And people call me freak." Skunky tugged, yanked, and pulled at his confinements, jamming his heels against the ground, trying to slide away.

I can tell you what people *never* called Skunky—smart.

Scooping my arm skyward, I enraged the lava beneath him, making it sputter. Several droplets landed on his ass, melting through the thin fabric in nanoseconds, singing his skin. "Where is she?" The words exploded from my lungs.

Skunky wailed and gripped the armrests, breaths quickening before his legs kicked in front of him. "I don't. *Know.*"

They never made it easy. Be it human or creature or deity, they all thought at some point I'd give them pity even if I didn't believe them. On a bounty hunt, I never came back empty-handed, so what would they all think would happen when it came to threatening the woman I loved?

"I don't believe you, Skunks." I hurled my arm forward, and the spearhead zoomed through the air attached to the chain, lodging into Skunky's calf. Two prongs sprung beneath his skin.

Skunky let out a blood-curdling scream that sounded like a mix between a screeching cat and a frog. Before he could catch his breath, I tugged the chain toward me, pulling it from his leg, a chunk of his flesh returning with it.

Drool dripped down Skunky's chin as he sputtered and writhed in pain. "He'll kill me if I tell you."

Flashes of what this "he" did to Aphrodite made my vision hazy.

"And what do you think *I'll* do?" I shouted the words, making the hanging light fixtures rattle. Balling my hand into a fist, I commanded the lava beneath him to swirl until it spiraled in lashes over his legs and arms, melting microscopic bits of skin.

Skunky grimaced and cried out before stomping his foot, harsh breaths flapping his cheeks, and the spit collecting at the corners of his mouth turning foamy. "It's not. Part. Of the deal. He will *crucify* me."

An impatient fury surged through me, fists shaking before I ground my teeth and launched the spearhead into his forearm, yanking it back. And again, into his shoulder, blood spurting as I summoned the blade back to me. Once more into his hand, I rendered the appendage lame as I pulled the center from it, taking bone and tendon.

"Talk now before you have no skin left to claim." I sunk my face into his, my eyes burning with agonized intensity— anarchy within one stare.

Skunky's eyes vibrated, chin dipping to his chest, his limbs slack.

"I don't think so, champ. No time for passing out." I snarled as I turned my back on him, throwing up a hand to make the lava sizzle up his spine.

His high-pitched shriek made my eardrums rattle, but he screamed, "Ithaca."

Urgency swelled in my chest, and I walked up to him, slapping each of his cheeks. "Now see, that wasn't so damn hard. Where in Ithaca? Who?"

Blood bubbled on Skunky's lips, and he vigorously shook his head.

"Answer me," I boomed, holding the spearpoint to his face, aiming it at an eye.

Skunky jerked and shook his head, tears streaking his cheeks before he finally whispered, "Narcissus."

Narcissus. That arrogant cunt.

The lava leaked from my forging arm, my gaze morphing into flickering flames as I pushed on the armrests, bringing me and Skunky's faces a hair apart. After flashing a satisfied grin, I moved my lips to his ear. "Give my regards to Hades."

"No, Heph, no, please." Skunky jumped in the chair as he yanked the chains, the heat from the lava pool beneath his seat building and licking his skin.

As I pushed away and turned for the door, the volcano erupted beneath him, pulling him into a molten lava grave that'd overtake him inch by inch.

When I exited the room, Orion stood at the doorway with his arms crossed, focused on the adjacent door and surrounding windows. Ares sat in a rusted chair, rubbing the back of his neck, his head raising once he heard my feet shuffle.

"Let's get the Tartarus out of here," I grumbled, breezing past them to get fresh air as fast as possible—as fresh as the District could offer.

"I assume the wails we hear mean you got your answer?" Ares asked before pushing to his feet.

"Fucking Narcissus took her to Ithaca." The very idea of that putrid worm taking her *anywhere* made me want to shatter mountains.

Orion flicked something from his nail. "I don't suppose 'ol Skunky gave up a specific address or cross-streets by chance? Ithaca is one of the largest subdivisions in the District."

Leave it to Orion to ask the essential questions. "No. I got too miffed looking at his face a second longer than necessary."

"Sounds about right," Ares said with a smirk.

Moving beside them, I grabbed one of Ares's massive paws and rested it on my shoulder. "We'll have Ares port us there. I can sniff her out from that point."

Orion slid a hand over his face before moving beside us. "Don't *ever* tell a woman you can 'sniff' them out, Heph."

"Why? S'not like she smells bad. Sweet and sultry, really." I shrugged and re-emphasized Ares' hand on my shoulder, raising a brow at Orion to do the same.

Snickering, Orion stood close enough for Ares to touch him. "Something tells me she wouldn't see it that way."

"Alright, you bickering biddies," Ares barked before materializing us to the heart of Ithaca.

Orion shivered. "Does anyone else's right ass cheek tingle whenever porting?"

"Something tingles, but it sure as shit ain't my ass." I elbowed Ares in the ribs before cutting my gaze to Orion. "Something you want to share, Orry?"

After flicking his light hair, Orion responded, "Can it, Lover Boy."

"Vlakás. This place reminds me of what Ithaca would look like if some hotshot corporation took it over. Looks nothing like its ancient self." Ares curled his lip as he sneered at the skyscrapers and holographic pillars bordering us.

Closing my eyes, I inhaled deeply, sorting out the hundreds of scents that hit my nostrils like a backdraft.

"I don't know why I settled on Daneland versus this place. Way more my scene. The way people dress, the scenery, and hot damn the cars." Orion pointed at a shiny chrome Bat-mobile-styled vehicle passing by. "Might have to pick one of those up."

"I'd like to think it's because you're not a sellout, cousin," Ares grumbled, cracking his knuckles as they followed their bloodhound—me.

A faint distinct scent floated through the air, and I stopped dead in my tracks.

"That may be, but Daneland is the equivalent to Suburbia in these parts." Orion's brow bobbed.

Ares lifted a single nostril in distaste.

Orion pointed at his expression. "Exactly."

"Would you two pipe down for a second?" A crinkle formed in my brow as I pinched my eyes shut, wiggling my fingers, concentrating on the sweet smell I'd gotten a hint of.

"You need quiet to *smell* things, Heph?" Ares asked, his voice gruff.

I glared over my shoulder.

Ares' palms flew up, and he slid backward. "Got it."

As weak as it started, Aphrodite's scent became suddenly overwhelming. It was enough to put me out of sorts and shake my head. "Wait. She's close. Real close. Maybe a block or two this way." Pointing, I strode in that direction.

"Or she's about to cross the street while the crosswalk is

red," Orion said, jutting his thumb the opposite way.

"Maláka," Ares mumbled, porting away.

I'd been warped into an eighty's movie, time slowing as I turned on my heel in time to witness Ares' shoulder colliding with an oncoming car, preventing it from hitting Aphrodite. Seeing her face as beautiful and resplendent as it had been before Narcissus took her from me was my hammer hitting the anvil—with each spark, renewed life. A pain twisted in my gut. I hadn't realized how much it truly pained me not to know if I'd ever have the chance to admit my feelings to her. Immortal deity or nay, nothing, and I do mean zilch, was ever guaranteed.

The moment I moved to run toward her, to sprint, Ares appeared with her on the street corner, his arm falling from her shoulders, and immediately stepped away.

"Phai," Aphrodite breathed out, her eyes glistening with tears like a dying star before she leaped at me, our chests colliding, her slender arms wrapping my neck.

Holding her to me, I smoothed her hair in languid strokes, hushing her—soothing her. "You're safe now, Ro. You're safe."

Through gentle sobbing, she sniffled and shoved her nose against my neck. "You think the Fates are a crock of shit, but we wind up on the same street corner?"

"You keep trying to convince me, love-y goddess. Don't ever stop trying." And she'd have for the rest of eternity to change my mind if I had anything to say about it.

"You were on your way to rescue me. How?" She pushed back, her petite fingers playing through my hair.

I didn't put her back on the ground, holding her tight and

not letting go for anything. "Did you think I wouldn't? But you—you escaped?" A beam of pride swelled in my chest.

"It's a long story. I—"

The volcano bubbled, bordering eruption at the sight of a thin gnarled scar tracing over Ro's shoulder. A harpy claw scar. "What happened? Did Narcissus do this?" The words came out in a fury of growls and rambles.

Aphrodite gasped as she peeled back my jacket. "Me? What happened to you? You've got two golf-ball-sized holes in your shoulder, Heph," she said, yelling the last part.

"I'll heal, Ro. This—" I frowned as I traced my thumb over the scar. "—is permanent."

"It doesn't matter," she pleaded, gripping my lapels.

I pulled her face closer, making our noses touch. "Did. Narcissus. Do this?"

She nodded as she bit her bottom lip, a crinkle forming in her brow. The fret in her expression was plain—she thought admitting to it would cause me to act on impulse.

The old Heph, despite the love of his life in his arms, would've stopped at nothing to incite revenge right then and there. Not anymore.

"I *will* take care of him, but right now, I'm not letting go of you when I just got you back." As I clenched my jaw, I searched her eyes.

Her gaze sparkled as a small smile graced her lips, and her legs wrapped around my waist, locking me in. "I have so much to say."

"There's something I need to tell you," I'd said simultaneously.

"You go first," we said in unison.

Orion cleared his throat nearby. I'd forgotten we weren't the only two beings in the universe. "So, Ares, you want to grab a drink or something?"

"Whiskey?" Ares grumbled.

"You read my mind." Orion clapped a hand over Ares' shoulder, and they walked off.

"You first, love-y goddess," I whispered, pressing my forehead against hers and moving one of my hands to her ass.

"I wasn't exactly being honest when I said I didn't know why my powers were going bonkers." Her eyes cast downward, her heartbeat pounding against my chest.

"Then you know the reason?"

With a nod, she lifted her gaze to mine and took a deep breath. "It's because the goddess of love is no longer *loved*."

Fucking Tartarus. I wanted to interrupt her right then but let her continue.

"Back when mortals still believed in us, their devotion to me was enough to last me for decades but now—" She trailed off, her tiny throat bobbing as she gulped. "And men? All they've ever been after from me is sex because of my reputation and looks. And it can't be platonic like the love from my son. We're talking l.o.v.e. *Love*."

I chuckled. Despite the hurt on her face from me seemingly laughing at her misfortune, I mused over it because maybe the Fates really were that clever. Shit.

She punched my shoulder. "Heph, it's not funny." She untangled her legs and wanted to slide to the ground, so I let her—especially knowing the volcano I was about to unleash.

"Oh, Ro. You've always pretended to be dense, but right

now—" I paused when her cheeks turned rosy, her bottom lip trembling as she shifted her back to me.

Oh, no, you don't. No more backs to each other. No more denial.

Grasping the crook of her elbow, I spun her, pulling her toward me, and planting my lips to hers. After a sharp intake of breath, her tongue plunged into my mouth—conquering, claiming—enough to make my brows bob. And then, the unexpected happened…we appeared in my apartment.

It started as heated and feral, our tongues curling and her going so far as to peel my jacket from my shoulders. Gently, I grabbed her wrists, halting her, slowing us down—for now. Despite the overwhelming urge to *take* her. Things needed to be said first. If I've learned anything the past twenty-four hours—don't take one fucking minute for granted.

She pulled away with a whimper but stayed in my arms. "Heph, are you saying what I think you're saying?"

"Yeah, Ro." Letting go, I trailed the back of my hand over her smooth cheek. "I love you. I have since we were kids."

"But you—but the bounty—" Her eyes blinked with the speed of a hummingbird.

Fuck. I hadn't even had the balls to admit to myself the real reason I'd taken that bounty—until now.

"Ro," I started, rubbing my knuckle under my bottom lip. "I took that bounty as an excuse to be around you."

"An excuse? When did we ever need an excuse to hang out?"

"It'd been years, Peach. Years. I was—" My throat tightened, and I matched it by pressing further into her. "—I was afraid you'd catch wind of something and call me out on it."

"Would that have been so horrible?" Her finger paused at my hairline, then trailed down my neck until it found a home in my jacket collar.

I blurted a laugh. "Fuck yeah, it would have if you didn't feel the same."

The tip of her nose turned crimson like Rudolph, her eyes filled with tears, and a single shimmering one rolled to her chin before I swept it away. "I love you too," she whispered.

I'd been punched in the gut many times in my insane existence, but those four words had me stumbling back on my heels as if I were roundhouse kicked by a cyclops. "You—you do? Are you serious?"

She laughed and cupped my face. "Of course, I am, you big, silly, sexy *lug*."

Every planet seemed to align, every neuron in existence pulsed, and every volcano in the known galaxy erupted simultaneously. We were meant to be—her and me—Hephaistos and Aphrodite. What ethereal lottery had I unknowingly entered and somehow managed to win?

She kissed me, softer than the first—borderline tender—her lips focusing on my top one, her tongue skirting the seam of my mouth but not forcing its way in. A bright flash of pink light filled the room, followed by an explosion of glitter and rose petals. I winced and sputtered, but through the haze of sparkles, Aphrodite stood beaming, her skin glowing in radiant shades of cherry blossom.

"Holy shit," I mumbled, frozen like a damned fool.

She swirled, floating on a wispy cloud of shimmering fog, running her hands through her hair, revitalizing it. Her clothes melted away until she stood before me naked as fuck and gorgeous to the very pore.

"I think it's about time we work off that tension, god of the forge." Her gaze flashed rose quartz before she sauntered toward me, her luscious tits bouncing with each step.

Quickly opening a holo screen to message Orion, I wrote:

Heph: My place. Keep a lookout. Have...business to attend to.

Orion: You got it.

eighteen

APHRODITE

THERE WERE FAR SAFER places I could've ported, given the hunters were still after us, but Heph's home *did* feel safe. The constant adrenaline spikes from potential danger at any moment also didn't hurt. Having my powers back after losing them felt like a rebirth—a rising phoenix from the god of the forge's flames, flickering and radiant. The god of fire, volcanoes, and Olympus' forge was finally mine, and he stood *right* in front of me. So, why did I have no frigging clue what to do with him? A rare occurrence for me. Heph had me dizzy and nervous in all the best ways.

In a desperate attempt to do something rather than stand there butt naked and frozen like Boreas in the summer heat, I raised my palm, sending a spiraling glow at Heph. It swirled around him, de-materializing his clothes with every pass. He locked our gazes as each inch of him revealed masculine, tanned perfection. A snarky grin slid over his lips as my powers neared his raging erection, my heart thundering in my chest, pausing before exposing him—*all* of him.

I chewed on my thumbnail as I perused my territory—carved muscle, so, so tall, a masculine scattering of hair over his chest, stomach, and limbs. And his cock? Any being who turned down Heph because of the face scar had no idea what they missed. Their loss. *All* mine.

I had my power back, but I couldn't pinpoint what Heph wanted, what he needed in a lover. It made me borderline disoriented. Should I pounce him? Go down on him? Ride his face? Or maybe none and all of it.

Heph curled his finger and beckoned me. "C'mere, love-y goddess."

Any being I'd been with in the past wanted me but feared what I was. Not Hephaistos. The confidence bursting from him like a molten geyser had my stomach in pleasured knots. I couldn't be sure if he wanted me to leap on him or take my time, but I'd been waiting an eternity for this moment, patience be damned.

I ported in front of him because I damn well could now, and I'd missed it, crashing my lips against his, scraping my nails against the back of his head. The kiss wasn't sweet like when we'd confessed our love for each other—this one was raw and ravenous—a winding top so taut from centuries of denial about to spin way out of fucking control. His tongue plunged into my mouth, and I sucked on it before he wrapped an arm around my waist, his hand grabbing my ass—*hard*. He whirled me around, and with a light nudge, my back fell onto his bed.

His bed. His domain—filled with reminders of who he was, why I fell for him, and scents of oil, smoke, and musk. I trailed my fingers down his arms and chest, dirtying him like when he forged the sword for me—*performed* for me.

He peeled back, glancing down at the black smudges coating his body, his skin sheening with sweat and grease. "Did you purposely make me filthy, Ro?"

Biting my lip, and grinning at him, I nodded.

He lowered himself between my legs with a smug grin. "You dirty, dirty, girl." He cupped one breast, kneading it, unabashedly blotching it with black streaks.

He'd been right when he said I didn't like to be stained or grimy. But with him, it was different. I wanted to be *soiled* by him—with him. Because it wasn't filth, it was passion and pride. Imperfections gained. My hips bucked, impatient and antsy for him, for the volcano god. A thousand years of failed words, masked feelings, and subdued pining catapulted all at once, translating through my fingertips as I groped him, clawed him, pulled him to me with every desire to *never* let go.

His tip played at my entrance, and Heph smiled down at me. So much packed into the tiniest expression—relief, passion, hope, and serenity. I traced a fingertip over his bottom lip, grinning back at him, hoping my smile packed the same punch for him as his did for me.

His gaze focused on my lips, eyes darkening before he thrust into me with abandon, filling me, slamming his forearms on each side of my head. My back arched from the bed, my powers bursting from my chest in response to the connection. A flash of radiant pink light, shimmering and welcoming. He rocked in and out of me, groaning and growling, pushing my head closer and closer to the wall where the "But Did You Die?" glowing sign hung above us.

He kissed, licked, and nibbled my neck, sliding my hands above my head and interlacing our fingers, holding me there. His thrusts slowed and he lifted his head to gaze down, pumping into me with languid strokes in a similar motion from our dance at the swinger's club. "Did you ever think about me when you were fucking someone else, Ro? Ever *wished* it was me?"

I bucked my hips, wanting him to pick up the pace again. "I couldn't tell you how many times, Heph."

"I tried so fucking hard to get the thought of you out of my head. The endless dreaming that I could be *with* you." He thrust once, deep and rough, making me gasp. "Because I never thought you'd be the one underneath me in a thousand years." He pumped again, his biceps flexing, hands wrenching against mine. "Never thought you could *love* me."

"Yes, yes," I whispered through a wistful moan.

He removed one hand and slid it down my face until my chin was in his grasp. "I'm *all* yours now, Aphrodite. Don't break me." His words were an equal mixture of plea and command.

Locking my eyes with his, diving into his fiery gaze, I shook my head. "I wouldn't dare, Phai. If we ever shattered—it'd be the end of times, and we'd wither away together."

The declaration made him come undone, and the furious thrusting picked up, one of his arms hitching under my leg, the other hand still holding one of mine above my head.

I used my free hand to trace over the scar on Heph's face, memorizing every dip and groove. He didn't shy away from my touch but shuddered against it, pumping faster, our bodies clapping with each meeting of our hips.

He'd closed his eyes when my fingers trailed his scar and blasted them open to reveal the fiery glow ignited in his gaze. "Do you want to feel the Forge, Ro?"

"Yes," I moaned, wrapping a hand over his neck, meeting him thrust for thrust.

The heat pooled first in my chest, delicious and warm, making my veins blaze orange beneath my skin. The sensation traveled through my stomach, pulsed down my legs, and surged once it reached my clit, making me cry out. Heph pinned my hand to the mattress tighter as I writhed under him. It'd begun to rain outside, the neon lights from surrounding buildings reflecting in the clear drops like flickering starbursts. Our bodies slid against one another, caked with dirt, grease, and sweat.

"The Forge is inside you, Ro." His cock pushed against my spot, and I dug my nails into his shoulder, shivers overcoming me. "*I'm* inside you. Claiming every wall, every freckle, every gasp escaping your throat." He traced his hand over my neck, holding it there, resting on my collarbones. "Come for me," he said through a whispered growl.

Fucking. Olympus.

The euphoria swirled in my stomach, building, and building until the climax overtook me. I cried out his name, his nickname, his shortened name—every damn label I'd ever given him. Heph buried his face against my neck, thrusting forward one last time, snarling into my hair as he released inside me.

Shuddering, I opened my eyes to gaze up at him. "Holy shit, Hephaistos."

"Don't think for a *second* that's the same show any other woman I've been with got from me." He kissed the tip of my nose. "You bring it out of me, goddess of love."

More. I needed more.

My powers swelled from my skin in pastel pinks as I pushed him back, straddling him, one hand on his chest.

"No," he said in a gruff tone.

I arched a brow. "No?"

A peculiar mix of fear and disappointment coursed through me.

"That's right. No." He sat up, stretching my legs behind him with me still perched on his lap. His fingers kneaded my hips before roughly grabbing them. "That first round was to get it out of our system. Now, you let *me* take control."

My stomach folded over itself, and I clenched his ribs with my thighs. From the first day I saw Heph sparring with Ares when we were teens I'd known that we belonged together— like a tang to its hilt. All the myths described me as love counterbalancing with war, but that's not what I needed. I needed someone as equally scarred, as equally lost with their identity. And someone to balance my passion and light with their own passion and callused hardness.

"*Let* you, hm?"

He nodded, pulling me closer, my clit slamming against his rock-hard stomach. "You're so used to being in control, having no choice but to *take* control. I can do it for you, Ro.

Do you trust me?"

The question seemed silly to me.

"With my ethereal life," I whispered.

"Good." A wild glint flashed in his gaze. "Now get up." He motioned with his head to the wall across from us.

My heart raced as I slunk from the bed, rivaling horses with a chariot. Heph slapped my ass with a stinging force, making me hiss yet smile at him over my shoulder. Once I reached the wall, I pressed my back to it, a fury of swirls and bubbles erupting in my stomach as I watched him stalk toward me.

He raised his palms, a plume of grey smoke and embers appearing before a pair of cuffs swung from his finger—the same sparkly cuffs he put on me during our hunt. Hephaistos had a kinky side. I should've seen this coming—shame on me for the *second* time.

"Before I put these on you, so you can't cheat and use your powers—" He lowered his mouth to mine, kissing me, darting his tongue between my lips for a fraction of a second, his beard tickling my cheek. "—make yourself a blindfold."

A breath pushed from my lungs at the mere thought of the vulnerability I'd have—blinded and powerless—at the mercy of the forge god. Goosebumps littered my skin before I flashed a crooked smile, waved a hand over my face, and put a pink blindfold with the words "Don't Be Gentle" on the side he could see. The world plunged into darkness, my other senses going into overdrive, picking up the chains rattling as he slipped the cuffs over my wrists.

His hot breath fanned my neck, his cheek pressed to my temple, and his lips brushed my ear. "Spread your legs."

Rolling my bottom lip through my teeth, I obliged, sliding them apart.

"Wider, Ro."

Sucking in a breath, I spread them even further, my ass pressing against the cold resin wall to steady me.

"Good girl," he whispered, smiling against my neck.

He *knew* I'd both hate him saying it while frigging craving to hear it again.

He lifted my cuffed hands above my head, securing the chain on something, forcing them to stay upright. A callused fingertip pressed between my collarbones, the forge's heat building in my chest. He upped the intensity, making tiny beads of sweat form between my breasts, at my hairline, and dimples of my lower back. Gasping, I reveled in the mix of slight discomfort overlapping with pleasure. His volcanic touch traveled to my breasts, both hands grabbing them, tweaking the nipples, making them as hard as marble.

Wetness soon covered one breast from his tongue, his beard scratching the sensitive skin there. He bit a nipple, making me yelp, soon followed by me biting my lip so hard I drew blood. He dragged his tongue the length of my stomach, pressing all fingertips right above my clit, pulsing the flames he commanded beneath my skin. I tried to pinch my knees together, to writhe at the warmth throbbing through me, but Heph slid something between my legs, cool metal pressing against each inner thigh, forcing my legs to stay spread.

The wetness disappeared, and his mouth pressed to my ear. "I'm going to show you the things I've wanted to do for *centuries* to you every waking moment we were together.

The reason I had to keep my distance. Otherwise, I would've gone fucking mad. And I'm going to start with licking and sucking every square inch of your cunt." He swirled a callused thumb over the very spot he claimed to devour. "But you're not allowed to come until I say so. Understand, love?"

He knew I wasn't a fan of that word, and him using it now with his commanding presence and my submissive one—had me sopping wet, some of the approval dripping down my thighs. I nodded in agreement.

His hand clasped my chin. "*Say* it, baby."

Baby. I couldn't recall anyone calling me that before and the way it sounded rolling from his tongue rivaled Terpsichore's soothing lullabies.

"Yes, Heph. Yes," I said through a fluttery moan.

The sound of his knees meeting the floor pounded in my ears. He grabbed my ass, holding me still as he made one long delicious lap over my folds from back to front. I gripped the chains of my cuffs, my head falling back, groaning. He swirled his tongue around my clit before flicking it with the tip. Whenever I shuddered or my body betrayed me, trying to curl inward, Heph would grab my ass tighter, forcing me to stay put.

When his mouth closed over that bundle of nerves—sucking on it—it took everything in me to follow what he asked and not come all over his sexy as sin face. I wanted myself laced in his beard.

Whimpering, convulsing, I whispered, "Heph, I think I'm going to—"

His lips left me and pressed to my mouth, kissing me, swirling his tongue with mine. Both of us shared the taste of my pussy, the juices collecting at the corners of my lips. He pulled away, and I felt my wrists lifted from the peg above my head before his cheek pressed to my forehead. "I said *wait*." He turned me around and shoved me against the wall, my palms pressing against it.

Never in my godly existence had a person taken the reins like this. If one were ever capable, they never had the gall to try. But with every fiber in me, was I ever thankful that Hephaistos *was* that person.

He slapped my ass—hard, leaving a pleasured sting behind. If I were mortal, it'd have left a red handprint for me to gaze at the next day and remember what transpired. I might use my powers later on to make it appear anyway. The tip of his cock brushed the cheek he'd just hit and his massive hands pressed over mine.

"Do you want it, Ro?" His voice was low and gritty.

More than anything in the entire cosmos forever and into the next life.

"Yes." I arched my back, presenting myself to him.

He teased me by shifting his cock from one cheek to the other and sliding between. "And what do you say?"

I balled my fists against the wall, and he clenched them within his grasp. "Please."

Sliding one hand away to position himself, he gripped my hands with his free one above us and pushed inside me from behind. His hand moved to my hip, pulling me back every time he thrust forward, his balls slapping against my clit with each stroke. His hand disappeared from mine, and I soon felt a single finger trailing down the length of my spine, igniting the heat with each vertebra he passed. He stopped thrusting and grabbed my hips, moving me forward and back over his cock. He growled and groaned behind me, his length throbbing inside me.

The blindfold suddenly disappeared, and the metal pressed between my legs, my eyes rapidly blinking to acclimate to the light. He pulled out of me and turned me around, pushing my back to the wall, and throwing my chained hands over his neck. I dug my nails into the back of his head, watching his eyes squint, a mischievous grin on his lips. I traced my toe up the side of his calf, gliding my knee over his hip, and he hooked one arm underneath it, pinning me against the wall with his chest.

He slid inside me, and I locked gazes with him, clawing my nails harder against his head. Groaning, he slapped one hand on the wall near my head, the other caressing my arm, sending a flurry of kisses down my skin as he pumped in and out of me.

"More than ten centuries of built tension. A millennium worth of flirting that actually *meant* something." He reached behind his head, grabbing the cuff chains and making them disappear in swirls of silver dust. "Use your powers on me, baby. Whatever you want." He sunk his face to plant his mouth to mine, taking a moment to suck on my bottom lip.

Heph had already been filled to the brim with sexual prowess, love, and passion, but a tinge more ecstasy never hurt anyone. Smiling, I pressed a hand to his chest, waves of pink fanning down my arm, pulsing into him. His thrusts halted, and he grunted against my cheek, his touch tensing on my hip.

"Feel that, Phai?" I nuzzled his face scar before dragging the tip of my tongue over it, still surging my power through him. "*Rapture* itself, babe."

"Fuck. You keep doing that, and I'm going to come." He beat his fist against the wall near my head, his hips pumping several times into me before stopping again.

"Do it. Come with me," I whispered, clenching myself around the length of him, swirling my power through my skin to share the same jubilation as I made him feel.

Panting, Heph hitched my knee higher, driving into me with such force my head banged against the wall, his palm shifting to cradle my skull. Embers floated around us, swirling with rose petals and shimmering pink dust as the rapture built and built. Heph kissed me—sweet and carnal all at once, an action without words. After the fifth thrust, we both came undone, shivering, quaking, and breathless. He let go of my leg, and I let it fall to the floor with a *thwap*, too satiated to worry about using any will to lower it slowly.

He cupped my cheek and smiled—genuine and resplendent. "Olympus. I played over and over again, fantasized even, of what sex would be like with you, and I've gotta say, my imagination could *not* do it justice."

"Oh, yeah?" I grinned and tugged once on his beard. "You'll have to tell me some of those fantasies sometime."

"Deal." He pressed a light kiss to my lips.

The glistening pink hue settling over my skin from my returned powers made me beam. "I think losing my powers helped put things in perspective, but I am so glad they're back.

I feel fresher than ever."

Heph's handsome grin turned conniving, and he slapped his still hard cock against my thigh. "See? All you needed was the Magical D, and Wham-O. Powers are back."

I swatted his shoulder. "Shut up, you."

He chuckled before pushing off the wall and taking a step back. "How much longer you think the boys will last out there?" He jutted his chin at the door, where undoubtedly an impatient Orion and Ares awaited.

"Are you kidding?" Smiling, I moved to the small dingy mirror above the sink in the kitchenette. "Those two owe you enough to give us years of favors like this." I pressed my forefinger to my cheek, creating a small glittering pink heart— an addition celebrating the new me.

"Mm. Wearing your heart on your cheek now, Peach?" Heph said from behind me, staring at my reflection in the mirror. His hands slid over my shoulders, massaging them before frowning as his skin brushed the harpy claw scar. "That son-of-a-bitch will get what's coming to him, Ro. Mark my words. I'm so sorry that happened to you."

Patting his hand, I turned to face him. "Oh, believe me when I say I'm coming with you to give Sussy a piece of my mind too. But honestly?" I glanced at the scar and shrugged. "I kind of like it."

"Yeah?" Heph's knuckles brushed my cheek.

"Yeah. It makes me imperfect. Makes me feel *real*—it's freeing."

Heph winced and rubbed the back of his neck. "Shit. I want to say something, but it's far too corny."

I tugged one of his hands. "Aw, come on, babe. I love your corn." A glint sparkled in my gaze as I smiled at him.

He sighed and took both of my hands in his, kissing the back of my hand before speaking. "A million scars could never make you any less perfect—to me."

I held back a laugh and canted my head to the side. "You're right. So, so, corny." He rolled his eyes and tried to pull away, but I yanked him back. "But also, extremely sweet. That's one of the many reasons I love you, Heph. Through the grit and grime, there's always been that rainbow too."

"Yeah, yeah." His beard hid most of it, but his cheeks flushed.

"The scar is also an ever-lasting reminder," I whispered, tracing a fingertip over the divot in his cheek.

"A reminder? Of what? How much of a fuckwit Narcissus is?"

Chuckling, I shook my head. "I've made a lot of mistakes throughout my life, Heph, but this reminds me of one of the worst." Cupping his cheek with my palm, I flashed a warm smile. "Taking so long to tell you how I felt."

Heph's shoulders relaxed as if what I was about to say made him tense. "Well, shit, Ro. In that case, should I lop off a limb since we're both equally guilty?"

"Forges, no. I like you with your limbs." I dropped my gaze to his still hard as steel cock. "Especially that one."

He made it bounce, grinning at me when I lifted my eyes back to his. "While we're still in this cheesy mood, come here. I want to show you something."

Holding one of my hands, he led me to his jacket crumpled on the floor. "As I said, I've loved you since we were kids, Aphrodite, but you've had my heart—" He dug into his pocket, producing the crystal swan I'd spied on his shelf days before. "—since you gave me this. Do you remember?"

I'd been so foolish when I saw it the first time. How could I forget?

"Yes," I whispered, nostrils burning from impending tears. "There was a birthday party on Olympus. I don't remember who for, but we were so, so young. Baby gods at that point. I knew you couldn't come to the party even if you wanted to and felt *horrible*." I held the swan between us, shining the pink neon through it, making fractals of light appear on the wall. "I made this for you and came down to give it to you as a consolation."

"Yeah. You did, baby. You were the only person who gave a flying shit about me that day. And I never forgot it." His jaw tightened as if he were holding back tears.

"And you've held onto it all this time?" A tear streaked my cheek.

With a gentle touch, he took it from me and set it back in its place amongst the gaming consoles. "Of course I did. It gave me hope that I wouldn't be seen as an outcast my entire life."

Pulling him to me, I trailed butterfly kisses over his scar and eyelids, down his nose, until I reached his mouth. He wrapped his arms around my waist and held me to him, sighing into my hair, his muscles relaxing. "I'm here, Heph. And I'm not going *anywhere*."

Someone cleared their throat behind us.

Heph's eyes flew open, and he pulled me behind him.

"Sorry, but um, Ares sent me in here to avoid potentially seeing his sister naked. I can see now his worry was warranted, but we've gotta get out of here, Heph. We killed two hunters and heard them alerting others through a comm system that you were back in your old place," Orion said, keeping his gaze on the floor.

"We'll be right out," Heph answered.

After giving a curt nod, Orion exited.

I swirled a hand around myself, making a hot pink wrap dress with capped sleeves and white sneaks with pink accents appear.

Heph turned. "We should—" His eyes roamed my body. "—get dressed."

"Whew. I can't tell you how crazy not enough wardrobe changes were." I ruffled my wavy hair.

Chuckling, Heph crossed his burly arms and tapped his foot. "What?"

"You mind giving me my clothes back? I have no problem fighting in the nude, but when my dick is flailing about, it tends to make me a tad nervous."

Biting into a smile, I snapped my fingers, making his dingy black pants, boots, and duster jacket appear on him—all dirt and grime still intact.

"Thanks, love." He dove in to kiss my cheek, his hand pressing my lower back. "We need to pick up Coney before continuing this little hunt for Oz."

"Coney? Who'd you leave him with?"

Heph trailed a hand through his beard and rattled his throat. "Uluu."

Uluu. Where had I heard that name?

Gasping, I hit his arm. "You left him with the *pasta* lady?"

"Ouch." He frowned, playfully batting my hand away. "Yeah. She never spits in or does anything else to my food, so I figured that makes her pretty trustworthy. Who else would I have left him with? Olaf?"

I folded my arms in a huff. "Tushy."

Bringing up that particular throwback made Heph smile. We'd say "tushy" versus "touché" to each other whenever the other won the banter. That is, *when* we were willing to admit it.

"Ready?" Heph held his hand out to me.

As I interlaced my fingers with his, I came to the striking realization of the true answer to his question. I *was* ready for the first time since crawling out of sea foam. I'm ready to be the best at my duties, to be Heph's partner and lover, and most of all—to forge my own destiny with the forge god himself.

NINETEEN

HEPH

FUCKING OLYMPUS.

If I were a mortal bloke, I'm convinced I'd be walking funny right about now like an Old West cowboy after a long horse ride. And that was only after banging Aphrodite *twice*. I'd kept my cool as I always did, but fuck if my nerves hadn't shot into overdrive. I'd venture to guess most people were intimidated by her—the ones who were fortunate enough for her to give them the time of day—that is. Hence, I knew my Ro needed a man with confidence, dominance, and the stamina of a Maenad. And I'd give it to her any time she asked.

"Oh, good. You at least thought of a practical thing like sneakers," Ares said with a huff, motioning at Aphrodite's ensemble. "What happens when you fall on your ass and show your bits to everyone?"

Aphrodite threw her hands to her hips. "Firstly, I won't be falling on my ass. And secondly, my dear brother—" She pulled at a hot pink pair of spandex shorts under her dress. "That's what the spanks are for."

"Vlakás," Ares mumbled, trailing a hand down his face.

"So, I take it things went—well?" Orion flashed me a cheeky grin.

I rolled my shoulders, flashes of Aphrodite blindfolded as I ate out her pussy, pulsing through my mind. "Well enough not to tell you a godsdamned thing. Don't try it."

"Aw, come on, Heph." Orion leaned closer. "It's Aphro-fucking-dite."

Orion was my best mate. He'd never do anything to betray my trust or intentionally hurt me—deep breath.

"It is. She's *right* there." I pointed at her several meters away, still talking to Ares, flicking Orion's nose in the process. "And now she's my girl, so watch what you say. We square?"

Orion scrunched his nose and slapped my hand away. "Yeah. We're square. You fucking dog." He threw his arm around my neck before I could deflect, rubbing his knuckles on the top of my head.

"Wow. People still give noogies?" Aphrodite asked before turning to Ares with finger raised. "And *don't* even think about it."

While Ares distracted Aphrodite, I leaned toward Orion's ear. "Listen, the Lunation Festival is coming up, and I figured Ro deserved a bit of a break amidst the chaos kind of deal, y'know? Thought I'd take her to my rooftop and—"

Orion waved a hand in my face. "Say no more. We got you, bro." He held up his fist for me to bump, so I did.

"And face the wrath of messing up your hair? I wouldn't dare, sis." As he passed, Ares challenged her with his stare, fake raising his arm, and making her lift her fists in defense. Chuckling, he pointed at her hands. "Are you going to punch me?"

"Maybe." Aphrodite lifted her chin and rolled her shoulders back, fists still up.

Elbowing Orion in the gut to get him off me, I moved beside Ares. "I made her a sword. We uh—we've started sparring."

Ares' expression melted and I dared say he looked—hurt. "You're learning to fight? Why did you never ask me?"

Sticking her bottom lip out, Aphrodite let her hands fall slack at her sides. "It's a recent development, Air. And rolling around on a mat seemed far more appealing with Heph?"

Ares scrunched his nose like someone took a shit in a nearby alley. "That's fair." He turned to face me, swelling his chest. "You make sure she knows what she's doing before she tries it in a real situation, yes?"

Aw, it was so cute when he tried to over-power me—to pretend I couldn't take him down right where he stood.

"I'd do nothing less, brother."

"What's the plan, Heph?" Orion asked, shoving his hands in his vest pockets.

"First, we give Narcissus a piece of our minds, then we go grab Coney before Uluu uses him in one of her meat sauces, and then continue the ridiculous hunt for Oz." The device breaking couldn't have happened at a less opportune moment. I not only made one god stranded from their usual time and place but *three*.

"If this Oz material is so hard to find, why'd you use it? Surely something else would suffice?" Orion flicked blonde strands from his face. Every time he did it, I wanted to show him how to curl it over his damn ear, pull it into an Ares "manly bun", or better yet? Chop it off.

"I could spend the entire day explaining how time travel works, but I'd end up talking in circles. I can tell you that it takes a strong material to act as a conduit. Oz is the strongest metal in the known universe." I steepled my fingers. "Therefore, I could've used another material in construction, but it wouldn't have performed as well, if at all. Worse yet, I could've ended up in the middle of a vast space instead of my desired destination."

"Now we know." Ares threw his palms out at his sides.

"And knowing is half the battle," I added, cutting Orion a grin.

Orion nodded. "Yo Joe."

"Oh, my gods," Aphrodite said, smiling and facepalming.

I pulled Ro to my side, wrapping my arm around her waist and nuzzling my nose against her temple. "You can pick the restraint next time, baby, if you can tell me what that's from."

Ares made a gagging sound behind us before walking away with his fingers plugging his ears.

"You're making this too easy on me." She gazed at me with heavy lids before whispering, "G.I. Joe."

And there it went. Pecker as hard as chromium—again.

"That's right. I'm a man of my word. Think about it." Bouncing my brow, I kissed her nose before motioning the gents to follow.

Having Ro lead the way, we stood in a line outside the building that housed Narcissus, staring up at it.

I snarled, my fists shaking. "Orion, would you do us the pleasure of telling us what room he's in?"

Orion's eyes turned bright yellow as he used his power to scan the building. I'd asked him several times to describe what it looked like when he used his hunting scan-y powers, and the best I could gather was a mix of the Predator's heat signature sight and Superman's x-ray vision. All the things this guy could see through almost seemed unfair. Almost.

"Top floor, back left corner room," Orion announced, his blue eyes returning to normal.

Turning to Aphrodite, I pressed my palms together. "Sweetheart, I have zero issues with you tagging along, but I want to be absolutely certain. You still want to come?"

"You're damn right I do." She pretended to roll up sleeves she didn't have.

"Gents?" I looked at them while taking hold of Aphrodite's hand, ready for her to port us.

Orion nodded. "We got the ground covered."

Ares grumbled.

"Hey, look at it this way, brother. You're getting practice for your new bodyguarding gig." I slid him a sly grin.

"Ay sto diaólo," Ares mumbled under his breath.

Aphrodite swooped her arm skyward, kicking up petals and gold dust, making us appear outside the door where Orion saw Narcissus. She scowled and marched forward, but I grabbed the back of her dress and coaxed her back, raising a finger to my lips to keep quiet. Her particular presence should be a shocking reveal.

Coaxing her behind me, I cracked my neck and slammed my boot into the door, splintering wood near the jam. I strode in with my arms wide, watching a terrified Narcissus spin on his heel. "Rise and shine there, biffy," I taunted with a cheeky smile.

"He-Hephaistos?" Narcissus stammered, his hands raising to his pretty precious face.

"Aw, you remember who I am. I'm flattered. That'll make this that much harder." I touched the side of my nose, flashing the forge in my gaze, making him whimper. "Or not."

"Oh, dear gods," Narcissus whimpered, cowering to a corner. "I don't understand. What did I do to you?"

"Not to me, mate." I stepped to the side.

Aphrodite lifted her chin and flicked her long hair. "Hey again, Sussy."

"Olympus above," Narcissus breathed out, his face going pale.

"You probably didn't figure Aphrodite was my lady love when you decided to kidnap and torture her into doing your bidding, didja?" Fury spiraled up my spine, and I made the veins in my fists glow a fierce orange.

"Oh, fuck. Oh, *fuck*." Narcissus turned to the wall as if it'd disappear, allowing him to escape.

"Oh, fuck, is right." I took a menacing step forward.

"Where's your crazy she-demon? You seem far less confident without her around. Or, oo, I know—care to take a potshot with a harpy claw again?" Aphrodite pulled her dress sleeve down her shoulder enough to reveal the scar.

That tore it. That fucking *tore* it.

Storming forward, wincing at Narcissus' pathetic screeching, I wrapped my hand around his neck and shoved him against the wall. "Where's the harpy claw?"

Aphrodite moved beside me with her arms folded, a scowl distorting her features, yet she remained as gorgeous as ever.

"In the—in the—" Narcissus stuttered and shook so badly, his eyes rolled back in his head as he tried to remember how to speak.

I slapped him in the face. "Words, Narcissus. Use 'em."

He blubbered and whimpered, pointing at a metal chest at the foot of the bed. "There."

Aphrodite whisked to the chest, tossing a smirk over her shoulder at me as she held a locked padlock. I snapped my fingers with an equally snarky grin, turning the padlock into ash. Rummaging sounds filled the room as Aphrodite pushed aside Olympus knew what in that chest until finally returning to my side with the claw in hand, resting it in my open palm.

"I swear I—I didn't mean it," Narcissus stammered as he pushed the back of his head against the wall.

"You didn't *mean* to hurt Aphrodite for your own gain? Is that what you're trying to fucking say?" I glowered at him, snarling as I tightened my grip on his neck, making him gurgle.

"No, I mean, what I meant to say was—" Snot gathered on Narcissus' lip as tears filled his eyes.

Aphrodite shook her head. "Excuses. Excuses. I never thought you could be any more pathetic, Sussy. I was wrong."

"I'll do anything. I swear." His crying turned into sobbing.

"Oh, we're not gonna kill ya." I patted Narcissus' cheek like we were old chums.

Aphrodite bit her lip, keeping her steely gaze on Narcissus and going along with every turn I took.

"You're—you're not?" Narcissus sniffled and gave a hint of a smile.

What an asshat.

"No, of course not, biffy." I patted his chest and jostled his shoulder. "Why, we're only going to show you the same courtesy as you showed the love goddess here."

"What?" Narcissus frowned and bounced his gaze between us, perplexed.

I pretended to tap the claw against my lips in thought. "Let's see. What, oh, what, does our dear Narcissus hold most dear?"

Narcissus' heels dug into the floor as he pushed into the wall, trying to shake his head, but I only held his neck tighter. "No, please. Not that." The words came out strained.

"Your pretty, pretty face." Before he could blubber any longer, I dragged the claw over one cheek, then the other, creating two haggard slashes on each side.

Ironically, my scar *still* looked far nastier, but I could've given him a centimeter-sized one, and it'd still have driven him bonkers.

I let go of his throat and took a step back as he cried out in agony, the poison from the harpy claw bubbling on his skin before his immortality took over to settle it. His hands shook on either side of his head and he dropped to his knees, ugly crying, sobbing, and out of breath.

Aphrodite crouched beside him and canted her head to one side. "You mentioned that curse before? I *do* have my powers back now."

What the Tartarus was she doing? Helping him? No. She had something else up her sleeve, and after I tossed the claw aside, I stood back to watch.

"You can lift the curse?" Narcissus looked at her, the claw marks on his face already morphing into lasting scars.

Aphrodite nodded, mischief gleaming in her stare. "Better." She swirled her hand, and a copper-framed mirror appeared in the air directly in front of Narcissus, making it impossible for him to not see his reflection.

Baller. Fucking. Move.

"No," Narcissus shouted before his expression fell, and he swiped the mirror from Aphrodite's grasp, trailing his fingertips over the reflection. "I'm in love," he whispered before rumbling and looking away. "With the most hideous creature in the world, but—" he looked again, craning his head from side to side. "Still so very in love."

Aphrodite dusted her hands of imaginary dirt as she stood.

I walked over, giving her the slow clap she well deserved. "You are positively diabolical to those who wronged you. I love it."

Her gaze took a sudden sultry turn as I got closer, and she grabbed my face, pulling me toward her and kissing me, her tongue lashing into my mouth. The wind rushed past us as she ported us away from the self-enamored Narcissus. The poor schmuck would be stuck for the rest of eternity in a torturous loop of loving himself but forced to look at what he perceived as an ugly version of himself.

She'd ported us to an alley, and I knew exactly where this was going. I pushed her against the wall, throwing her legs around my waist, and hitching her dress up her hips.

Conveniently, she'd made the spandex underwear disappear, and the sight of her bare pussy greeted me. Growling, I made quick work of my belt, unzipped my pants, and drove into her. She clenched my cock like a godsdamned vice, tightening my balls and spine. I paused inside her, claiming her mouth with mine as I used one hand to support her ass, the other pressing against the wall above her head as leverage.

I pulled away from the kiss to look at her, her gaze meeting mine. She bit her lower lip, ensnaring me without one ounce of power needed. As I continued to pump in and out of her, I kneaded her ass and pulled it toward my hips repeatedly, keeping our eyes locked on each other.

Should we have been worried about a bounty hunter attacking at any moment? Probably. But call me crazy. I *think* that was part of the appeal.

She pulled my head toward her, burying her face against my neck, letting out muted pants and sultry moans that echoed in my ears. "Harder, Heph. Fuck me harder. Make me come," she whispered against my skin.

Answering her desires, I pounded into her, the back of her head thumping against the alley wall. She gasped and grinned at me as she wrapped her arms around my neck, her head tilting skyward, the neon glow from surrounding signs giving her skin a blue hue, mixing with her natural pink gleam and creating purple shimmers. Grunting, I thrust into her a final two times with harsh, concentrated strokes before coming inside her, the base of my spine tingling.

I blew a harsh breath against her neck, moving my hand from the wall to cup her chin. "You cheeky little minx."

"First of many, many times, Heph." She used the tip of her tongue to lick her lips. "*Many.*"

Giving her mouth a quick peck, I smiled before guiding her back to solid ground. She tugged the hem of her dress down and swirled an arm around herself, fixing her hair and whatever else happened when she did that.

I quickly sniffed the surrounding air, smelling nothing out of the ordinary, and nodded. "Let's get back to Ares and Orion before they barge in on Narcissus, thinking there's trouble."

"*You* may have enough favors built up from those two to last several lifetimes, but me? I'm going to owe *them* for how many times we ask them to keep watch so we can bump uglies." Aphrodite slipped her hand into mine, her slender thumb grazing my knuckles.

"Something tells me Orion would easily come up with several requests, and Ares? He won't hold any of this against you. You and I both know that." I winked at her before curling her to my side and kissing her head.

"Oh, Ares. Such a tough, macho dude on the outside, but for the right woman? Absolute pudding on the inside." Aphrodite's radiant smile made her eyes sparkle. "Don't tell him I told you that." She used a single finger to tap my nose.

After crossing my fingers behind my back, I replied, "My lips are sealed, baby." With the goddess of love holding me in a side hug, we walked the alley's length.

Something told me we'd be shagging like rabbits for the unforeseeable future. And that was no pun directed at Coney. Aphrodite had an insatiable appetite that I fucking *loved* to feed.

twenty

APHRODITE

LET THE RECORD SHOW that I cannot get enough of this man—of Hephaistos. Finally able to be with him in every way I ever desired was like scratching a decade-old itch you could never quite reach. It's cliché to say, I know, but of the thousands of lovers I'd had through the centuries, not a soul could satisfy me the way Heph could. And I'll probably let some time go before fessing up to him about it—no need to inflate the ego that much quite yet.

After our impromptu quickie when I'd been rendered incredibly horny after watching Heph defend my honor, we rounded the corner to an awaiting Orion and Ares. They did a double take once spotting us, expecting us to arrive from the opposite direction.

Orion squinted and folded his arms. "You two boned, didn't you?"

"Maybe," Heph answered, flicking a toothpick between

his teeth.

Ares rolled his eyes and tugged his beard.

"Uh-huh. This is what you both get for letting the tension build up for a thousand years." Orion shook his head and kicked an empty candy wrapper on the sidewalk.

"No, this is what *we* get," Ares grumbled.

"Alright, let's pick up your rodent companion so we can keep looking for Oz. The sooner I get back, the sooner I can relieve this anxiety bubbling that I left my iron on at home." Orion scrunched his nose as he stared off into oblivion.

"You iron?" Ares asked.

"How else do you think I keep the creases out?" He smoothed a hand down his vest with a coy grin.

"Well, I *do* need to get back, Heph. And soon," Ares shouted over his shoulder as we all walked.

"I'm doing things as fast as I can, tough guy." Heph slipped his palm against mine, interlacing our fingers as he adjusted the toothpick in his mouth with the other hand.

I sighed, knowing things could be going *a lot* faster were it not for the one person we knew had Oz—frigging Hippolytus.

Orion turned, walking backward as he spoke to us. "As much as I enjoy taking in the sights—"

On cue, a man wearing only jeans cut off at mid-shin, boots, and several chains around his neck walked past us, working up a loogie that he spat into the street.

Just when I thought Ithaca harbored the more *elite* patrons.

"Is there a reason we're not porting to Uluu's Eatery? Isn't it in The Dez?" Orion jabbed his thumb in the other direction.

Heph frowned. "Would you believe me if I told you I forgot

we had two porters in the group?"

The group. I can't say I've ever been a part of an ensemble—a love goddess, a war god, a hunter god, and a god of the forge. The shit we could all get into.

"Last one there is a wet blanket," I shouted at Ares before porting Heph and me to The Dez.

Heph chuckled into my hair as we appeared on the corner near Uluu's food stand, waiting on the other two to show up mere seconds later.

"Joke's on you, sis." Ares pointed at his chest with a thumb. "I'm already a wet blanket."

"And this is something to celebrate, Air?" Smiling, I hung an arm over Heph's shoulder.

Ares flicked his hands at me before turning away. "Vlakás."

With as much discreetness as possible, Orion scratched his right butt cheek, glowering.

"Uluu," Heph said, leading me to the vendor stand. "How are you, dearest?"

Uluu smirked as she squeezed sauce into a carton for a customer, handing it off after they scanned their wrist for payment. "Better than you, I imagine." Uluu paused, examining me.

"Aphrodite." Flashing a warm smile, I extended a hand.

I couldn't remember the last time I'd used my real name without needing to bite my tongue. Liberating didn't begin to describe it.

Uluu blinked at me as if she weren't used to good manners before wiping her hand on her apron and sliding her palm against mine. "Uluu. Heph has said quite a bit about you."

Heph coughed into his fist. "Where's Coney, then?"

"Oh, he has, has he?" I grinned at Heph before elbowing his ribs. "You've talked about me to your *pasta* lady?"

"Oh, you know, Ro. Little things like, 'Saw Ro today, and she looked beautiful as always.'" Heph leaned forward and made a "hurry-up" gesture at Uluu, eyes searching behind the counter, underneath it, and on the ground.

"That's not how I remember it, Heph. Something about not being able to stand being around her, not because you didn't want to, but because you didn't know how long you could hold back?" Uluu flashed a sly grin at me. "Almost sounded like you were addicted to a drug if you ask me."

Addicted to love.

Okay, I loved the guy. Better rescue him.

Raising on the balls of my feet, I kissed Heph's cheek. "Well, that makes two of us."

Heph's shoulders relaxed, and Uluu frowned, almost as if disappointed I hadn't played along for more than thirty seconds. She ducked behind the counter and returned with a sleepy-eyed Coney in her palms, who perked up as soon as he spied Heph.

"He wasn't any trouble for you, I hope?" Heph's smile brightened as Coney hopped into his arms, immediately flopping to his back to let Heph scratch his tummy.

"Nah. He even helped me make a few extra sales. I never thought of having a mascot. Maybe now I should. A ferret or something." Uluu snickered and patted Coney's head.

"Well, aren't you the little entrepreneur?" Heph cooed at his rabbit, Coney's whiskers twitching as he pawed Heph's finger.

I rubbed Coney's cheek, Heph and I preening over the fluffy bundle of cuteness as if he were our own newborn. The thought sent flutters through my stomach, but different flutters from lust-fueled ones.

"I appreciate it, Uluu. How's about four helpings for the road, eh?" Heph handed me Coney, and I gladly curled him into the crook of my arm.

"Oh, I don't want an—" Orion leaned in, raising a finger.

Heph planted a hand in Orion's face and idly pushed him away. "Orion there will have extra *extra* sauce, Uluu, my dear."

Uluu dished out four cartons of pasta, and Heph handed them to each party member. The four of us moved to a vacant street corner, Ares digging into his pasta like he'd been starved for weeks. Orion flipped open the top of his carton, took one whiff, gagged, and threw it away.

"Hey, what if I wanted that?" Ares asked with a mouth full of food.

Smiling at my goof of a big brother, I leaned against Heph and used a pair of glowing chopsticks to scoop some pasta into my mouth. I'd underestimated how long the noodles were, and the red sauce splashed over my chin as I sucked it into my mouth.

Heph chuckled and dipped his mouth to mine, licking the sauce away and giving my cheek a quick peck. "You like it?"

"It's delicious. I can see why you're so obsessed with it." I covered my mouth with my hand to swallow the rest of the food.

"Mm," Heph moaned, diving into my neck to kiss it. "Must be why I'm so obsessed with *you*, then."

Giggling, I craned my neck, urging him to kiss it more.

"Because I taste like pasta?"

He pulled away with a furrowed brow. "I was going more for the delicious approach, but now that you mention it—"

With widened eyes and a slack jaw, I playfully hit his shoulder. I *loved* that despite us finally admitting reciprocal feelings for each other, our dynamic hadn't changed one bit. The playful, innocent flirting had blossomed into a simple, meaningful way to express our love for each other.

"I still can't believe you have a pet rabbit," Ares grumbled beside us, throwing his empty carton into the nearest trash bin.

"You're just jealous that any pet you'd get probably wouldn't like you." Heph bumped my shoulder with his.

A scowl formed over Ares' features.

"Oh, what about a pig?" Orion snapped his fingers. "One of those pot-belly ones? That seems up your alley."

"Vlakás. You're *hilarious.*"

"I'll be honest, Heph, when you first told me you got a rabbit, I thought you'd been referring to the vibrating variety." Orion bobbed his brow.

Heph winked at Orion. "Not all of us enjoy our asses buzzing, mate."

Glaring at Heph, Orion pointed in his face, making the deer head tattoo on his right bicep stretch. "I told you that in confidence."

"Yes, you did," Heph replied, flashing a grin.

The smirk on Orion's face faded, and he threw his arm out to the side, producing a golden bow. He notched an arrow, pulled back, aiming, and in the same instant, shot the arrow. It whizzed through the air, landing in someone easily over fifty meters away.

Heph paused mid-bite of pasta, blinking. "I assume that was someone bad? I couldn't smell the guy."

Orion rolled his shoulders back, the astute concentration on his face disappearing. "Hunter. There are bound to be more."

"Could you at least let them get closer?" Ares asked.

Orion lowered his bow with a quirked brow. "Why would I do that when distance is an advantage?"

Ares pointed at himself, leaning closer to Orion. "So, I can kill them."

Orion folded his arms. "Is anyone else not disturbed that an arrow launched into a man in the middle of a crowded street, and no one batted an eyelash? People are stepping *over* him."

"Not weird for here, mate." Heph tossed his carton away and stuck a toothpick in his mouth.

"See? You're part of the problem, Heph." Orion shook his head, making strands of golden hair fall over his gaze.

Heph lifted the toothpick. "Or—am I the solution?"

"Mm, I'll take some of that solution," I purred, hugging Heph's side.

Heph playfully nipped the side of my head with a growl.

Orion and Ares exchanged glances before Orion walked over, snapping his fingers. "Listen. These hunters are after you two, not us. Why don't you port to my place, enjoy this revelation it took you centuries to figure out, and let us do some sleuthing for Oz."

My heart sang a hymn the Muses themselves would've fawned over.

Heph shook his head and sliced a hand through the air.

"I'm not a fan of having my mates do my dirty work for me."

"Don't think of it like that. We're family, Heph. Besides—" Ares slid a pair of Aviator shades on. "You'd be sparing me from seeing you continuously macking on my sister."

Heph chewed on his bottom lip, and I hugged him tighter for reassurance. "I don't know."

"The Lunation Festival is tomorrow anyway. Remember?" Orion's brow bobbed.

The Lunation Festival?

"Alright, alright. If you *must* twist my arm to lay low. But consider any favors you both feel you still owe me satisfied after this behemoth of one."

Orion and Ares nodded at each other before Ares leaned forward, sliding the sunglasses to the tip of his nose. "Nope. This one's on the house."

"Not sure what I bloody well did to deserve this, but I'll take it." Heph pretended to sniffle and dabbed the corners of each eye with his knuckle.

Positively beaming, I smiled at my big brother and mouthed, "Thank you." He pressed his hands together and bowed before I ported us to Orion's apartment.

"Now then, how many surfaces do you think we can screw on before tomorrow so we can hold it over Orion's head, eh?" Heph rubbed his hands together.

As I walked back to Heph after securing Coney in his cushioned drawer, my brightened grin faded, the realization of our unsolved situation hovering over me like one of Dad's rainclouds. "Heph, we *need* to get our hands on some Oz. This isn't fair to those two to be stuck here when we have the means to fix it."

"Fair to *them*? Last I checked, I stranded you here too." Heph took my hands in his, the calluses on his thumbs grazing between my knuckles.

My upper lip curved, and I shuffled closer to him. "It hasn't been all that bad."

"Listen, Peach." He kissed my forehead. "I've put you through a lot of shit since bringing us here. The Lunation Festival is tomorrow, and I want to take you—the calm before the storm. We can celebrate from my rooftop, and Orion has already agreed to keep watch."

Nerves prickled my skin. "Calm before the storm? What does that mean?"

He drew circles with a single finger on my palms. "Because after tomorrow, I'll dig to the planet's very damn core with my bare hands if that's what it takes to get to the Oz."

And I'd seen what he could do with his bare hands both sexually *and* lethally.

"All I'm asking is that you try not to worry and *be* with me. Yeah?" He slipped a hand around my neck, kneading his strong fingers into my tense muscles.

How had I been so blind to him? To this? He'd make the universe's volcanoes erupt simultaneously to keep me safe.

Nodding, I placed a feather-light kiss on the tip of his nose. "Alright. But Lunation Festival? The last time you took me to that, it didn't seem to be much. Just an excuse for debauchery outside under a full moon."

Not that I gave a flying frig when and where Heph wanted to celebrate *anything* with me.

"That was years ago." He slid one hand to my lower back and took my other hand in his, slowly waltzing us through the living room. "They've improved it since the District discovered how much money they can save by shutting down *all* the lights for a solid four universal hours."

"All the lights?"

Pushing a hand on my hip, he spun me out, holding onto my hand to reel me back in. "All of them. The only illumination is the bright white moon and glitter of the stars."

I settled into Heph's grasp, letting him lead us around the room as if we danced on air. "Sounds like I'll need an ensemble to fit the occasion."

"That's right." His beard tickled my cheek as he pressed the sides of our faces together, his lips grazing my ear, his voice deep and rumbly against my skin.

"I say we start with screwing against that clear resin wall I saw upstairs." I peeled back, pointing to the bedroom at the end of the winding metal stairwell.

Heph slipped a hand to my ass, swatting it. "Devious. Nothing like an ass print smudge to tell your mate how thankful you are."

We christened Orion's apartment on said wall, the living room floor, and the L-shaped leather couch, and even managed to find a swing hanging behind Orion's bedroom door. We drew the line at the kitchen counter and thought twice about his bed before settling for the floor there too. After round eight, I wrapped us in a shimmering gold blanket, and we fell asleep with the neon-blazed view of the Daneland skyline watching over us through the windows.

We stood on the rooftop, waiting for the District to shut down all the lights once the moon became its brightest. I wanted to wait until that precise moment to create a dress for myself, to let the sights and sounds of the festival inspire me.

"Should be happening right about—" Heph stood at my side and lifted a finger, a playful smile curving his lips. "—now."

Darkness spilled over the surrounding subdivisions, cheers from patrons lining the district streets echoing around us. Once my eyes adjusted to the sudden lack of neon, the moon's shining light shadowed everything it touched in a glowing blanket of white. The stars above twinkled with vibrant radiance, their numbers seemingly multiplying now that they had time to shine.

Closing my eyes, I swirled my hands around my body, conjuring the dress which begged to be seen—a black tea cup-styled dress with a galaxy pattern. The cosmic dust within each nebula would change color along with my emotions like a mood ring. The black tulle tucked under the skirt portion of the dress gave it body and fluff, the top forming a halter with lapels. And finally, a pair of clear heels sparkling with shooting stars.

I clicked my heels together as I turned to face Heph, twirling one of the loose ringlets I'd morphed my hair into around one finger. "Well, what do you think?"

Heph blew out a breath as he took me in, his dark eyes starting from my forehead and taking their time to roam downward. "Your creativity continues to blow my mind, babe." He stepped forward, slipping his hands over my hips, gaze focused on the glittering heart adorning my cheek that I'd changed from pink to silver, matching the moon. "C'mere, love-y goddess."

He led us to the roof's edge, guiding me down until we sat next to each other, our feet dangling. "Love your dress, but it *is* missing something."

"Oh?" I frowned.

"Accessories." Heph wrapped a hand around my wrist, and cool metal settled over my skin. When he moved his palm away, a silver bracelet remained—two swans forming a heart, scattered roses, and a crescent moon. "To remember the occasion."

My eyes hazed as tears built up and I swallowed them back. Brushing my thumb over the uniquely created jewelry he'd forged only for me, I whispered, "It's beautiful."

Heph kissed the corner of my brow before setting a bottle of fizzy strawberry drink near me, followed by a metal container with a bright yellow label that read: Live Free Pie Hard.

Music blared from the streets below, techno mixed with electric guitar and deep bass. Tiny fractals of color reflected off buildings from the celebrants cracking glow sticks.

"What is this?" I smiled at him while spying on people below twirling yellow, blue, and green glow sticks and howling at the sky.

"Pie in a can. Sounds disgusting, but, it honest to Olympus, tastes like it came right out of the oven." Using the tab in the corner, he peeled the top of the can back, steam wafting from it. "Even heats itself. See?"

"Are they all the same flavor?" Sticking my tongue to the corner of my mouth, I opened my own, closing my eyes as the buttery pie crust smell filled the air.

"Nope. Always a surprise. Hopefully, mine's not mincemeat." Heph scrunched his nose as he sniffed it.

"Do I eat this with my fingers or—?"

Heph palmed his forehead. "I'm right daft. Forgot spoons. Good thing I carry extras." With a charming wink, he snapped his fingers, making two iron spoons appear, and handing me one.

Digging in, I spooned some of the fruity pastry into my mouth and closed my eyes with a blissful sigh. "Peach."

"Well, ain't that ironic."

Flashing my eyes open, I smiled. "What's yours?"

He quirked his head from side to side as he tasted his pie. "Razzle."

"Razzle? What's that?"

"Sort of a mix between raspberry and blackberry."

I scooted closer to him, looping my arm with his, continuing to dish out pie from my can, and marveling at the beautiful view of the star-lit sky. "Where's Ares and Orion, by the way?"

Heph peered down, squinting, before pointing. "Right there on the corner."

They stood firm with their arms folded, heads on a constant swivel from the dozens of partiers passing them.

"They look like bouncers down there. Poor guys." I finished my can, scraping out every last crumb.

"Ares should be right at home then. Orion is probably chomping at the bit to join the party." Heph snickered and smiled at me licking my can dry. "Has anyone ever told you you're utterly adorable?"

Flicking a crumb from my lips with my thumb, I beamed at him. "Not anyone I believed or cared about, no."

Heph leaned forward, kissing me, mixing the fruity flavors of our pies with one quick lap of his tongue over mine. "Well, you're adorable. And I still can't believe you're mine."

The nebulas in my dress morphed from blue to deep crimson, matching the flush forming in my cheeks.

"What's with the color changing?" Heph asked, his voice laced with deviance and gravel.

My insides folded over themselves as I scraped my fingernails across the cloth covering his chest. "The dress matches my mood."

"What did blue mean?" Heph pressed a hand to my lower back, pulling me closer.

"Happiness," I whispered.

The dress exposed my entire back, and Heph trailed his touch down my spine. "And red?"

Gulping, I tilted my chin, yearning to feel his lips against mine. "Lust."

Heph's eyes darkened, and he continued his sensual torture of my skin, dragging his fingers up and down. "We're all alone up here, Ro. Only the moon and stars as witnesses."

"Nyx could be watching. Maybe Erebus too?" I bit my lip, mischief playing in my gaze.

Heph grumbled and hung his head low. "If you want the Magical D again, I'd suggest not mentioning primordials and their panache for voyeurism."

I shrugged the jacket off his shoulders. "As if that'd make a difference to you."

Heat ignited in Heph's eyes, and his hands were in my hair, pulling me closer to him. "You're right. I wouldn't give a flyin' fuck."

Kissing him, devouring him, I made our clothes disappear, turning my dress into a galactic animated blanket. With each movement, the fabric would respond to us, mold to us, and cradle our every motion. Heph's hand slid to the back of my head and he slowly lowered me to the ground, the blanket circling beneath me to cushion my skull. He stared down at me, smiling as if he were the happiest being alive, a sight that not only warmed my heart, but burst it.

"You're a treasure, Ro. Gemstones and filigree. Never forget it," Heph whispered against my lips, feathering butterfly kisses over my nose and cheeks.

I traced first the scar on his face, trailing my touch down the length of it, across his chest, and to the harpy scars on his shoulder that mirrored mine. "That makes you my key then, Phai."

Heph groaned as he dragged the tip of his nose down my throat, inhaling me, and paused between my breasts, resting his forehead for a beat. He nuzzled his cheek against one breast while massaging the other, the stars brightening in the sky above us as if in reaction to our offering—us in our purest, rawest form.

He loomed over me, hovering his chest near mine as he coaxed one of my legs up, my knee pressing to his hip. He hooked an arm under my thigh, and his hardness teased my entrance as he lowered himself. The nebulas in the blanket blazed crimson until Heph pushed inside me, turning them all colors of the rainbow—shifting, marbling, and pulsing. I gasped and stared at him, digging my fingers into his hardened shoulders as they tensed, keeping his weight off me.

All veins within Heph's body glowed radiant orange beneath his skin, his gaze pulsing in the same vibrant color. His thrusts were slow, rolling, and deliberate. Our previous times together had been a carnal, animalistic claiming of each other—but this time, atop a rooftop in the Neosphere District with the moon spilling white light over our naked bodies and the thumping techno music blaring below from celebration—we made love.

He deepened his thrusts, pushing harder, but pausing until I tightened around him. His lips pressed to mine, tenderness behind the kiss that left me trembling. He pulled back, keeping our noses a breath apart, and stared into my eyes. "I love you. And I came so fucking close to saying it for the first time years ago in this very spot, during the *same* festival."

My entire being reacted to his words, chest humming, the blanket curling and spiraling around us, still flashing rotating vibrant colors. A pink shimmer surrounded us, radiating from my skin in pulsing waves. Pressing one hand to the back of his head, I kept his gaze. "I love you too, Hephaistos."

He growled before moving his lips to my neck, kissing it, and driving into me over and over, his thumb moving to swirl my clit. My back arched and I kept my grip on his head and neck, grounding myself as the rhapsody built. Heph's heat from his glowing veins, and lava from Olympus forges pooled into me, igniting my insides in a blissful fire. As he gave one final thrust, coming inside me, our eyes locking, a white glow I'd never seen illuminated from myself settled over us like misting rain.

Panting, I didn't look away from him, the nebulas in the blanket settling into pale shades of yellow from the relaxed satiation I felt. I raked my fingers through his beard, smiling at him. "Can we do this forever?"

He let out a raspy chuckle. "Considering what we *are*, I'd say that's a definite possibility, Peach."

The soft, brassy undertones of a saxophone playing in the distance made Heph perk up before leaping to his feet, and holding his hand to me. I bit my lip at the sight of his still hard cock bouncing. Bringing the galactic blanket with me, I draped it around us and followed him to the opposite roof's edge. Heph sat first, and I slid onto his lap, his burly arms wrapping around me and holding me against him.

"Any guesses on what song Mr. Saxophone will play next?" Heph's fingers drummed against my hip to the sax melody, a song I hadn't recognized.

Nestling against Heph's chest, I let out a contented sigh. "I'm going to go with *Baker Street*."

"Oo, good one. Hm. I'll say *Careless Whisper*."

Giggling, nuzzling into him further as if I could anymore, I kissed his cheek. "Why does that not surprise me?"

We both quirked our ears as the sax player's current song faded out. After only a few riffs played, we smiled at each other as it kicked into the chorus. *Take My Breath Away* by Berlin. Gasping, I sat up straight, feeling a familiar flutter pitter-pattering against my stomach.

Far. Too. Familiar.

"Um, Heph," I said through a squeak, gulping.

"Yeah, baby?"

I licked my lips and turned to face him. "I'm pregnant."

He slow-blinked once. Twice. And his brows drew together. "I know we're gods, but even still—doesn't that seem, I don't know, fast?"

There was no mistaking it because not only was the feeling familiar, but I'd felt it in the exact same way before because the fluttering…

Wings.

"No, Heph. I'm pregnant." I placed a hand on my stomach. "With Eros."

TWENTY-ONE

HEPH

A FAINT HUM BUZZED in my ears, drowning out all sounds. My vision blurred until Ro's soft voice repeating my name pulled me back to reality.

"Heph? Are you okay?" Aphrodite clung to my forearm, concern pinching her forehead.

"Yeah. I'm—I think I'm processing?" I scratched my chin before dragging my hands through my beard repeatedly.

She was preggo with Eros. And with the timing and how her eyes snapped to mine when she'd said it suggested something I couldn't rightly wrap my head around.

"Eros is your son, Heph." A lump the size of a ruby formed in her throat, fear leaking from her pores, the scent filling the air.

Don't fuck this up, Heph. This is as crazy of a revelation for her as it is for you. And right now, it's your damn job to tell her everything will be right as Reese's Pieces.

Gripping her shoulders, I took a deep breath and nodded. "How did you think he came about before?"

"I—" She started, her eyes searching my face, her mouth open, but no words followed.

Screaming on the inside would've been a fair comparison to how I'd felt with the news. It's not as if I didn't want to be a dad, but I also never got to be, nor would I. Not to a kid, anyway.

"It's alright, baby. Tell me." I sent warmth to her cheeks through my fingertips.

She covered one of my hands with hers, her skin ice cold. "I thought I was so lonely my powers—created him."

"You mean with no outside—" I pointed at my pecker. "—interference?"

"Heph, Zeus made me from sea foam, and Hera made you appear inside her out of spite for her husband. Would Eros not having a dad really seem that far-fetched?"

Bugger. She had me there.

"So—" I scooted closer to her, staring into those sapphire eyes I know matched Eros's. "—I'm a, uh, a dad, eh?"

Tears filled her eyes and several escaped in glistening trickles down her cheeks. "Is it horrible that I'm as freaked out as happy?"

"Not horrible at all. I'm struggling with conflicting feelings myself at present." I dragged my knuckles across her face, wiping away the tears.

"Oh, no." She gasped, her hands flying to her mouth, and pulled away from me. "You don't—I mean, how could I just assume you—"

You're doing a bang-up job not fucking this up, ya gobshite.

I grabbed her hands and pressed them between mine, catching her gaze. "Ro, deep breaths. I never said I wasn't happy about being his dad. But try to understand that you raised Eros. You've been his mum since he was born. I'll never have that. All I get is a grown god of love that I somehow have to let know—he's got a daddy."

"Wait. You'll never have that?" She clenched her eyes shut and shook her head. "So much of this doesn't make any sense. How is he being born in the future when he's already been born in the past?"

The volcano sizzled in my stomach. "A paradox," I answered, my voice so low the blaring music from the festival almost carried it away.

"A what?"

Rubbing my chin, I mulled my words before speaking out loud. Time travel could be so incredibly fucked. "A paradox. Time travel, space, dimensions—it can all be right screwy, babe. What's going on here is what they call a causal loop."

"What does that *mean*, Heph?" Aphrodite clung the galactic blanket to her chest.

My face scar suddenly burned and itched, and I scraped a finger over it. "It's when a future event causes a past event that could in turn, become the cause *for* the future event. And both events exist simultaneously in spacetime."

That sounded even more ass backward saying it out loud.

"Both exist…" Aphrodite said, trailing off as she stood and chewed on her thumbnail.

Despite her walking to the other side of the roof, the blanket still covered my goods, and I followed her, keeping quiet.

She stared at the party-goers below dancing circles in the streets, howling, drinking, doing drugs, and some went so far as to strip their clothes. "If what you're saying is true, Hephaistos, I *need* to get back." She turned to face me, an expression I hadn't seen on her face in some time flushing her features—a lioness fearing for her cub. "Because it's possible if I don't, Eros will never exist, isn't it?"

Fucking bollocks.

"It's—possible. But we're—" I started, pulling her to me.

"—not going to let that happen," Aphrodite finished, the nebulas in the galaxy blanket she'd created mixing with black and swirls of gray.

I couldn't be sure what each color represented, but from the pinch in her brow and the Arctic-like temperature settling over her skin, I'd guess fear and worry.

"Never, babe. Trust me." Kissing her knuckles, I kept her hand at my lips. "I told you I'd do whatever it takes to get that Oz. And now more than ever, I mean it."

She gripped my hand tighter, using the other to touch my scar, the coolness of her skin soothing it. "You know what we need to do."

Every radar went off in my body, my mind—my cosmic fucking *entity*. She was a breath away from bringing up Hippolytus again, and with a dozen emotions swarming through me like a godsdamned cyclone, I wasn't sure I could hold the eruption back as easily this time.

"Ro—" I said but stopped short, overlapping scents, hundreds of them flooding my nostrils. Ares and Orion. "Babe, port us, port us *now*. Ares and Orion are being overwhelmed."

When we appeared at street level, my jacket and clothes were back on, and Ro in her pink jacket ensemble and sneaks. Flocks of birds tormented Ares, Orion, and any surrounding partiers that had the ill fortune of stumbling onto the wrong corner at the very wrong time.

Ares aimlessly swung his sword at any bird that dive bombed him with their bronzed beaks. "Heph, are you trying to tell me that Hippolytus wants revenge so fucking badly he resurrected Stymphalian birds?"

Ah yes. *That's* why they smelled so familiar.

"Weren't *you* the one that created them, war god?" Orion shouted, lifting his bow to launch an arrow through two birds.

"Maláka," Ares growled, stabbing his sword through a bird who'd swooped to claw his shoulder with its metallic talons. "That was over a thousand years ago, and I only stupidly did it for my mother, not knowing her intent."

Aphrodite lunged past me, the court sword I'd forged for her appearing in her extended hand, the blade catching bird shit from landing on a drunken party-goer passing by. "I seem to remember their shit being *poisonous*, Ares?"

"What? Do you want me to apologize for the god of war making them lethal?" Ares threw his arms out at his sides, one bird flying into the side of his face, leaving a strip of tiny white feathers on his bottom lip. Snarling, he sputtered and pointed at me with his sword. "Tell me you still have that damn rattle."

Fortunately for us, the Neosphere District inhabitants were either far too distracted by the festivities or so pissed on alcohol, they didn't notice the dozens of man-eating birds.

The rattle Ares spoke of was a particular iron piece I'd created centuries ago per request of Athena for nearly the same situation—the birds terrorizing crowds of people. Grinning, I spun my hand around, before producing said rattle in my palm. My celestial arsenal had unending storage and I'd never discard anything I forged. Even weapons and armor I created for others had copies within my stash as mementos.

"Orion, your arrows, if you please?" I held my hand out.

Aphrodite let out a feminine grunt, her little sword slashing through the air with conscious movement. Considering we'd only had one lesson thus far and most of that time was spent mentally fucking each other, her moves were impressive.

"Heph," Orion shouted next to me.

I jolted to attention, fumbling with the small jar of hydra venom I'd produced. "Right. Tips, please."

"Care to explain what for?" Orion tilted his body closer as he bunched the arrows in his grasp and held the pointy bits out.

I drizzled the venom on each and nodded. "These birds have an extra special aversion for hydra. Shoot as many as you can with the venom arrows, and eventually, the rest will bugger off."

"Easy enough." Orion notched several arrows at once to the bow's string and landed each in a bird with precise accuracy.

"Show off," I grumbled.

Orion cut his gaze to me while keeping his head forward, a cocky grin egging his lips.

Once he shot all eight arrows, the birds began to squawk and scatter, flying off in all directions. Soon, bird shit and feathers were all that remained, spread over the pavement like an aviary murder scene.

"Oh, sure. Excellent idea, Heph. They're just going to go terrorize elsewhere." Ares rested the sword's blade on one shoulder.

"You say that like it's a bad thing. At some point, somewhere nearby will need assistance getting rid of the flying nightmares. They'll need someone who knows how to deal with them. I call it—job security."

"Get rid of one pest only to have another," Orion said, nudging his chin at a band of approaching bounty hunters.

They were from all walks of life and variety—men, women, questionables, light, dark, little cybernetics, or fully-replaced limbs. And they each sported an assortment of weapons, including bats, rifles, swords, and randomly—a purple dildo long enough to wrap around my arm twice. I wouldn't want to be the dude who got taken out by that particular accouterment.

"The birds were supposed to distract you," a shorter fellow the size of a Hobbit sporting a bowler hat said. "And now we get to handle this the spicier way."

"Oh, good." Igniting the forge within my arm, I willed my hammer axe to my grasp. "Because I do *love* spice."

The hunters charged forward with the party still moving in full swing around us, the moon's light and shadow enveloping the clashing of weapons. Orion backed away, hoisting himself atop a dumpster for aerial advantage with his arrows. After forging another quiver full, I tossed them to Orion. Ares roared like a bloody grizzly before slashing his sword across several hunters. I bashed one in the face with the hammer side of my weapon, flipping the axe part around to slam it into the neck of the next approaching hunter.

"Enough," Aphrodite yelled, her skin pulsing a radiant pink glow, her eyes matching.

She dove into the middle of the action, hurling her arms forward, and a surge of pink shimmering energy shot from her hands, a single pale bolt of lightning swirling within it. Her blonde hair flew up around her, framing her face as she let out a warrior cry, the energy disintegrating any poor schmuck that came in contact with it into glitter and dust. She was Storm and Jubilee from *X-Men* bloody fucking combined. Any hunter fortunate enough to have not been in Aphrodite's way, threw their weapons to the pavement and ran, shrieking like cats with their tails caught under the rocking chair.

The energy fizzled away, and Aphrodite's eyes returned to normal. She stared at her palms, arms shaking, her expression resembling mortified. She blew out a breath, her chest pumping up and down before her gaze kicked to mine. "I—I don't know how."

I didn't say anything at first. My eyes darted between Ares and Orion, who had the same look I was sure I had—what the fuck was that?

Finally shaking the cobwebs away, I approached Aphrodite with fanned palms. "Ro? Baby? You alright?"

"I think so?" Her eyes glistened with tears as she continued to eye her hands like foreign objects. "I don't know how I did that, Heph."

Ares furrowed his brow and stepped closer. "Try it again, Aph."

"But you know—" I pointed away from us. "In that direction."

Aphrodite licked her lips and opened her hands at the open alley. Her jaw tightened as she concentrated, a light growl bubbling at the back of her throat. Pink shimmers, gold dust, and a radiating light flowed from her hands, but no energy blast or lightning followed.

Sighing, Aphrodite dropped her hands at her sides. "It's no use. I don't know how I did it. All I can tell you is that it happened when this overwhelming fear consumed me. Heph, you must turn me over to Hippolytus. Please don't argue with me."

Argue with her? After that display?

At one point, I'd subconsciously covered my godsdamned balls, fearing evisceration.

Closing the distance between us, I gave a curt shake of my head. "Ro, we've talked about this. It's too risky. Don't ask me to purposefully put you in harm's way. Please, love."

Orion slow-blinked, and he slid closer to Aphrodite, staring at her as if at any moment she'd suddenly remember how to use her new powers and direct them on him.

"I've got my powers back. I can handle Hippo and his damn goons. I'm tired of waiting—" She slid a hand over her stomach, that same cinch forming on the skin between her eyes. "—especially now."

Orion stepped closer with a quirked brow after securing the bow on his back.

"We shouldn't be talking about this here," Ares said, motioning to us to grab hold of each other.

As I didn't let Aphrodite's gaze drop from mine for a millisecond, I took her hand and clapped my other to Ares's shoulder. He ported us to Orion's apartment, and Aphrodite shrugged away with a disgruntled growl, her face falling into her hands.

"How can you not trust me, Heph? You. Of all people?"

Frowning, I kept my distance from her. "I never *ever* said that. You're one of the very few people I *do* trust, babe. Implicitly. You can't—I mean—after what you told me mere *minutes* ago, how do you expect me to react, hm?"

Ares and Orion exchanged glances.

"Alright, alright." Ares slid between us with his palms out. "Whatever you two are going on about obviously affects Orion and me too, so would you be so kind as to fill us the fuck in? And, sis, don't think we're throwing the small matter of that energy blast you somehow did under the rug."

Aphrodite dragged a hand through her hair, tugging on it. I tried to get her to look at me, to let her know that I'd tell them if she couldn't, but to my dismay, she looked anywhere but at me.

"Eros—" Aphrodite wrapped her arms around herself, her gaze finally meeting mine, eyes glassy. "—is Heph's son."

"The fuck?" Orion blurted, his widened eyes darting to me.

Ares squinted at Aphrodite before throwing me a glare that could boil the Baltic Sea. "What the Tartarus is she trying to say, brother?"

"Rein it in there, warthog. We both only found out about it today. It's a paradox time traveling anomaly that we don't have the time to explain right now." I chewed on my lip and walked the perimeter of the area rug in the living room. "But she has to get back stat or we run the risk of him—" I'd only just found out the cherub was my kid and the thought of him gone made my throat tighten. "—never existing."

"This is the second time you've brought up this paradox shit. And now you're saying my nephew is at risk. So, take the time to explain. Would you?" Ares said, crimson flashing in his gaze.

Furiously scratching the back of my head, I hitch-stepped to the billiard table and grabbed two balls. "This one represents the past." I set it at one end. "This one? The future." Moving the past ball forward, I made the future ball curve back around to give the past a nudge, forcing it in another direction. "The original ball has its trajectory, but because spacetime can exist simultaneously, the future can inadvertently go back to cause that past event."

Orion's eyes formed slits. "So—" He elongated the "o" and twirled his finger in the air. "The past *is* the future."

I beat my palms against the pool table's edge. "Precisely."

"There see. Was that so hard to explain?" Ares plopped his ass on the back of the couch.

Frowning, I opened my mouth to respond, but Orion interrupted me. "Then what's the problem, Heph? Let her go to Hippolytus if he has a stash."

The volcano bubbled under my skin, and I crossed the room to my old mate, poking him in the chest. "You don't get it. He wanted to turn her into some sex slave. I *know* he's got power dampeners because I *made* them for him."

"Maláka," Ares breathed out.

Aphrodite's hand slid over my bicep, pulling my attention to her. "Heph, you what?"

"It was years ago—just another job. I didn't know any of this was going to happen. I—" I shut my trap before rambling like a damn fool.

Aphrodite placed a finger over my lips. "I know you're worried about both of us." She took my hand and put it on her stomach, the tiny beats of a pair of wings brushing my fingertips. "And I adore you for it, but you have to let me do this, Phai. My powers are back tenfold, and I promise you, Hippo won't get the chance to get close enough to even *think* about putting dampeners on me."

"We still also need to figure out this new power of yours, Aphrodite," Ares said with a harsh undertone.

Aphrodite's shoulders slumped, but she stood still in front of me, her hand slipping from my mouth to rest on a shoulder. "Ares, I don't *know* how I did it."

"Passion," Orion said, garnering all of our attention.

"Come again?" I asked, raising a brow.

Orion walked closer, dragging a hand through his long unruly hair. "She's the goddess of love and passion. I'd guess that passion can elevate beyond a physical or emotional state within someone, but rather a manifestation of it."

"Since when were you such a nerd?" Ares huffed.

Orion bumped his shoulder against Ares's. "Have you ever *not* been a brute?"

The thought of not only handing Aphrodite off to Hippolytus but playing the part of betraying her, had my stomach in knots. Aphrodite raised on her feet, planting the tiniest kiss on the edge of my lips.

"You know this has me feeling like absolute shit, right?"

She trailed the back of her hand down my face scar, nodding. "I'm not excited about it. But we can and *will* do this. Not only for Eros but for them too." Aphrodite nudged her head at a still arguing Ares and Orion. "They've got lives to get back to, Heph."

"If part of your reasoning is me, sis, then don't worry about me. I can figure out another way to get back, another—" Ares stammered, cutting his hand through the air in front of him.

Aphrodite touched her brother's forearm. "Brother, you know as well as I do that finding Oz is the fastest option, even *if* there's another way back aside from Heph's device."

Ares's nostril bounced, his gaze casting to his feet. "And you're positive your powers can handle them? I don't know how I'd live with myself if—"

"Yes, Ares." Aphrodite tugged his hand, making him look at her again. "I'll be fine."

"I think it's about time you two put a little more faith in the love goddess." Orion folded his arms and leaned on the wall. "She wouldn't be putting herself and her kid at risk if she didn't think she could handle it."

Aphrodite gave Orion a small smile, eliciting a nod of affirmation from him.

I growled, furious at the entire fucking universe for our situation. "We better fucking do this before I lose my nerve."

A snarling sigh escaped Ares's chest. "I can port with you to bring you back. I'll stay out of sight so Hippolytus doesn't catch wind of something."

"It's going to be fine, baby. I promise you. And the sooner I get back, the sooner we can tell Eros. Together." She took both my hands, squeezing them.

Tell him that I was his dad. His father—another situation that had me in a twisted mix of excitement and nausea.

Ares didn't let me stew on it, porting us outside Hippo's compound, only to slip out of sight as promised. I couldn't meet Aphrodite's eyes as I made the glimmering cuffs appear. Cuffs I'd stupidly used to bring her in as a bounty, only to use them for an entirely different purpose later.

Aphrodite lifted her wrists in front of my face, nodding to me as one last confirmation that this *was* happening and we weren't turning our backs now. "It's like a Band-Aid. No sense in taking an eternity to rid yourself of it."

Only the love-y goddess could manage a smile out of me at a time like this. "Bad analogy, babe. I'd sooner rub dirt in the wound before putting on a Band-Aid."

"Oh, yeah?" She took the cuffs from me, putting them on herself. "What if it were Mario Band-Aids?"

A light chuckle escaped my chest. "Tushy."

She smiled and tugged my hand toward the door.

I didn't budge. "Before we go in there, I have to ask you one thing, Ro."

"What is it?"

"He *obviously* gets his good looks from me." I placed a hand on my chest, grinning as she slapped my shoulder. "He has *your* eyes."

"Your cleft chin you keep hidden in your beard now?" Aphrodite slid her finger through the hair on my chin to wiggle it in the cleft.

"Yes, that too. But where the Tartarus did the wings come

from?"

Aphrodite rubbed her lips together and circled a finger around the glittering pink heart she'd added to her cheek. "I have my theories, but it's pretty corny."

Kissing that same heart on her cheek, I winked at her. "I love your popcorn."

Her smile spread wider. "When you told me you loved me. Honest to Olympus, I felt like I could *soar*."

The lava in my veins simmered to a tempered lull. "That's not corny, babe. You're basically saying Eros is an actual product of our love." I cocked my head from side to side. "I mean, I did feel like gagging a bit, but still—"

She swatted my chest before giving me a playful shove, still grinning.

"You do whatever you need to do in there to stay safe. Please, Ro. *Whatever* you need to do." I pulled her to me, hugging her and breathing all of her in.

"I promise. People always think I'm a lover, not a fighter. But I'm both, Heph." She pulled back, running her knuckle under her eye to squelch the tear that'd built up.

"I know you are."

After kissing her forehead, I rolled my shoulders back, prepping myself to act like the infamous bounty hunter who had little to no mercy for anyone. And in I walked with the love of my life in handcuffs, not to dominate her in the bedroom, but to give her up for a damn bounty. Time travel really can be fucked.

TWENTY-TWO

HEPH

"RO, ONE LAST THING," I whispered against the side of her head as I slipped a hand over one cuff and pulsed magic through it. "I'm sending you in there with real dampeners hoping he won't put his *own* on you, so I made a weak spot on the right cuff. When the time is right, all you gotta do is pull it, the cuffs will fall free, and you can use your powers. Understand?"

Aphrodite nodded and stared at me with brightened eyes—a light in the edging darkness.

The slimy expression playing on Hippolytus' face when we entered was almost enough to make me call off the entire fucking thing, lop Hippo's head off and play a *real* game of "The Floor is Lava" with his pervy goons.

"Well, well, well. What do we have here?" Hippo sat in a leather burgundy lounge chair, legs crossed and hands steepled.

Tightening my jaw, I lightly shoved between Aphrodite's shoulder blades, pushing her in front of Hippo. "I can quite literally dodge a lot of bullets, but that last stint you pulled with the birds?" I sneered at the back of Ro's head. "She's not worth it."

Man-eating birds. A dozen cyclops. A ravenous group of sexual deviants. I'd deal with it all repeatedly until the end of time for her.

"Ah. It took that, did it?" Hippo moved his pale hands to the armrests, tapping a single finger against the wood. "You'll forgive me if I don't believe you had such a sudden change of heart."

Fuck. Why couldn't this be easy?

"It's true," Aphrodite said in a strained voice. "The scar on my shoulder?"

Hippo's gaze darted to the scar, and he pushed from his seat, crossing the room for a closer look. "That's new."

"Yeah. A harpy claw." Aphrodite glared at me. "That bastard did it because I *talked* too much."

The way Aphrodite could slip into the role needed of her was both an artform to behold and a diabolical mind fuck. I knew with every breath she played pretend, but *hearing* the words still cut like a scythe to the stomach.

"Yack, yack, yack. That's all this woman does. Not sure what I ever saw in her in the first place." I curled a lip back in disgust.

Hippo squinted first at her, then me, staring us down and dissecting us. "Mm, yes. It's why I prefer my own company. For who knows me better than well—me?"

Such a nutter.

"She's all yours, Hip. I'll be collecting that bounty reward now." I made "come at me" gestures with my hands.

He made no motion to one of his people to retrieve a parcel, nor did he turn away to get it himself. Instead, he clasped his hands behind his back and stood in front of me. "I'm curious as to why you changed your mind. For such an iconic bounty hunter of the District, you put your entire career at risk for this woman. Why?"

Speaking of people who talk too godsdamned much.

"Haven't you ever simply wanted to get your dick wet?" I held a finger up before placing it on my lips. "Right. Sex is icky to you."

Aphrodite puffed her chest, her nails making light scraping sounds against the cuffs as she picked at them.

"Still. All of the theatrics for some pussy, Heph? Seems farfetched."

I'd throw him so far, *he* couldn't be *fetched*, the sleazy fuck knuckle.

Chuckling, I grabbed the back of Aphrodite's neck and pulled her between us. "Are you kidding? This is the goddess of love, Hip. Any man would *kill* at a shot between those thighs." I let my eyes roam her neck to her tits, the feral glint in my gaze *not* fake. "In fact, one more for the road, sweetheart?" I kissed her, pressing my hand at the back of her head and shoving my tongue into her mouth.

She kissed me back for a fraction of a second before she went into her acting mode, beating at my chest and pushing me away. Her nail caught my cheek, leaving behind a scratch and a burning sting.

"Asshole," Aphrodite said through a snarl, wiping the back

of her hand over her mouth.

Nice touch.

Flashing her a devious grin, I dragged a finger over the cut on my face, faint hints of blood staining my skin. "Anyhow, been there. *Done* that. And I'm tired of running from all your hunters and freak shows."

Hippolytus slipped his hands into the pockets of his sleek, far too tight for my liking, black slacks. "Uh-huh. You won't mind if I give my crew a little sample before closing the contract then, would you? Given all the complications and everything." He waved his finger in the air, and a group of people entered from a corridor, slinking their way to Aphrodite.

Fucking Olympus.

One man slid his hand over Aphrodite's stomach, and I suppressed the urge to turn them all to ash where they stood. A woman traced her fingers across Aphrodite's neck before inhaling the scent wafting from her hair.

This was a bad idea. How did she think for one second I could stand idly by while these greedy pieces of dogshit touched *my* goddess? My skin. My everything.

My boot didn't make it an inch off the floor before Aphrodite flashed her gaze to mine, the shimmering pink energy pulsing in her eyes too quickly for anyone else to catch—an unspoken reassurance to trust her. Aphrodite flinched as another man's hand grabbed her ass.

I needed the Oz, and I needed it *now*.

"Right. They look cozy. Hip, currency, and Oz? The Oz first, preferably." I couldn't look at Ro, otherwise, I'd risk fucking up the entire operation. Keeping my eyes glued on

Hippo, I held my palm out.

Hippolytus licked the corner of his lips, nodded, and moved behind Aphrodite being groped by several pairs of hands, forcing me to see it again. "Of course. Dimitri, would you be a doll and grab this man's reward?" He'd said it into the man's ear, keeping his sleazy eyes traced on me.

The forge ignited on its own beneath my jacket sleeve from the lava boiling inside, and I fought it back before it reached my hand, giving us away.

"Heph, let me assure you." Hippo hung an arm around Aphrodite's shoulders, his fingers grazing her cheek, but she tilted away. "If I sense any funny business, any at all—I'll make the cyclops and birds look like child's play. Bounty or not. Are we clear?"

Flexing my jaw, I shifted my stance to hide my furious unease and forced a smile. "Like cellophane, champ. Though I have to ask—where in the world did you find access to mythological beings?"

Hippo's jaw twitched. "I have connections you couldn't dream of, volcano god. And that classified information isn't part of the bounty contract."

Of course, it wasn't. Somehow it felt like this would come back to bite me in the ass.

Dimitri returned and handed me a zipped black bag. Snatching it from him, I immediately rummaged through it, finding the first piece of Oz and holding it up to the light. Real. Thank Olympus.

"Aw, think I'm pulling the wool over your eyes, Heph?" A serpent's smile slithered across Hippo's lips as he lowered his mouth to Aphrodite's face and licked her damn cheek.

A heated tingle shot down my spine, and I lunged forward. "I'd never think that of you, Hip. But you *do* have something there." I pointed at nothing on his chest, but he fell for it all the same, and I slapped him in the face with a snarky grin.

I'd been grasping at straws with that maneuver but it befuddled him enough to get the Tartarus away from her.

"Before I leave you all to your—" I shifted a glance to Aphrodite's chest. "—devices—I'd like to see that you close the contract. Right here. Right now."

Hippolytus snickered. "So mistrusting, Hephaistos."

"You know as well as I do the concept of trust when it comes to bounties in this place." I pointed at his wrist, my jaw flexing from the continued impatience. "Contract. Close it."

"Yes, yes."

The holo device displayed the bounty with me and Aphrodite's faces, the reward amount still making my head spin. I stared at it until the word "Closed" flashed in blazing crimson before disappearing entirely once Hippolytus lowered his arm.

"I do hope we can do business again in the future." Grinning, Hippo traced the back of his hand over Aphrodite's neck.

"Not if I can help it, Hip. Not if I can fucking help it. You all have fun." I turned my gaze to Aphrodite, giving her a subtle nod. "No hard feelings, love-y goddess. Business is business." After flashing a sparking wink at her, I turned on my heel and damn near sprinted for the door.

As soon as I was outside, when my feet hit the foyer, I prayed to the forges Ro would do whatever she needed to do to keep them off her and buy me some time. I didn't give her or Hippolytus another glance before my shoulder slammed into the door. If I'd looked, there'd have been no stopping the lava from roaring. I'd spent all my fucking patience.

Ares met me at the curb, his eyes searching my face, recognizing the fury spiraling. "You got it?"

I gave a curt nod, he grabbed my shoulder, and we ported to Orion's apartment.

"Bloody fucking shit," I roared, tossing the bag across the room, not paying attention to the direction.

Orion lunged in front of me, snatching the bag by its strap before it flew into his stereo system. "Heph, listen to me, brother. I know this is hard on you, but you need to keep your head in the game to fix the device and go get your woman."

Hard on me? Hard? More like I could topple every marble pillar in Olympus with my bare fists, I felt so furious.

"Don't try to say for one moment you could somehow *empathize* with me, Rion." I pointed at Orion and then turned it on Ares. "And especially not you."

Ares glared at me, uncrossing his arms as he prowled forward. "Do you forget I was fucking married? And those bastards *killed her*? I know the kind of angered torture catapulting through you, so I'm going to let that one go. But don't take my rare act of kindness for granted."

Fuck. He *had* been married. To an Amazon—a mortal Amazon. And not only was she killed, but brutally. And he hadn't been with anyone since. Admittedly, an asshole move on my part.

"Sorry, Air. I didn't mean—" I slumped into the nearest

chair and held my face in my hands.

Ares clapped a hand on my shoulder. "Shut up, brother. Like Orion said, get your head clear."

"Everything you need is on the kitchen counter, Heph." Orion motioned his head at an array of tools and the broken porting device on a towel. "I swung by your place to grab it so you could work on it here."

Something light and frail bumped against my foot. I peeked through my fingers to find Coney fumbling over my boot, trying to sit on it. Managing a weak smile, I scooped the rabbit into my hand and curled him against my chest, his soft fur calming my raging nerves.

"Alright, let's get to it then." I pushed to my feet, carrying Coney with me and resting him on the counter. After taking off my jacket, I wiggled my fingers over the tools, surveying if all needed were here. "Ares, would you grab the Oz from the bag?"

I hung the jacket over the back of the chair after popping a toothpick from the inside pocket to chew on. Ares placed the Oz in my opened palm, and I created a vat to melt it down and make it more palpable. Ironically, I'd broken the device more than it had been during my wee temper tantrum, but an easy enough crack repair. I turned my finger into a soldering iron, snatching one of the solders, and went to work. The tiny sparks flying from the process had images of Aphrodite's expression as she watched me forge her sword swirling through my brain. It made me lose focus and the solder slipped from my grasp.

"Shit," I yelled, throwing the device on the table. "How could I have *left* her in there? At one point, Hippolytus licked her face. Licked. It."

"You know godsdamned well I'm not sitting on this situation well either, Heph." Ares leaned on the table, the veins in his hands so prominent even *I* took notice. "But I'm just as guilty as many others in Aphrodite's life who underestimated her. Are you trying to tell me the guy she *chose* does too?" The corners of Ares's jaw bounced, his hands clenching, the swirls of fury blazing red lightning in his eyes.

No. That wasn't me. Since we were kids, I knew Aphrodite was far more than glitz, glam, and curves. Did I give her shit over it as often as I could? Yeah. It's all part of the dynamic. But questioning her now, and worse, being called out on it by your little brother?

I stuck the toothpick back in my mouth and cracked my neck before turning my attention to the device.

"That's what I thought," Ares mumbled before pushing off the table to back away, giving me space.

Soldering the crack without error, I snatched a chipping tool and got to work replacing all the parts that required Oz to power them. Coney started making circles on the counter's corner, his poofy tail raising before there were light pitter-patter sounds in the otherwise quiet room.

"Did your rabbit just shit on my kitchen counter?" Orion asked from the living room.

Risking a peek, I confirmed that, yes, he had. Six tiny brown balls rested on the counter. "What are you going on about? Those are clearly Coco Puffs."

Orion glared at me as he rose from the sofa and breezed into the kitchen to snatch a paper towel. The glaring continued as he scooped the pellet-sized poop and walked away. The chipping tool jammed in the middle of the fourth Oz installation, forcing me to wiggle it. *Snap*.

"Bugger," I yelled, slamming the tool onto the counter and holding the edges of it as the world spun around me.

A bottle appeared on the counter a moment later.

"Here. Drink that. Calm the fuck down and get this device *done*, Heph." Orion stuck a stern finger in my face.

I batted it away. "A frothy? What's that going to do aside from tasting like a malty, delicious beverage?"

"It's not beer. It's Ambrosia wine I 'borrowed' from Dion the last time we hung out."

Dionysos, the lucky jackass, could turn any liquid into Ambrosia wine. The only form of inebriation offered to the godly variety.

"That'll work." I swiped the bottle and tilted my head back for a long swig. The bubbly, sweet honey fizzled down my throat, and my shoulders halfway relaxed. That'd be enough. I didn't need to be sloshed to retrieve my love-y goddess.

Hours passed, and after destroying another four soldering tools, finishing an entire bottle of wine, and enough cursing to make a sailor blush, I'd fixed the device. Shooting to my feet in triumph, I fluttered my fingers over the buttons.

"I should probably attempt a port across the room before trying to port across town, let alone another time." After fiddling with the coordinates, I pushed my thumb to the grooved red button I'd purposely made stick out to avoid accidentally porting myself straight to Tartarus or Olympus knows where else.

The world blurred in blue whirls for a nanosecond before I appeared behind Ares. He didn't immediately notice, and I took the opportunity to tug his hair.

"Vlakás," Ares shouted, swiveling to face me with his fists raised.

I flicked my hand over Ares' fist, keeping my attention focused on the device, tossing it in my palm. "Fellahs, it works."

Orion shook his head. "What are you waiting for then?"

"Be right back," I replied with a wide grin, my thumb slipping over the button to port me to an awaiting damsel. "I'm here to res—"

On the one hand, relief washed over me at not porting into the scene I thought I'd be arriving in, but on the other hand, my insides twisted at what I *did* see. The group of men and women that'd been groping Aphrodite before I left were in the middle of an all-out orgy. Guy on guy, a woman with her legs in the air getting railed by another man, two women taking turns licking and sucking the other's tits. And where was my love-y goddess? Perched on Hippo's lounging chair, dressed in a pink negligee with a goblet in one hand, a golden bowl of grapes in the other, popping them into her mouth as a shirtless male goon fanned her with a palm frond.

She dropped the bowl, the small purple fruit rolling across the floor. Her face brightened when she saw me, and she pushed from the chair, batting the palm frond away. "Heph," she shouted, absently tossing the goblet aside, not caring about the red liquid staining the white carpet. She leaped into my arms, her shimmering face pressing to my cheek. "About time you showed up, *jack*."

I inhaled her scent, my touch tracing the soft negligee across her back, her skin glowing beneath the sheer fabric. "Yeah? You don't seem to be having a bad go of it."

"Are you kidding?" She pushed back, gripping my arms and using her thumb to point over her shoulder at the unfolding orgy. "I wasn't sure how much longer you would be and what I'd do if I had to call that off. I can't leave them in that state."

"Why not?"

She crossed her arms, accentuating the triangular pink fabric covering her breasts. "They'd forget to eat food or drink water and eventually slowly, I don't know, *die*?"

The man fucking the other man slapped him in the ass, making him cry out in appreciation.

"Doesn't seem like such a bad way to go to me." Grinning, I tickled her stomach through the gauzy pink fabric. She giggled before swatting my hand. "What happened after I left?"

"The moment that door clicked, I did your little cuffs trick and worked my magic. Having all those worshipping hands on me back in the day might've gotten me my jollies, but now? Gag." She pointed at her open mouth.

She did it—used powers unique to her to buy me some time without ever putting herself in a compromising situation. I'd been an idiot for ever doubting her in the first place.

"Where's Hippo?" I cocked a brow, squinting at the bouncing, sweaty bodies, not seeing him among them.

"The whole sexcapades deal wouldn't have worked, and I didn't know what to do with him, so I—" She scratched her head and pointed behind me. "Made him mesmerized with a corner."

The sight of Hippolytus with his face in the corner of the room like a scolded child made me laugh—loudly. "I'm putting that sight to memory as we speak. Well played, babe. Well played."

She tossed her hair over one shoulder. "It's not my best work, but not too shabby for a moment's notice."

"Although I'd completely understand if you wanted to leave him that way. He's a fucking grub." I sneered at his back.

"No. Yes, his revenge scheme was a bit over the top, but I still did him dirty, Phai. I'll be the bigger person here and offer a truce."

No shit.

"Really? How do you figure you'll do that?" As I scratched my chin, I peeked over Aphrodite's shoulder at the continued sex fest in the background of our conversation.

Funny how the sexual moans, groans, and wails hadn't phased either of us.

"The way his type thinks and feels toward sex is because they don't find themselves attracted to most people if any. It took some searching, but I dug into my cerebral love finder mumbo jumbo, and found him. The one singular person in existence in this time that he'd not only be attracted to but eventually could love."

"I don't follow. Aren't you messing with the Fates in that regard?"

She pinched the bridge of her nose. "About that. I had to pull a few strings with them—" She paused to snort and smile. "Strings. Get it?"

A love-smacked grin graced my lips.

"Anyway, I'll owe them a favor, but it leaves my conscience clear. I've already planted the seed in Hippo's mind, and it'll be up to him if he wishes to pursue it." She brushed her hands before resting them on her hips.

"And you did all of this in the time I've been gone?" I pointed at the ground with a quirked brow.

"Yup." She shrugged as if harnessing and organizing a man's fate in a matter of hours was a walk in the park.

Slipping my hand to the back of her neck, I pulled her to me and dipped my mouth to hers, kissing her. Our lips slid over the other, our eyes pinching shut, and as we pulled away, we stood still, holding each other, knowing the part that came next.

"Heph," Aphrodite whispered, nuzzling my neck.

I rested my chin on her head. "I know. We need to get you home."

Sniffling, she stepped back, dragging a knuckle under her nose before splaying her hand at the sex group. No sooner had the spell been lifted, they all collapsed to the ground, wheezing and groaning.

"I'm so thirsty, but I can't feel my feet to move," a woman whined.

A man stared between his legs. "I think my dick is swollen."

"Oh, please. They've only been at it for three hours." Aphrodite flicked her hair from her face. "Such babies." A tiny smile tugged at her mouth before disappearing into a frown.

"You ready, love-y goddess?" I slid a hand over her stomach, etching the feel of those tiny wings pressing against my fingertips across my mind.

"You better come to me as soon as you can, Hephaistos. Don't leave me waiting." She gripped my forearm—hard, her nails digging into my skin.

Grunting, I patted her hand. "I promise. All I need to do is take Ares and Orion back. But I also need to ensure Hip closed the contract for good. I trust him about as much as a Titan doing calculus."

"As *soon* as you can," she whispered again, fanning her hand behind me to undo the curse on Hippolytus, but waited.

As I brought the blue portal to life with the device, I brushed my lips against hers, edging her backward until she stood at the threshold. With tears glistening in her eyes, pink swirls of magic floated from her fingers toward Hippolytus. She backed into the portal with her hands clasped under her chin.

I knew I'd see her again, but watching her slip into the portal made my gut wrench. The volcanoes simmered within me, and I prayed to any god of Olympus that'd damn well listen spacetime wouldn't figure out a way to fuck us over. And if not for anything else, make Eros—alive.

twenty-three

APHRODITE

THE WORLD BLURRED IN waves of blue marbling, Heph's face shimmering away as I reappeared in my office. A breath pushed from my lungs, and I collapsed in my chair, almost missing it, clapping a hand to my chest. Would my time in the future screw with some shift in time? Cause another loop? Would Heph make it back?

Nausea bubbled in my stomach, and I pressed a hand over it. Gasping, I pushed from the chair. I never thought I'd be relieved not to feel my son's wings beating against my belly. And what's more, I could sense him, the way I'd always been able to do—to know where he was at all times. Eros existed. It worked.

The door flew open, and I produced the sword Heph made me, holding it above my head.

"Aphrodite?" Thalia screeched, her eyes darting between the blade and my stern face. "You're alive."

How long had I been gone? So much had changed in what seemed such a short time. Sighing, wooziness pulling at my bones, I rested the sword on the desk and leaned on it.

"I'm alive, Thalia. Sorry I couldn't contact you. I—"

Euphrosyne burst through the door, the tight raven ringlets of her curly hair bouncing as she paused at the doorway with her hand on the knob, caramel eyes wide. "Holy shit. Where have you *been*, Aph?"

All of it happened too fast—too much and way too fast.

"Did someone say Aphrodite?" Aglaia's rich voice asked from the lobby before she, too, appeared, bumping into Euphrosyne in the process. Her platinum blonde hair hung to the middle of her back, and she tossed it over one shoulder.

Rubbing my temples, I sat on the desk's edge. "Please tell me there aren't any clients in here. You've all said my real name countless times."

"Oh, we've had the place closed the moment we realized you were missing," Euphrosyne answered, a crease forming in the terracotta skin above her dark brows.

"Closed down?" I pushed from the desk. "Imagine the profits we're losing, imagine the margins, why would—"

"Dite." Thalia placed a hesitant hand on my shoulder. "What happened?"

"And why are you wearing a see-through nightie?" Aglaia asked, swooping a finger over my ensemble.

Glancing down at the pink chiffon still hugging my form, I groaned and swirled an arm around myself. Seconds later, I appeared in a simple light pink fitted tee, jeans, and white Keds.

All three Graces widened their eyes, and Aglaia leaned

toward Euphrosyne, whispering, "Is she wearing jeans and a t-shirt?"

"Uh-huh. And sneakers. *Sneakers*," Euphrosyne whispered back.

"Yeah. I'm wearing simple. Sort of lacking inspiration at the moment."

Thalia gently curled her arm around me and rubbed my shoulder. "Dite, what happened? Tell us."

Staring blankly at a crack in the wood paneling on the floor, I spoke the truth in a monotone. "I lost my powers because I thought no one loved me, Heph took a bounty Hippolytus put on me, I ended up in the year 2104, a swingers club, a rabbit, a cybernetic cyborg, mind-blowing sex with Heph, confessions of love, and now I'm back."

Silence filled the small space, and I welcomed it.

Euphrosyne waved a hand in front of her face. "That—was a lot."

"And there's more. That was Cliff's Notes version."

"So, you and Heph?" Aglaia's light brows bobbed.

Thalia jostled me. "There's that, and I'm still hung up on swingers club?"

And now I knew where their priorities lay.

"Yeah," I pushed out, already missing my forge god with such fierceness it made my lungs burn. "And Heph he—" An image of my son—our son—and Heph next to each other shimmered over my brain like a mirage. "—he's Eros's dad."

"What?" Thalia and Aglaia shouted in unison.

Euphrosyne threw her palms up. "That tears it. This calls for drastic measures." She snapped her fingers, making us all appear in the Graces' vast bathhouse.

Corinthian pillars lined the borders of the squared bathing area, decks of white and gray marble surrounding it. Milk mixed in with the steamy hot water, rose petals floating on top. Pitchers of Ambrosia wine rested at every corner, along with a goblet for each of us. She'd made us appear in the bath topless with our hair pinned to the top of our heads in a messy bun—the more exposed skin to the milky water, the more nurturing it could be.

I waded backward until my butt hit one of four benches. Sitting, I pushed my back to the wall and dipped low enough for my head to rest on the edge, my breasts covered just above the nipples. Thalia moved next to me with a goblet in each hand, offering me one.

"Thanks, Lia." I mustered a weak smile.

Thalia gasped and pointed at my shoulder. "Is that a *scar*?"

I'd forgotten about it until now.

"Harpy claw. Another long story."

Aglaia cocked her head to one side. "You don't seem that bothered by it."

Cupping a handful of water into my palm, I trickled it over the scar. "It doesn't. I see it as a symbol of something I finally overcame. A reminder that I have strength even as the goddess of love."

Thalia rested her head against mine, offering a one-armed hug.

Euphrosyne unabashedly sat on the edge with her feet dangling in the water, breasts on full display. Not as if we hadn't all seen each other naked numerous times through the ages. "Alright. Hephaistos. I take it you finally admitted your insane crush on him?"

"I think it's a tad more than a crush, Phro." Aglaia winked at me and tipped her glass in my direction before settling onto a bench across from us.

My grip tightened on the goblet of its own will, and a pomegranate-sized lump formed in my throat. I took a sip of wine to settle what it would of my nerves. "He's the love of my life, Graces."

"Aww," they cooed with their hands pressed to their chests, making pouty faces.

"What's not to like about a man like Heph, anyway? Muscles for days. A fighter. Funny. Good-looking. And if you ask me? Scars are sex-ay." Aglaia made a chef's kiss gesture before grinning at me and sipping her cup.

Her description made me smile genuinely at the thought of my volcano god. *My* Heph. "Beyond that, he's incredibly loyal, caring and never hesitates to put me first."

"Not to mention he's your kid's dad?" Thalia bumped our shoulders together, making the foggy water ripple around us.

"Yeah," I squeaked, sinking further into the water. "That too."

"How does that work? He's a grown man, and didn't you say *you* made yourself pregnant with him?" Euphrosyne crossed her legs and leaned back on her palms.

"I did, but going to the future and sleeping with Heph, multiple, multiple times did the trick." I chugged the rest of my wine, and no sooner had I lowered the goblet from my lips, Thalia was filling it to the brim again with a sparkling smile.

"I still don't get it." Aglaia shrugged.

"Please don't make me try to explain. I'd royally screw it up, but it all has something to do with spacetime and loops and mumbo jumbo."

"Let's get to the important bit." Euphrosyne leaned forward, wine in hand and a devious glint in her gaze. "*Multiple* times with the Hephster?"

Heat rushed to my cheeks. "For the first time in our immortal existence, I'm going to play the part of a prude." I hid my face with the goblet.

I caught Aglaia's eye roll from the corner of my eye. "Will you at least give us each one yes or no question?"

I'd be lying if I said I wasn't chomping at the bit to spill some dirty details as we always had to each other, but things were different with Heph. And maybe this would get them to move on. Unlikely, but no harm, no foul.

"Fair enough." I sat up straighter. "Go for it."

"Did he use handcuffs?" Euphrosyne poured more wine into her cup.

Phro always going straight for the jugular.

The feel of the cool metal pressing against my skin and him forcing my hands above me blindfolded…

I pinched my knees together and answered with an even-toned "Yes."

"I knew it. I knew that man was a closet kink show." Euphrosyne slapped her thigh.

Thalia cleared her throat, her face already matching the ruby color of her hair. "Did he—" She leaned toward me and finished in a low whisper. "—do you against a wall?"

Sweet Thalia.

Smiling at the others with their hands cupped over their ears, I nodded. "Yes, he did *do* me against a wall…several times."

Thalia's cheeks blazed hotter.

Aglaia fanned herself. "And did he use toys? Vibrators and the like?"

I traced a milky finger between my breasts. "No. No need."

"Olympus," Euphrosyne breathed out, sloshing her wine in the goblet before sipping it.

"If you two have such a star-crossed love, where the Tartarus is he, anyway?" Aglaia's tone bordered on the defensive—a defense for *me*.

"He had to bring me back to make sure Eros existed. The whole loop junk I don't want to get into."

"Alright, so he brought you back. Why isn't he here now?" Euphrosyne arched a brow.

Why *hadn't* he come back yet?

"Something I'm trying not to think about." I clipped my words before finishing the remaining wine in my glass.

"Sorry," Aglaia said, slouching into the bench seat.

"It's fine. I'm exhausted. I appreciate you all doing this and letting me vent, but I think I'll get some shut-eye. See you all tomorrow at the office?" I stood, milky water droplets trickling in a warped circle around me.

"The office?" Thalia lifted her bright green eyes to meet my gaze. "Are you sure you don't want a little more time off?"

Shaking my head, I stepped out of the bath and made a camisole and pajama shorts appear. "I need the distraction."

"See you at eight sharp then, boss." Euphrosyne lifted her

goblet to me.

Before any of them could give me an ounce more grief, I ported to my bedroom, flopping onto my fluffy white comforter as soon as I appeared. Groaning, I shoved my face into two of the eight pink pillows I kept on my bed and tried to fall asleep.

The next day came quickly and still no signs of Heph. Sleep hardly happened because I'd wake up in a hopeful panic with every tiny noise, thinking it was him, only to deflate with disappointment. My idea to distract myself at work had been going about as well as my attempts at sleeping. I sat at my desk, mindlessly spinning in my chair, and staring at the ceiling when Thalia's voice booming from my intercom almost made me slip to the floor. After yelping and grabbing the desk's edge to steady myself, I cleared my throat.

"Vena?"

I closed my eyes and rubbed the bridge of my nose. "I'm sorry. Yes, I'm here."

"There's a potential client in the lobby who wishes to meet with you. Are you able to see them now?"

No?

"Sure. Send them in." I smoothed my magenta dress shirt and ruffled my hair, shifting papers on my desk as if I'd been doing something more constructive than dizzying myself in my chair.

A tall man in a grey polo and dark jeans walked in, his dark blonde faux hawk, shaved sharp jawline, and confident bright smile telling me nearly everything I needed to know about him. But I'd be out of business if I didn't get his type in my office every other week.

His hazel gaze snapped over his shoulder as he pointed at the door. "Should I close this?"

Standing, I played with my shirt buttons. "Yes, please."

Without dropping his smile, he shut the door with a light click and turned to face me, extending his hand. "Kyle Miller."

"Pleasure to meet you, Kyle." After shaking, I sat and folded my hands on the desk. "How can I help you?"

"I'm going to cut straight to the chase here, Vena, if you don't mind?" His voice was low but not as deep as Heph's, and I missed that grittiness I loved so much.

"That'd be a breath of fresh air, Kyle. By all means." Grabbing a pen from the holder at the corner of my desk, I rolled it between two fingers and leaned back.

"There's this woman."

Here we go.

"I'm crazy about her, you know?" He pressed his forearms on my desk, making the lean muscle of his biceps twitch. "But I have no idea if she feels the same. There are signs, I think, but I could be misreading them."

"Alright. And what exactly are you seeking our services for?"

As if I had to ask—I didn't. Vena had to.

"There's a wedding coming up soon that I know we're both invited to. I thought if I showed up with a date, I could see if it would make her jealous." He raked a hand through his hair. "I'd feel terrible bringing a *real* date, though."

My mind had drifted mid-sentence from the explanation he spewed that I already knew.

"And you want us to provide said date as a failsafe." I set the pen back on the desk—well, more like slammed it with more force than intended.

His brow quirked, gaze dropping to the abused pen before lifting back to my face. "Yes. Exactly."

"No." I puffed my chest.

Kyle gave two quick blinks and looked around. "I'm sorry. No?"

Calmly interlacing my fingers, I lifted my chin. "That's right. I'm denying service. If you had come in here a month ago, hell, even two weeks ago, I would've assigned you an escort without hesitation. But you know what, Mr. Miller?" I leaned forward. "I'm tired of people coming in here trying to solve their problems by other means than simply *talking* about them."

And yes, I *was* speaking to myself too. Probably more pissed at my own actions versus the mortal in front of me, but he needed to hear it before he made my same mistakes.

Kyle flattened his palms on the desk. "I—don't follow."

Maybe I needed a blazing red sign behind me that read: Talk it Out or Get Out.

Not feeling the patience to sit any longer, I pushed to my feet and crossed my arms. "Have you ever thought about telling her how you feel, Mr. Miller?"

"Sure. Plenty of times."

"Then why haven't you? What's the worst that could happen?"

I rode a thin line grilling a client, but I needed the affirmation as much as he needed a swift kick in the ass.

Kyle beat his forefinger against the hardwood. "I'd think—rejection?"

"Love—" I sat on the edge of my desk near him and rested my hands on my lap. "Is all about fear and taking chances—*embracing* them. It's what makes love so special and unique."

"I guess—" He leaned back, slumping, and blowing out a breath. "—I never thought about it that way."

"Tell her how you feel, Kyle. Leave the deception out of it. Trust me. And I think you'll be surprised that she may be experiencing the same thing as you—fear of rejection."

He nodded but squinted one eye at me. "You purposely lost money giving me advice like this. Why?"

"Because I don't like seeing others walk down a path I know personally is the wrong one when I can step in to help." I extended my hand to him.

He hesitated at first but stood and shook it. "Thank you. And I mean that. I didn't expect this."

Neither did I, kid. Neither did I.

But I liked it. *Really* liked it.

I followed him to my office door and waved as he breezed through the lobby. Leaning against the doorframe, I flinched at Thalia's perplexed expression once she marched in front of me.

"What happened?" She motioned with her head toward the exit.

"What do you mean?"

"Did you not sign him on? He was a textbook case."

My powers hummed under my skin. "No, I didn't. I told him to talk to her. To tell her how he feels."

Thalia's jaw dropped. "You—did? Wow, Aph. You've… changed."

Had I? Because I didn't *feel* different. I felt—alive.

"I don't think I have, Thal. I think I'm just not afraid of being myself anymore."

Thalia clasped her hands together. "Huh. Wow. Well, I love it. I'm going to grab some lunch. You want something?"

My smart watch buzzed on my wrist with an incoming text, making my heart throttle into a gallop when I saw the name: Cupie. My nickname for Eros since he was a toddler.

"Uh, sure. Yeah. Whatever you're having." My voice trailed off.

"You sure? I'm having tofu."

The haze cleared long enough for me to say, "Then I'll have chicken."

Thalia smiled and clicked her heels together. "You got it. Be back in a jiff."

The walk back to my desk turned into a trek through hip-high mud. Eros texted me. At some point, the conversation of him not only having a dad but who that dad was would have to happen.

Holding my breath, I flopped into my chair and pulled up the message on my phone.

Cupie: Mom, I heard you're back. Are you okay? Where were you?

I scraped my nails over my throat before typing up a response.

Me: I'm fine. I'm safe. But it's a long story. Too long for texting.

Cupie: Then pop over to Toronto. You haven't seen Hedone in a while, anyway.

Hedone. My granddaughter.

Frig, frig, triple frig.

I pressed the corner of my phone into my temple. Heph gained a son *and* a granddaughter—I wouldn't blame him in the slightest for freaking out.

Me: Sure. Give me a few days, okay?

Bouncing dots on a screen had never made me more nervous.

Cupie: Alright, mom. Talk to you later. Love you.

Me: Love you too.

I dropped my phone on the desk and held my head in my hands to keep it from spinning. A moment later, I picked it back up to type another text.

Me: Air, are you back?

And waited.

My knee bounced under the desk, and I grabbed the phone with both hands as the damn bouncing dots appeared.

Big Bro: Yeah. Got in yesterday. What's up?

Me: Can you meet me somewhere? I need to talk.

Big Bro: Naí, of course. Where?

Me: A bar. Any bar.

Big Bro: Now you're speaking my language.

TWENTY-FOUR

HEPH

IT TOOK EVERYTHING IN me to force that reassuring smile as Ro disappeared through the portal. The last thing I wanted to do was fucking *smile*, but I knew it was what she needed. I'd tear down Olympus and rebuild it from its foundation if it's what would make my goddess happy. When the portal disappeared, I let the scowl carve into my features. After shoving the device into my pocket, I turned, stalked across the room, and slammed my forearm against Hippolytus's chest, pinning him to the wall.

Hippo laughed. Fucking *cackled* in my face. "Someone's an angry puss."

"Let *me* make something clear to you, Hip." I slid my arm to his throat, pushing hard enough he wouldn't be able to speak but not enough pressure to constrict his breathing. "The only reason I didn't lop your fucking head off as soon as she left is because for whatever godsdamned reason, she saw it in her heart to *apologize* to you."

Hippo tried to push me away, and I kneed him in the dick, making him grunt and gurgle in an attempt to speak.

"Nuh-uh. I'm not done." Keeping my arm at his collarbone, I used the other hand to grab his face, forcing him to look me in the eye. "If you ever come after Aphrodite again. If you ever send someone after her again, it won't be a cyclops, birds, or endless bounty hunters, Hippolytus." I beat the back of his head against the wall. "It'll be me taking *days* to dip your fucking body into a volcano, and I'll start with your big toes."

Hippo's throat bobbed under my arm.

"*Now,* are we clear, Hip?" Giving him one last shove, I dropped my arm and stepped back, the lava seething in my bones.

Hippo rubbed his neck, a sadistic grin quirking his upper lip.

"Something funny, champ?" I made my hammer axe appear.

"You have no idea the forces you're meddling with, Hephaistos." He stood straight and stuck his arms out to each side. "You can't touch me."

"Yeah? I'd say that bruise on your neck says otherwise."

The villainous smile had yet to disappear from Hippo's face. "What makes you think all of this is only about *her*? Or perhaps she's a piece in an incomplete puzzle."

Why did the bad guys always feel the need to speak in riddles?

"Going to take this as you spitting on Aphrodite's apology, then?"

Say yes, you pathetic excuse for an air breather. Give me a

reason, *any* reason, to bash your fucking skull in.

Hippo stroked a hand over his silky-smooth chin. "No. Not entirely. But I also don't trust her. Who's to say this man she claims could be the only love of my life isn't also a serial killer, a money launderer, or gods forbid, a construction worker." He sneered and shivered.

What the fuck?

"As if you're a saint, you damn hypocrite." I pointed my weapon at him. "And what the Tartarus do you have against construction workers?"

Hippo folded his hands behind his back. "My disdain for your girlfriend remains until I know her so-called apology is sound. And do not get your hopes up for my sovereign to back down as easily."

His sovereign?

Glaring at him, I shifted my stance. "What are you yammering about?"

Hippo waved his finger at me like scolding a child. He even made the *tsking* sound. "You didn't think I'd tell you who they are, did you? Oh, and by the way. You asked me to cancel the conjoined bounty, but the one on Aphrodite alone? It's still very much active."

My heart fell to my gut, a searing heat striking down my spine, and I pounced. "You conniving son of a—"

"Ta," Hippo said, waving and—disappearing in a swirl of inky black smoke.

The axe lodged in the wall, and I growled, yanking it out and seething at the hole it'd left behind. I knew Hippolytus had no means to port anywhere any more than I did, and I'm a fucking Olympian god. This "sovereign," whoever they were, seemed not only bad news but the *worst* news. He could've been bluffing about the bounty on Ro. He *better* have been fucking bluffing.

As I walked toward the exit, ignoring the naked group of people still groaning and whining in the corner, I pulled up the bounty listings on my wrist holo device. Flicking my fingers to scroll, I froze, a tingle shuddering over the back of my neck. Not only had he not been bluffing, but the photo of Aphrodite showed a clear view of her face now, and the reward amount—doubled.

"Fucking Olympus," I growled, slapping my hand over the device to close the program.

The wrist device chimed with an incoming text message.

Orion: Did you forget about us?

"Fuck," I yelled from the street corner.

Producing another portal, I stormed through it and jumped into Orion's apartment. Ares paced the living room, and Orion sat at his coffee table playing Solitaire with a pack of nudie holo cards.

Ares whipped around to face me. "Maláka. What took you so long?"

My eye twitched as I stared into oblivion.

"And why do you have that look on your face?" Orion tossed the remaining cards on the table and stood.

"I know I've asked you two for too many favors as it is, but I need one more." The twitch moved into my cheek.

"Heph, I need to get back." Ares stepped in front of me, hitting the back of one hand against the opposite palm, emphasizing his point.

Orion searched my face before squinting. "This has to do with Aphrodite again, doesn't it?"

"Shit. Does this place have it out for her or something?" Ares interlaced his hands behind his head and huffed. "What is it, and how long is this going to take?"

"Not long. And I don't even need you to break a sweat fighting anything."

"I don't like this favor already," Ares mumbled.

Orion leaned on the couch and crossed his ankles. "What are we doing, Heph?"

"Hippolytus never canceled the bounty on Ro. And—he doubled the reward. I know a guy who can wipe it from the system, but he's never done it and will be hard to convince." I tossed the portal device from one palm to the other. "I figure it would help with the intimidation side of things if you two were there. Yeah?"

"You want us to stand there and look…mean?" Ares' tone turned monotone and unenthused.

I stuck my bottom lip out, contemplating his simplistic phrasing. "Pretty much."

Orion pushed from the sofa and snapped his fingers. "Let's go."

I didn't deserve these two as mates, I swear it.

"Do you want me to port us there?" Ares asked after letting out a gruff sigh.

Grinning, I pushed the portal ignition button on the device. "No need, brother. I'm back in business, remember?"

Orion saluted me as he walked past and jumped in first.

Ares threw his jacket on and hung his hands on the furry lapels. "You know your portals make me want to hurl by the time I make it to the other side, right?"

"Maybe try holding your breath?" I arched a brow.

He mumbled incoherently in Greek, the only words I caught being colorful phrases to express his distaste for portal jumping. Once Ares stepped in, I jumped behind him and met them a block away from The Bounty Emporium.

"Alright. A little intel before we do this." After shoving the porting device back in my pocket, I dragged a hand through my hair, my eye still twitching. "This dude, Olaf, is a hard head. He's self-righteous, would sell out anyone without flinching if the price were high enough, and he's the only bounty gig in town which makes him abundantly confident."

Ares cracked his knuckles. "Why don't we beat his brains in and call it a day? Or better yet? Kill him."

"Killing would make it far too easy on him. I'm more of a fan of prolonged torture, myself."

And found that to be increasingly more accurate with Aphrodite back in my life, *especially* now.

"How are you going to convince him?" Orion scratched the stubble on his cheek. "Threaten his reputation?"

"That is a grand idea, Orry. I think I'll use it." I stepped forward.

Ares pushed my chest, halting me. "Are you trying to tell me you didn't have a *plan*?"

"Ah, Air." After adjusting his lapels, I tugged a strand of his long hair that'd fallen from the manly bun. "You know I'm better flying from the seam of my trousers."

"And I'm better when handling you in smaller doses."

"Adapt and overcome, brother. You're going to be seeing a lot more of me now." I patted his shoulder and slipped past him, ignoring more of his Greek grumbling.

The look on Olaf's face when he spotted me in the distance was all too satisfying. Several bounty hunters stood in line, and Olaf paused mid-transaction to gulp and avert his gaze as if we hadn't already made eye contact.

"Olaf," I shouted, slamming my hand onto the counter and shoving aside the current hunter awaiting payment. "Biffy. Old friend. Chum."

Olaf fiddled with the floating chair's controls, making it bob chaotically. "Heph, to uh—to what do I owe the visit? Didn't see your name on any bounty contracts."

Ares and Orion stepped behind me, making Olaf's eyes bulge.

"Listen here, you dodgy cunt." I leaned on the counter, forcing our faces closer. "You're going to do me a favor, or I'll sully your reputation."

"No." Olaf punched the controller of his stool left to right, making it spin circles. "No, no, no. I know what you're going to ask, Heph. And I can't do it."

"Bullshit," Orion chimed in from behind me.

Fire blazed in my eyes, and I balled my hands into fists. "Blondie is right, Laf. Everything can be canceled. Even *people*."

Ares stepped beside me, cracking his knuckles.

Olaf guided his stool as far back as the tiny kiosk would allow, the metal chair repeatedly clunking against the far wall.

"Cancel the bounty on Aphrodite *now*. Make it look like it never existed, Olaf." I beat my finger on the counter, the fire in my gaze raging.

Olaf eyed the protective casing he was in before shaking his head with pursed lips.

"Ladies and gents," I announced, turning to face the impatient line of awaiting bounty hunters. "Did you know that Olaf here has stiffed me on not two but *three* bounties?" Holding three fingers up, I grinned at the cacophony of murmurs and gasps floating through the air.

None of that was true, but a bounty dealer's rep was *everything* in the District.

Olaf floated closer to the partition. "That's crazy. They'll never believe that."

"Won't they?" I brought my face as close to the glass as I could without touching my nose to it. "Who are they going to believe? The sniveling prat who takes a portion of their bounty rewards or one of the most renowned bounty hunters in the outer systems. Hm?"

Olaf chewed on his lips and rubbed his leg stump, Aphrodite's bounty displaying on his holo screen.

That's right. Fucking do it.

Olaf's finger hovered over a button before zooming backward on his stool and shaking his head. "Nope. No. I can't."

"Maláka. Enough of this," Ares roared, pushing past me.

He gripped a corner of the partition and, with one quick tug, tore the frame from its hinges, creating a hole large enough for two of the three of us to make it through. I sighed, holding my face in my hand.

I may as well let him finish his tirade at this point.

Olaf screeched like an adolescent girl as Ares barged his way in, arms flexed and poised at his sides. Ares threw a booted foot forward, kicking Olaf's stool from under him. He launched his arm out, grabbing Olaf by the shirt before he hit the ground, and held him there as Olaf clawed his arm.

"You're going to cancel the bounty so we can all move the fuck on. Do you understand me, worm?" Ares's lip bounced in a snarl, and he carried Olaf to the holo screen, shoving him at it.

"Hey, Raging Bull," Orion beckoned. Once Ares cut his gaze to him, he added, "You don't think Heph or me could've done that? There's a reason we were trying to keep a low profile."

"What?" Ares spat.

Sighing, I glanced at my watch. "You've got approximately thirty seconds to get him to cancel that bounty, Air."

"Or *what*?"

"The Emporium is District property. They've rigged every inch to alert enforcers of foul play," Olaf said, making the grave mistake of *smiling* at Ares.

"Maláka," Ares roared, shoving Olaf's face closer to the holo. "Do you think I give a flying fuck about enforcement? Cancel the bounty *now,* or I'll make all of your limbs *match*."

My brother might have been the god of war, but he could just as easily be a god of passion. The man could make Titans cower from one snarling lip bounce, I swear.

"Alright, alright," Olaf stammered, his hand shaking as he

moved it toward the screen.

"And don't fuck it up," Ares added.

Gulping, Olaf pressed a button, and the red cancellation blazed the screen. "There. See? It's done."

"I want it gone, Laf. It never existed. Remember?" I snapped my gaze to a brooding Ares before directing it back to Olaf.

Through a babble of whimpers, Olaf swiped several more screens before pressing a final button, and the bounty glitched away in a blur of numbers and symbols. "There. It's done, it's done. Now put me back on my stool."

"I should make you *crawl* back to it. Gamó to theó sou." Ares carried Olaf far enough he could toss him back to the stool, but there was no "placing" him back about it.

The faint digital sirens blared in the distance, and I quickly pulled up the bounty database, scrolling through every area Olaf could've hidden the bounty instead of deleting it. The sirens grew louder and louder with each passing screen.

Satisfied Ares's intimidation techniques worked on 'ol Laf, I snapped my jacket sleeve back over my wrist. "Right. We should go—*now*."

Ares grabbed my arm, followed by Orion's, and we appeared in Orion's apartment.

"Ah, here we are again, gents. Home sweet home." Exhaustion pulled at my bones as I leaned against the living room couch.

"Any other favors you're going to pull out of your ass, Heph, or am I free to go now?" Ares stepped before me, fishing for the porting device in my pocket.

"Hey, now. You haven't even bought me dinner first."

Smirking, I shoved him away and removed the device, spiraling a portal to the past. "There you are."

"I'll catch you fools later," Ares said, walking toward the portal.

I stepped forward with an out-stretched hand. "Wait."

Ares paused in front of the warbly portal, the blue swirls clashing against the red casting in his eyes as he looked over his shoulder. "Naí?"

"Are we—" I rubbed the back of my neck. "Are we good? The whole Aphrodite thing?"

A deep chuckle thundered from Ares's gut. "Honestly? I'm glad it's you, brother. But if you want—" He crossed the room and pointed in my face. "If you hurt her, I swear on my father's reign I'll—"

"You'll *what*, tough guy?" I bit back a grin.

A smile crept over his lips, and he slapped my face. "Nothing. I know you won't hurt her. Besides, her wrath would be far deadlier than anything I could manage to do to you, so I'm not worried."

"Thanks, brother. For everything." I held out my forearm.

"Anytime. But you owe me a new armor set." Ares locked arms with me before pulling me into a side hug and leaping through the portal.

Re-adjusting the coordinates on the device, I made a second portal to the past appear with a direct passage to Orion's place. "You ready, Orry?"

"Actually, I think I'll stay for a bit."

I spun on my heel with raised brows. "Come again?"

Orion sat on his couch, cozy, with Coney resting on his lap

in a ball. "I'm starting to take to this place, I think. It's not like there's anything for me in the past."

"What about Artemis?" After squelching the portal and securing the device in my pocket, I flopped next to Orion on the couch, and scratched Coney's head.

"I'll still hunt with her once a month. We always use her hunting grounds, which isn't a part of that world." Orion shrugged and leaned his head to rest on the couch's back.

"You just like the copious amounts of tail here, don't you?"

Still leaning back, he gave me a sly grin, a sparkle glinting in his eyes. "It doesn't hurt. Shouldn't you be getting back to Aphrodite? She's probably getting fidgety right about now."

Everything that'd been muddied from taking that bounty on Aphrodite seemed settled. And yet why did I get the gut-wrenching feeling it'd only begun?

"This is far from over, you know," I mumbled, pressing my forearms to the tops of my thighs with a deep sigh.

Orion sat up and scooped Coney to the seat between us. "How do you figure that?"

The Sovereign. I couldn't get Hip's words out of my head. What did it all mean?

"There's something bigger at play here. Far bigger than those pion cunts Narcissus and Hippolytus are capable of, that's for damn sure." The exhaustion that'd rattled my bones seeped into my veins, but I fought its will to pull me under. "I'm wondering if Ro is *safer* in the past."

"Shit, Hephaistos. This again?"

I straightened and threw my arms out at my sides. "Fucking what?"

He twisted his torso to face me, resting an arm on the couch's back. "We're biffies, right?"

The question of our level of friendship seemed ludicrous.

"'course. You're my best mate."

"Alright, then I say this with the utmost kind regard for your wellbeing, Heph. You're making decisions for her again, you asshat." He shoved my shoulder. "Not to mention, if this thing you're referring to is so powerful, do you not think it can time travel?"

Always the fucking voice of reason.

Frowning, I let my arms droop. "I suppose that's possible."

"And call me crazy, but wouldn't the safest place for her be with you? At your side?"

And now there'd be no living with him.

"You're right, you asswipe. Alright?"

"Now get the Tartarus out of here. You have a goddess to go back to and a son to meet." He first pushed me from the couch with his hand, followed by a kick in the ass from his boot.

A son.

I hadn't forgotten about it, but porting back to Aphrodite was one step closer to meeting Eros in a new light. Would he be angry? Would he believe us? Would he *hate* me?

"Heph," Orion shouted.

Cutting my gaze to him with wide eyes, I blinked at him.

"Go," he whispered.

Giving a curt nod, I spun up a portal and appeared in Aphrodite's house. Moving through several rooms, I found her sitting on the edge of her bed, trailing her fingers over the sword's hilt I'd made her. She looked so sad and worried. It tore a hole in my heart.

Had she thought I wouldn't come back for her?

I kept quiet as I snuck behind her, trying not to let the honeyed scents exuding from her make me trip on the area rug. Leaning forward, I lowered my lips to her ear.

"Hey ya, Peach."

twenty-five

APHRODITE

THERE HAD TO BE a sort of irony for a goddess of love to feel unsure of herself. I'd led thousands of people to their partners, lovers, and confidants. Even created circumstances and scenarios for people to discover passion—experience it in its truest form. And yet, I sat in a corner booth of a dive bar, nursing a warm beer, waiting for my older brother to show up and set me straight.

When Ares stepped through the front door, the older woman wearing a Harley Davidson vest, chaps, and boots at the bar, finally lifted her head. No matter where he was, my brother always managed to make an entrance without effort. Mortal women were drawn to the carnal energy he exuded like an alpha wolf, and the men had the battle-frenzied urge surging through their veins from his presence.

Ares had his dark hair in his usual style of half up, half down, the up part pulled into a bun. He scanned the room, searching for me, and I waved a hand over my head. As he made his way past scattered tables, the mahogany bar, and broken jukebox, he shoved the sleeves of his burgundy Henley shirt and plopped in the booth seat across from me.

"Vlakás, sis. Couldn't have picked a bar with even a *two*-star rating?" Surveying our environment, Ares combed a hand through his beard.

I shrugged and continued to scrape the bottle's label from the glass. "I feel shitty. Therefore, I surround myself with shitty."

"Is this about Heph?"

Shooting my gaze to my brother's, I ran out of label to pluck and resorted to using my nail to pick at the sticky leftover residue. "Maybe."

"Wait a minute." Ares squinted before scooting closer. "Is my super confident, take-charge sister *worrying* a guy is standing her up?"

"It is not your job to make fun of me right now, Air." I threw the discarded labeling at him.

With a swift swipe of his hand in front of his face, he deflected the sticky paper, chuckling. "I'm your big brother. It *is* my job to give you a hard time and *then* offer sage advice."

As I caught Ares's gaze, my powers hummed in my chest. A radiant glow surrounded my brother, a sight I'd never witnessed with him and doubted if I ever would. But the timing made little sense because Ares—was in love.

Ares's eyes narrowed, his gaze watching me cant my head side to side. "Fuck. Not sure why I thought I could hide it from *you*."

"Didn't you *just* get back into 'town'?" I made air quotes.

Ares glanced around as if the two other patrons and bartender watching a boxing match gave a rat's ass about our conversation. "Do you know how bizarre it is to get back home only to realize my life suddenly glitched into the future?"

Looping spacetime. Unreal.

"There is the small matter of my son?"

Ares slouched and closed his eyes. "Vlakás. Eros. Yeah, sorry."

Now that he had stopped hiding it, the shimmering glow beamed around him, making a breath catch in my throat. "And it's a—fated bond."

"Yeah." Ares nodded, a satiated half-smile pulling at his lips. "Who would've ever guessed war would have a fated bond? With a mortal woman, no less."

I'd known Ares had been fated to meet her as a means of balance and connection. But there were limitations to love's all-knowing power because I could not have told Ares any of it and had no way of knowing when and where. "Are you going to tell me about her?"

Ares stretched his arms the width of the booth's back. "You'll meet her in due time, Aph. Right now, it's about you. What's eating at you?"

Grimacing, I lifted the beer bottle to my lips and took a sip, gagging over the flavor and the metallic undertones it took on from the warmth.

"Since when do you like beer?" Ares held back a laugh as he watched me attempt another sip.

I smacked my lips together. "Still don't, but I needed something to look busy while I sat here wallowing in my own self-pity."

"Aph." Ares beckoned, leaning his forearms on the table and tapping my hand with a single finger. "Talk to me."

Zipping my back straight, I clutched the bottle with both hands. "I have this crippling fear that Heph will change his mind about us. Or that he doesn't want to be a dad, or—"

When had I become self-conscious enough to doubt my worth?

"Hey. Enough of talking like that." Ares *tsked* and flicked his hand at me.

Scowling, I shot him an icy glare. "Excuse me?"

"You know Heph worships the ground you walk on. Probably even the gum that sticks to your shoe from said ground. You think you're going to get rid of him that easily?"

I sneered at the mention of gum on my shoe and sighed. "That's the thing, Air. I don't know any of it."

"What are you talking about? You can't sense the love he has for you? The passion?"

I traced heart patterns on the tabletop, the last one pulsing in a quick neon pink before fading away. "Nope. If it would've been that easy, we'd have gotten together years ago." Flattening my palms on the table, I mustered the courage to meet my brother's gaze. "We both lived in fear of the other not feeling the same. And my powers could never detect it one way or the other."

Ares flashed a warm smile before leaning back. "Do you hear yourself, sis?"

"I don't follow." Pushing my back to the seat, I rested my hands on my lap.

"The universe made it a challenge for you, sure, but all this tells me is the feelings you and Heph have for each other are simply the same basis for most relationships—"

How strange it felt to have the tables turned. So many times, I'd been the one in his shoes, advising on love, loss, and companionship.

"And that is?"

The warm smile on his face turned downright gooey. "Blind faith."

"Love looks good on you, Air." I reached across the table to poke him. "Real good."

"Yeah, yeah. Now, stop doubting yourself *and* Heph, live for the moment, and for the love of Olympus, let me finish that beer?" He jutted his chin at the bottle with only three sips taken from it.

I laughed, happy tears forming in my eyes, and slid the bottle across the table to him. Ares caught it and downed the hoppy liquid within three gulps, wiping the back of his hand over his beard once finished.

"You're okay with this, though. Me and Heph?"

Ares stifled a belch with a fist pressed to his chest before shaking his head at me. "Vlakás. You two, I swear. You're both going to do what you want regardless of my opinion, and you *should*. But if my blessing means that much to you, I'm damn glad it's Heph of all the numbskulls you could've picked, sis."

Snorting a laugh, I continued to trace hearts on the table, visions of Heph smiling down at me fluttering through my mind. "He can be a crazy, silly man sometimes. But he's my perfect level of silly, you know?"

"I do. And I'm glad you're finally getting to be more yourself."

Mental and emotional exhaustion claimed far more of a toll on me than any physical variety could ever do. Yawning, I dragged a hand over my face. "I should get some rest. I appreciate you hanging out with me, big bro."

"Anytime, but hey—" Ares moved next to me in the booth so we both faced the same direction with a clear view of the entire bar. "We haven't played it in a while. For old time's sake, how about a quick game of All's Fair?"

All's Fair. A childish game we played as tiny gods with mortals as our pawn pieces. We'd each use our powers, making the mortals either want to fight each other or kiss and hug. One of us would eventually get tired or bored and lose concentration and the other would be declared the winner.

"You're on, brother."

As I stretched my hands, Ares wiggled his fingers, his palm resting on the table. Tiny tendrils of red fog swirled his knuckles before settling into the air—a quick and subtle display undetectable to the mortal eye.

The biker woman at the bar slammed her fists down and pointed at the bartender. "Would it kill you to pour drinks with over a thimble full of liquor?"

The bartender snapped his gaze from the boxing match playing on the hanging television to the sudden irate customer, frowning. "What the hell are you talking about, Bernice? Half the time, you order a damn beer."

Oh, this was almost too easy. Ares didn't stand a chance.

Tossing my hair over one shoulder, I exaggerated cracking

my knuckles by interlacing my fingers and turning my palms away. Ares continued to work his magic, his gaze pulsing red as he eyed me side-long. Smiling, I fanned my hand, sending the swirls of my magic into the air in rotating tendrils of shimmering pink and gold.

"Ah, hell. Why are we fighting? The only reason I come into this shit dive is to see you," Biker Woman said, wringing her hands together.

The bartender threw a towel over his shoulder and leaned on the bar in front of her. "Really? You hardly say a word when you're sitting here."

"Because I'm too nervous to talk to you. Most guys are intimidated by me and the hog I ride."

A flash of white shone through the bartender's peppered beard in a radiant smile. "Yeah? Well, I think it's damn sexy."

Ares grunted beside me, balling his hand into a fist, the red fog growing denser, floating from his arm and into his hand.

Biker Woman had been grinning, but now her face contorted into a scowl. "Sexy? Why? Because I'm a woman?"

"What?" The bartender slapped the towel between them. "You can't take a compliment?"

Okay. That tore it.

Pinching my brows together, I opened my hand, fully facing my palm at them. The pink shimmers glowed brighter within my power.

"I'm afraid," Biker Woman whispered.

The bartender's expression melted, and he bent forward, slipping his hand over hers. "There's no reason to be."

Plucking the tip of my tongue against my teeth, I fanned my

hand, ready to bring these two love birds home. The bartender moved his lips to hers, and they shared a brief kiss.

"Shit," Ares grumbled beside me, dousing his power and shaking his head. "I give up."

After performing a small victory dance from the confinements of the booth, I elbowed my brother in the side. "If it makes you feel any better, you were doomed from the start. No sooner had I tapped into these two, I could tell they'd been pining for each other for months."

"Hm," Ares started, repeatedly raking his fingers through his beard. "Two people pining but too afraid to tell the other. Why does that sound so familiar?"

"Ha. Ha."

"Are we still eighty-twenty? I lost track in the last decade."

I had eighty percent of the wins to Ares's twenty.

"Yup." Flashing him a winner's smile, I tugged on his sleeve before shimmying across the booth seat. "I'm going to scoot. Let me know if you hear from Heph."

"Won't need to, sis. You'll see him real soon. Trust me."

And I did trust Ares. But waiting for a man I'd recently discovered was my *own* aphrodisiac gave me all forms of unfamiliar impatience.

Finding a suitable area outside and away from prying eyes, I ported myself home. I'd made my sanctuary as cozy as possible when I first designed it, but these past few days, no manner of interior decorating could help escape the fact—it felt empty. No vibrance. No nerdy corners of gaming consoles and Legos. No adorable little bunny greeting me. I always did have a thing for rabbits.

Walking into my bedroom, I eyed the pale pink chandelier hanging from the ceiling, speckles of stardust flickering for the lights versus bulbs. A sheer curtain hung over the single window in the room, white strings of lights behind it, an opaque backing shielding the sun from outside. Several paintings I'd collected through the years adorned the walls, but they missed something. After tapping my finger against my lips, I snapped my fingers, making a pink neon heart appear above the headboard.

There were hidden alcoves in this place that I'd kept a shielding spell over. Disguised pieces of myself I feared anyone finding out about—floor-to-ceiling shelves of romance books, my pink action figure collection, the array of tabletop games only the Graces knew of. Things had changed, however, so why did I care what people thought? Not to mention, who the Tartarus did I ever have in here *aside* from the Graces?

"Screw it," I whispered, moving to the side room with the office mirage.

After swiping my hand through the air, the office décor shimmered away. Pink and white shelves with a ladder on tracks to reach the highest points appeared, filled with books divided into categories and spine colors. A rotating turnstile with my favorite tabletop games, including *Catan* and one based on the movie *Labyrinth*, including a bag of varied number-sided dice resting in the corner. A transparent portion of the shelving housed my action figure collection, all forms of pink variants of known toys or characters known for the default coloring. Grinning, I flickered my fingers at the shelving, beaming pink and white backlighting—an idea I admittedly stole from Heph's console display.

Satisfied to see this piece of myself again, I strolled to my bedroom and sulked on the fluffy white comforter. After staring at my rose-patterned area rug, I summoned the sword Heph created for me. The goddess of love not only wielding a weapon but enjoying it. Written myths be damned, I say. Heph had a point—maybe we *did* write our destinies.

Scents of fire and oil surrounded me, and I tensed, wrapping my hand around the sword's hilt. Warm breath skirted down my neck before a whispered, "Hey ya, Peach," fluttered against my skin.

Gasping, I pushed to my feet, whirling around and slanting the blade near—Heph's throat. "Heph?"

Heph darted his gaze to the sword before tracing back to me. "Nice reflexes. Hope I didn't make you that mad taking a bit to get back?"

"Heph," I blubbered, dropping the sword and fast crawling over the bed to reach him. Uncontrollable sobbing overtook me as I hugged him, craving his sturdy arms around me.

Heph wrapped my waist with one arm, the other hand combing my hair before resting on the back of my head. "Ro, baby. Did you think I changed my mind?"

"I wasn't sure what to think," I mumbled against his chest.

Heph sank to his knees, resting me on the edge of the bed and settling between my legs. "Well, sweetheart, I'm in this for the long haul so long as you'll have me."

Smiling and beaming, I took his face in both hands, brushed my lips with his, and smacked him on the shoulder. "Where *were* you all this time?"

Heph winced and squeezed my thighs. "'spose I deserved that. It's an honest to Olympus good excuse."

Folding my arms in a mock huff, I arched a brow. "I'm listening."

"The bounty Hip claimed he dropped on us? He told a half-truth." He slid the jacket from his shoulders, tossing it on the bed beside me.

"Which part was true?"

Heph scooted me further onto the bed using one arm, the other supporting him as he crawled over me. "He took the bounty down on *us*, but not the one still up on *you*. Even raised the reward amount."

"What?" I breathed out, momentary panic rattling my bones.

Heph gave two pecks to my lips before moving to my neck, and sucking on it. "Relax. I took care of it. That's why it took me a few days."

Closing my eyes, I chewed on my lip as his trail of kisses reached my stomach, his fingers pushing the camisole to my ribs. "Did you kill anyone?"

"As a matter of fact—" Heph slid a hand down my shorts, those hardened fingertips finding my folds. "—no. Didn't have to."

Letting out a moaning sigh, I tangled my fingers in Heph's chocolate hair. "And—" I gulped, feeling one finger slip inside me. "—and, Hippo?"

"Will have to keep an eye on him. He sorta…disappeared." Heph slid a second finger inside, using his thumb to work my clit as he pumped in and out of me in languid strokes.

I clenched around him, my nails scraping Heph's scalp, and

pushed out a breathy, "What?"

"There's something bigger at play here, Peach." He moved his mouth back to my stomach, his beard tickling my skin as he swirled his tongue around my belly button. "But it's nothing we can't handle. We're a fucking force to be reckoned with." A third finger pressed into me, one gliding back and forth over my spot.

It's nothing *we* can't handle. The words alone were almost enough to send me over the edge.

"But what—" My legs shook as he timed his circling thumb with each rub and thrust. "—what's your plan?"

He kissed me, his tongue pushing between my lips to reunite with mine, and suckled on my bottom lip as he pulled away. "*Our* plan, should be enjoying the quiet time granted to us. I want to take every possible moment I have to be with my love-y goddess."

His finger pumping picked up the pace, and my back arched from the bed, hands gripping his shoulders, his neck. A chime sound went off on my phone. I ignored it. That was until it chimed a second time, and I caught the name flashing on my smartwatch.

"Shit," I said, out of breath and sorts. "It's Eros."

Heph froze, fingers resting inside me but not moving. "The irony of that is disturbing."

"Heph, we need to talk to him. It's been eating me up, and he's worried about why I've been so quiet and distant."

Heph tapped his thumb against my clit, making my hips jerk. "And you want to do that now? *Right* now?"

"Yes?" I elongated the "e" as I contemplated how to answer

him.

Stopping mid finger bang wasn't exactly something I wanted to do, but I also knew I wouldn't be able to stop thinking about my son worrying.

Heph sighed and rested his forehead on my stomach before slipping out of me. "Yeah. You're right. The sooner we do this, the sooner I see how mad he is at me for knocking up his mum." He smirked and adjusted my shorts.

"He can't be too mad. It's why he exists." I propped on my elbows and traced a hand down Heph's face scar.

Heph nodded and stared at the new neon heart blazing above us on the wall. "That new?"

"Yeah. Found myself missing the neon." A smile grazed my lips—thankful and content.

Heph's eyes sparkled as if grinning, but the action didn't follow through to his mouth.

"Eros is a smart man with an insanely good head on his shoulders, Phai. Not sure where he got that from *either* of us. He'll be shellshocked at first, but he'll come around. And I *know* he won't hate you."

Heph slid from the bed and slapped each side of his face before circling his beard with one hand. "Right. We better get to it, Ro, before I wuss out."

Standing, I morphed a simple t-shirt, jeans, and sneakers to my form and took Heph's hand. We appeared in front of Eros's door, and I paused with my hand raised, ready to knock.

TWENTY-SIX

HEPH

IT'S NOT AS IF I never met Eros before now, but not in this manner and with this new knowledge. I'd always felt some unexplained connection to him but chalked it up to my feelings toward Aphrodite at the time. Hephaistos—intergalactic bounty hunter, slayer of monsters, and commander of volcanoes now trembling over the idea of being a daddy. There were crazier things in the world, I suppose.

Aphrodite paused with her fist raised to the door, her gaze cutting to me, the gleam in her eye tying a knot in my gut.

"What?" I whispered, wincing as I prepared for impact.

"You also have a granddaughter," she blurted before slamming her knuckles against the door several times.

An invisible cyclops' foot kicked me in the nuts, and I grabbed the doorframe to steady myself. Before I had a moment to process the family I'd inherited, to practice in my head for the umpteenth time what I would say to my son, the door whisked open—and there he stood.

Eros quirked a brow as he shifted his gaze between us. "Mom." He squinted at me, drumming his fingers on the wall inside the apartment. "Don't take this the wrong way, Heph. But what are *you* doing here?"

I stood dumbfounded, staring at him. A pair of blue eyes that were the exact replicas of Aphrodite's. The same slant in his nose as mine, the same jawline. And when he'd smiled upon seeing his mum on the other side of the door before spotting my ratty mug, it took the same shape as hers. If I'd doubted Ro for a second about him being our son, not that I had, but there'd be no mistaking it now.

Aphrodite let out a nervous laugh and wrapped a hand around my bicep to guide me. "We need to talk, Cupie."

The tip of Eros's tongue skirted the corner of his mouth, his gaze still scanning me before stepping aside. "Alright. This is nothing bad, is it?"

I sure hope not.

"Nope. Not bad. Just—news." Ro's voice had suddenly gained an octave, a trait of hers when she was an adorable bumbling bundle of nerves.

Eros shut the door behind us, rolled his neck and shoulders, and a broad set of bright white wings flared from his back. They stretched to the tips, feathers rustling before he folded them behind him with a deep sigh.

Majestic. There was no other word to describe them. And our *love* created them. Fucking unreal.

Aphrodite tapped her fingertips together, and all I wanted to do was hug her to my side, but I knew she wanted to ease everyone into this slowly. "You wouldn't happen to have any Ambrosia wine lying around, would you?"

The skin between Eros's eyes wrinkled, and he bit back a smile. "You, drinking before noon? This has to be *some* news."

"Please, Eros?" Aphrodite slid her hands into her back pockets.

"Yeah, uh, okay. Pretty sure there's some left in the fridge from our anniversary."

Anniversary with his soulmate no doubt.

"The Missus, huh?" Words inexplicably remembered how to form over my tongue.

Eros's head ducked into the fridge, returning with a plain brown jug half full of liquid. The arch of his wings twitched as he reached into a cabinet, producing three glasses and filling them.

"Yeah. She's off flying and working." Eros handed me a glass, still giving me the peculiar side-long gaze.

"Thanks. Cheers." I tipped my glass before sipping.

Aphrodite curled both hands around her cup and waited for Eros to sit across from us before guzzling some down.

"Alright, Mom, out with it. The anticipation is killing me, and the tension in here is thicker than granite." Eros adjusted, putting the chair's back between his torso and the wings.

I decided to grow a pair and leaned forward. "Your mum and I are—together."

"That's it?" Eros looked between us before chuckling. "That's your news? As a fellow god of love, Mom, all I have to say to that is—about damn time." Eros lifted his glass.

Ro and I exchanged glances before we obliged, raising our cups and sipping.

"Well, I'm glad to hear that because Heph, he's—" Aphrodite took a deep breath and straightened her back. "—he's your dad."

Eros sputtered wine, misting it in the air between us. His eyes widened, and he dragged his hand over his mouth. "How? I mean, wait—" He set the wine glass on a table behind him and waved his hands. "I don't mean *how*. I'd rather not hear that. I mean, you told me *you* made me." Eros glared at me before softening his expression and looking back to his mum. "Alone."

I suppose I deserved that too. A lot of that going around today.

"I *did* think that. Because one day you—appeared." Aphrodite rose, moving to stand in front of Eros with her palms pressed together. "Where I've been, and why I couldn't contact anyone, is with Heph. In the future. In the Neosphere District."

Leaving the whole bounty deal out of the equation made her an absolute gem. Explaining spacetime would be bad enough without adding in the bit on my poor decision-making skills.

The gleaming white feathers in Eros's wings bristled, and he rubbed the dark stubble on his chin. "Alright, so you were in the future. How does that circle back to me?"

Swigging back the rest of my wine, I spread my legs wider and hung my hands between them. "Ro and I didn't admit our feelings to each other until the future. Which left everything in the past hanging in the balance until the situation arose." I paused to gauge his reaction to how batshit crazy I sounded.

Eros squinted one eye, his cheek twitching, the cleft in his chin wrinkling. "Go on."

"It's called a causal loop where events can co-exist through different time spectrums. Spacetime, to be exact. You were born in the past but *conceived* in the future."

Eros blew a harsh breath and slumped in his chair, holding his head in his hands. "Time is an odd, odd bird."

Aphrodite took several hesitant steps forward before resting her hand on our son's shoulder. "What are you thinking? How much do you hate me?"

"Hate you?" Eros lifted his head, a single wavy piece of dark hair falling over his forehead that he batted away. He patted Aphrodite's hand. "Why would I hate you? You had no idea. I guess I—" His Adam's apple bobbed as he gulped, and his gaze met mine. "—I feel a bit robbed."

You and me both, kid.

"I know and I'm so sorry for that, Cupie." Ro's voice wavered as if on the verge of tears.

Rising, I moved to her side, rubbing her arms to soothe her.

"I have no idea why this happened to us the way it did. It could be the universe's way of punishing me because punishing *you* is far worse for me."

"Hey, Mom. Don't talk like that." Eros stood and took one of Aphrodite's hands in his. The three of us stood in the same space for the first time since discovering we were a family, my son and I comforting the woman I loved who could only find it in her heart to blame herself.

"Look, Heph, I hope you understand that I'll need a little time to let this sink in." Eros rubbed the back of his neck, wings drooping.

"I've known longer than you have, and I'm still processing it, kid. Take all the time you need. Not expecting you to call me pops anytime soon." I offered my hand for a shake. "But any time you want to make up for lost years and throw down some rugby or go hunting 'er some shit, say the word, and I'm there."

A thick laugh escaped Eros's chest, and he shook my hand—confident and firm. "Deal."

"Olympus," Aphrodite squeaked, hands fanning her face, cheeks turning rosy.

We had twenty seconds tops before Aphrodite burst into happy, blubbering tears.

"Ro." I cupped her chin.

Eros rubbed her shoulder. "Mom, please don't cry."

And here came the waterworks.

"I can't help it," she stammered through sobs of joyful tears, each one falling, shimmering more than the last. Aphrodite hopped up to wrap an arm around our shoulders, forcing us into a three-way hug.

I kissed Ro's cheek and patted her back, nodding to my son, who damn near mimicked my actions.

"Listen, I need to open the bar, but did you want to say hi to Hedone really quick?" Eros asked.

Sniffling and dabbing her eyes, Aphrodite stepped back. "Is she in her room?"

"Yeah, napping. But no reason you can't make a quiet visit."

And Hedone must've been the granddaughter Ro sprung on me at the last minute.

"Heph? You up for that?" Aphrodite outstretched her hand

to me.

My heart hammered in my chest, and I still took her hand with a shrug. "I've already dived in this deep, I might as well shoot to touch the bottom, eh?"

I let Aphrodite crack open the door, considering I had the finesse of a wild boar at keeping quiet. The room remained dark save for a scattering of wall lights spilling a calming blue like a water's reflection. A white crib with curved drapes surrounding its edges nestled in the center, a mobile hanging above it with rotating birds, stars, and moons, *Fly Me to the Moon* by Frank Sinatra lightly playing from it.

My heart made a thunderclap in my chest as Aphrodite led me to the crib. I tightened my grip on her hand, and Ro squeezed back, offering me a warm smile. I'd been staring at Aphrodite, and despite standing right next to a little cherub who was also my granddaughter, I had yet to look down at her. Still smiling, Aphrodite pointed.

I had no idea ice chips remained at the corners of my heart, but one look at her and they melted, collecting in a gooey puddle in my stomach. A baby goddess with the tiniest set of tan wings and a head of fiery red hair slept soundlessly, her miniature chest rising and falling with every breath she took.

"She's—" I rubbed the calluses on my right hand together, reminding myself of the rough and gruff nature I lived by, but still somehow found moments for softness. "—beautiful."

"Isn't she?" Aphrodite whispered, resting her head on my shoulder. "And I hear she's quite the handful since figuring out how her wings work."

Visions of what my son may have looked like at this age

sparked in my mind. Did he have the same chubby cheeks? The same wings?

"Did Eros look like this?"

Ro nuzzled my arm. "Somewhat. He was far chubbier, had a mess of wavy brown hair—" She ruffled my head of dark locks with a grin. "—and his wings were gray at that age."

"Like ash." I glanced down at her with hooded lids.

She tilted her head back to look at me, reeling me in with those blue whirlpools she called eyes. "Yeah. Like *ash*."

"You think Eros would like a new bow? I'm not sure how to connect with him at this point other than—"

One of Ro's fingers pressed to my lips, silencing me. "He'd *love* a new bow. Especially from Olympus' forge god and his *dad*."

"Can we head back to your place, Ro?" I gave a final glance at Hedone, who let out a small yawn, tiny spit bubbles forming at the corners of her mouth.

"Of course, let's go say goodbye to Eros." Aphrodite reached a gentle hand to Hedone's head, stroking it. "Sleep well, little cherub."

The sight had my heart singing as much as breaking. I knew precisely what Eros meant when he said he'd felt robbed. The fury spun in me, blazing up my spine and arms. I'd never see a baby Eros cradled in Ro's arms. Never be on constant guard he'd fly into a ceiling fan or laugh at Ro when he'd let out a surprise whizz in her face. Fucking. Robbed.

I took a moment, putting the sight of Hedone in her crib to memory. To try by some warped sense of hope, the universe would intertwine lost remembrance of Eros to my mind, making some of it, any of it, come back to me.

"Ready?" Aphrodite whispered, cupping my elbow.

Once I nodded, she ported us back to her apartment—to a room I hadn't remembered existing before. Bookshelves with hundreds of titles lined the walls, a turning display with board games, and even a special shelf section for dozens of toys and action figures backlit with a neon pink hue.

"And what, pray tell, is all this, love-y goddess?"

To say I was impressed would've been a gross understatement. I was fucking floored.

"A side of me I never show anybody. This doesn't freak you out, right?" Aphrodite scratched the tip of her perky nose.

Still ogling the nerdom surrounding us, I took her hand and placed it on my pants, where a raging boner ensued underneath. "That answer your question, babe?"

Her cheeks flushed crimson, and she bit her thumbnail, peculiarly seeming nervous to show it all to me—a forge god with a Lego collection and cubicles of gaming systems.

"Here. I wanted to show you something," Ro said, snatching a velvet bag from the top of the gameboard turnstile. She removed a chrome twenty-sided die and placed it in my palm. "This one always reminded me of you."

The die shone in bright reflective silver, tiny fake rivets at the corners of every number. "Ah. Is that why the numbers are worn off in places? Rubbing one out with it?" Bobbing my brows, I lowered the die near my dick.

Giggling, she thwacked my arm. "No. I use it the most."

How this goddess thought herself to be anything less than perfect at any given moment baffled me.

Trailing my thumb under her bottom lip, I kissed her and smiled against her cheek. "Why would you assume I'd think any of this weird? It's not like you have a Jar-Jar Binks shrine somewhere, right?"

She squinted one eye and looked away.

Any erection I had? Gone. Dead. Buried. "Ro? You don't… right?"

After a few beats, she burst into laughter, pointing at me. "Meesa so got you."

"Olympus," I pushed out, pretending to hold my chest from an impending heart attack.

Aphrodite slipped her arms around my neck, resting her chin on my chest and peering up at me. "Are you okay, Phai?"

"A little overwhelmed. But then I think about how only weeks ago I thought I'd live the rest of eternal existence alone, and now—" I pressed my lips to the top of her head. "I've got not only you, but an entire family."

"Pretty wild, right?"

The urge to call Aphrodite *something*, a label of some kind, made an itch form at the base of my spine. The term "girlfriend" didn't describe what we had well enough. "Lover" was only a centimeter of the pie. And the idea of calling her something beyond that fit about as well as two perfectly forged chain links.

"Ro," I started, grasping each of her shoulders and coaxing her back so I could look her in the face. "We've been friends for centuries, know each other better than anyone else, Tartarus, even *ourselves* at times. And we've both loved each other for far longer than either of us is willing to admit."

A pink spark ignited in those moonstone eyes. "Agreed on all accounts. What's this about?"

"Why don't we make the myth real, Ro?" My grip tightened on her. "Except the uh—the whole cheating on me with your brother deal. That could be a real drag."

Her skin shimmered in vibrant pinks and silvers, her breaths pausing. "Hephaistos, are you—"

"Marry me, Ro."

An anvil dropped to the pit of my stomach when she didn't answer right away.

"No," she said with a straight face.

The anvil tore through my gut, leaving a hole the size of Uranus. "I'm sorry. No?"

"Marriage is for kings and queens to keep their reign. I want something more with you, Heph." She took my hands, interlaced our fingers, and pulled them to her chest.

More than marriage…

"Are you saying—"

"I want an eternity bond with you." She licked her lips, the anguish in her eyes waiting for my answer, mirroring mine.

The Fates rarely performed eternity bonds. Fated bonds, soulmates, and all other forms of connecting one's soul to another in our world were far more manageable once you *found* that other said someone. But eternity bonds?

"You know that has to be blessed by the Fates, right? And we'd need witnesses. If we called on them and all we got back were crickets—think about how bleedin' embarrassing that'd be."

She shook her head and pulled me tighter against her. "They

won't deny us. This connection we have? What'd you say earlier? We're a force to be reckoned with?"

Hair fell over her gaze, and I brushed it across her forehead. "I suppose there's something special about *choosing* your destiny, hm?"

"I do have one request before we do this." She bounced on her heels and held up a single finger.

"Oh, more?"

She nudged me in the gut, making me grunt. "A date. We've never been on one, and seeing as our lives are about to get all kinds of blissfully looney, I'd like one last moment to feel—normal."

"A…date? Like, pick you up at half seven, reservations at a fancy to-do restaurant. A *date*?"

"Mmhm. In the District."

I slid my hand under her shirt, trailing my touch over her taut stomach. "The District, eh? I thought you hated that place."

"It's—grown on me," she answered through a wistful sigh.

I kissed her neck, giving it a quick nip before letting out a raspy moan. "Deal. But let me stay the night, love-y goddess. Even the *thought* of an eternal bond with you has me all forms of horny and in between." Pulling her bra aside, I traced a thumb over one nipple, groaning as I felt it pebble against my touch.

"I wouldn't have let you leave anyway, forge-god." Her head tilted back, urging me to suck the nipple I'd been teasing with my fingers.

"Well, then. *Lay* down, Ro," I commanded, pulling a wicked

grin over my lips. I twirled our favorite pair of handcuffs around a single finger and stalked toward her sprawled, naked, and ever-ready to be mine *forever*.

twenty-seven

APHRODITE

WHEN HEPH TOOK US to his place in the District, I hadn't expected him to tell me he'd be right back and return to "pick me up" like an ordinary mortal date. He left me in his apartment with a snuggling Coney resting in my lap and my roaming eyes, unable to stop gazing at all the paraphernalia littered everywhere. Eyeing the neon signs decorating his walls, I flicked my wrist, making the pink heart appear nestled right by the gaming console cubby he kept my crystal swan.

Cradling Coney in the crook of my arm, I stood and twirled my wrist several more times, conjuring shimmering pink drapes, white-starred twinkling lights, several filigrees throw pillows for the bed and a small white wooden vanity in the one vacant corner. Turning a circle to gauge my handiwork, I puckered my lips.

"Think I did too much, Coney?" I nuzzled my cheek against his. "You're right. The pillows are overkill. And I haven't told him I want to live here permanently yet, have I?"

Resting Coney on the vanity table, I stood in front of the mirror, running my hands over my chest and stomach. What to wear? What to wear?

Starting at my head, I swirled my magic, designing my hair into a high, wavy ponytail secured with a glowing holographic white band. I conjured a strapless satin metallic pink dress, a strip of folded fabric covering both breasts, and a transparent boned bodice traveling to my waist. Cloth draped from the chest piece, hanging in a diagonal and pinning to another part of flowy satin that surrounded my hips, exposed the entirety of my legs, and fell to my ankles. Touching a fingertip to the heart on my cheek, I made it extra glittery.

"Knock, knock," Heph's voice sounded from the other side of the metal door. "Are you decent?"

When he walked in, a breath caught in my throat. I hadn't expected him to wear a suit—black dress slacks, shiny wing-tipped shoes, a white shirt with black jacket, and a skinny black tie. Moisture formed between my legs, and I rolled my bottom lip past my teeth.

Heph fast-blinked at me, perusing his evening date, and taking his time. "I'd say 'damn' to not catching you in the nude, but you look breathtaking, Ro."

Turning a circle to let him get the scenic view, I slipped my hands to my hips. "Look who's talking. I don't think I've ever seen you clean up like this."

"Yeah." He grimaced, pulling the tie around his neck. "Threads like these are always so constricting. I can't remember the last time I wore them. A bounty hunt, perhaps? Maybe?"

"Well, you look stellar, babe." My body hummed for him, skin tingling with pink shimmers of affection.

He bowed before picking Coney up and carrying him to his rabbit fort Heph constructed out of Legos—a two-story bunny resort with a ramp to the second floor, a grassy area for dirty business, food and water dispensers, and plenty of things to chew on.

"Ready?" Heph offered his arm, and I took it, swooping the dress's train behind me as we exited.

Eyes from Desolation Row's other inhabitants darted at us like laser beams. They weren't looks of surprise or disdain but perplexed. Considering we both looked like we belonged in Ithaca rather than the slums, I couldn't blame their curiosity.

"Where are we going?" I asked as Heph led us to the curb.

"A place in Daneland. Best fish I've ever had, and it has fancy fake fish tanks and the like." Heph approached a vehicle that reminded me of a mix between a Lamborghini and the frigging Batmobile—equal amounts of chrome and shiny black metal. It had clean, sharp lines and sat low enough to the ground that it was clear this thing could go *fast*.

"Damn, Heph. Is this yours?" I turned to the side, admiring my reflection in the car door.

Heph chuckled as he opened the vertically extending door for me. "Oh, no. I get around via portal. But you wanted things normal, so I borrowed her from Orion."

"Thank you," I flashed a smile before hitching my dress and sitting.

The interior was unlike anything I'd seen before, even with the mystical life I led. Blue holo menus and buttons covered a sleek white dashboard, and the steering wheel, a rectangular shape, only extended once Heph took the driver's seat. He swiped his hand over the holo in the middle console, and the opaque hexagon pattern covering the windshield dematerialized in a fizzle of blue.

"Want me to drive or set it on auto?" Heph asked, drumming his fingers on the steering wheel.

Crossing my legs, I leaned past him to check how high the speedometer went—over one hundred eighty kilometers. "That depends. Can you go faster if you drive it manually?"

"You bet your pretty perky ass I can." The grin that slid over Heph's lips had my insides twisting into a bout of endless sensual knots. He fanned his palm over another menu, and music blasted through the cabin—a grungy techno song with scratching electric guitar, digitalized drums, and a male voice singing.

Sounds of pistons shifting and the light engine whirring filled my ears as Heph pulled onto the street. He took advantage of my request and sought every opportunity to go as fast as possible, weaving through slower traffic, flying through caution lights, and drifting when taking tight turns. The adrenaline rush combined with speed and the grin that never left Heph's face, had me beaming inside and out. An older version of me might've been gripping my chair, but not this particular model of Aphrodite.

After several blocks, we pulled into a parking garage with floating holo numbers marking the spots. Once parked, the holo surrounded the vehicle, securing it with granted access given only to the owner. Otherwise, an alarm would sound as a warning to the perp and if they ignored it? The ground tased them, and the enforcers would arrive to cart them off.

As soon as we entered the restaurant, called "Fisk," two large tanks with holographic simulated water lined the sides, complete with dozens of animated fish of all varieties and colors. A maître d in a simple black pants suit ensemble and her hair styled in an "o" around a silver apparatus approached us stone-faced.

"Two?" She brought up a holo map from her wrist device, the strip of neon purple that started at her bottom lip and continued down her chin, glowing from the holo.

"Yes, please," Heph answered.

She motioned with two fingers for us to follow and led us to a seating area with several squared tables, two chairs at each. A shimmering canopy hung over each place setting, and our table had a prime view of the Daneland cityscape through the windows—tall buildings nestled side by side flush to each other of every primary color. Each with a dozen windows, glowing neon strobes bordering every other in a given row. A concrete boardwalk separated the buildings from a vast body of dark water, the rainbow lights reflecting on the surface.

"Isn't the water toxic around here? How are there still fish?" I took a seat as Heph pulled it out for me and helped scoot me closer to the table.

Heph tugged on his tie and sat across from me, taking a moment to scan the surrounding customers before resting his palms on the table. "Daneland had cautionary barriers in place to preserve their imported fish which sequestered this one particular lake from the rest. That's why this place is so expensive and hard to get a reservation."

"Oh?" I tossed my ponytail over a shoulder and leaned back, crossing my legs and exposing them both from the skirts. "And how did you manage to get one at the last minute?"

"I happen to be an infamous bounty hunter." He snapped the silver napkin open, draping it over one knee. "Aw, love-y goddess, did you not realize how renowned I am here?"

"I guess I hadn't. It's almost enough to demand you take me right here on the table and say to Tartarus with dinner." With a wicked curve to my lip, I bit my thumbnail, staring at him across the table, the reflective water light from the tanks casting delicious shadows over his face.

"Mm. Is that so?" He stared back at me with a devious glint in his eye before his foot wrapped around my chair leg, pulling me closer. "You're much too far away over there."

Resting my elbows on the table, I interlaced my fingers and set my chin atop my hands, smiling at him like a lovesick fool. "I love you, Phai."

"Love you too, Ro." A sheepish smile crept on his lips, and he grabbed the glass decanter filled with a glowing purple liquid, filling our glasses. "But can I ask what I did to warrant a sudden blurb of affection?"

I took the glass from him, sipping—grape-flavored with undertones of caraway and citrus. "Nothing. Just needed to be said, is all."

"I'll take it." Heph pressed a button in the middle of the table, pulling up a holo menu of an array of fish dishes prepared differently. "You trust me to order for you?"

"Of course I do." I pointed at him with my glass-holding

hand. "So long as it *is* fish and not some random animal you don't tell me about."

He grinned, the light of the menu glinting from his chocolate eyes. "Here we are. Grilled halibut with horseradish sauce. Safe enough, right?"

"Sounds perfect."

Just like this moment, the forge god sitting next to me, my newly-formed godly life…

Within seconds of Heph ordering our food, it arrived in the hands of a shorter fellow with a bald head, and a swirly patterned tattoo covering the back of his skull. He reached through the opening of our canopy, resting our plates on the table before whisking away as if he were but a passing spring breeze.

"This looks delicious," I said, scooping a fork into my hand to dig into the spiced white fish, asparagus sprigs, and a mix between lingonberries and horseradish sauce, but paused mid-bite. "Heph?"

Heph sat rigidly, his hands gripping the table's edges as he filled his cheeks with air, staring at his plate.

"Hephaistos, you look like you're about to be sick."

His lip curled back, and his eye twitched. "It didn't say anything about *asparagus*."

"What do you have against asparagus?" I shoved a sprig into my mouth. "It's not as if it makes *our* pee stink."

"No, no. It's not about the piss, Ro." He balled his fist over his mouth and looked away from his plate. "Please get rid of it."

"Okay," I said suspiciously, leaning over his plate to scoop the asparagus onto mine. "Do I even want to ask?"

Heph shook his head and blew air through his nose before

eating his fish. "No, because I truly don't want to explain. All you need to know is that it was a former female encounter with bizarre—tastes."

I stopped chewing, slapping my hand over my mouth to keep the food in as I choked back a laugh. "Oh. Olympus, Heph. Any other crazy bedroom stories I should know about?"

He closed his eyes and moaned while eating the fish. "That one took the cake, but there was also one who was obsessed with gnomes."

"As in lawn gnomes? In her yard?"

"No, no." He stabbed the next piece of fish with more fervor. "Shelves of them. In her bedroom, like those creepy porcelain dolls, only gnomes. I'm not sure which is worse."

I bit my lips together to keep myself from laughing again.

"Needless to say, I couldn't stand all those beady judgmental eyes staring at me, so I high-tailed it out of there." He gave a proud curt nod.

"Can't say I have anything near as crazy as yours. Back when mortals believed in us, most of them would become terrified when they realized who I was, and now? They have this crippling fear I'll judge their every move, and they can't live up to my expectations." Smirking, I took a sip of my drink, swirling it in the glass to let it breathe.

"Are you saying you *never* judged mortals' performances?" Heph leaned on his forearm, bringing our faces closer, a snarky grin plastered to his lips.

"That—" I gave him a quick peck. "—is neither here nor there."

Heph didn't take his eyes off me for more than a few

seconds, as if I'd disappear from him again.

Smiling, I rested my chin on my hand. "Pick a couple in here. Any couple will do."

"Yeah? What for?"

I stretched my arms toward the ceiling. "I haven't had my powers for a long time. It's good to give them a stretch."

Heph chuckled and swiveled in his seat, scoping his choices and pointing at a table with two women. "How's about them?"

Squinting, I willed my powers to read them and abruptly shook my head. "Nope. They're related. And that version of this particular love goddess is dead and buried. Pick another."

"Alright then. Them." Heph nudged his head at a table near us with an older woman and a young man who physically appeared half her age.

"That—" I shifted on my seat. "—I can work with."

Discreetly wiggling my fingers, I sent the shimmering powers of passion and lust toward them. The woman had been staring at the table, but shot her gaze to the young man once my power hit her, gripping the table. The young man's eyes grew feral, and he tore off his tie, standing and moving to lift the woman into his arms and out of the restaurant.

Smiling, I waved at them as they passed before resting my chin back in my hand and peering at a befuddled Heph.

"I'd say, and call me crazy, but you haven't lost your touch, Ro." Heph chuckled and sipped his drink.

"I certainly hope not." I traced my finger over the dark hair on his knuckles, curving a sultry grin.

His gaze shot to our hands. "Careful now. Our dinner will end faster than Athena running to show off at Trivia Night."

"What you got, forge-god?" Arching a brow, I shifted my gaze to the mortals surrounding us.

"Hm." Heph rubbed his chin, the hand resting on the table closest to me turning black as he morphed his arm into the forge.

One woman at the table of two he'd pointed out earlier picked up her fork that'd turned into multiple forks melted together. "What the hell?"

The other woman furrowed her brow, picking up what used to be her butter knife. "Is this a—mace?"

I slapped a hand over my mouth, squelching the laughter that burst from my lungs.

"Bout the best I can do, love." Heph turned back to face me, smiling, his eyes glistening with mischief.

Several screams leaked through the windows outside, a group of people running from a different group of people chasing them. I glanced in their direction but cleared my throat and snapped my gaze back to my plate.

Heph's face appeared in front of mine. "You want to interfere, don't you?"

"What? Don't be absurd. We're enjoying a pleasant evening." The next bite of food proved harder to swallow.

"You. Do." Heph let out a gruff chuckle. "I think I created a monster."

He had no idea.

Clanking my fork to the plate, I uncrossed my legs, stomping my heels to the ground. "Okay fine. I do."

"Uh-huh. What happened to normal?"

I wiped my mouth with the cloth napkin. "This has been

wonderful, but I guess I realized that normal for people like us is—overrated?"

"I couldn't agree more." He tugged on his tie, loosening it to hang limp around his neck, and swiped his wrist over the device in the middle of the table to pay. "Shall we, then?"

Flashing a broad smile, I tossed the napkin to the table and stood, slipping my arm with this, excitement sizzling over my skin. I could've changed our clothes with one snap of my fingers, but there was something especially tantalizing about us fighting in evening wear attire I had to test.

Once we reached the foyer, I ported us to the end of the docks, where the apparent baddies had cornered a group of people. The relief it gave to freely use my real name in public and port out in the open was pure ecstasy.

Snarling, Heph tore the tie from his neck and tossed it aside along with the jacket to roll up his shirt sleeve and ignite the forge. "Pardon the fuck out of us for the *interruption*, biffies."

"Mind your own damn business. This doesn't concern you," a man with a mullet, glowing red eyes, and circuit boards over both cheeks spat.

"They're trying to rob us," a woman with a red cocktail dress cowering against a pylon cried out.

A woman with hair shaved on one side and the other half dyed bright green armed with a spiked bat raised it toward the screeching woman's head. "You'll shut your fucking mouth if you know what's good for you."

I hurled my magic at the threatening bat woman, lashing her with a blast of sparkles and making her drop her weapon. In the same instance, Heph materialized his hammer axe. The four would-be robbers turned to face us, two armed with rifles.

"Run," I shouted to the three they'd threatened.

The high slit in my dress made for flexible maneuverability as I whirled in circles, sending spirals of pink energy any time one lunged at me. I'd tried to summon the more powerful energy mixed with lightning sparks, but still came up short. Heph swung his axe at one rifle, slicing it in half before slamming the blunt side of it into their face, rendering them unconscious. I thought of making my sword appear but acted cautiously because I'd still only used it a handful of times. My magic, however, felt closer to home.

We'd only been battling them for mere minutes before two held their bloody noses and, through strained voices, shouted, "Let's get the hell out of here."

I swirled my dress behind me, letting my powers bubble in my palm to ensure they weren't bluffing. Heph stepped beside me, dousing the blazing forge from his arm, that tanned muscular forearm re-appearing. Lust rippled through me, mixed with adrenaline, and I kissed him, leaping and wrapping my legs around his waist.

He smiled against my lips and kissed me back. Grabbing my ass, he pulled me tighter against him. I ported us to his apartment, still kissing him, devouring him, imagining what sex would be like once we were eternally bonded. His hand slid into the slit of my dress, fingers slipping inside me.

I pulled back, already breathless and ravenous. "Do you still have that chained choker?"

"You're so fucking naughty, Peach." He bit the air in front of me, smiling as he dragged his hand around my neck, the requested choker appearing unattached to a dress this time.

Wiggling my fingers at our clothes, I made them disappear as pink glitter and ash floated into the air. I licked his bottom lip, rubbing myself against his stomach, my legs still wrapped around him. "How do you want me?"

His eyes blazed with darkness and need, his hand fisting the chain hanging between my breasts. Gently but with a firm tug, he guided me downward until I slid from his hips and rested on my knees, the tip of his cock grazing my lips. With his hand still entwined with the chain, he pulled me forward. I looked up at him as I took him into my mouth, keeping our gazes locked.

He groaned as I began to suck, flicking the head with casual laps of my tongue, and stroking his shaft in tandem. I took more of him until I could feel it hitting the back of my throat. He palmed my head, making me pause, and using the chain, pulled my mouth on and off him—full-on fucking my mouth, and I couldn't get enough of it.

Growling, he pulled me to my feet with the chain, his head dipping to my breasts, licking, sucking, and biting my nipples. "Lay on your stomach." He nudged his chin at the bed, leading me to it with the chain, the volcanic lava surging within him glowing in his veins and igniting in his gaze.

Licking my lips, I lay down with my ass in the air. Heph kept hold of the chain, keeping it taut, grabbing my hips, and hoisting them higher. His mouth pressed to my pussy from behind, tongue slathering my folds before plunging inside me. I bunched the sheets in my palms, whimpering, and writhing.

Without warning, Heph pushed my ass down, my hips

pressing into the bed, and his cock dove into me, his chest pressing against my back. He rolled in and out, kissing the back of my head, and my cheek. His grip tightened on the chain, the other arm wrapping around my shoulders, holding me steady as he pounded me.

"Cross your ankles," he whispered against my hair.

I did, and the intensity soared tenfold, making me cry out.

"You're going to come with me, Ro." His words fluttered over my ear, gritty and in *complete* control.

Nodding, I bit my lip, already on the verge of crashing over the edge before him. He grunted as he thrust faster, his balls slapping against my ass.

"Now baby," he hoarsely whispered, his body tensing behind me as he gave one final pulse and paused inside me to allow the climax to roll over him in waves.

I screamed into the sheets, my magic swirling around us as rapture seized me.

The tautness on the chain slackened as Heph let go and rolled to his back. I smiled at him, peeking one eye from my hair that'd fallen over my face, tracing a finger down the sparkling chain. Heph grinned back, chuckling, and parting the hair away.

"So, what do you say, Phai?" I propped on my elbows. "Will you bond with me?"

"Hey, I'm supposed to be the one proposing to *you*." He dragged a finger down the length of my nose.

I sat up and curled my arms around my knees. "Then ask me again."

"Aphrodite," he sat back on his haunches and held my

hands. "As we sit here naked as sin, satiated and gleaming with sweat, would you do me the honor of eternally binding yourself to me?"

That couldn't have been more of a unique proposal from the volcano god.

I laughed, my vision blurring with tears, and tackled him, landing on top. "Yes, Hephaistos. A million times, yes."

"Grand," he teased, lazily dragging a finger over my breasts. "When would you like to do this, Ro? Where?"

"I was thinking maybe somewhere here in the Fringes? Between the Graces and me we could make some pretty decent scenery and be away from the crowds."

"Whatever you want, baby. I've heard the dudes are usually just there to say, 'I do,' and more or less go along for the ride." He chuckled, running his thumb over the heart on my cheek.

"I'm going to need at least a day to come up with this dress. I want it to be something to *really* wow you." Heph's mouth opened, and I clapped a hand over it. "And don't you say anything I do will wow you. I mean it."

He held his palms up and I lowered my hand. "Alright, I'll hang out with the mates tomorrow then."

"Ooo, like a bachelor party?" I rested my chin on his chest, swirling my finger over the light scattering of dark hair.

"Sure. Why not? Did you want me to wear something specific for this shindig?"

I pressed a kiss to his pec. "I want you to be you, Heph. You could show up naked for all I care."

"Now, if I do that, Ares will get all hot and bothered. It could be quite the distraction."

Laughing, I swatted his shoulder and nestled my head in the crook of his shoulder. "Eternity, Phai."

"Gia aioniótita," he whispered.

TWENTY-EIGHT

HEPH

"ALRIGHT, YOU TWATS, THINK." I sat at a picnic-styled table with Ares and Eros across from me, Orion to my right. We'd decided on the ever-growing popular mortal sport of axe-throwing in the modern world back on Earth for my makeshift "bachelor party." "Who the fuck could this *sovereign* possibly be?"

Ares groaned, swigging back more Ambrosia wine before plopping his head on the table. "We've been through this, Heph. *Three* times."

"Oh, excuse me if I want to know what we're up against," I scoffed, snatching my bottle and sloshing more wine into my gullet.

Orion scratched the stubble under his chin. "How could you begin to guess what we're up against if you don't know who or what it is? You're going to drive yourself crazy over this."

"I, for one, am glad the conversation shifted away from my mom." Eros rolled the sleeves of his plaid shirt to his elbows.

Ares grumbled as he lifted his head and reached across the table to rapidly tap me on the forearm. "Aderfé, listen to me. Your question will answer itself soon enough. For now, agáli-agáli gínetai i agourida méli. Naí?"

Whenever Ares started drinking in copious amounts, he spoke more Greek, favoring proverbs above all else.

"*You* be patient," I mumbled, sipping more wine.

Alright, what he said was far more profound than a simple one-word suggestion, but thinking in Greek tended to give me a godly migraine.

Ares flicked his hands at me as if I could not be helped.

"Did we come here to yap or sling some metal?" Orion looked around at the group.

Slapping my hands on the table, I shot to my feet. "Right you are, Orry. Right you are. Throwing sharp objects is precisely what I need to distract myself."

As I moved to the target area, Eros turned his back to Ares and pointed between his shoulder blades. "Hey, Unc, itch my back, will you?"

What an odd request.

Ares dropped a glare at my son's back and leaned away. "What the hell for?"

"*They*," Eros emphasized without saying the actual word. "Have gotten spoiled lately and make me itch to release them way more often than ever."

His wings. Not sure how I could've forgotten them after seeing their entire span not even a day ago.

A bin of axes rested behind the throwing line, and I rummaged through them, grimacing at the shoddy excuses for weapons. Most of them didn't even have the entire handle intact, much less serve as anything beyond a butter knife.

"Why don't you use the wall or something?" Ares turned away, grabbing his bottle with both hands to indicate they were otherwise engaged.

Eros rolled his eyes.

"Oh, scratch the boy's back for Olympus' sake, you grumpy knob," I shouted, still perusing the axe selections and settling on the one that made me sneer the least.

Growling, Ares re-positioned on the bench and quickly ran his fingers over Eros's back before snapping his hand away.

"Did you *do* anything? That felt like a gust of wind." Eros arched a brow over his shoulder.

Ares slammed the bottle on the table and pointed at him. "Vlakás. If your leg starts bouncing like a damn skýlos, I'm done. Akoús?"

"I think I can resist considering I'm *not* a canine."

After giving a curt nod, Ares used both hands and furiously scratched Eros's back, being sure to move vertically and horizontally.

Eros's hand curled into a fist on the table before he let out a loud moan.

Ares abruptly stopped, flew his palms up, and stood. "Nope. Done."

"What?" Eros cut his gaze to Orion, half-smiling before attempting to wipe the grin away. "I can't help you have a soothing—touch."

Eros kept a straight face for ten seconds before he and Orion burst into uproarious laughter.

Ares snarled and shoved his palm in Eros's face, fingers spread wide and smacking the back of his hand with the other.

Not only a single moutza but a double. A lovely Greek gesture for a good 'ol-fashioned: Fuck you.

Eros didn't flinch as he let his uncle mime his disapproval, him and Orion still chuckling at the war god's expense.

Ares shook his head and took several swigs from his bottle, waltzing near me. "Now I see how he's definitely *your* son."

I winked at my brother and tossed the axe between my palms, checking its balance.

"Olympus. Are you going to play Hot Potato with it or throw the damn thing?" Ares threw his arm out at the target, baiting me.

Always one for obliging my dear, dear brother, I wound up, threw the axe—and it smacked against the target sideways without so much as trying to land home. "Fuck me dead."

I did a double-take. That couldn't be right.

Ares slapped a hand over his mouth to keep Ambrosia wine from spewing out as he burst into laughter, pointing and stumbling over his feet. "The god of axes can't throw them to save his life."

Making the walk of shame to retrieve my failed axe, I snatched it from the ground and observed its structure again. "It's the gods awful craftsmanship."

"Sure you're throwing with the correct hand, Heph?" Orion asked from the table, his hands interlaced behind his head, a dick-eating smile cracking his lips.

"I don't see either of you archers up here giving it a shot. Do I?" I pointed between Orion and my son with the axe handle.

Eros's eyes widened, and he put a hand on his chest.

"Oh, ho. Calling out your own son, huh?" Orion quipped.

Ares yanked the axe from my grasp. "Let me show you how it's done." With his bottle in one hand and the axe in the other, he squinted at the target and readied to throw.

"Um, sir?" A shaky male voice said from behind us. A younger man nearly a foot shorter than us with a polo of the establishment's name stood staring up at us and gulping.

"Yes?" Ares asked, his tone incredulous.

The poor kid's chin shook, and he gulped again before pointing at a sign hanging on an adjacent wall. "We ask that all drinks be left at the table when standing at the—at the tossing line, sir."

Ares stood toe-to-toe with the kid, his eyes flashing crimson. "Or. What?"

"Uh, I, uh—" The kid leaned away, arms jittery at his sides, eyes never blinking.

Patting Ares's arm, I coaxed him like one would the Hulk. "Come on, brother. Sun's getting real low."

Ares growled at the kid before turning and walking away. Orion offered the employee a friendly radiant smile, attempting to diffuse the situation with his inherent charm.

Axe in hand, Ares launched it from the table and into the target, still holding his drink—bullseye. "And that is how you throw an axe, *bro*. Oh, and I wasn't at the tossing line." Glaring at the employee who hitch-stepped and sprinted off, Ares chugged more wine.

"Did anyone ever tell you how cute you are when angry? Your cheeks get all rosy, your left eye twitches, and that ever so slight curl of your lip?" I flashed a grin. "Adorable."

Ares didn't acknowledge me and shook his head, sitting on the bench sideways with legs spread wide. He hunched forward and looked at Eros. "You came outta that thing's balls. Remember that."

Eros squinted one eye. "Well, thanks for *that* horrifying mental image."

"Why yes, brother, I'll get that axe for you," I yelled to Ares, walking to the target and yanking the weapon, making stray straw fly.

Grimacing, I tossed the axe back into its bucket and scanned the area to spy if anyone was looking. I crouched behind one partition, ignited the forge on my arm, and produced my own godsdamned axe.

"Cheater," Orion shouted, cupping his mouth and grinning.

"Cheating is what *you* do at cards, mate. This is called— improvising." I flicked my thumb on the point of the blade, eyes closing at the satisfying *ping* sound it gave.

Raising the axe above my head, praying to the forges this attempt would hand me my dignity back, I launched it. Bullseye—in the same hole Ares had left behind.

"Shit. Nice, Heph," Eros said.

Was it pathetic I'd felt an extra smidge of pride knowing the statement came from my *son* versus just another chum?

With a flourish, I bowed, ensuring I made eye contact with Ares as I pointed at the axe. "Did you see, brother? See it?"

"Yeah, yeah. Yours didn't hit like a wrecking ball, though." Ares snickered and combed his fingers through his beard.

That'd always been one of Ares's mottos: If you can't beat

'em, hit it as hard as you can.

Pulling the axe from the target, I whirled on my heel to face them. "What about Eris? She and Ro seem to always be in a tiff."

"Here we go again," Ares said in a huff, tilting his head back to finish his bottle.

Orion propped his feet on the bench, crossing his legs at the ankle. "No way. She's evil incarnate, sure. But sending others to do her dirty work? Not her style."

"The beef between those two is different anyway. They're not out to kill each other. More like, make each other's lives a living Tartarus kind of deal?" Eros shrugged and took a sip of his wine.

I tapped my chin with the blunt end of the axe blade. "The Erinyes?"

"What would Aphrodite have done to incur their wrath? They need to be provoked. Has she ever even met them?" Orion scrunched his nose and looked to Eros for confirmation.

Eros shook his head. "Don't look at me. Mom and I just started having an amicable relationship for the past couple of years."

"Why do you assume this is only about her, aderfé? Hm?" Ares chimed in, digging his hand into a bowl of corn nuts in the table's center.

"Funny you should say that because Hippolytus said the same thing." Impatience and fury swirled my spine, and I turned to the target, hurling the axe to drive the energy elsewhere.

"Maybe she's a catalyst for something?" Orion puckered his lips.

Ares crunched on the corn nuts, juggling some in his hand like dice. "And how the hell are we supposed to know what for?"

A pain throbbed in my temple, and I closed my eyes, rubbing it. "This whole thing is somehow giving me a bleedin' headache."

"Told you it'd drive you crazy, Heph." Orion set his feet on the floor and walked over to me, clapping a hand on my shoulder. "You're bonding with a goddess tomorrow. Focus on that, and we'll jump in head first afterward."

"I'm sure Mom would want to be part of your investigation anyway. *Especially* if it involves her." Eros held his hand out, motioning for the axe. "Now let me see if this somehow runs in the family, considering I've only ever been great at archery."

Smirking, I slapped the axe handle into his palm. "Honest to gods, not sure where you got that from. I'm horrible with a bow."

"I'll say," Ares added, his voice muffled from a mouthful of corn nuts.

Orion jostled Eros's shoulders from behind. "Must be a skipped gene from Apollo because your aim is about as crappy, Rosy."

"Ass." Eros shoved the handle into Orion's side with a sly grin. "Alright, step aside."

Eros zeroed in on his target, raised the axe, and launched. It hit just to the right of the target but whizzed through the air like he'd done it dozens of times before.

"Not bad at all—" Son. I wanted to call him my son just then but bit my tongue. There'd be a time for us to ease into this new dynamic. "Mind if I give you a few pointers?"

When Eros smiled, a shimmer of Ro's same grin gleaned in my mind. Thankfulness coursed through me, knowing our separation this time was by design and not because some conceited psychopath wanted a curse lifted. It still fired me up to no end the mark he left on her, but the serene look on her face when she told me she *liked* it, made any anger melt away.

"Be my guest." Eros yanked the axe from the target and held it out to me.

Eyeing the target, I shifted my stance to face it full-on. "You've got the aim, and there's power behind your swing. The one thing you could work on if you want to hit that target every time is your follow through." I lifted the axe above my intended target and slowly lowered it until I was in line. "Observe." The axe whistled through the air and slammed into the straw in the precise spot I'd landed it the last time.

"Ah, I think I see." Eros showed me by doing a mock throw, his fingers extending this time to push the flow in his desired direction.

"Precisely." I grinned and retrieved the axe, tossing it to him. "Again."

When Eros threw it, I saw myself in him, his poise nearly identical to mine. It was enough to make my nose burn. I gave a gruff sniff and rolled my shoulders back.

"Boom. Bullseye," Eros shouted, laughing and pointing at Orion. "Suck it, O."

"I'll stick with the elegance of bows and drinking," Orion replied, raising his bottle before sipping.

Eros walked back with the axe, glancing at his watch with a frown. "Shit. I need to get back." He handed me the axe and held his hand out to shake. "Appreciate the pointers, and I'm sorry I can't make it to the ceremony tomorrow. Hedone is a full-time job at this stage."

I shook his hand and waved off the last comment. "No need to apologize. I'm only glad you don't hate my grimy black guts."

"Not sure I have a reason to hate you. You love my mom. It's pretty clear. I should know." Eros nudged my shoulder. "And Mom wouldn't be bonding with you if you didn't treat her well."

There went my damn nose again. I cast my gaze on my boots and nodded. "Thanks for that, kid."

Eros patted my back before breezing to Ares. "Come on, Uncle. Let's get your hammered ass home."

"I'm fine," Ares growled, flapping his lips in a *pfft*.

Orion cut me a coy grin as he propped one knee on the bench seat. "Never port under the influence, Ares."

Eros hooked his arm with the war god's, guiding him toward the exit.

"You shut your pretty-ass face, Orion." Ares pointed at him and dove for the last few remaining corn nuts before letting Eros take him outside.

Orion dragged a hand through his hair and rested his head on the back wall. "Well, I'd say that went pretty well."

"Ares didn't break anything, and I managed not to make an ass of myself in front of my boy. Not half bad." I gave a one-shoulder shrug and twirled the axe.

"You staying at my place tonight? Coney's already there."

After taking a quick scan around us, I made the axe

disappear. "Do you mind? I actually need to uh—borrow some clothes."

"Clothes? From me?" Orion finished his bottle and stood.

It'd been embarrassing enough asking without him questioning it.

"Yeah. For tomorrow." I scratched my face scar. "Ro said to wear whatever I want, but I can't show up in this heap." Gesturing to the dirtied duster jacket and black pants, I spun a single circle. "And you and I seem about the same size, except for my *much* broader shoulders."

Orion stood next to me with his arms folded and shaking his head. "Only you would ask for a favor and insult someone in the same sentence."

"Is that a—yes?"

He punched my shoulder. "Yeah, I can hook you up with something. Let's head back."

No sooner had we appeared in Orion's loft, Coney hopped from his drawer and over to me. I had been neglecting him a tad as of late, the poor little fur ball. Picking him up, I laid him on his back in the bend at my elbow and scratched his belly, grinning as his left back leg kicked and his eyes closed.

"Sorry, we haven't had as much time together lately, Cone. But daddy has been busy getting you a mommy. You remember, Ro, right?"

Coney nuzzled further against me as if he understood.

Orion chuckled at my side. "And you never thought you'd make a good dad."

"I have yet to raise a miniature godly being, Orry. A rabbit can be mostly self-sufficient. I couldn't have left a winged baby to bide their own time, right?"

My mind wandered, curious as to what Aphrodite had been working up for this so-called wowing dress. If I knew her, she created a dozen dresses and put so much pressure on herself that none of them were perfect enough for her. And then the Graces would make her see the voice of reason, and all would be well in the universe. The imagery brought a cozy, familiar smile to my face.

"Well, come take a look at my closet, Heph." Orion signaled for me to follow him up the stairs to his bedroom.

He led me into a walk-in closet that was slightly smaller than my place in The Dez. Clothes were organized by style, cut, and color and hung in pristine fashion, with one wall dedicated to shelves full of various foot coverings.

"Forges, mate. Do you even wear half this shit?" Still holding Coney, I used my free hand to push hangers aside in the "dress shirt" section. It was like shopping at a fucking department store.

"You'd be surprised. Aphrodite isn't the only one that likes clothes." His blue eyes glinted as he walked the perimeter of the closet, grabbing items and draping them over an arm. "I think this will suit you fine, Heph. Not overly formal and not clothes covered in dried harpy guts."

Setting Coney on the floor, I took the clothes with a bemused expression. "I'll have you know those guts serve as mementos."

"Whatever you say." Orion leaned against the door frame. "How does it feel, by the way?"

Stripping to only my boxers, I slipped on a pair of black

pants, a tight black v-neck shirt, and a sleek black bomber-styled leather jacket with shiny silver zippers down the arms. "How does what feel?"

Orion pointed at the full-length mirror hidden in the corner. "Knowing tomorrow, you're going to be bonded for eternity. That's some heavy shit, Heph. It's not just marriage—it's soul binding."

Should I have had cold feet? Nervous? Anxious? Because I wasn't any of it. Ro and I had known each other for so long that it'd have felt more out of place to *avoid* doing it.

"It's Aphrodite, biffy. She's my world." After giving him a reassuring smile, I turned to the mirror, checked myself out, and adjusted the jacket. "Seems only fair to give her the universe back in return."

Orion appeared behind me, looking at me through the mirror's reflection. "I'm happy for you, bro. I am. And I can only hope someone is as crazy about me one day, huh?" He adjusted one zipper that was misaligned on the jacket and nodded.

"They'd have to be prettier than you, or it'd never work out, though, I'm afraid." Sparking a devious grin at him in the reflection, I nodded back. "Virto. This'll work perfectly. Thanks, brother."

"Anytime." He grabbed my shoulders from behind and shook me, plastering a wide goofy-ass smile.

With a deep breath, I took a final gaze at the clothes I'd be wearing tomorrow. Threads I'd be donning as I pledged the rest of my godly existence to the only woman, the only goddess, who not only ever gave two shits about me but also found in her heart—to love me.

twenty-nine

APHRODITE

"THIS IS SO FRUSTRATING," I said through a growl.

Seven dresses lay on my bed—poofy dresses, mermaid, flowy, cocktail—of all colors and fabrics imaginable. And not one of them satisfied me. It had to be beyond the perfect dress. A dress to make the halls of Olympus itself shine with radiance upon looking at it. All three Graces surrounded the bed, rubbing their chins and sifting through the dresses they'd spent the past several hours cooing over as I made them and agreeing when I eventually said I hated it.

"Aph, there are so many gorgeous dresses here. One of them surely is—" Thalia started but snapped her mouth shut when I lifted my hand.

Falling into a slump in my ivory high-back chair, I frowned. "I appreciate what you're trying to do, Thal, but this will only happen once in my entire existence. None of these dresses scream 'eternity' to me."

Euphrosyne tapped her lips as she paraded the bed, sporting her Coffee, Curls, Chaos shirt before snapping her fingers, making her tight dark ringlets bounce. "I got it. You obviously liked certain aspects of all these dresses, right?"

"Yes?"

"Why not pick your favorites and combine them?" Euphrosyne threw her hands to her hips.

It wasn't a half-bad idea. I wanted so much out of the dress that I'd poured every idea into each one instead of blending them.

"That—could work." With a newfound giddy-up in my stride, I leaped from the chair and back to the bed, pointing at the dress I'd made the bottom like overlapping rose petals. "The bottom will look like this."

"Ooo, yes. And are you still going to do a color fade? I noticed you did that on several, but not all." Aglaia hooked her arm with mine and rested her head on my shoulder.

The Graces didn't realize I took notice, but they often made subtle decisions to help guide me, disguising it as if only I steered the ship.

Biting my lip, I scanned the array of colors I chose for each dress, representing an entire rainbow. But who was I kidding? Most of my clothes, bedroom, and life revolved around one particular color—pink. "Hm. What do you think if I started the top as powder pink going into a gradient at mid-thigh and gradually getting into a darker pink?"

Thalia clapped her hands together, jumping. "That sounds lovely."

"You need to keep the plunging neckline of this one

because you have a killer rack, Aph." Euphrosyne pointed at a sapphire dress.

"And I'm sure Heph would appreciate it," Aglaia said, tickling my side.

Laughing, I playfully batted her away and eyed the dresses, noting each one had some form of shimmer and sparkle. "The entire bodice shimmering?"

"Obviously," Euphrosyne teased.

On one dress, I'd created draping extensions from the train connecting to my wrists. Thoughts of Heph slipping those cuffs on me made it ache between my legs. "I think I've got it, Graces. And I'll ask Heph to provide the final touch for me."

"Well, let's see it, woman." Euphrosyne shot her arms out at her sides, tapping her foot and feigning impatience.

"But be quick about it. Heph is due to port in any minute." Thalia gestured at the gold ornate-patterned clock hanging above the door.

I couldn't believe we'd been at this since yesterday. I'd created several dresses into the wee hours of the night, and we fell asleep exhausted, sprawled on my bed *amidst* the dresses.

Inhaling a deep breath through my nose, I closed my eyes and swirled an arm at my feet, working my way up until I decided last minute on a hairstyle. The Graces stared at me slack-jawed and silent when I stood in full ceremonial garb.

"Can one of you say something?" A nervous chuckle floated from my belly. "Anything?"

"Aph," Aglaia started, crossing the room to take my hand. "I say this with the utmost honesty. This is by far the most epically gorgeous dress you've created. Ever."

Tears welled in my eyes, and I looked to the other two Graces, who emphatically nodded, holding back their tears.

"Really?" I whispered, moving to the mirror to marvel at my creation. A breath caught in my throat. The bottom of the dress floated around me in subtle suspended animation like piles of dark pink rose petals gently caressed by the wind. A piece of fabric extended on either side from the back of the bodice, connecting at my wrists where I planned to ask Heph to create shimmering arm bands to hold. The pink gradient grew lighter as it traveled up my body, the plunge-lined bodice comprised of varying un-matched shapes, shimmering and sparkling in such a pale pink it almost looked white. The sides of the bodice were opaque with bursting lines of gemstones like fireworks. My hair was half up, bunches pulled into three wavy sections behind me, charms of crescent moons and stars scattered throughout the design, including the charm Heph had made for me during the Lunation Festival. The pink heart on my cheek glistened, and the harpy scar on full display on my shoulder only added to the radiance coursing through me.

This was it. This was the dress.

"You look beautiful, Aph. But I believe you're missing one final touch," Euphrosyne said, squeezing my shoulders from behind me. "Graces."

The three goddesses who'd been my best friends, aside from Heph, circled me and raised their palms.

Euphrosyne extended her hand, sending shimmering swirls of onyx toward the dress's train. "For a joyous union."

"And for that union to remain ever shining," Aglaia continued, her glittering gold powers floating from her fingertips.

Thalia smiled and stepped closer, crouching and fanning both palms at my dress. "And may it forever bloom, Aphrodite." Silver starbursts shone, mixed with the other Graces' blessings.

Their magic settled into the rose petals of my gown, joining in the subtle animation and giving it vibrant life—Thalia's silver stars, Aglaia's gold dust, Euphrosyne's glittering onyx.

"There," Aglaia whispered, kissing my cheek. "You better make it disappear for now, though. Would hate for him not to be surprised."

And I couldn't wait to see the look on his face. He thought no matter what I produced, I'd wow him beyond belief, but this dress—would potentially make him tear up, only to have him blame the wind. I snapped my fingers, making the dress fizzle away.

"Thalia, since only one of us can go, Aglaia and I talked, and we think it should be you." Euphrosyne smiled warmly.

"Me?" Thalia looked between us, her hand bunching her shirt under her chin.

Aglaia hugged Thalia. "You've been at Aph's side more than any of us and also put in the most work at Sans Solo. It's about time we pick up some of the slack."

A tear crept down Thalia's cheek. "I don't know what to say."

A warbly blue portal appeared in the middle of the room, pushing my stomach into somersaults, my nipples puckering at the mere thought of him stepping out. Heph jumped through, wearing a black leather bomber jacket, black v-neck shirt, pants, boots, and silver belt. I pinched my thighs together, my pinky absently tracing my bottom lip.

"Graces," Heph addressed the girls with a nod. "Love-y goddess." When his chocolate gaze fell on me, his volcano lava could've melted me into a bubbling puddle.

"Well, don't you clean up nice," Euphrosyne cooed, jokingly sucking on her lip and ogling him.

"You do us proud with those decorations, Thalia." Aglaia poked the tip of Thalia's nose.

Heph sidled up to me, his massive hand curling over my hip, the feral playfulness dancing in his gaze not even close to a man with "wedding day" jitters. "You ready for this?"

Rising to my tippy-toes, I wrapped my arms around his neck, grazing a feathered kiss over his lips. "More than ever, Phai."

"Ares and Orion are already at the spot waiting, making sure no bums wander through." Heph bent lower to press his forehead to mine, grinning.

I laughed, and hugged him tighter. "Daphne should be on her way and Thalia's coming with us."

"Looks like the gang's all here then." Heph stepped back and took my hand, spinning up another portal and motioning to Thalia.

Euphrosyne and Aglaia sent a dozen air kisses our way, tears streaking their cheeks as they waved, and we stepped into the portal. We appeared in the open-spaced wastelands of the Fringes, away from the crowds of the District and, most importantly—curious people. Ares, Orion, and Daphne waited, trotting over once they spotted us arriving.

After we exchanged pleasantries, I turned to Thalia. "Would

you do us the honors, Grace?"

"It would be my pleasure," she replied, curtsying with a sparkling grin.

She spun in a circle, taking note of her canvas. Fanning her hand behind us, a circular display of tan and white feathers, matching the dirt of the Fringes, but granting it softness, appeared. Wriggling her fingers, she made sprigs of green throughout with pink and white roses. White icicle fairy string lights hung from the top, falling to the bottom like a lighted curtain. A single piece of tan fabric slung over the top, falling off center to the side. On each end stood small squared displays with lit candles and rose flower arrangements.

"Breathtaking, Thalia," Daphne breathed out, the fairy lights glimmering in her eyes. "Mind if I add one final touch?"

Thalia's brow rose, and she stepped aside. "Be my guest."

Daphne swirled her hands, creating greenery around the altar, soft grasses, meadow flowers, and other forms of plants with long, luscious leaves protruding from the dank dirt. She'd made them appear in a perfect circle around the altar, making this particular spot not look as drab as the rest of the Fringes.

"Very nice, Daph." Thalia playfully swatted her on the shoulder, her surprise evident by her widened eyes.

Daphne flashed a sparkling grin and looked at me for approval.

"I love it. Thank you. Both of you."

Thalia beamed and bounced on her heels. "Wait until you see her dress."

I looked up at Heph, gulping. Nerves pricked my skin. Not because of anything about to transpire, but I couldn't predict

Heph's reaction, despite how well I knew him.

"I'm ready to be floored, Ro." Heph turned to face me, brushing his knuckles across my cheek.

Peeking at an awaiting Ares and Orion, who looked almost as curious as Heph, I closed my eyes and, with the shimmers granted to me from the Graces, made the dress materialize thread by thread. Once done, I couldn't open my eyes, trying to imagine Heph's expression and thoughts.

The sound of Daphne's gasp gave me the courage to finally look at Heph. He stood dumbfounded, his eyes roaming my every curve, his jaw repeatedly tightening. He coughed and cleared his throat, and after a light sniffle, I caught the glisten in his eyes that he choked back. I wouldn't call him out on it. At least not today. The sight of me brought the forge-god to tears—a man who slayed harpies, dismembered and tortured those who threatened the ones he loved, and had volcanoes under his command—he had me *swooning*.

"You—" He cleared his throat and stepped closer. "You were right."

"About?" I placed a gentle hand to his scar.

His callused palm slipped over my knuckles. "You pure floored me. You look—I'd say gorgeous or beautiful, but those words don't seem to cut it. You look—" He paused and took both of my wrists, holding my arms out at my sides to ogle me more. "—transcendent."

All I could do was smile, my cheeks hurting from the strain. "I hoped you could give me the final touch. Need something for my wrists?"

Heph's gaze darkened, no doubt thinking about our

scandalous escapades with restraints. The veins in his hands glowed orange, and a wide silver band appeared on each of my wrists, connecting the draped fabric. "That what you're looking for, Peach?"

Pressing my hand to the scar he once thought defined him but in actuality, became a *part* of him, I grinned. "*You* are. You're all I've ever looked for in a partner."

He took my hand, kissing my palm, never tearing his eyes away. "Let's do this, love-y goddess."

Ares appeared at my side, gently cupping my elbow as he leaned in to kiss my cheek. "You look beautiful, sis," he whispered, a hint of a smile appearing from his beard.

"Thank you." I beamed at him and smiled at the sight of Coney resting in the curve of Daphne's arm.

"You positive you want to do this, adrefoúla? Not too late to back out." Ares bit back a smile, lightly nudging my shoulder with his fist.

"Appreciate the concern, big bro. But I'm good—no." I grinned. "I'm great."

He squeezed my arm before backing away and standing next to Orion.

Ares and Orion stood at a distance behind Heph, while Thalia and Daphne stood behind me. Standing in front of the altar Thalia created, I took Heph's hands. I'd seen countless deities seek a blessing from the Fates, very few receiving it, but the procedure remained the same.

"I need you to close your eyes, Hephaistos and think to *yourself* why you seek the Fates' blessing. Don't say it out loud."

Heph had already closed his eyes but popped one back

open. "Can I tell you later?"

Laughing, I squeezed his hands. "Sure."

Pinching my eyes shut and rubbing my thumbs between Heph's knuckles, I settled on my own thoughts.

Hephaistos. Why should we be together forever? Why were we *worthy*? He saw past the beauty and glitter, helped me not fear to bring out my true self, and supported me in ways he may not have been aware of. He remained my rock to hold onto in raging rapids, my best friend, a lover who understood what I needed, and to top it off, he gifted me one of the most precious gifts I felt I'd given to the world—Eros.

"Ro, what's happening?" Heph whispered.

A rolling breeze curled through my hair, and I flickered my eyes open. A yellow lighted orb blazed between us. The Fates were answering our pleas. My vision turned blurry from tears, and I tugged Heph's hands.

"You can open your eyes, Heph."

When he did, he squinted at the orb and tensed. "Is that—?"

"Yes," I whispered.

The orb brightened and shimmered, rising above our heads before light bursts darted for our chests, capturing us in its radiant embrace. Heph grunted and arched an eyebrow at me as if to confirm if this was supposed to happen. I smiled at him, watching the Fates' blessing circle him, the lighted orb floating between us, keeping the connection.

The inside of my right forearm burned, and I hissed, turning my arm over. A tattoo grazed my skin, a Greek meander key in a diamond shape, a knotted endless design representing eternity since ancient times. Heph kept one of our hands intertwined as he pushed the jacket sleeve of his right arm up, revealing a matching tattoo in the precise spot mine was. We locked gazes, realizing in the same instant what it all meant.

Bonded. Eternally. Forever. For as long as we both shared celestial breath.

The orb pulsed twice, settling over us before fizzling away wholly. I leaped into Heph's arms, kissing him, the newly formed bond making my chest hum from the contact. Our witnesses, our friends, brothers, and sisters, whistled, clapped, and whooped behind us—the sounds of them celebrating fading into our ears.

Heph held me, his forearms supporting my butt as he smiled. "I love you."

"I love you too," I squeaked out, the animated petals of my dress wavering between us.

The fairy lights in our circular altar suddenly went out, the joyful cheers from our friends dying away altogether. Heph sniffed the air, lowering me to the ground as he instinctively curled an arm around me and coaxed me behind him.

"I don't understand it. It's not like it's being battery-powered," Thalia said, repeatedly snapping her fingers at the display, expecting her powers to revive it.

"It's not because of you, Thalia." Ares pointed to the District buildings in the distance, the lights dousing in gradual succession block by block.

Animated darkness swirled over us, curling around our bodies like smoke mixed with black fog. I lifted my arms, half expecting the mysterious vapor to burn me.

"Well, at least whatever this is was kind enough to wait until after the ceremony." Heph shrugged his jacket off, tossing it to the ground, already igniting the forge within his arm. "Literally *right* after."

Before bonding, Heph and I had a strong connection, but with the Fates' blessing, we'd be the epitome of a "power couple." Thinning my lips, I gazed down at the new tattoo adorning my skin, tracing it and making the symbol shimmer. And as a dozen harpies plunged from the darkness surrounding us, I produced my court sword, slicing the air in front of me with shimmering gold, ready to show the world the true meaning of—the eternity bond.

THIRTY

HEPH

IT WAS A PECULIAR feeling being bonded to someone—*truly* bonded. And I don't mean it in the sense of something terrible or uncomfortable—but at first…overpowering. The protective instinct I'd had for Aphrodite before bonding was raging, and now? Fucking cataclysmic. What started as an urge to dig to a planet's core to save her, transformed into erupting all the volcanoes in an entire galaxy if anyone tried to take her away from me.

"Daph, take Thalia and get out of here," Aphrodite commanded, holding her sword at her side.

Concern cinched Daphne's brow as she curled Coney tighter against her. "But what about you, Aph?"

The harpies screeched above us, the mysterious darkness swirling in the air, carrying them like black paint in water.

"Daphne. *Now.* That's an order. Please." Aphrodite cut her gaze long enough for them to catch the plead written all over her face before focusing back on the winged nightmares looming.

"Alright, alright." Daphne pressed a hand to Thalia's back, and they sprinted away.

Fear had driven my worry over her entering Hippolytus's lair again—alone and only armed with her hidden powers. Despite it spiraling from the care I had for her, it seemed foolish to have ever doubted her at the start. Because what is love if not one of the most potent forces in the known cosmos? Aphrodite always had a warrior's heart, and all she needed was the opportunity to realize it—embrace it. I couldn't know how long eternity would be for either of us, but if that were the final gift I gave her, I could turn into stardust and memories, becoming one with Chaos blissfully happy.

Ares produced his sword and shifted to my side, Ro on the other, and Orion hovering behind me with his bow drawn and ready. Five harpies swarmed the air above us, talons poised, and teeth bared. I twirled the axe in my palm, glaring at the creatures who'd become a rivet in my side—a constant burrowing one.

"Remember. Watch for their godsdamned claws," I growled to the family surrounding me.

Thick darkness curled in the air around us with animated shadows that had no rhyme or reason for existing, given the lack of light. One harpy screamed and dove, flapping its wings as it stretched its talons, aimed for Ares. Ares deflected the first blow, but the harpy proved too quick when he slashed at its foot, hoping to remove it.

"Maláka," Ares shouted, spinning on his heel to keep the harpies in his sights.

Between the four of us, we had every angle covered, rotating with each other as we took turns slashing, prodding, and hammering the winged banshees. Aphrodite created shimmering pink energy shields to deflect their blows, occasionally countering with the sword.

We needed to spar more and *actually* spar.

Forcing my thoughts away from sexual deviance with my eternal goddess, I grunted and hurled my hammer skyward, clocking one harpy under the chin. It nosedived to the ground, skidding to a stop, using the talons on its wings to sit upright. Before it could go airborne again, I pulled away from the group long enough to slam the blunt side of the hammer across its face, making green sludge spew from its mouth. Now disoriented, I twirled the handle to the holo axe blade and, in one swift slice, separated its head from its shoulders.

A chill mixed with static shock fused up my spine, making me wince. My eye twitched, and an overwhelming sense to turn, to shout—I spun.

"Aphrodite, on your left," I cried out as a harpy dove from Aphrodite's blind side.

Aphrodite's eyes widened, and at the last possible instant, she swung her blade at the harpy's claws, removing three of the five before it had a chance to slice her.

What the Tartarus was *that*? The eternity bond?

The harpy flapped its wings, screeching bloody murder, green liquid dripping from the three missing claws. An energized fury erupted in me, slicing into my mind, and infusing my bones. My vision turned red. Holding the axe like a javelin, I launched the weapon at the harpy, pinning its wing to a nearby rusted metal sign. The harpy shrilled in agony, pulling away, only tearing a giant hole in its wing.

An arrow whizzed past my head as I stalked toward the fallen harpy, the volcano within me igniting every vein beneath my skin into blistering fire. The arrow pinned the other wing to the sign, Orion giving me a curt nod in the distance. Leaving the axe in place to keep the harpy from escaping, I invoked a great sword, using several slashes to rid the harpy of any other claws that could find a home in my flesh. The harpy opened its mouth, letting out one shrill cry, the tips of its wings vibrating.

"I've battled you ugly pieces of shit for centuries because the more I eradicated, the brighter the universe there'd be." I grabbed its face with one hand, being sure to keep my fingers away from its canines, violently snapping at me. "But now that you've purposely gone after my goddess, my woman—" Lowering my face closer, I let the raging lava ignite in my gaze. "—you've made it personal."

After taking one glance over my shoulder to ensure Ares and Orion had Aphrodite's back—they did—I poured all my strength into my grip on the harpy's head. I willed the forges and commanded the volcanoes to lend me their power. It wasn't about a manifestation of passion but a pure, brute physical display of it. My hand and arm shook, my teeth grinding and the head soon collapsed within my grasp, green brain matter and chunks of skull flying around me. Part of a jaw bone was all that remained, dangling between two of my fingers.

Still clenching my jaw, I tossed the bone aside and cracked my neck. Caked harpy guts on my clothes used to remind me of mistakes made, enemies vanquished—but I no longer needed it and made it all fucking disappear. I turned to Aphrodite standing in front of Ares and Orion, their height matching mine, looming over her like impenetrable towers. I'd never been a man into the artsy-fartsy wonders of the world, but the way my Ro fought in that rose petal dress floating with her like spirited clouds, her light hair swirling with every turn—it looked damn right *poetic*.

I no longer needed a reminder because I'd bonded myself to the reason I couldn't ever let my guard down: Aphrodite, my love-y goddess. And I'd give her every last bit of my strength, mind, brawn, and life for as long as the universe would allow me.

I yanked the axe free from the still pinned harpy wing, retrieving Orion's arrow, and sprinted back to the group. A harpy swooped near Aphrodite and she took a knee, pulsing a wave of energy above her. Ares stabbed his blade in front of her, blocking the blow. Orion rose behind them, poised with a notched arrow, and after two readjustments he launched it straight through the harpy's eye. Its wings slackened and it fell to the ground in a gnarled heap.

What started as three harpies multiplied into a dozen, emerging from nothing but the ebullient darkness still intertwining us. Ares and I took turns on either side of each other, slashing and slicing with each clawed attack. Aphrodite held her own, getting several quick stabs and slashes with her smaller blade. Battling these "shadow" harpies was akin to lopping off hydra heads. With every one of them we killed, three more would spawn from the inky blackness in its place.

Aphrodite spun circles, the slight panic spreading over

her face with every flinch and urge not to blink. Several surrounded her, and that same tingling surge I'd felt earlier wrenched my spine. Kicking the harpy I'd been fighting in the chest, I turned and lunged behind Aphrodite, wrapping my forge arm over her shoulder and covering her chest from behind. A harpy's claw bounced off my impenetrable arm, making orange sparks fly. I gave Ro a quick peck on the cheek before bumping her arm that held the sword, encouraging her to slash the harpy with me in unison when it circled back.

She peeked over her shoulder, smiling at me as she roused power in her palm in glittering pinks and golds. The harpy dove at us, and Aphrodite blasted her magic at it, disorienting it long enough for us to deliver the killing blows with our weapons.

The harpies continued to appear in unending waves of screeching terror, clawing, biting, and making our lives a living Tartarus. But we were a relentless lot, and whoever was the puppet master controlling them didn't realize we'd all meet Chaos before giving up on *any* of us. As if acknowledging my unspoken threat, the harpies all paused mid-air, their heads darting to a single crow cawing, perched on the same rusty sign I'd pinned a harpy.

We all stood with our weapons raised, giving each other sidelong glances of "what the fuck's"? The inky floating darkness began to sink away, pulling toward the crow as if it were the one controlling it, the harpies disappearing along with the fog. When all harpies were gone and the darkness flittered from the air, the crow stared at us, giving one final caw before flying away. Ares picked up a rock and, with an angered snarl, hurled it at the bird, missing it.

Rule number four: Harpies never surrender…

"Did the bird offend you somehow, Ares?" Orion asked, bemusement in his tone as he loosened his grip on the bow.

Ares tossed his sword to the other hand. "I didn't like the way it looked at me."

Aphrodite fluttered her fingers, making the court sword disappear, and ran her hands down the shimmering bodice of her dress. She stared at her hand like a stranger, the skin between her eyes crinkling.

"You alright?" I touched the small of her back.

She shook her head. "I don't get it. I still can't perform that lightning power. Even watching my family attacked by creepy harpies."

"We'll practice and figure it out. You'll find it again." Dragging the back of my hand down her cheek, I wiggled her chin to look at me.

A warm smile graced her lips. "I suppose this should be one of those moments I don't overthink why all those harpies suddenly stopped attacking because of some crow and be thankful for the temporary quiet?"

"Aw," I said, wrapping an arm around her shoulders, pulling her to my side, and kissing her head. "You're learning."

She elbowed me in the ribs but slid her fingers over my forearm, tracing my hair, and tilted her chin to look up at me with hooded lids. The city lights returned in succession on each block, and soon, even our altar lights shone brightly behind us.

"Where the fuck did those harpies come from? Was it that

weird floating oil or what?" Orion positioned the bow on his back.

Ares paced a square in the dirt, the adrenaline still pulsing in his veins. "Someone's testing us. Whatever *that* was—was only the tip of the iceberg, I guarantee it."

"The calm before the storm," Aphrodite whispered, still scraping her nails over my skin.

"You're going to need a lot more than an army of harpies to wear us down, Mystery Twat Waffle," I shouted into the wind.

"Oh, good, Heph. You don't know who or what it is, and you're yelling threats at it." Orion shook his head.

"They have *clearly* vacated the premises, or perhaps they're the rock. Or—" I gasped. "Maybe the wind itself. Whoever they are, they're a fucking coward."

"I need to get home. But you come get me whenever you need backup, brother. Do you hear me? When. Ever." Ares made his sword disappear and gave me a firm nod.

"And maybe that new goddess of yours can join in on the fun next time, hm?" I drummed my fingers at one end of the plunging neckline of Aphrodite's dress, right over her breastbone.

"Oh, she will. She'd be pissed if I didn't invite her for *another* battle." Ares stood in front of Aphrodite and held his arms out to her. "Adrefoúla."

An actual embrace? My, my, this woman really did do a number on the war god.

Aphrodite hugged him, pinching her eyes shut and squishing her cheek against his chest. "Thank you for coming. Thank you for everything, Ares."

"No need for thanks, Aph." He squeezed her shoulders and turned to me. "I saw Daphne and Thalia run off that way. Mind giving Thalia and me a lift back?"

Nodding, I kissed Ro's temple. "I'll be but a moment, Peach. Orion?"

"Not going anywhere, Heph." Orion did a deep squat, his heels hovering from the ground, and he rested his arms on his thighs.

The mere moments separated from Aphrodite through time as I took Ares and Thalia back to their respective homes left my chest hollow as if she had kept my heart with her. A deep sadness and nausea soon followed, and I felt like a steamroller had run over me—*twice*—by the time I got back to her. My boots no more momentarily touched dirt, and Ro leaped into my arms, a breathy sigh pushing against my ear.

"Miss me, baby?" I grinned against her jaw, brushing my beard over her cheek, and holding her to me with one arm.

"I'd heard about the separation side effects that came with a bond, but the word of mouth and scrolls don't do the feeling justice." She pressed her forehead against the side of my head, taking deep inhales.

"You felt that too?" I swatted her ass with my free hand. "Because misery *does* love company."

She peeled back, lips quivering like she wanted to smile but didn't want to give me the satisfaction. "Shut up, you *twat*."

Chuckling, I rested her on the ground, gave the corner of her brow a quick peck, and walked to an awaiting Daphne and Orion. "No more crows, harpies, or inky jizz smoke while I was gone, I take it?"

"Nope. Not even a damn tumbleweed." Orion shrugged. "What are you two still doing here, by the way?"

We first looked at each other and then behind us.

"What are you going on about?" I took Aphrodite's hand, my middle finger idly making circles against her palm.

"You two just spent the moments after your ceremony battling harpies. Call it a hunch, but most may want to spend their evening doing something—else?" Orion raised a light brow, Daphne giggling at his side, her cheeks blushing.

"I don't know. Battling harpies sounds like a typical Tuesday afternoon." Aphrodite smiled and looked at me from the corner of her eye, her delicious pink tongue ever so slightly licking her lower lip.

"Would you two get *out* of here?" Orion flicked his hand at us. "I'll make sure Daphne gets home safe, and Coney might as well have a room at my place at this point. We're all good here. Now *go*."

"I'll see you tomorrow, mate." Winking at Orion, I turned toward my eternal. "Love-y goddess, care to do the honors?"

She smiled and turned to Daphne. "Thanks for being here, Daph."

"We'll see each other soon, Dite. Go, go." Daphne did a little hop, making Coney jiggle from the curve of her arm.

Wrapping her arms around my neck, Ro stepped forward and kissed me as she ported us. I kneaded her lower back and peeled away, scanning my apartment with a devious smirk. "Wait a minute. We're cheating here, Ro."

"Cheating?"

"Uh-huh. Port us to the hallway."

Her ruby lips parted, and she shifted her gaze to the door before looking back at me. "Why?"

"Ro." I trailed my knuckles over one of her cheeks, then the other. "Port us. To. The hallway. A few doors down would be preferred."

She nuzzled her cheek against my touch and did as I requested.

"Perfect." Before she had a moment to protest, I hoisted her over one shoulder with her ass pointed at the ceiling—fireman style.

"Heph," she squealed before that blissful infectious laughter of hers followed.

I smacked her ass and carried her down the hallway, passing several neighbors who whistled and wooed at us. "I do believe there's a mortal custom of carrying the bride over the threshold?"

Peeking at her over my shoulder, I saw her hands covering her face, her cheeks rosy but smiling. "I don't think this is the proper carry they talk about, *jack*."

"Tomato, potato, baby." Using my boot, I pushed the door open and carried my goddess inside, whisking it shut with my free hand.

"Can we get to the best part now?"

Grinning, I let Aphrodite slide down my body until her toes reached the floor. "Everything is the best part, Ro. Though I'll admit what's to come next *is* up there with my favorites."

A serene smile graced her lips as she beamed at me, her slender fingers tracing the v-neck of my shirt, concentrating on the bit of hair peeping out. I stayed silent, watching her.

Her usual expression when we were about to fuck had a carnality—a desire to be controlled and taken. But this time? Her expression remained soft, inviting and I knew she needed something different from me tonight. She lifted her hand to make our clothes disappear, and I grasped her wrist.

"Wait." I kissed the inside of her forearm directly over the new tattoo we both shared. "Allow me."

I could hear her heartbeat as if it were my own, booming and pulsing in my ears as I made slow, calculated moves to stand behind her. Grazing my knuckles against her skin, dragging them down the length of her spine, I clasped the zipper and slowly undid it tooth by fucking tooth. With it undone, I took each of her wrists, making the metal bracelets I'd created for her disappear, allowing the fabric to drape free. Still behind her, I slid the dress down, pausing to cup her tits, pebbling the nipples between two fingers. She moaned and let the back of her head fall onto my shoulder.

I stopped stripping her once the dress hung at her hips, leaving her topless in front of me. After dragging the rough texture of my fingertips across her skin, I made several circles over the harpy claw on her shoulder and pressed my lips to it before turning her to face me.

"Hey," she whispered, her skin shimmering a radiant light pink.

Grinning, I took her hand and placed it on my shirt's hem. "Hey."

Biting her lip, she slid her hands under my shirt, groaning once her fingers grazed my abs. She pushed the shirt up, and I lifted my arms to let her pull it free and away. Her gaze traveled over my muscles, fingernails scraping the hair on my chest, and stomach, the bit that disappeared into my trousers. She kissed my harpy claw scars, mine running far deeper than hers. I'd only been glad *I* suffered multiple lashings and not her.

"A gal has to feel pretty lucky getting to stare at this for eternity." She dipped her fingers in my pants, her fingernail grazing the base of my cock.

Growling, I bunched the dress resting at her waist in my grasp. "Every bit of it is yours, Ro. I'm flaming iron fresh from the hearth, ready for you to pound as you see fit." As I pulled the dress past her ass, letting it fall in a pile at our feet, the rose petal train still glittering and floating, I sunk to my knees.

She stepped out of the dress, and I stared at a thin pink piece of lace, her pussy hiding and waiting behind it. Curling my fingers on each side of her hips, I swirled my tongue around her belly button as I pulled them down, taking several seconds to suck her clit. The need to bury my cock inside her was gasping for breath with no air—another new and peculiar feeling I'd chalk up to the bond. I led her to the bed, guiding her to her back, and made quick work of my pants. The hungry glint in her gaze and playing on her lips had me hard as an untapped diamond.

"No fun bracelets?" Aphrodite lifted her hands, smiling, lying there naked, gorgeous, and waiting—for me. *Me.*

As much as I loved when we got kinky, I also knew my Ro more than anyone. She didn't think I could hear the gentle purr collecting in her throat, the softness in her stare, and how her finger traced her bottom lip—tonight, she wanted to be *cherished.*

"Not this time, baby." I crawled onto the bed, my hand trailing up her shin to rest on her knee. "Just let me love you. Can you do that?"

She bit her fingernail, nodding, her skin shimmering more than I'd ever seen it. Her legs opened for me, and one wrapped around my waist, pulling me toward her.

Moving over her, I slowly pushed inside, the wetness, the softness clenching around me so tightly it made me moan. I took her hands in mine, interlacing our fingers and gripping them on each side of her head. When our hips met, my cock buried as deep as it could, and the tattoos on our forearms glistened. A surge similar to the one I'd felt battling the harpies sizzled up my spine, and I started to roll my hips, pumping in and out of her—slow at first before picking up the pace and slowing again.

"Heph," Aphrodite cried out, her one hand threading in my hair behind my head, the other gripping my ass as I ground into her.

Her powers floated from her skin, embracing us, making my veins ignite with my own forge magic. The fires roared within me and I sat back on my haunches, bringing Ro's knees together, pushing them tighter against her, my chest resting against her shins as I pumped. I kissed her knee, smiling as her eyes opened, gazing up at me as if there wasn't another being in all the cosmos.

Yanking her legs apart, I sat back again, holding her limbs by the calves, keeping them raised. Her back arched from the bed before a feminine snarl escaped her throat, and she reached between her legs for me. Her hands greedily roamed her territory, paying the most attention to my stomach but taking time to pinch my nipples, making me grunt and smile. I threw her legs over my shoulders, sinking to bring our faces closer, still pounding into her with even strokes.

"You ready to come with me, baby?" I trailed my tongue over her bottom lip, staring into her moonstone eyes that eclipsed any other thought I'd have tried to summon.

"Yes," Aphrodite moaned, grabbing onto the back of my head, and kissing me. She tasted like strawberries and sin—the perfect mix of sweet and wicked. "Olympus, Heph, yes," she cried out.

My soft thrusts turned outright primal as I drove into her, fucked her, made love to her, the headboard beating against the wall like a hammer to an anvil. My spine seized as I came inside her, hips bucking, fists digging into the mattress. Another wave, a sensation I'd never felt from any other sex in my godly life, rippled in my stomach—a tightening, twisting.

Aphrodite screamed, her nails digging into my shoulders, two of them breaking my skin. Her back fully arched off the bed, her head dipping backward, and hips pressing into my ribs as I kept hold of her. Sweat beads collected between her tits, and I licked them away as she continued to shiver through her release until finally, she sunk boneless to the bed, entirely spent.

"Holy fucking shit." Aphrodite clapped a hand over her face, out of breath and chuckling. "I don't even know what that was. I've never—" Her gaze cut to mine, staring up at me with widened sapphire eyes.

"Ro, love." I moved the hair sticking to her forehead. "Did

your scrolls mention anything about shared orgasms with bonding?"

She gasped and bit back a smile. "No. But that'd sure explain a lot."

I combed my beard with a hand. "I'm unsure if I should feel lucky as a guy to experience a shade of a female orgasm or be absolutely mortified."

"Think of it this way—" Aphrodite finger-walked up my stomach, pressing her palm to my chest once she reached it. "—double the fun?"

Snickering, I kissed her lips before slowly pulling out of her and lying back with open arms. She crawled toward me and rested her head on my chest, our height difference perfectly aligning our bodies for me to rest my chin on the top of her head comfortably.

"How much about this bond do you know, sweetheart?" I slipped one hand behind my head and wrapped the arm closest to her around her shoulders. "I got these peculiar sensations during battle. As if I could sense you were in danger seconds before it happened."

"That's the biggest part of it. The bond heightens any connection we had before—beyond physical and emotional. This takes it to an almost...cosmic level?"

"Huh. Interesting. Can we sense each other's emotions and shit? Not that I have a hard time reading you as it is." I traced my fingers up and down her arm, the silkiness of her skin making my dick hard, ready for more.

"I don't know. What am I feeling?"

Pausing, I closed my eyes. "Overly satiated and ravenous

from the magical D."

She kneed my thigh, laughing. "I'm serious, Phai."

"Ow," I said with a chuckle. "You're happy. Content."

She cooed into my neck. "Mm. I am. And you forge-god—" Moving to sit on me, straddling me, she tapped her fingers on my chest. "You finally have confidence bursting from you. Inside—" Her fingers fluttered over my face scar. "—and out."

We'd given each other the same gift it turned out—the courage to be ourselves.

I grabbed her hips, grinding against her, groaning at how wet she was still. "Maybe we *can* sense each other's emotions. If even a teensy bit."

She bit her lip, her neck flushing like when she got overly nervous. "Do your Prime voice."

"My—" I paused and couldn't help but chuckle at the random request. "My *Prime* voice? As in…Optimus Prime?"

"You used to do it all the time in the nineteen eighties. You don't remember?"

The light chuckle turned into a hearty one. "Of course, I remember, baby. I'm only shocked *you* do."

"For me?"

I cleared my throat and dug into century-old memories. Dropping my voice lower than it already was, I said, "As long as power flows through any of my circuits, Aphrodite, I will fuck you."

"That. Is. *Hot*," she squealed with delight, clapping her hands before collapsing on top of me and giving me a quick kiss.

"Olympus, do I wish I knew about this nerdy side of you a long time ago. May have given me the courage to come clean sooner." I bumped her cheek with my knuckle.

"It's as much my fault for hiding it. No harm, no foul." She rested her chin on her hands, her chest pressed against my ribs. "Heph, do you think all the time hopping you do—the time hopping I've suddenly done—because of the crazy spacetime stuff you always talk about—do you think it's changed things for any other gods?"

There was the million-dollar question. The thought had crossed my mind more than once, but with how long I'd remained in the future, I figured events had settled by this point.

"It's—possible? But let's be honest, most of the gods could *use* a change."

"True." She beat a finger against her hand, gaze falling to my chest.

I lifted her chin to look at me. "Besides, what's the craziest thing that could happen? Zeus settling into the marriage lifestyle?"

We both went quiet before bursting into laughter.

"I mostly ask because—" She inched forward to tickle her nose against my beard. "—I want to stay here."

"Really? You've said countless times how this place isn't your scene. I'd be more than happy to go back to the past. You know that, right?"

She nodded. "I know you would. You'd do damn near anything for me despite it making you miserable, Heph. I do know that about you. And that's more reason I want to stay. This place makes you happy and all this time spent here with you, it's *so* you, and therefore, it feels more like home than anywhere else."

415

"Damn, baby." I hugged her tight. "But what about your business?"

"A business the Graces can handle. Besides, I want to start something new."

As if my life couldn't get any more surreal. I'm bonded to my dream girl at her request and get to spend the rest of eternity with the goddess I've loved since I was a kid. She's an absolute tigress in the sack, and now? She wants to live *here*.

I grabbed her shoulders and pushed her back far enough to see her face. "Like?"

"Figure I could shadow as a relationship therapist—no need to call myself anything but Aphrodite here. Let them think what they want to think, but it's a way for those who need help to find me. And I *love* making people happy, Heph. I really do."

"I don't know what to say." Smiling like a godsdamned idiot, I gripped her shoulders tighter.

"Say we'll find a bigger place to fit you, me, Coney, and *all* of our nerd stuff."

Laughter poured out of me. "Deal. Absolute fucking deal, love-y goddess."

"And when whatever it was that attacked us today comes back because it will, we'll be ready." She sat back and lifted the arm with the tattoo still glistening.

I sat up, curling her legs around me and pressing my tattoo to hers. "I pity whoever tries to come between this, Ro. And speaking of future battles—there's the matter of your bonding present."

"Present?" Aphrodite's skin glimmered, her smile matching

its gleam.

After the day with my mates throwing axes, I'd gone home to forge something for Aphrodite that took me nearly a dozen tries and pounds of scrap metal to get right.

I materialized the silver and gold scale mail with bits of chainmail shoulder pauldrons. Her eyes lit up before glistening with tears, her hands cupping her nose and mouth.

"Heph, you—you made the goddess of love *armor*?"

Repositioning us, I slipped the pauldrons over her head and fitted them to her. The overlapping gold and silver scales formed a triangular pattern around her neck, the design continuing over each shoulder, a thicker piece forming around her neck similar to the choker I'd summoned in the swingers club.

A thin piece of chain mail hung from the scale mail between her tits, and I rubbed it with two fingers. "I wasn't lying when I said I always thought you were a warrior. And all true warriors need armor. So, why the fuck not?"

"This is gorgeous. Feminine but fierce all at once."

I cupped her chin. "Perfect words to describe you, Peach."

She smiled and trailed her hands over her exposed breasts. "Not to question your handiwork, babe, but it seems to be missing key—components?"

"You are correct. You still need a breastplate, grieves, gauntlets—all of it. My deal to you, my dear goddess, is I'll make another piece of armor for each time you agree to spar with me. *Really* spar. Though afterward, if we want to screw like monkeys on the mat, it would also be perfectly suitable."

She squealed and tackled me, the shoulder pauldrons

clanking together. "We have so much to offer this universe, Hephaistos. Me *and* you."

A secret kept hidden deep across the known galaxies: Worlds can be created without the need to conquer if first *forged* with love.

epilogue

APHRODITE

Several months later...

A COUPLE BICKERED ON the other side of my desk, and I let them for the time being, waiting for the right moment to intervene. My new business in the Neosphere District, which I lovingly named *Love Potion Number Right* because this place loved its gimmicks, had only been open for the past month. But word spread quickly of the owner, who called herself Aphrodite, working actual magic. They didn't know what to think. Was I a sorceress? The *real* Aphrodite? Not that I admitted to anyone who happened to guess. It'd take longer to explain than the realization took to settle in.

It took me a couple of months to pick a location and find a suitable place for the business. As much as Ithaca would've fit my profile as Aphrodite, the patrons who lived there wouldn't benefit as much from my services as other places. They wouldn't appreciate it. And not to mention, most of them were in relationships for all the wrong reasons or cheated on their partners every which way from Sunday. No thanks. Daneland was the perfect place and had some of the most calming views of the docks and water with the rainbow-colored houses in the backdrop. And my office suite, situated on the highest floor of the building, faced it.

"May I interrupt?" I interjected when both of them managed to take a breath. The pink pencil skirt hugged my legs as I crossed them.

The man, a thirty-two-year-old security guard with a geometric haircut, widened his eyes at me. "Shit. Sorry. We're here paying for your services and not letting you do your job."

"I still do not understand what you have against cybernetics, Hank. I don't." The woman, a thirty-one-year-old bartender sporting a teal mohawk, huffed at her boyfriend and turned her back on him.

Briefly glancing at the clock hanging on the back wall, knowing Heph would be here any minute to pick me up for lunch, I decided to bring this puppy home. "What *do* you have against them, Hank? Mind sharing?"

Hank sighed, holding his head low as if he'd already been defeated. "She doesn't need them. Cybernetics started as advanced synthetic parts for people who lost limbs, or went blind, or had failing organs. Now? People use them like fucking plastic surgery. I mean, hell, they've even made it a *thing* by urging people to be more 'minty.'"

Strategically, I kept my mouth shut, waiting for this to sink into the woman's head. My powers hummed around these two, which told me they were a supreme match if they could get their heads out of their asses.

"Plastic surgery?" She guffawed and slapped her hands against the chair's armrest. "It's not as if I'm getting a new pair of tits, Hank. I've stood all day at that job for twenty years. My knees are shot. All I wanted was cybernetic replacements, so I never have to worry about it again."

And there we had it. Despite his narrow-minded views, Hank could genuinely understand people if he listened to them. This would pull at his heartstrings.

"I had no idea." Hank placed his hand on her shoulder. "Are you in pain, Sylvie?"

Sylvie frowned and turned to face him. "Sometimes. If I stand too long."

"Shit. I'm so sorry."

"The key here, my friends—is communication. Believe me. I know this can cause a lifetime of pain and suffering if you don't figure it out sooner rather than later. Virto?" I held my hands out.

"How do you do that without barely talking to us?" Sylvie asked, wrapping her hand with Hank's.

Winking at them, making a sparkling glint in my eyes, I blew on my palm. Pink dust and gold glitter floated into the air, settling over them but disappearing before it made contact. "Magic." I'd just granted them a night of mind-blowing sex to set their priorities straight again.

They both slow-blinked at me and made no motion to move until I rose from my chair.

"Thank you, Aphrodite. *Thank you*," Hank said.

"You're more than welcome. You can see Thalia at the front

desk on your way out for payment. You two have a fabulous night." I grinned, knowing full well they would and then some.

Thalia was one of the Graces helping out this week, but all three had elected to rotate, with the other two keeping Sans Solo afloat back in the past.

"Knock. Knock." Daphne knocked and poked her head in the crack of the door. "How you doing, boss?"

I'd done as promised and got Daphne away from a life with the Doves, offering her an opportunity to use skills she learned there but under no circumstances ever for anything sexual. Some people simply needed company—someone to talk to about their problems or interests—a person to rest their head in their lap as they got their hair stroked. And not only was Daphne great at it, but clients also started *requesting* her services.

"Blech. Please don't call me that." I laughed, throwing stray pens into the holder on my desk and straightening my Funko POP collection I'd brought from the past when Heph and I got a new place together in Daneland.

She snapped her fingers, tapping her fingernails against the doorframe. "That's right. You're having lunch with Heph today, aren't you?"

"Yup. I'm all yours tomorrow, though." Winking at her, I slid the white vinyl jacket from the back of my chair and slipped it over my shoulders.

"Ooo, does your man know of our heated affair?" She grinned and bobbed her brow before laughing.

"He does *not*. Is there Jell-O involved?" Heph said from the doorway, casually leaning on it like the gorgeous hunk of badass he was.

My skin sizzled for him, an ache pooling between my thighs that had me crossing the room and kissing him, not caring Daphne still stood nearby. "Hey, babe."

A jovial snarl gathered in the back of his throat as he slipped an arm around me. "Mm. Peach. What a greeting."

We'd tested the limits of the separation clause countless times, and only when we were divided by space and time did we experience the worst of it. Being apart with a city between us or even remaining on the same planet was mildly agitating at best and mostly made us both horny beyond belief.

"And on that note, I'm out of here before you start screwing on the desk. Have a good day," Daphne said, laughing and waving as she exited, closing the door behind her.

"How's work?" I played with the lapels of his jacket—his crisp *new* jacket, lacking all signs of harpy guts.

"Taking off, I'd say. Taking off. Orion's becoming quite the popular bounty hunter. Think he's trying to compete with *me*." Heph smirked and shook his head.

Heph started his own bounty service, taking the monopoly away from Olaf. He'd hired someone to handle the administrative work of assigning and rewarding bounties so he could continue to hunt. And Orion, having decided to stay in the District, soon became one of his regulars.

"Yeah? Think you'll put Olaf out of business soon?"

Heph slipped a finger under my chin, lifting it and bending down to kiss me. "I give it a month."

My toes wanted to curl inside my heels, and I took a shaky breath. "Where did you uh—where'd you want to go to lunch?

And please don't say Uluu's again."

"Nah. Thought we'd order some delivery and eat at the loft."

My heart swooned. Positively soared.

"You—you want to Netflix and chill with me?"

Heph squinted and circled his finger as if solving an algebraic equation. "Well, Netflix doesn't exist anymore, but I'm sure we can find something to watch, and if chill means fooling around on our big new couch, then yeah."

Would it have been far too cliché to cry?

Forcing the tears back, I jumped and wrapped my arms around his neck. "I adore you."

"I adore you too, Ro, but I'm a bit surprised you're this excited I wanted to stay in." He chuckled and slid a hand into my hair.

"I like staying in sometimes," I said with a mouse-like tone, lifting my head to look at him, fingers wringing behind his neck.

He kissed the tip of my nose. "Then take us home."

I ported us to our two-story open floor plan loft atop the tallest Daneland building. In the center of the first floor was our extra-large holo TV display with Heph's gaming consoles surrounding it, the black leather curved couch with a rounded glass coffee table in the center, and a swirly hexagon light hanging overhead. The right corner housed Heph's Lego displays, my bookshelves, and the table to play my tabletop games on Heph made with pink felt and raised sides to catch the dice. We set up the full bar in the back, complete with several wooden stools that Heph carved designs of anvils, roses, volcanoes, and swans into. Behind the bar, backlit with pink and white neon, was my action figure collection. Upstairs remained our bedroom sanctuary with Coney having an entire half of the room all to himself.

"Food should be here soon." Heph kissed my cheek and tossed his jacket over the back of the couch. "Ambrosia wine?" He snapped his fingers at me as he backpedaled toward the bar.

"Sure," I said, grinning.

There were rare moments I found myself not smiling as of late—life with Heph. Despite how I used to feel, life here in the Neosphere District had become pure bliss. We'd also gotten lucky on how relatively quiet things had been lately. There'd been the usual crime activity, the occasional supernatural creatures, and of course, endless harpy invasions—but no signs of the strange shadow harpies we'd encountered.

The charm sound went off, and a robotic female voice said, "Front door."

"Must be the food. I'll grab it," Heph said, handing me a goblet of wine as he shimmied past, opening the automated dolly delivering services used for top-floor complexes.

Smiling, I sat on the couch, curling my legs underneath me, and waving my hand to turn on the holo, searching for something to watch.

"Here we are," Heph sat next to me, resting white squared cartons with animated noodle logos on the table.

"Heph. You didn't."

Heph shook his head. "Not Uluu's. Look." He shoved one carton in my face, showing the name *Tortellini in Love.*

Laughing, I swiped the container from him. "You really are

obsessed with noodles, aren't you?"

"Ah, but these are stuffed. Like *you'll* be later." A wicked grin curved his lips, and he popped his carton open.

We found some random movie about a guitar player who'd tour local bars and clubs as a disguised assassin, his guitar morphing into an unexpected machine gun. Beyond those minor details, I couldn't recall much, considering we were all over each other within fifteen minutes of finishing our food. We'd made love on the couch, the floor to ceiling windows spilling rainbow light from surrounding buildings against our bare skin.

I'd summoned a silk blanket with the same animated galaxy print from my Lunation Festival dress. We wrapped it around us as we cuddled on the couch afterward, catching the tail end of the movie and trying to make sense of it.

Heph lay behind me, his arm wrapped around my front. "I didn't want to sour the mood, but you know I can't and won't keep things from you, Ro."

A pit formed in my stomach, and I peered at him over my shoulder. "What is it?"

"There've been more and more crow sightings." His brow furrowed into a scowl.

"Think it could be a different crow?"

Heph shook his head, fire reflecting in his eyes. "Unlikely. If you haven't noticed, there isn't a lot of animal life that survived—certain species of dogs, cats, rabbits, and the like. And then you have the damn rats and cockroaches that always survive, the bloody bastards. But zero birds. None."

"We've gotten pretty lucky it's been this long, I suppose. It was only a matter of time, and we all knew that, Heph."

He nodded, interlacing his fingers with mine and sighing. "I know. But whatever this is, it's *big*. I can't shake the feeling that some real shit's about to happen."

"And if it does—" I turned to face him, palming the scar on his cheek. "—we'll deal with it. And we'll take care of it."

"I know. Still it—" He blew out a breath and cleared his throat. "—it fucking scares me, Ro."

It scared him to lose me. Scared him to lose Orion, Ares, or anyone else who agreed to fight with us. He didn't have to say the reason because I could feel it torturing him to his bones. It made my heart wrench.

Bringing our faces closer and closing my eyes, I kissed him, willing serenity through our bond to calm him. He sighed against me, his beard tickling my chin, and then…

Zap.

A short burst of lightning sparked between our lips, emanating from mine. I yelped and jumped back, my hand flying to my mouth.

Heph bit back a smile and rubbed his chin. "Ow."

"Olympus, did I—" I fell forward, my hands scrambling for his face, and instead, making our foreheads bump.

"Ro, calm down." Heph roared with laughter and grabbed my shoulders, steadying me. "If you hadn't hurt me before, now you knocked me senseless. That was a good thing, right?"

I traced a finger over my lips, my skin still tingling from the shock, and nodded.

"What did you feel when it happened? I sensed fear but couldn't be sure if that was my own." He rubbed my arms, patience unique to him settling between us.

"Like before, fear was the biggest part, but also passion and—" Gulping, I caught Heph's gaze. "—overwhelming happiness. Phai, this is the best I've felt in forever. I don't want it taken away as soon as we've found it."

Heph pulled me to him, wrapping his comforting, strong arms around me and stroking my hair. "That won't happen. I won't let it. *We* won't let it."

Heph was right. And that meant being prepared.

Biting my lip, I tightened my grip around him. "I could always reach out to Hekate?"

Heph grumbled. "Are we that desperate we need to recruit a witch to our ranks?"

"Heph," I shouted, smiling and swatting his chest. "She's a goddess of magic."

"Witchy magic, Ro."

Tracing a fingertip over one of his dark brows, I let out a wistful sigh. "She might be able to help us though, babe."

"I'll make you a deal, Peach. We try to figure it out on our own and if shit starts to hit the fan, we'll make the call." He slid a hand over my knee and gripped it.

I needed to learn how to use my new power on command, but first—I spied my armor set on display in the corner, only one piece left for Heph to forge—the grieves.

"Why don't we spar, Heph?" And regardless of my own fear catapulting through me, I offered him a smile capable of melting steel without the aid of fire. Because despite the unknown of what was to come, I had complete confidence in us. And *they* were the ones—who should be scared.

PRONUNCIATION GUIDE AND GLOSSARY

Aglaia (uh-glay-uh)

Aphrodite (af-ruh-dy-tee)

Ares (air-eez)

Biffy (biff-ee) – a District word referring to a close friend. Can also be used as an insult.

Daphne (daff-nee)

Dionysos (dee-oh-nee-sOHs)

Eris (air-iss)

Erinyes (air-iNN-eez) – also known as "The Furies" – goddesses of vengeance in Greek myth.

Eros (air-OHss)

Euphrosyne (yoo-frOH-zeh-nee)

Hedone (hEE-doh-nee)

Hephaistos (heh-fais-tuhs)

Hippolytus (huh-paa-luh-tuhs)

Lupe (lEE-pee)

Minty – a District word to describe the level of cybernetics one has installed.

Nakas (nAH-kAHz) – a digital form of District currency.

Narcissus (nar-si-suhss)

Olaf – (oh-lAHf)

Orion (oh-rye-ehn)

Ostilanide (oz-tehl-ah-nyde) – the strongest metal in the known universe. Often shortened to "Oz."

Stymphalian Birds (stihm-fail-ee-ehn) – monstrous birds of Greek myth.

Thalia (tAHl-ee-yAH)

Uluu (oo-loo)

Virto (vER-tOH) – a District word to show an understanding, appreciation of, or exclamation of excitement.

Catch the first book in the Contemporary Mythos series:

HADES

The King of the Underworld may have found a woman
truly capable of melting his cold, dark heart.

HADES (Contemporary Mythos, #1)
BUY IT ON AMAZON

CATCH APHRODITE, HEPH, AND ARES
in the following Contemporary Mythos series books:

ARES

ARES (Contemporary Mythos, #3)

EROS

EROS (Contemporary Mythos, #4)

BUY THEM ON AMAZON

STAY TUNED!

WWW.CARLYSPADE.COM

ACKNOWLEDGEMENTS

FIRST, TO MY HUSBAND, who continues to be a massive inspiration for my hero characters. Heph was no exception. I chalk his wit, fierce loyalty, and badassery to your direct influence.

To AK, my continued critique partner who never fails to be honest with me (without being mean about it) and always, *always* makes these stories that much better with your amazing feedback and reactions.

To all of my beta readers who, with your feedback, helped this story blossom and develop into something beyond its intent.

To Jhi, who ensured every Greek phrase for Ares in this book was an honest translation and allowed me to not rely solely on Google!

To Cerys, who, despite beta reading this lightning fast, continued to be a sounding board afterward as I worked through revisions. Your enthusiasm for these characters helped me develop them into something more than intended, and we have *you* to thank for that.

And finally, to you, the reader. Thank you for taking a chance on a cyberpunk fantasy romance world featuring my version of Greek mythology characters. This story has been an idea on paper for over four years. (Way before the concept of the Contemporary Mythos series was even a thought.) I love creating worlds from the ground up, and featuring my versions of Heph and Ro made for a fantastic experience. I'd never intended on this going beyond one book. I didn't think this book would push past the hundred thousand words threshold. An ensemble cast was an afterthought as I continued to draft, and I'm so thankful the Muses planted that particular seed in my brain. With each passing revision, OLAF transgressed from a romance-based action story to a story about the importance of communication, being part of a family, and having the courage to be yourself. From the bottom of my heart, thank you. And you haven't seen the last of the Neosphere District or this cast of characters because, quite frankly, I'm not ready to let go.